ESCARCHA

HORACIO BOOK 1

NINE REALMS SAGA
BOOK 13

KEN LANGE

Escarcha
Ken Lange

Published by Ken Lange
Copyright © 2024, Ken Lange
Edited by Elizabeth Robbins
Cover Art by Natania Barron

A big thank you to my better half for believing in me enough to let me do this.

1

THIS IS IMPORTANT

March 2nd

Puebla, Mexico, Earth

You know those advertisements for memory foam mattresses that say they don't transfer movement? Yeah, that was a goddamn lie. How did I know? Well, the edge of the bed just dipped down like someone had taken a seat. Hopefully that was my wife, otherwise I was about to have a very bad day. There was a slight distortion as their body weight shifted and a delicate hand touched my shoulder.

Lilith's soft voice cut through my sleep addled mind. "Hey, I need you to wake up."

"What?" Scrunching my eyes closed, I pulled the blanket up around my neck as I tried to make sense of the words. Eventually they came into focus. "Why?" Even though I tried to keep the irritation out of my voice, I failed. "What time is it?"

"Almost five." She patted my shoulder. "Come on, this is important."

I wiped away the grit that'd settled into the corners of my eyes. "I got in at three...you can't expect me to function on an hour and a half's sleep."

For a second, I thought I saw her brown eyes glow amber. No, that had to be my subconscious trying to interfere with the waking world. Even so, that didn't make her any less beautiful. She was tall —right at one point seven five meters—with refined features, smooth ebony skin, and super fit. As gorgeous as she was on the outside, it paled in comparison to her compassion, intellect, and generosity. In my eyes, she was the absolute picture of perfection, inside and out.

Even though she flashed me a brilliant smile, there was something dangerous in her tone. "You can sleep on the way, but I need you to come with me now." She gestured at the door. "The way I see it, you have two choices." Her index finger flicked up. "One, get up on your own." The look she shot me told me that'd better be the one I picked. "Personally, that's my favorite." Her next finger popped up. "Or two, I'll have Jose scoop you up like the little princess you're being and carry you out."

That woke me up. Just why the hell was the head of her security team here at the house? Shit, something serious must've happened. "Jose's here?"

Her smile slightly faltered. "Yes...so are the others."

Okay, for her to have the whole team here, something was definitely wrong. That alone pulled me mostly out of my stupor. "How long do I have?"

Glancing at her watch, she tensed the muscles in her jaw. "Ten minutes?" She glanced out the open patio doors and squinted. "Maybe less, the company helicopter is on its way."

I had so many questions, but they could wait. Throwing the blanket off, I sat up then kissed her on the cheek and got to my feet. "I'll be ready."

She placed a hand on my arm. "Did you find the girl?"

I'd spent the better part of the week in Mexico City searching for an eight-year-old who'd gone missing. To be more specific, she'd been kidnapped. Thankfully, she was physically fine; the mental part would probably take a whole lot of therapy to work through. "Yeah, she's home with her family."

Her tone hardened. "And the people who did it?"

"They won't be an issue going forward." I patted her hand. "I passed their info off to Hector."

Lilith gave me a suspicious look. "You mean the hoodlum you grew up with?"

That wouldn't be how I'd describe Hector Matos even if it technically fit. He liked to say he was a businessman. Which was true... he did run one. On the surface, it was a networking firm that specialized in collecting data for other corporations. Once you went a little deeper, it turned a bit darker. A lot of the information that went through his company was sensitive in nature. His clients ranged from governments to the grandmother down the street. Hector wasn't particular, so long as the people in question could pay for his services or had information worth selling. This meant he knew a lot of people, and some of those were straight up criminals.

Seeing how our businesses aligned, we worked well together, with me providing him certain bits of information in return for a favor here and there. Last night, I cashed in one of my chits when I asked him to pass along the info to one of his clients. You see, one of the local cartel leader's sons vanished about a year ago, so I doubted they'd survive the day. At a guess, their final moments on this planet were going to suck. Eventually, they'd tell the man everything he wanted to know, thus bringing their usefulness to an end, at which point they'd pass into the great beyond.

"You know he hates it when you call him that."

She winked. "Then he shouldn't skip out on dinner invitations."

Groaning, I kissed her on the cheek. "I'll let him know."

Without another word, I dragged my sorry ass to the shower. By the time the chopper landed six minutes later, I was pulling on my boots.

Upon exiting the bath, I came to an abrupt halt. "Hey, buddy, I wasn't expecting to see you in my bedroom."

Jose Infante was a little taller than me, at one point nine meters, and ran the line between being lean and heavily muscled. He had the kind of body that made a lot of people envious, with his perfectly chiseled abs, pecs and arms. It wasn't like he skipped leg day either, but somehow it was all perfectly proportioned in such a way it didn't show through his tailored suits. Like everyone else that worked for Ōmeyōcān-Mictlān—the company my wife ran—he was overly goodlooking.

The man had the perfect combination of salt and pepper hair that made judging his age difficult. He was for sure over the age of thirty, but it was impossible to say more than that. And that beard of his only accentuated his already square jawline. Thankfully, he, like all the others that worked for her, didn't seem to notice they'd won the genetic lottery. He was easy-going, polite, and when called for, absolutely ruthless.

"Morning Horacio." Awkwardly returning the wave, he gave me a big smile. "Lilith sent me up to wait for you. She's downstairs collecting a few essentials."

I glanced out the window to see the chopper sitting out in the distance with its rotors still moving at full tilt. If she brought her full team, I had a guess who the pilot was. "Issac?"

Jose glanced out the doors then nodded. "You got it."

Issac Duval and Jose must've worked out at the same gym since they had similar physiques, but where Jose wore custom suits that'd fit in anywhere, Issac did not. That wasn't to say he didn't wear slacks and a jacket because he did, even if they weren't the usual affair. Then there was the issue of the shirts. Instead of a button up, he went for a pastel tee. Oh, what did I mean by not the normal affair? Well, the jacket and slacks were made of linen—all the same cut and in a variety of colors. For whatever reason though, he seemed to heavily favor white. Also, it was clear the style of suit—if that's what you could call it —were designed with a hotter and more humid environment in mind.

I didn't want to hurt the guy's feelings, but it was kind of retro in all the wrong ways, but then again, so was his hair. It was nice enough, but it was about shoulder length—mine was too so that wasn't where the judgement was coming from. No, the judgement came from the fact he had it feathered back like something straight out of the eighties with blonde highlights and enough hair product to choke a horse. Worse still, he carried a pair of thick, black rimmed sunglasses he habitually stuffed in his front jacket pocket or twirled in his hand.

The way I saw it, he either needed to wear the goddamn things or leave them at home, because using them as some sort of fidget spinner was unsettling. While I found his fashion taste questionable, he was good at what he did, and that was all that mattered. Well, there was that and the man could cook.

I gestured at the door. "Shall we go?"

Stepping back, he waved me through. "Christopher is in the kitchen—he's supposed to be scrounging us up, something we can eat on the way."

"Sounds good."

We stepped out into the industrial sized hallway. You'd think walking around in a giant space where the floors and walls were made of anodized steel it'd be noisy, but due to the judicious placement of the artwork and textured floors, that wasn't a problem. Yeah, I didn't buy that bullshit excuse either when Lilith said it, but as it turned out, she was right.

Two landings later, and a quick trip down the hall, I found myself in the kitchen. Christopher Reynaud was a tall, lean man who looked as if he did a lot of distance running. His curly, long, black hair had the look of a man who'd just gotten out of bed and ran his hand through it to put it in place. It had that sexy, yet messy, bedhead look that probably drove his lovers crazy. He was the kind of man that could wear anything and look like he'd just stepped off a photoshoot of some sort. To that end, he normally wore slacks and a button up shirt that he kept half buttoned—and that was being generous. Given the way he looked and the toned flesh underneath, no one complained.

He gave us a big smile. "Hey, it's almost ready."

Frowning, Jose's gaze passed over the empty stove. "Really? Uh... I'm not seeing anything."

Opening the fridge, he grabbed a much too full box of cereal with both hands. "Cereal!" He gave us a serious look. "You know breakfast is the single most important meal of the day."

Before I could say anything, Lilith's voice cut through the quiet behind me. "What is a cereal box doing in my refrigerator?"

Placing a bowl on the table, Christopher chuckled. "You guys are going to LOVE this."

It was then I bore witnessed to one of the greatest culinary crimes to ever exist happen in real time right in front of me. A way too happy Christopher carefully opened the plastic before squeezing out what looked to be sludge into the waiting dish.

Horror sounded in Jose's tone. "What sort of abomination is this?"

"What?" Genuinely puzzled, Christopher looked up to see our stricken faces. "Haven't any of you ever had cereal before?"

I held out my hands and took a step back. "Are you telling me that you pour the milk into the bag first, then place it in the fridge before eating it?"

He stared at me for a long moment before shrugging. "Well, you have to squeeze it, so the consistency turns out right, but yeah... how do you eat it?"

"Not like that!" Jose clapped his hand over his face and sighed. "The rest of the world either pours milk into the bowl first then cereal or the other way around." He gestured at the sludge. "No one in their right mind does this."

Offended, he stood up straighter. "That's not true, that's how I eat it...it's how my dad taught me to make it."

His father needed to be placed under arrest for psychological warfare against his own child.

Resignation sounded in Lilith's tone. "We'll grab a protein bar and go."

"Pass." I gestured at the pantry. "You know I hate those things... they're vile."

She narrowed her eyes at the old argument. "You need to eat something."

Reaching into the pantry, I grabbed a couple packets of Jerky.

"Yeah, but we've discussed this." Edging around Christopher, I opened the fridge and snagged a cherry slushie out of the drawer that kept them at just the right temperature. "Anyone else want one?

Annoyance sounded in her tone as she reached into her purse to pull out one of her company's death bars and opened it as she stared at me. "Suit yourself."

Jose longingly looked at the jerky before turning his attention to the protein bar and sighing. "I'll have a bar."

"Suck up."

Before we could say anything else, Jamie Sanchez opened the door and stepped in. "Everything's been cleared." His voice trailed off as his gaze landed on the bowl on the table then up at Christopher. "Are you fucking serious?"

Jamie was the tallest of Lilith's security team, coming in at two meters flat-footed. No, that didn't include the hair on his head, since he was bald. His perfectly manicured snow-white beard stood out against his dark skin. However, his most arresting feature was his gray eyes. They seemed to have the ability to look right through your soul. Out of all of them, he was the scariest. He was nice enough…quiet and rather direct, but nice.

Christopher winced. "What?"

"I've told you about that." Jamie pointed at the bowl.

He grimaced. "How was I to know you weren't messing with me."

Jamie's eyes closed for a long second, then he slowly opened them. "Dispose of that outside, and let's go." He glanced over at Lilith. "I'll make sure the people on the ground have something waiting on us we can eat in the car."

Lilith held out her protein bar. "I'm fine."

He didn't shrink back from it, but the look he gave the sickly gray thing in her hand spoke volumes. "I'll tell you what I told my mother; I'd rather starve than try to choke down one of those atrocities."

She rolled her eyes then looked over at the rest of us. "You heard the man. Let's go."

Jamie tapped Lilith's shoulder as she turned to leave. "Ms. Gama said she'll be there as soon as she can get free."

Frowning, Lilith nodded. "Thanks."

Outside, Luis Islas and Martin Navarro escorted us to the helicopter. Luis was a nice enough guy; he too was tall, good looking with just the right amount of scruff to come off as sensual. Martin was the same, and they were both lean-ish men. They were a bit thinner than Issac and Jose but thicker than Christopher. They, like Jose, wore custom dark suits that hid their physiques.

As for the helicopter itself, it was one of the fancy ones I normally spotted at Ōmeyōcān-Mictlān headquarters. It'd also be my first time in it—Lilith normally didn't go for this sort of thing unless it was for a business trip. It was my understanding it was normally used to transport goods between the facility here in town and the satellite labs.

Glancing through the front window, I spotted Issac wearing his trademark white linen jacket, pants, and boat shoes. That couldn't be proper flight equipment, but I wasn't about to point that out for fear of Lilith murdering me on the spot. She clearly wanted to get to wherever we were headed quickly.

Once we were strapped in and the doors closed, the chopper jumped into the air quicker than I thought possible, then it began to speed off toward the north at a pace that had to be breaking several laws.

Yeah, there was something important happening, but for whatever reason Lilith didn't want to share what that was just yet. Hopefully, that'd change soon.

2

OLD FRIEND

Teotihuacan, Mexico, Earth

Obviously, I hadn't quite grasped the concept of what Jamie meant when he said everything had been cleared. At the time, I thought he was referring to the flight plan, and to be fair, that was probably included in the statement. However, there were a few things I hadn't expected, such as our chopper being capable of near supersonic speeds. That alone was cause for concern, though it did cut the trip down to fifteen minutes. More importantly, how was I to guess we'd be landing in the visitor parking lot leading into the Teotihuacan ruins?

Up to this point, I thought pressing Lilith for information wasn't necessary, but given the circumstances, that was changing quickly. "Honey, what's going on?"

"Give me a few and I'll explain everything." She gestured at the door. "We need to get the chopper out of here as quickly as possible. Once it's gone, we can go over the details." Tapping the mic on her headphones, she said, "Issac, were you able to make arrangements with the locals?"

His tone was smooth and slick. "Of course I was." He chuckled.

"Hell, I was even able to find a white Testarossa to make the trip back here a quick one."

She shot an exasperated look his way. "Fine, but don't cause any unnecessary trouble."

"You got it, boss." His mic cut off.

Unbuckling my seatbelt, I followed Jose and the others out. Lilith was the last to exit. The rotor blades spun faster, and the helicopter was gone so quickly it was hard to believe it'd ever been there.

The second it was quiet, Lilith tugged out her phone. A moment later, every mobile present dinged with a message alert. "That's a composite photo of the man we'll be searching for this morning." Tears filled the corners of her eyes, and her voice cracked as she spoke. "Study it closely. I don't want to miss out on finding Cain because you overlooked an important detail."

Cain was her eldest son, and the possibility of him being here garnered my full attention.

I should probably explain. Lilith had three children, two of which were still alive, Cain and Vasile. The former was supposedly in what I equated to Interpol's witness protection program. He was some sort of elite soldier that dealt with a lot of the off-the-book stuff. From what I understood, he encountered his middle brother, Abel, during his final deployment. Turned out Abel was a psycho and Cain had to put him down.

Hey, before you ask, yes, I'm aware of the irony. No, I didn't have a clue why they'd gone with that naming scheme.

Anyway, it turned out Abel's former employers were super angry with Cain forcing him to go on the run. At some point afterward, he entered the program and vanished.

As for Vasile, he was supposed to be in law enforcement up north. Even though he was within a few thousand miles, there never seemed a right time for them to get together. I had to assume there were some family dynamics there she didn't want to get into, because thirty years was a long time to not even take a day to say hi. I figured when she was ready, she'd tell me what was really going on. Until then, I didn't want to infringe on how she conducted herself with her children, no matter my own viewpoint.

Two taps later, I was looking at the composite photo she'd sent over. Cain had dark skin like his mother's. He had kind chestnut-colored eyes and a bald head. Even though the image showed the man from the shoulders up, I could see he was muscular. When you combined that with his face, I was certain he wouldn't have any trouble finding a companion.

I glanced around to see the others were looking at the same image with wonder written across their expressions.

Clearing my throat, I asked, "Where do you want us to start?"

Lilith gave me a comforting smile. "You'll be with me." She gestured at the others. "The rest of you spread out." Her tone hardened. "I don't think I have to tell you all how important this is to me."

Jose shook his head. "We'll handle it."

As we started to walk towards the complex, cars began filing in behind us to fill up the spots they'd cleared for the chopper to land. By the time we made it through the gate, the first lot was full and there had to be at least three hundred people hot on our heels. Their presence would make this much more difficult, though Cain did seem like he'd be a hard man to miss.

Twenty minutes in, I was suddenly struck with the realization I'd been relocated from what had long ago been a very impressive city to the ninth level of hell. Please allow me to explain. Let's start with the fact that there were way too many people. While I found the ruins here intriguing as hell—I mean this whole area used to be flooded, and they used boats to move from one pyramid to the next...that was just cool as hell. Sadly, only a few others seemed to give a shit about it, the rest were here for themselves.

What did I mean by that? Most of them were *influencers*—god, I hated that word. What was an *influencer* anyway? Seriously, just give it a little thought—was being a semi-attractive twenty-something wearing skin-tight outfits rambling incoherently about things that didn't matter truly count as influence?

And if it did, wasn't that kind of—well you get the picture; I didn't approve, and I didn't have to. People were entitled to their opinions even if they were often wrong, or at the very least, misinformed.

To make things worse, Z, the latest and greatest internet platform, was filled to the brim with them. Z was a subsidiary of Muzos —an evil megacorporation that'd bought out Facebook, Tik-Toc, Myspace—hey, I was just as shocked as you to find out it still existed, as well as all the others. Yeah, I always thought there was some sort of law preventing such a monopoly too, but with enough money, I guess anything was possible. Now, if you wanted a social media account, Z was the only place to be—you know, because of the whole monopoly thing.

One of my many problems with Z was the fact it was owned by what amounted to a set of cartoon-type villains, Edward Munns and Geoffery Yanos. A second and probably far more sinister reason why I didn't like Z was due to its branding. Sure, a stylized Z didn't sound evil, but when you placed a horizontal slash through the center, it took on a whole different meaning. Due to said meaning, I had to wonder how they got the trademark pushed through around the world. Seriously, I'd like to know who looked at this damn thing and said it was fine. Then to see them turn around and use it in recruitment campaigns was giving off some serious dystopian vibes.

Anyway, everywhere we turned there were cellphone rigs being used to record *content*—and I used that term loosely—for their channels. Thankfully, this seemed a bit more family-friendly than what the authorities encountered last week. Apparently, a pair of creators using Z's more adult-themed channels snuck in late one night and was filming porn atop the Pyramid of the Moon. I have nothing against porn, but come on, be respectful enough to get the permits.

Between the rigging, the internet sensations, their entourage, fans, and actual tourists, the place was packed to the gills. Where I thought spotting Cain would be a simple thing, it was anything but. Issac recruited a few techies from the area to fly drones over the site, in hopes of spotting him with their cameras. Still, though, we didn't seem to be making any progress.

Technically, it was a nice enough day—clear skies, a cool breeze, and it was right around twenty-one degrees Celsius. Nice, right? Well, I wasn't feeling it. My general aggravation level was reaching heights I wasn't comfortable with. Maybe it was the people—specifically the attention-seeking pricks making our job that much harder —yeah this was their fault for being in the way.

I stepped forward only for someone to push me back. "Hey! Watch it, old man. I'm filming here." The twenty-something blonde wearing a barely-there bikini waved me away. "Get out of my shot. You're ruining everything."

My irritation turned into a seething hate, and I took a step forward. Fear bloomed in the woman's eyes as she scrambled back.

A gentle hand slipped around my forearm. "Let it go." Lilith leaned in to kiss me on the cheek. "You're tired, and you are in her shot."

I let her tug me away from the vapid little shit without saying a word. When I glanced back, I was surprised to find a half dozen of Ōmeyōcān-Mictlān's security personnel dismantling her gear.

"Thank you."

Leaning against my arm, she said, "No problem." She flashed a vindictive look over her shoulder. "Some people need to learn they aren't as special as they think they are."

Yeah, fucking with Lilith in her current mood wouldn't serve anyone well.

Out of nowhere, she handed me a slushie. "Here, its peach."

Taking it, I took a long sip from the straw. "Where'd you get this?"

A small smile crossed her lips. "A girl has to have some secrets, and this is one of mine."

"Thanks."

I knew I should've pushed the issue, because seriously, where in the hell was she keeping the thing? On the other hand, I wasn't about to push any boundaries. Why? Because I liked all my parts and pieces where they were. In the mood she was in, I wasn't willing to risk questioning her judgement over a freaking slushie.

Plus, I wasn't at my best.

All I'd had to eat so far was a couple bags of jerky. Then there was the lack of sleep. I mean, I was awake and alert, but my senses were somewhat dulled from the constant go, go, go of the last ten days. To make matters worse, my wife was stressed out over her long, lost son, and I wasn't doing a lot to help.

By this point, she seemed more exhausted than I'd ever seen her. Her gaze continued to sweep over the crowd, hoping beyond hope she'd find Cain. My heart sank, because my gut was telling me he wasn't here, but I didn't have the heart to tell her.

Wrapping my arm around her waist, I pulled her close for a moment before letting her go. "Love you."

A small smile crossed her lips. "I love you, too." She reached out and took my hand, squeezing it tight. "Thank you."

I winked. "Thank you, too."

We continued to weave our way through the crowd, then a tall woman with long sapphire hair and cool blue—almost white eyes stepped in our path. Lilith came to an abrupt halt as she squeezed my hand even tighter. Obviously, she recognized this stranger from somewhere. Turning my attention to the newcomer, I really took the time to size her up. She had an air of authority about herself that demanded respect. The tailored surgical-white pant suit seemed to accentuate her confidence and power. Then there was the way she held herself that screamed that she was a dangerous woman. Her every movement was an exercise in control. There seemed to be some sort of predator just under the surface straining to be let loose.

As she eyed Lilith, a hint of remorse marred her preternatural beauty. When she spoke, the regret was palpable. "I'm sorry to say, you missed him." She glanced out to the north. "Even if you'd left the moment you realized, you would've been too late." The corners of her eyes became wet. "I'm sorry."

My mind was having difficulty comprehending the woman in

front of me. It wasn't just the physical either, there was something unearthly about her as if she didn't belong to this world. Everything about her was alien—those cool blue eyes seemed ageless, almost as if she'd borne witness to the birth of the universe itself. Then there was her voice; it held a siren's call as if her words could ensnare the soul.

Wait, what was happening to me? In that moment, the strange sensation that'd settled over me was gone, broken. It didn't change her exactly, but whatever was going on with her was gone now.

It was then she turned her attention to me. "How—interesting."

Lilith's voice had a dangerous tone to it. "Mab."

Holding up her hands, she shook her head. "I promise you, that was unintentional." She gestured at herself. "Though I am impressed he shrugged it off so easily. Most men caught within my power never resurface from it, even if it isn't my intention."

Lilith's shoulders slumped. "I know, old friend." Her gaze passed over the Pyramid of the Sun. "Are you sure? Cain's gone?"

It was clear Mab didn't want to answer, but she nodded. "Yes." Shaking her head, she said, "I'd hoped to get here quickly enough, but by the time I arrived, he'd vanished." She gestured out toward Mexico City. "I have people searching, but I have to warn you, they aren't the only ones."

Anger flashed in Lilith's eyes, and for a split second I thought they glowed amber again. "The Onyx Mind?"

She nodded. "That's our guess." A small smile crossed her lips. "Though, it looks like he has a companion—a woman." There was a slight hesitation before she spoke again. "My people seem to think she could be his child."

Happiness spread across Lilith's face in an instant. "Truly."

"It's a guess, but I think it's a good one."

Relief spread across her face. "Since I can't be with him, I'm glad to know he won't be alone."

Mab's gaze landed on me. "Speaking of alone." She gestured at me. "Is this the stray?"

Running her hand over her face, Lilith sighed. "How many times do I have to tell you, the word is orphan." She bumped her shoulder into mine. "And yes, this is my husband, Horacio Garcia." Gesturing at Mab, she smiled. "Honey, this is Mab."

So, that was a weird word choice, though maybe this wasn't her first language. Still though, how had she known about me being an orphan? It wasn't as if I hid it, but I didn't know this lady. As to me being an orphan, I'd been adopted early, and my adoptive father was wonderful. Back in his younger days, he was a fireman. One day, he responded to a call involving a tenement in the process of burning down. To that end, they were able to rescue most of the people living there. I'd been found wrapped in a blanket in the basement, alone and crying. When it became clear no one was stepping forward to claim me, he and mom adopted me. Shortly after her death when I was two, he took early retirement from the department and opened a gym-slash-dojo so he could raise me.

A wicked smile crossed the woman's lips as she raked her gaze over my body. "Long dark hair, warm brown eyes, and those cheekbones." She pulled air in through her teeth. "Then there's that jawline—that caramel skin...and he's just the right height. Very nice." Biting her lip, she let out a low humming sound. "For a stray, I can see the appeal."

Suddenly, I felt like I was a dog at Westminster being considered for best in show. The predatory look she was giving me made me feel like she was about to start shoving fingers in places while cupping stuff she shouldn't. Granted, my wife occasionally invited extra participants home for a bit of fun, but right here, right now, wasn't what I'd call appropriate.

Even while she continued to scan the area, Lilith shot her old friend a dirty look. "Again, not a stray, and being an orphan has no bearing on his genetics." Annoyance flashed across her face. "Also, stop messing with me. This isn't the time."

Mab's smile vanished and she hung her head. "Again, I'm sorry." She turned to me with a sad smile. "It was a pleasure to make your acquaintance."

"Likewise." I let out a long breath before patting my wife on the shoulder. "I'm sorry we missed him."

She placed her hand over my own. "Thanks." Her gaze trailed off in the distance. "I knew it was a bit of a longshot when I came, but I had to try."

I hugged her tightly. "Of course you did." Following her gaze north, I said, "We could try to catch up."

The moment we separated, Mab stood there holding a golden box. It was large enough I would've spotted it earlier, and there definitely wasn't enough room to hide it inside her suit, so where the hell did it come from?

Eyeing the box with trepidation, Lilith's voice was barely above a whisper. "No, we can't."

"What do you mean, we can't?" I gestured out in the distance. "Give me a day, and I'll find the trail; you know I will."

She shook her head. "That won't work."

Was she high? "Why not?"

Her old friend eyed the object in her hand with great distaste. "Because it's time."

Obviously, I'd missed something important. Glaring at Mab, I took a step forward. "And what the hell does that mean?"

Something primal flashed in her eyes as she swelled to her full height.

Tugging me back, Lilith placed herself between me and Mab. "Hey, I've got this." She watched her friend, who seemed to calm. "Thank you." She thumbed over her shoulder at me. "Let me say goodbye?"

Stepping aside, Mab nodded. "Of course."

What the hell did she mean by goodbye?

Lilith pulled me off to the side and the world around us seemed to blur as tears ran down her cheeks. "I'm sorry…" Her voice trailed off. "I should've told you…I just couldn't. I didn't want to ruin anything."

Instinctively, I reached out to wipe away the tears. "It's fine… whatever it is we can work it out together."

Lilith flinched. "Th...that's sweet of you, but you don't under-stand." She gestured at Mab. "She's here to take me—" Her voice cracked. "...into protective custody."

What the hell was she talking about? "I don't understand."

The tears continued to fall as pain and regret filled her voice. "I...ah...it's hard to explain." She hung her head. "Do you remember what I told you about my ex-husband?"

How in the hell could I forget? The guy was an abusive asshole with attachment issues. That was a polite way of saying he stalked her after she got away from the prick. Not only did he track her down, but he poisoned the guy she was seeing at the time. From there, her life was a series of escapes with small windows of peace in between.

"If you're worried about what he'll do to me, don't. I can take care of myself."

A sad smile crossed her lips. "Yes, you can." She wiped her cheeks. "Unfortunately for all of us, he isn't the only problem." Her gaze tracked over my shoulder toward home. "Through no fault of your own, you don't have a clue what Ōmeyōcān-Mictlān does."

"I wouldn't say I don't have a clue." Ōmeyōcān-Mictlān was a combination think-tank, research and development center, manu-facturer of next-generation technology, and a major supplier of goods that had the possibility to change the world, given enough time. "But you're right about me not knowing specifics."

Lilith beamed. "Right...your work. I do appreciate you not digging—though that'll come back to bite you in the ass soon."

I blinked. "Why is that?"

Melancholy filled her halfhearted attempt at laughter. "Because as of this morning, you are the CEO...full ownership has been transferred over." She glanced at Mab. "When I heard Lamia's call, I knew things would get complicated and my location would leak."

"I feel like I'm repeating myself here, but I don't understand, and who the hell is Lamia?" I shrugged. "Also, what does any of this have to do with Ōmeyōcān-Mictlān?"

Her expression hardened. "There are those who want my

secrets…want me specifically because of what I know." Balling her fists, she growled. "Once they figure out where I am, they won't stop." She held out her hand to stop my obvious retort. "You don't understand; the forces aligned against me would burn this world to ash if they thought they could control me."

My wife was a lot of things, but dramatic wasn't one of them… not normally anyway. "Do you think there's a chance you might be overestimating yourself?"

She gave me a look that said she thought I was a special type of stupid. "There will come a time in the next few years that you'll look back at this conversation and think to yourself how sorely I understated the fact."

I glanced over at Mab. "Is she with Interpol?"

Her eyes went wide, then she shook her head. "Ah, no." A genuine laugh escaped her. "She works for a higher authority."

There was a higher authority? I thought Interpol was the highest legal authority on the planet. "Judging by the answer, you're not going to tell me who she works for, are you?"

Her amusement instantly faded. "No, I am not." She leaned forward and kissed me on the cheek. "I'm doing this to protect you and those that work for me." Shaking her head, she let out an annoyed grunt. "It's not forever, but it might as well be as far as you're concerned."

There was so much being said while not being verbalized and I knew I was missing most of the conversation. "When's the trial?"

Confusion swept over her expression. "Trial?" Then as if realizing what I meant she shrugged. "You could say it started in earnest today." Her voice was barely a whisper. "Though I doubt you'll hear anything about it for a few years at most." Pride shone in her eyes as her tone firmed. "Say what you like about my son; he isn't subtle."

"Wait, you mean Cain?" How the hell was he involved? "What's he got to do with this?"

Lilith beamed. "Yes." Clearly ignoring my second question, she looked up at the pyramid. "I'm sorry I missed him."

My heart sank at the hurt in her voice. "I'm sorry about that."

She waved away the words. "It's not your fault or mine—it's just a shitty set of circumstances, is all."

Unable to stop myself, I asked, "Did he know you were here?"

She shook her head. "No…I couldn't risk anyone finding out."

Damn, that had to be rough. "I'm sorry."

"It's okay." She wrapped her arms around me and pulled me in for a tight embrace. "I'm going to miss you, Horacio Garcia."

Holding her close, I sighed. "I expect you to come back to me, you know."

"I will." She shrugged. "Though, it will be a while…and you should live your life to the fullest."

What the hell did that mean? "Excuse me?"

Pressing against me hard, she kissed my lips. "In time, you'll understand. Don't waste your life waiting on me…though we're still married and that's not going to change. In the meantime, though, you've got a hall pass."

My mind ground to a halt. "Are you telling me to date?"

"Just focus on the here and now." She gave me a wink. "Though, I expect you to lead a healthy life, and that includes certain activities."

This was a super uncomfortable topic to be discussed so openly. "Fine, whatever, we'll figure it out…okay?"

"Of course." She kissed me again. "It's time."

Suddenly, Mab stood next to her. Turning, Mab gave me a slight bow. "It's been a genuine pleasure."

Wish I could say the same…and I did even if it was a lie. "And you."

Mab held out the box to Lilith. "Are you ready?"

"No." She squared her shoulders. "But that doesn't matter."

Rubbing my hand over my face, I blinked. When I opened them again, they were gone. "What the hell?"

A soft, lilting voice to my right startled me. "Yes, that's Mab in a nutshell."

After nearly jumping out of my skin, I turned. Just to my right elbow stood Gisele Gama. Gisele was half a head shorter than me, though her body was proportioned in such a way she looked long and lean. Her long, dark hair was pulled back to drape past her shoulders. She had a refined beauty that spoke of passion and depth. Her poise was that of some long-forgotten queen, which I imagined served her well as Lilith's second. It was her job to keep the clocks turning and manage the day-to-day affairs of Ōmeyōcān-Mictlān while Lilith all but lived in the lab.

"Gisele?"

The smile she flashed me was both warm and filled with sadness. "I'm honored you remember me."

How could I forget? Anytime I visited the compound, it was her job to escort me to and from the lab. "I take it you finished up at the office."

Lifting her hand, she held out a tablet in my direction. "I did." Her tone was soft and comforting. "I had my hands full transferring ownership of the company to you on short notice. Thankfully, most of the paperwork had already been pushed through years ago, but there are still formalities that need to be followed."

Panic began to set in. "What?" I glanced around hoping to see Lilith somewhere nearby laughing at this strange prank. "No...this isn't right."

"I apologize for any confusion you have, but I assure you, this is correct." She lowered the tablet. "Look, I know this is sudden... and with Lilith stepping away, you're obviously distressed." Tucking the tablet into her case, she patted my back. "Go home, talk with Jose or one of the others...if that doesn't suit you, I'll be happy to send someone or come myself." Her tone lowered to a near whisper. "We will all miss her. She was your wife, but she was our companion as well. We've known her for...well what feels like forever. I think a bit of shared grief will help...talking it through with people who understand has a way of easing the pain."

Shame hit me like a brick. It was true, while they may've been employed by her, she'd known each and every one of them longer than she'd known me. She'd been their friend, rushed to the hospital to see their kids being born, and so much more.

Hanging my head, I nodded. "Thank you." I held my hand out for the tablet. "I assume you need me to sign some things."

She nodded. "Yes." Handing it over, she tapped the screen. "Here you go."

I shook my head. "Where do I sign?"

Gisele pointed. "That gives me permission to keep doing my job."

After reading the section, I used my finger to sign the document

With that done, I moved to the next screen and took several minutes to work my way through the corpo-speak. "Everything seems in order." I continued to scroll to the end of the text, only to find there was no signature line. "Ah, there's no place for me to technically assume my duties, such as they are."

Gisele grinned. "Press your thumb against the indentation there —Lilith has it keyed to your biosignature. Once it confirms it's you, we're done."

Pressing my thumb to the indentation, I said, "Next you'll be wanting my first born too."

Gisele shook her head. "Nah, that went out of style back in the dark ages."

As young as she was, she probably thought anything more than fifteen years ago qualified. Mumbling more to myself than her, I said, "Youngsters."

She arched an eyebrow. "How long have you known me?"

The comment caught me by surprise, then I thought about it. She'd been working for Lilith for years before I came into the picture thirty years ago. That was when I took another hard look at her. "Damn, talk about some good genetics." I shook my head. "You don't look a day over thirty."

Snorting a laugh, she quickly covered her mouth. "Sorry." She cleared her throat. "It's...well, let's just say I haven't heard that in— more years than I'd like to admit."

Really? She was a beautiful woman, and men weren't known for their subtlety. "I find that hard to believe."

She rolled her eyes then took the tablet. "Whatever." Her expression faltered. "Will you need a lift home, or will you be finding your own way back?"

Whew...yeah, I wasn't up for making it home alone. "I could use a ride, if it isn't too much trouble."

A chuckle escaped her. "You know it's not." She gestured for me to follow. "Come along."

It was only after she started walking that I noticed a dozen new figures move out of the crowd and fall instep around us. Jose's team was waiting for me at the gate, all of us looking rougher for the day's experience.

3

NOT TODAY, MY FRIEND

December 21ˢᵗ

Puebla, Mexico, Earth

Living in a city nestled in the mountains had its advantages, such as the near constant breeze keeping the air clear and clean. Then there was the fact it never got too hot or too cold. Even in the depths of winter, all I needed was a medium-weight leather jacket to stave off the nip in the air. As I strolled down the street, I caught snippets of holiday songs whenever a door was opened.

Above me, a dozen rows of long, brightly colored lights hung there waiting for their moment to bathe the cobblestones underfoot in a sea of blueish white. Meter tall stars were hung from every light pole, just itching to glow to life and dazzle the children as they cycled through their vibrant color schemes. The little ones would look up with awe in their eyes and think of the presents waiting for them at home. Thanks to the city's subtropical highland climate, the fountain in the square rarely froze. Due to that little oversight of nature, the city took the liberty of draping hundreds of artificial icicles around it.

In the square, I spotted several people dashing around trying to find the perfect gift. I guessed this was what it was supposed to be like, but I couldn't be sure. Growing up, Christmas hadn't been a big holiday—mom passed away on Christmas Eve and it was hard on my father. His big holiday was the day of the dead. I think it was his way of honoring mom.

Even now, I was sure my father was at home going through his daily routine. I checked my watch: 11:30. Yeah, he'd be running the crossword puzzle right about now. Once he finished that, he'd make himself some lunch and take a nap. He was highly upset when the government tried to abolish the siesta under the guise of saving the buses.

They claimed it put a huge strain on the transportation system. In reality—according to the papers—they were trying to appease the corporations who wanted to increase productivity. Again, my pops said that was a lie too; the corporations only wanted to tighten their grip on the individual in an attempt to build the same abusive work culture they had in the United States and other parts of the world. Anyway, after his nap, he'd take a stroll through the park, catch a show of some sort before dinner, and head home.

I visited him a few times a week, and he'd even drop by the office, especially when he wanted to bum lunch. The whole wanting a free meal thing wasn't restricted to my father, since Hector often did the same. Today, for instance, he offered to meet me at the little mom and pop torta shop down the street from my office—the real one, not whatever they had for me at Ōmeyōcān-Mictlān. While I technically ran what was arguably the most powerful company on the planet, I had a day job that I understood and liked. Which was why I was in Centro and not in their compound on the north-western edge of the city.

Gisele understood and didn't make much of a fuss over my choice, but she did have one caveat; Lilith's security team was mine now. What'd that mean? Well, where I went, they went whether I liked it or not. Mind you, they weren't intrusive, and most of the time it helped having a few extra hands around. Though, on a day like today, it had the potential to feel a bit crowded.

Rounding the corner, I entered the little shop. Hector was off in the corner. When he saw me, he waved me over. "Right on time." He held out one of the plates in front of him. "I just picked up the food."

At a smidge over two meters and ninety-one kilograms of muscle, Hector was a big man. Between the two of us, he was normally what most people referred to as the handsome one. That wasn't me putting myself down. Not to be vain, but I wasn't hard to look at. Hector, however, was just annoyingly handsome. Back when we were young boys, this frustrated me because very few people gave me a second look since we were always together. I'd gotten fed up with it one day and said something to him. That was when he sat me down and explained things from his point of view.

"Yes, I get a lot of attention." He shrugged off the comment. "But it's only because of the way I look." Pointing at me, he said, "The women that look at you see you for who you are. They aren't blinded by something as petty as a pretty face."

That was when I shut my mouth. He had a point. The man never sought out the one-night stand—he was forever looking for the great love of his life. It wasn't until years later I found out he hadn't lost his virginity until he was in college.

I meandered over and gave him a hug as he rose out of his seat. "Good to see ya, buddy." Glancing down at the plate, I lifted the bread with my finger. It looked right—sliced avocado, breaded chicken cutlet, Oaxaca cheese, freshly sliced onions, some dried pápalo leaves, and a chipotle adobo. Arching an eyebrow, I said, "This is chicken, right?"

"Of course." A shit eating grin crossed his lips. "When have I ever gotten that wrong?"

Mind you, the pork version wasn't wrong. It just wasn't my favorite. "Every time you think you can get away with it."

Hector gestured at the seat. "Not today, my friend." His gaze tracked over the room. "Are your friends with you?"

I glanced over my shoulder but didn't spot anyone. "They should be."

"Invite them in." He turned to the lady at the counter. "I've got a few more coming, so just take their order and bring me the bill when they're done."

The old woman behind the counter blushed and nodded. "Thank you, Mr. Matos."

Placing his hand over his heart, he acted as if she'd wounded him. "Lucia, how many times must I tell you, it's Hector."

Lucia held up her left hand. "It's Mr. Matos." There was a glint in her eye as her gaze tracked over him. "Now if I were single, that'd be a different story."

He burst out laughing. "Fair enough."

Jose gave me a curious look as he strode through the door. "I thought you wanted a private conversation."

"Yeah, me too." I gestured over at Hector and smiled. "But he wants to make this a family affair."

Jose arched an eyebrow in his direction. "Are you sure?"

Hector's expression turned serious. "Come, we have much to talk about."

Issac, Christopher, Luis, Jamie, and Martin strode in and quickly ordered. While they were busy getting their food, Hector and I moved some tables together to make room for everyone.

Once everyone was seated, I gave Hector an expectant look. "So, what's up?"

"That's a loaded question, my friend." His gaze tracked out of the open door, and he frowned. "Are you familiar with a man named Barry Lawson?"

Oh, for fucks sake. "Yeah, the prick has been relentless in his attempts to schedule a meeting with me." Then I had a sinking feeling. "Tell me you didn't—"

Halfway to his feet, Hector wagged an accusing finger at me. "Dude, you know me better than that."

Yeah, that was shitty of me to even think. "Sorry man."

Flipping me the bird, he plopped into his seat. "Man, now I'm halfway tempted to keep what I know to myself." He shot me a dirty look. "Wow—do you really think so little of me?"

I shrunk back in my chair. "I really am sorry...the guy has been out there trying to bribe anyone and everyone to trick me into a meeting." Gesturing at the door, I sighed. "He even tried to corner my dad."

"Wait, he went after Miguel?" His eyes went wide with anger and horror. "Is he okay?"

Did he think the guy was dangerous? "Yeah, Barry is persistent but he's just a lawyer. It isn't as if the guy is muscle for some cartel."

Hector's anger at me seemed to have faded when he learned about my dad. "I wouldn't be so sure." He plucked a thumb drive out of his pocket and slid it over to me. "Look, that's everything I can find on the guy."

Picking it up, I eyed it then stashed it. "Is there something on this bugging you?"

"A lot of things." Hector drummed his fingers against the table. "Look, you know the people I deal with, and I've got a lot of connections, but this guy has me beat out on every front."

Did I miss something? "What's that supposed to mean?"

Pushing his uneaten torta out of the way, he placed his elbows against the edge of the table. "Well, for starters, Barry Lawson didn't exist a year ago." His fingers continued to tap out a rhythm against the tabletop. It was one of his more serious ticks that told me the situation was well and truly out of hand. "And whoever created this new identity for him made it bulletproof. There aren't any holes in it…everything is perfectly legal, and for all intents and purposes, he is exactly who he says he is."

Jose cocked his head to the side. "What gave him away?"

"A few things." He shook his head. "Take a look at the venture capitalist group he supposedly represents. I mean, it's existed for years but it'd barely been functional until Barry showed up eight months ago. That was when things started moving. Then there's the money—it's been flowing for the better part of twenty years. It looks like he's had multiple cards issued in his name, and he even took out a loan for a house he's since paid off. Thing is, that house doesn't exist." He got a faraway look in his eyes. "Then, there are the card charges…an automated charge of a few thousand pesos would hit it then get paid off the next day. Not a single one of them were swiped in person until—"

Issac swallowed his bite. "Until eight months ago."

Hector pointed at him. "Exactly." He shrugged. "There's more—like a lot more, but the important part is, whoever is backing him has a whole lot of clout and the kind of money they use to buy countries."

Jose glanced at the others before giving them a curt nod.

Jamie got to his feet. "I need to make a call and send some texts." He hooked a thumb over his shoulder. "I'll be right back."

Hector watched him go before turning to Jose. "He won't find any more than I did." He gestured at me. "Maybe take a look at the data on the jump drive first."

Holding up his phone, Jose gave him a half-hearted smile. "Already on it."

"What?" His eyebrows knitted themselves together. "How are you able to access it from there?"

Jose gave him a sly smile. "Trade secret."

Looking a little unsettled, Hector arched an eyebrow at me. "You know your people are just as scary as Barry is, right?"

I waved away the comment. "We went through this years ago. It's fine."

Hector and I did a little digging into the company when I first started dating Lilith, Ōmeyōcān-Mictlān wasn't what it appeared, and neither were the people working there. We were able to track the company's origins back nearly two hundred years. It seemed to pass from one holding company to another with a number of different figureheads over the years. As for Lilith and her people, they seemed to have just stepped into their positions the moment the company was formed about five years before I met her. It was a weird setup, but since the company had a long history of helping, I chose to ignore it.

Grumbling, he picked up his torta. "If you say so."

Hector and I ate our food in silence while the others alternately picked at theirs and sifted through their phones. By the time we were finished, Hector looked even more stressed than he had.

When his plate was empty, I gestured at the door. "I'll walk you out. Once we're done here, I'll head back to the office. Any big holiday plans?"

A small smile crossed his lips. "I'm picking up Esmerelda and the kids for dinner at my parents."

Esmerelda Millan was Hector's ex-wife and the mother of his two kids, Paulina and Jaun. Esmerelda was a successful actress, absolutely stunning, and sweet. The problem was, Hector's job prevented him from basking in the limelight next to her, which was an issue but something they worked through, eventually. The final straw came when his job put him at odds with one of the studios in Mexico City, and she had to make a choice between a husband she liked and a job she loved. They were still on good terms, and even though they were divorced, they were still seeing each other regularly, so maybe this was the key that'd fix their relationship.

I gave him a hug. "Alright, just take care of yourself." Straightening his collar, I smiled. "But I'm glad she's joining you for the holidays this year."

A big smile crossed his lips. "Me too." His gaze landed on Jose. "Are you going to be okay?" His voice lowered to a near whisper. "You know you're welcome at my parents place...this is your first holiday alone since Lilith—well since she went away."

Her being gone hurt, but that wasn't due to the holidays. "You know I've never been big on Christmas." I gave him a wink. "Go have fun...and if you're lucky, you'll find a little something from me under the tree."

His whole body went rigid. "Did you break into my house again?"

"No." It was the truth too, I had Jamie do it. "But I do have my ways."

He ran his hand over his face. "Tell me it's at least family friendly."

Goddamn it, he needed to let that go. Back when he and

Esmerelda got married, I sent over a year's supply of massage oils, a massage table with all the extras, and a few other things. Then the dumbass lugged the unopened gift over to his parent's house to celebrate with them. How was I to know he'd do that?

"Yes, it's family friendly."

Gisele was kind enough to scoop up a few things for him and the family. His was a prototype tablet that worked off the new Network she was currently experimenting with. Once it was done, it'd replace the internet and be available worldwide and beyond. I wasn't sure what the solar system would need with unlimited wi-fi, but whatever. It was as if she were planning ahead for some unseen future. As for the kids and Esmerelda, they received a scaled back version of the same tablet.

Hector winked. "Good." He leaned in to whisper in my ear. "Not that the massage table hasn't come in useful, but I don't need another kid right now."

Hanging my head, I let out a long breath. "Dude, way too much information." I pointed out the door. "Go...and thanks for the heads up."

He grinned. "No problem."

With that, he turned and left. Now, all I had to do was figure out who this Barry creep was and what the hell he wanted. Speaking of creepy, I lifted my phone to take a better look at the guy. He was a pale, hairless man who seemed to celebrate his eccentricities. In the photo, he wore a white and black cow print suit with a canary yellow shirt. It seemed to bring out his hazel eyes. According to the stat sheet Hector had on the guy, he was one point eight three meters tall and roughly fifty-five kilograms. Given his height, such a small amount of weight was highly impressive. To sum him up in a few words, he was a slight, weaselly man with beady little eyes that screamed malevolence.

After hearing about the man and doing a bit of reading, I knew ignoring him wasn't going to work. One day he'd find me, and that day would suck. Just looking at the picture gave me the ick, so I couldn't even imagine what being in his presence would be like. Let me be clear, it wasn't his overall look that bothered me, it was the details in the bio and the fact he was a lawyer...and not the kind that sought justice. He was the kind of guy who used the law to create contracts that'd harm the other party. There was something in his eyes that told me he likely enjoyed the pain and suffering he caused.

My gut was telling me he was going to be a long-term problem.

Grumbling to myself, I said, "Fuck this guy and whatever he wants."

I glanced at the photo again. Yeah, it'd be a cold day in hell before I'd ever sit down with this prick and have a civil conversation.

There was something untrustworthy about the guy that bothered me on a fundamental level.

Jose glanced up at me. "Sorry, I missed that."

"It was nothing." I turned my screen toward him. "I just can't see me sitting down with this guy on purpose."

His expression darkened. "Smart move." He pointed at his phone. "Hector's correct; his identity is airtight, but there's definitely something off about it. We're doing our best to dig into it, but we're not making much in the way of progress."

Jamie stepped in, looking like he was ready to murder someone. "Everyone needs to stop what they're doing." He waved his phone around before tucking it away. "Ms. Gama will be handling things from here." The look on his face said that was the last thing he wanted. "Seems like we rocked a few boats, and we're getting calls from several low-level bureaucrats connected with the Archive."

Issac tilted his seat onto the ground and gave Jamie a hard look. "I see."

It was clear they weren't going to share, so I thumbed over my shoulder. "We should go."

My phone beeped and I glanced down to see a message from Hector.

. . .

Hey buddy, I forgot to pay Lucia, could you handle that for me?

That prick.

I strode over to the counter and handed Lucia a five hundred peso note. "Thank you. It was wonderful as always."

She beamed and tucked the money away. "You're most welcome. See you soon."

With that, we walked out and headed for the office. After what Jamie said, I couldn't shake the feeling that dealing with Barry was going to be worse than I imagined.

4

WHEN YOU'RE READY

September 9ᵗʰ

   Puebla, Mexico, Earth

My gaze flickered from the fistful of papers in my hand to the literal stack of folders lying on the desk in front of me and from them to Gisele. I didn't say anything as I continued to sift through what looked like an organized attack against some organization called the Archive. I'd heard the name in passing a few times, but no one bothered to sit me down and tell me what it was. That looked like it might be changing.

Frowning, I flipped back to the front of the document to review the highlight reel, such as it was. First up was a newspaper article that'd been translated from French.

Man Mutilated on the Steps of Notre Dame.

The photo that followed showed the outline of a body beneath a rough canvas tarp stained dark with gore. It was clear the heavily wounded man had been running, and equally clear his pursuers had caught up to him. Large swaths of the stone steps were covered in blood where he'd fought for every centimeter he could. In the end it wasn't enough.

The article read:

Reports are still coming in about prominent businessman and philanthropist, Alfred Monet. From what the police have pieced together from camera footage at the church, Mr. Monet entered the restricted zone at 1:58 a.m. pursued by nine masked assailants. They tackled him to the ground, stabbed him several times, and cut out at least one of his internal organs while he was still alive.

Below the snippet was a notation from Gisele about the man's importance. Alfred Monet, European Governor for the Archive. There was a small V annotation next to his name, but it didn't seem to correspond with anything else in the report. It mentioned he was due in Rome later in the day for some sort of meeting that'd had its own issues. My big question was why was he running toward a burned-out church with little to no security in the middle of the night? It wasn't like he was going to be granted sanctuary. Even if he had been granted such a boon from some clergy member, I doubted the guys who gutted him like a fish would've paid it any mind.

Moving on, the next article that'd been translated for me was out of Hong Kong.

Woman Burned at the Stake.

Somehow Gisele got her hands on the unedited photo to show the stake in question had been shoved through the woman's anal cavity and out through her shoulder. By all accounts, she'd somehow lived through the trauma, only to be doused in some sort of accelerant and lit on fire. What remained wasn't visibly identifiable as a woman. All I could tell was it was human at one time, but that was about it. The charring was so bad I wasn't sure the head was still attached, as it seemed to all blend together in one big, long lump.

Local restaurant owner, Van Hang, was tied to a post, doused in petrol, and set afire outside her home in broad daylight around nine this morning. While the motives are unclear, there is some speculation that the Triad is involved.

Another notation from Gisele marked this Van Hang as a triumvirate—whatever that was—out of Asia. There was that same weird V annotation again, but just like Alfred, there was no explanation.

Flipping to the next, I found a clipping from Cape Town.

Severed Head of a Woman Found on Spike.

This time, whoever did the killing shoved her severed head atop a large ceremonial spike that'd been driven into the ground.

Local artist Aitan Kaya was found brutally murdered in her driveway at two this morning. Neighbors complained to the police of shouts and screaming. By the time they arrived, Ms. Kaya was already dead.

The note marked her as a triumvirate out of southern Africa. Then there was that stupid V annotation again.

On to the next.

. . .

House Fire in Covington, Louisiana.

The charred remains of what had once been an expensive two-story house appeared in the photo.

Local city official's house was set ablaze...neighbors called the fire department shortly after eight p.m. No body has been found yet.

Gisele's note said this house belonged to one Elizabeth Dodd, who was a Prefect for this Archive organization. And again, there was a strange V annotation.

Part of me wanted to ask what it meant, but I chose to focus on the details of the report first. That could come later.

What came next wasn't a regular article but one from the Historical District in New Orleans.

Three Abandoned Vehicles Found in the Garden District.

I couldn't help but wince at the photo. It looked like the old F-150 mentioned at the bottom of the photo T-boned the SUV at a relatively high speed. Then to make matters worse, a dump truck filled to capacity had a head on collision with it. What'd once been a big car was now small enough to fit in most people's living rooms. Then there were what looked to be three bodies off to the side, though the picture was too dark to be sure.

The incident was called into police around eight p.m. after a neighbor had a tire crash through their front window. NOPD has sent a special investi-

gations unit, the Uncommon Crimes Department (UCD), to check into what happened. Officer Jeremy Riggs was first on the scene.

According to what we know, there was a multiple car accident involving a black SUV and two other vehicles, resulting in four fatalities. At least one of the drivers is unaccounted for.

Finally, I got back to the Rome incident.

Building Collapses Near Vatican.

Photo of an ancient three-story stone building that'd caved in followed.

Shortly after one a.m., a small fire broke out in the residence, causing the gas line to explode. At the time, the owners, who have been unavailable for comment, were throwing a party of some sort. We can confirm at least eighteen people are dead. Several of the guests escaped the blaze but haven't been seen since. The police are currently looking for them so they can be questioned as to what happened.

Frustrated, I placed the pages down and glanced up at Gisele. "I saw most of this, and more, back in August when it happened." Pushing the papers toward her, I shrugged. "Why bring this to me now?"

Her gaze flickered down to the folders then up at me. "I feel we need to clarify a few things before we can properly get started."

What the hell was she talking about? "Uh—okay, sure, clarify away."

Gisele retrieved a tablet from her bag then glanced back at Jose. "You've made sure we won't be disturbed, correct?"

He nodded. "Your team is covering the entrance. No one will make their way in."

"Good." She turned to look at me then pressed her thumb against the indentation at the bottom. Suddenly, every article she'd shown me appeared in a hologram between us. Then with a wave of her hand, they all stacked themselves neatly off to the side. A second flick of her hand called up four photos, only one of which I knew. Pointing at the first, she said, "Of course you're familiar with Cain."

That'd be a stretch. "I wouldn't say familiar—I mean, I know he's Lilith's son, and I've seen his photo before—though this is a new one."

Gisele gave me a sad smile. "Right, my apologies." Reaching up she tapped the photo. Suddenly, a spinning globe bloomed into existence beneath it. It stopped when Europe took center stage then zoomed in to show Romania before dropping down to focus on an older Art Deco style building in Bucharest. "We believe this is his current residence, though he has ties to Brasilia as well."

A few dozen articles centered around the disappearance of a woman named Namisia began to populate. These were somehow tied to some ghost train that'd been circling Romania for decades but hadn't been seen in months. Crime scene photos from a place called Club V showed the building in ruins before being bought out and refurbished by new owners. There were literally thousands of reports showing an abnormally high number of missing persons throughout the country. On top of that, there were reports of high-level corruption, along with a spike in crime rates. Then back in July, everything took a sudden turn for the better, and no one seemed to know why.

I read over the details then glanced up at Namisia and finally Cain. "Let me guess, Cain is working again?" Pointing at the very attractive woman, I said, "And he put an end to the bullshit she was running?"

Gisele gave me a quick wink. "Very good." She slowly moved him to one side. "Okay, when you're ready, we'll revisit Cain."

"Hey, I'm ready."

The look she gave me damn near made me crap my pants. "No, you're not." Tapping the next photo, a name appeared underneath it, Viktor Warden. "This is Viktor; he runs Warden Global." She gave me a curious look. "Are you familiar with them?"

Actually, I was. "Yeah, they're a security firm that runs humanitarian aid around the world. For a bunch of heavily armed people, they do a lot of good. They make sure those in need get it, and anyone who tries to stop them regrets that decision rather quickly."

She bobbed her head from side to side as she thought it over. "That's good enough for now."

She pointed at Viktor, and two photos appeared beneath him. One was an extremely attractive dark-haired woman, and the other was a man with long black hair, a dark complexion, brown eyes, strong handsome features that were very similar to—no. I glanced over at Cain then back at the other man.

Stunned, I mumbled. "Is that Vasile?"

A sly grin crossed her lips. "It is." She pointed at Viktor. "That's his father."

I blinked. "Viktor Warden—the head of Warden Global—the man who has what amounts to the largest standing army on the planet is Lilith's ex?"

"Yes." She rolled her shoulders. "Now, the important thing to know about Warden Global is, they are one of our major customers." Her hand flashed up to stop my obvious question. "And no, Viktor, nor anyone else who works for him knows that Lilith used to own the company. Furthermore, none of them had a clue of her whereabouts since she and Viktor split."

Okay, that was a lot to take in. "Uh-huh."

Tapping the next photo, she smiled. "This is Gavin Randall. He's the head of the vigiles—think of them as Interpol but for the Archive—shit." She bit her lip. "Sorry, they killed that name a week or so back; they're going by the Witan now, but it looks like—"

"Hold on." Unable to stop myself, I snatched up the folder. "The Archive? The people that died worked for them, right?"

Her body tensed, then she nodded. "Yes."

I pointed at Gavin. "And he's the head of their police force?"

She nodded. "That's correct." Pointing at the papers in my hand, she said, "If you'll look back at the article from New Orleans…he was in the SUV when the attack happened." Her tone hardened. "Those attacks were coordinated and took place at nearly the exact same moment."

I felt my jaw drop as I glanced between the papers in my hand and the man she'd just pointed out. "Is that why they changed their name?"

Gisele wobbled her hand back and forth. "It's a bit more complicated, but when the former head of the Archive was killed—" She gestured at the last photo. "Jade Baker took over. It was her opinion they should make a clean break from the old thus the whole rebranding and structural overhaul."

Well, then, that—that was a lot. "Okay, so if Warden Global is one of our largest customers, I'm guessing the Witan is as well."

A big smile crossed her lips. "They are now…not so much previously. Lilith wouldn't do business with Lazarus."

What was it with the people in her life and all these biblical names? "Christ, his parents must've hated him."

Arching an eyebrow, she asked, "What makes you say that?"

"The name."

Her jaw tightened. "Ah…yes…quite right." She cleared her throat. "The main reason I'm bringing this up to you now is because the world around us is rapidly changing. Between what happened in August, Viktor losing his daughter and finding his son not long after, he's not exactly in a good place. Then we've got the restructured Witan that's in the process of cleaning house while another organization has coopted the Archive monicker for less than ethical reasons."

"Do we know who picked it up?"

Disgust washed over her expression. "A group called the Twelve; they have known ties with terrorists and multiple hate groups around the world. But the real problem is their ties with Muzos, since they seem to be bankrolling this shit show."

Fucking Muzos. "That's not great news."

"It gets worse. I assure you." She shook her head. "But that can wait for now, though, I just need you to be very careful. Mr. Lawson has stepped up his attempts to contact you, while at the same time filing multiple lawsuits against the company. One way or another, I'm sure he'll make himself known at the worst possible moment."

I leaned back in my chair. "Great, not only do I have to worry about Muzos and the Twelve, but I have to dodge Barry too." Shrugging, I grumbled. "You know being rich and running a powerful company is supposed to be fun, right?"

Her tone had a dangerous edge to it. "Not with Edward and Geoffrey in the picture it's not. They are two of the vilest people I've ever met."

Wincing, I sat the folder atop the desk. "Wait, you've been in the same room as those two?"

"It was a long time ago, but yes." Her fingers drummed against the arm of her chair. "They lost a lot more than they expected due to the situation. Sadly, though, they survived the encounter."

While I had to agree the world would be a better place without them in it, I wasn't sure I wanted to be the one who killed them. "That's a little ominous."

Fury burned in her eyes. "Trust me, I wouldn't lose sleep over their demise, and neither should you; they've got more blood on their hands than you'll ever know."

Yeah, pushing this issue wasn't in my best interest. "So, what's our next step here?"

Her gaze tracked up to the hologram. "Now that you're aware of the players, I'll send over some of the pertinent data. Once you've worked your way through that, we'll move to the next stage."

"It feels like you're prepping me for something." I folded my arms. "You know I'm never going to sit on the board of directors...right?"

The tension in her body melted in an instant and she burst out laughing. "Oh...yeah, I know that. And yes, I'm prepping you for something but not for that." She pointed at Cain. "I'm prepping you for him…and the others as well, but yeah, just read what I send you…check it against your own sources then ask for me." She got to her feet. "Also, think about curtailing your jobs in the near future. I don't want Barry getting to you through that."

I nodded. "That's reasonable." My gaze danced around the images. "By the way, I knew Lilith was working on the hologram thing, but this is beyond my expectations…so congrats on that." Then a thought hit me. "Hey, do you think I should talk to my father about moving?"

She waved away my words. "We already bought the building he lives in and the ones next to it. We have a number of people stationed there to watch over him." Her fist clenched before she tapped the screen to disperse the images. "Barry will never get that close to your family again."

"Thank you."

Gisele gave me a slight bow. "My pleasure." She thumbed over her shoulder. "I'll see myself out." Glancing down at her watch, she said, "Maybe think about taking the rest of the day off."

That wasn't a half bad idea. "Hey, could you keep an eye on Hector, too?"

She waved the tablet in my direction. "Trust me, I already am."

I wasn't sure what that meant, and she was through the door before I could ask.

5

THEY ARE THE MAN

March 2nd

Teotihuacan, Mexico, Earth

Between a worldwide pandemic and a missing friend, I was having trouble appreciating what was admittedly a spectacular sunset. Even in my frazzled state, I couldn't help but stand at the foot of the Pyramid of the Sun astonished by the awe-inspiring backdrop. It was as if the gods decided today was the day they'd pay homage to the ancient structure. What could I say, the ruby reds and vibrant oranges really made it stand out like a beacon lost in time.

Tearing my gaze away from the sight, I did my best to find my friend.

Whoa, slow it down. Yeah, I am completely aware I shouldn't be out and about. Hey—HEY, tone down the judgement. Do you really think I want to be here? The whole world has gone mad, so, no I don't. Contrary to most others, I've been enjoying the me time quarantine has given me. Look, I've been able to catch up on my reading. Not only that, but I started and finished that series I'd been meaning to get to for the last couple of years. So, yeah, leaving home wasn't in the cards today, but you know what they say… duty calls.

Before you ask, no, I did not learn to bake. Here's the deal, I like to cook. For me, it's relaxing and fun, baking, however, is not. That's more like chemistry you get to eat, and that's not my bag. Sure, I like the end results, but I'm the kind of guy who measures with his heart. That kind of shit will ruin a cake or whatever type of bread you're trying to make, along with anything else that needs an exact measurement to work.

Christ, I can't see how people enjoy it. For me, it's nothing but hours upon hours of stress.

Oh, you want to know why I'm here. That's simple; about four hours ago, Hector texted me saying he was in trouble. Seeing how he's my best friend, I came to lend a hand.

Hey, I'm sorry to bother you, but I got myself in a bit of a bind. Esmerelda made a reservation for the ruins at Teotihuacan. Since they're only letting one hundred people a day visit, I thought it'd be safe, and it is...we're not infected, but someone stole my car. With the Gaia Contagion running rampant out there, I don't feel safe taking an uber...could you please come pick us up? I swear I'll make it up to you.

Of course, I called, but he'd been forced to cut the conversation short since his phone was about to die. Not feeling like I had a whole lot of options, I called Eli to tell him where we were headed. Eli was the head of the trimmed-back security team assigned to me at home. Jose and the others needed some time off before attending continuing education classes back at headquarters.

So, yeah, that was why I was here. It took me a minute to get things moving, and since I wasn't taking the express chopper, I got here about an hour ago. Since then, I'd done nothing but search for Hector and his family. Sadly, they weren't turning up, and I was starting to get concerned.

Oh, wait, I should probably explain the whole pandemic thing. On October sixteenth, the first case of the Gaia Contagion was confirmed in Montreal, Canada. Yeah, I was just as shocked as you to see the Canadians involved. Anyway, the pathogen apparently had a few paths it could take. The first was arguably the best, in that the person encountering it was immune, thus no side effects. Then came the second-best outcome, you got superpowers.

I know, you're wondering how that isn't number one. Well, that's simple, the diet, but I need to explain the final path before we get to that. Trust me, it'll become crystal clear momentarily.

The third, and by far the worst, option came in the form of a horrific and excruciating death. To be clear, the person's body mass would suddenly increase...sometimes this was due to their bones expanding, sprouting thorns and ripping through the flesh. Other times, it meant they turned into blob-like creatures that drown on their own fluids, and those were the kinder ways to die to this contagion.

Now, back to the diet required to keep those with superpowers alive. Those who acquired powers would need to consume either the flesh or drinks infused with powdered bone or some other disgusting thing from those who were killed by the infection. This made them outcasts as well as cannibals.

The only thing keeping the second group from being snatched up by unscrupulous individuals or killed on sight were the combined efforts of Warden Global and the Witan. They were doing all they could to make sure those affected lived the best life they could, given their fate.

My phone dinged.

I glanced down to see it was from Eli.

We're coming up empty handed over here. We'll make another sweep before pinging his phone and sending a recovery team to its location.

Frowning, I tapped out a reply.

· · ·

How long?

His response was nearly instant.

Give us half an hour.

Checking my watch, I sighed and began typing.

Okay.

For whatever reason, just hitting K or Ok seemed wrong. Maybe it was my age, but I felt the whole word should be spelled out. Of course, I believed in punctuation as well. This whole thing about it being considered passive aggressive by the younger generation was absolute nonsense.

Personally, I blamed Muzos. Okay, that may've been the only thing they weren't totally responsible for. What did I mean by that? Where do you want to start?

Let's see, there's the divisive nature of their platform that gives terrorists and hate groups a place to spew their toxic rhetoric. They let them bully, drown the public in lies, and generally factcheck anything they disagree, with then ban the sane users, turning it into nothing but a cesspool where only the vile seem to swim to the top.

Not a good enough example for you?

Alright, let's look at global warming.

Yes, I am quite aware other people got that ball rolling a while back, but Muzos and friends have really been pushing the envelope as of late. Seriously, they've yet to encounter an environmental protection act they haven't been willing to violate. Then there's their stance on renewable and clean energy—they absolutely refuse to participate. To be clear, they actively work against it at every opportunity, choosing to support the coal and oil industry. To be specific, they've chosen to support the worst of the worst—those that refuse to pay a living wage, place their people in continuous danger, and give them outdated equipment. Worse yet, whenever their employees die, they collect the life insurance policy the company has taken out on them.

Roll back your indignation about how that can't happen and look up dead peasant insurance...yeah, that's some pretty evil shit, isn't it? Now, you see, they don't need the person's consent, they don't have to pay the family, they don't have to do shit other than collect on the death they likely caused.

I could go on, but I think you get the point. Edward Munns and Geoffrey Yanos were the epitome of that cartoon villain trying to bring about a capitalist hellscape that'll leave the planet a scorched husk. In their opinion, if the Earth died, that was just the cost of doing business. Of course, what else could you expect from a company who popularized then weaponized their corporate logo, the stylized Z with the slash in the center. I mean, they straight up stole that from the nazis.

Goddamn it, I was spiraling. Then again, why shouldn't I? My wife was god-knew where, preparing to face off against monsters like Edward and Geoffrey.

What? Are you seriously defending these assholes? They're billionaire pricks with more money than any two people could ever spend if they tried. Let me spell it out for the slow folks out there. They aren't defiant. They aren't part of some great resistance fighting against the man—they ARE the man. I don't know how people can't see this, but they've turned their greed and influence against the world itself, and they won't stop until everyone is on their knees.

Granted, they weren't the only ones, but they were the most public.

In the last few months, I'd come to learn there were a lot of hidden powers. For instance, the Black Circle was once a catchall for a global syndicate. Then, for reasons yet to be revealed to me, roughly a third of their leadership splintered off, taking the Twelve with them. It was these pricks that'd revived the Archive moniker with the help of—you guessed it, Muzos. As Gisele said, they were bankrolling the whole affair. Hell, they were trying to revive a recently defunct hate group called the Gotteskinder.

Again, though, there were a lot of hidden creeps out there. One group of infected were led by someone calling himself Khaos. Then there were a group of escaped prisoners out of Greece that'd banded together to create their own little criminal organizations. Not like they were alone; there was some organization calling themselves the Vampire Courts. God, who in the hell thought that was a good idea? Did they really think they were vampires? It didn't matter; it looked like that was the organization Cain was bound and determined to put in the ground. By all accounts, he was doing a damn good job too. More or less, there were literally thousands of evil little shits out there looking to do harm. Thankfully, not all of them were as well funded as the Archive.

A man cleared his throat somewhere close by and I nearly jumped out of my skin. Turning, I spotted a tall, wiry man with an all too pointy chin wearing an ill-fitting police uniform. "Buenas noches, senor." His gaze panned over the area. "Are you waiting for someone?"

I gave him a crooked smile. "Just a text."

Stepping closer, his accent suddenly vanished. "So, you are alone." A malevolent smile crossed his lips. "Good, that'll make things easier."

His sudden change in demeanor took me off guard. Stumbling back, I caught a glint of something silvery flash in the light. "What—"

My voice suddenly vanished. Something warm splashed down my chest. There wasn't any pain, but the crimson spilling down my shirt told me all I needed to know. I'd been cut. The blade must've been sharp, because I never felt a thing. It was clear the man had some talent given the speed and precision of the cut.

My conscious mind told me there was no surviving this, and I was oddly okay with it. What I wasn't okay with was this asshole walking away. One way or another, this would end in mutual destruction.

Thump, thump, thump.

My heart was hammering away. At this rate, it was only a matter of a few seconds before I lost control of my body. I wasn't sure how I was so clear in this moment, but I was. It was as if time slowed to a crawl for me, allowing me to exact my final act of defiance. On instinct, I rushed forward. Shock wrote itself across his face. He clearly hadn't anticipated the fact I would or could fight back. Sucked to be him. My father started my training before I could walk, and after he bought the gym, it only intensified from there.

Blood leaked out of my mouth as my lips twisted themselves into a feral smile. In his moment of inaction, I grabbed his wrist and twisted it around to point the blade he was holding at his chest. With all the strength I could manage, I pushed. I felt the knife skitter off his rib before it slid through and into his heart. His eyes were wide in horror, then they began to dull. His knees buckled, and he collapsed onto the ground, quite dead.

Thump...thump...thump.

My heart was slowing.

Staggering back, my heel caught on something hard and sharp. My fine motor skills were shot at this point. Losing my balance, I tipped back. I fell in slow motion. My shoulders slammed into something hard and angular. It should've hurt, but it didn't...I mean, there was some discomfort, but somewhere in the dark recesses of my mind, I knew I should've been screaming. My lower back and ass were next. They were given the same treatment as my shoulders, but what'd been a dull thud was barely registering now.

Finally, there was a barely audible crack as the back of my head hit the unforgiving surface below, but I didn't lose consciousness right away. For whatever reason, I was lying at an odd angle, looking up at the fading sun. Unable to move my head, I contented myself with the fact it was a truly spectacular sunset this evening.

Thump... Thump... Thump.

My heart continued to slow. I wasn't long for this world, and that was okay. I'd done enough. All my life, I'd heard stories about other peoples' near-death experiences. According to them, their whole life seemed to flash before their eyes. That wasn't the case for me. I thought of Lilith and how much I loved her, but that was it. There weren't any regrets—okay, maybe collecting on Hector's lunch tab would've been nice.

My brain sent the command to my lips for them to move into a smile, but the muscles didn't respond.

Thump.

Thump.

Thump.

Yeah, I was too far gone for that.

Thump.

Darkness ringed my vision as it began to tunnel.

Thump.

I couldn't feel my body anymore. Part of me wanted to float off into the aether, but I stubbornly refused. A flash of white danced through my eyes followed quickly by one of crimson. They were so very pretty.

Thu...

It really had been a beautiful sunset.

6

I DON'T BELONG TO YOU

March 3rd

Out in the distance, a light flickered and died several times before finally catching. It was weak, barely able to push back the darkness surrounding it. I, however, was left adrift in the endless black of this strange abyss I found myself in. Turning my attention back to the tiny spark of light, I tried to focus on the details. It was a glowing white sphere with crimson script of some ancient language that'd long ago been lost to the universe inscribed upon its surface.

According to the quacks selling their new age bullshit, I was supposed to go toward the light. That was normally reason enough for me to plant my feet and staunchly refuse to move an inch. Today, however, it was the only point of interest in this—well I didn't know what this was.

Maybe this was purgatory or perhaps its unkind little brother, hell…either way, I didn't know, and I didn't particularly care either. On the other hand, standing here wasn't going to do me any good, so I decided to investigate.

As I started to take a step forward, something wrapped itself around my legs and began to pull. Planting myself in place, I refused to be moved. It didn't stop whatever it was from trying to drag me off, but I did stop sliding backward.

Pain shot through me as I took my first lurching step forward. Grunting, I brought my other leg up to meet the first. Each step cost me more and more energy, leaving me nearly exhausted after the tenth one. A quick jerk from the thing around my legs brought me to the ground, hard. Refusing to give up, I dug my fingers into the hard-packed earth and clawed my way forward.

Snarling, I said, "Fuck off, I don't belong to you."

For whatever reason, the thing wrapped around me loosened for a moment. I scrambled forward enough to slap my hand inside the circle of light. It flared to life, pushing back the shadowy tendrils trying to drag me away.

Okay, this wasn't purgatory—this had to be hell, and the only thing that was keeping me safe was the source of light overhead. Though, now that I got a closer look at it, it wasn't actually a light—it was all of existence rolled into one tiny minute sphere no bigger than my thumbnail. Even so, it contained the power of creation as well as that of oblivion. It could wipe the slate clean and remake the universe in its image if it so wished.

Was this god?

After several seconds of thought I knew it wasn't. This—whatever it was—couldn't be labeled; it simply was.

Collapsing on the spot, I lay there in awe of this one moment of perfection, then I looked out into the void.

Yeah, that was hell. I knew if the light disappeared, I'd be left alone in the dark. Maybe it wouldn't be so bad. Then again, the only version of hell I knew to exist was the one with all the fire and brimstone run by none other than the devil.

To say I wasn't exactly a devotee of any organized religion would be an understatement. Seriously, up until this moment I hadn't been sure there was an afterlife, and if there was, I doubted it'd be restricted to a single religion. It was my humble opinion that if you lived a decent life, i.e. not an evil prick, you'd go to whatever version of heaven you believed in or just cease to exist. I was kind of on the fence with that. As to the subject of hell, that had to be reserved for serial killers, Hitler, the person who weaponized robocalls, whoever created chihuahuas, and chihuahuas themselves.

For the record, chihuahuas were the worst. They were evil incarnate with their tiny rage-filled bodies, constant yipping, and willingness to attack everyone and anyone they could reach. How did I know? When I was four or five, dad let me go out to play. The moment he ducked inside, a pack of the bug-eyed fucks attacked me. By the time my dad found me, I was bleeding profusely and was on the verge of death. It took almost two hundred stitches to put me back together. Ever since they'd shown me their true colors, I knew who they were, even if the general public didn't.

Slowly, one of the dark tendrils braved the light and wrapped itself around my leg and yanked back hard. Turning, I slapped my hands against the rough-hewn floor looking for purchase. Scrabbling, I found a groove with my fingernails and dug in. I felt chunks of flesh and what felt like a piece of my soul be stripped away in an instant.

Suppressing the urge to vomit, I began the grueling process of clawing my way back to the light. Whimpering, and groaning with every centimeter, I felt tears running down my cheeks onto the cold, uncaring floor. Each time the tendrils stripped away a piece of me, it sent a chorus of agony into my mind's eye, leaving it frayed and on the verge of collapse. All I knew as if I let go for even a second, they'd take me, and once they had me, there was no escape.

Suddenly, the sphere pulsed. A flash of light washed over me. The tendril's grip vanished in that instant, and I crawled toward the center and collapsed.

I would not surrender to the darkness.

Then the light collapsed in on itself as it dropped into my chest and vanished.

Oh, fuck.

It was official, I was done. Turning over, I lay on my back. The way I saw it, if the devil was coming for his due, I might as well be comfortable.

Nothing happened. The tendrils seemed to be gone for good, but I was still alone in the dark lying on some stupidly hard stone. Seriously, it was as if the devil didn't take my comfort into consideration. That was kind of an asshole move on his part, if you asked me.

On that note, maybe I should voice my concerns in the hopes he would do better in the future. "Hey, Lucifer, if you're listening, you really need to work on your reception area." I vaguely gestured around at the dark. "This whole darkness thing sucks, and would it kill you to put some seats in the lobby? For fucks sake, man, have some goddamn pride. You're running a business here."

That was about the time it hit me; he was in the whole eternal torment, suffering, and bleaching the soul clean of impurities side of things. What did he care if I was a little uncomfortable or not?

Then I started thinking about it. "You know, if I were in charge of the whole afterlife thing, I'd let everyone—okay almost everyone, have a chance at paradise." I nodded. "Yeah, this whole if you don't believe in me thing is an ego trip belonging to pricks like the guys who run Muzos." Glancing up—not that it mattered, everything was so dark I couldn't see. "And you don't want to be compared to those guys, trust me."

Something cool and gentle brushed against my body. That sure as fuck wasn't the tendrils; they were anything but gentle. Huh... was that a breeze? Did hell have wind? Nah, if it had wind, it'd be carrying heat and sulfur, right? It was hell after all.

Suddenly, I was no longer able to speak. *'Right, pissing off the cloven hoof guy was probably a bad idea.'* It was then I realized movement wasn't an option either. *'Satan was a petty little shit. Seriously, anyone who couldn't take a little constructive criticism didn't need to be in charge.'*

Then, as if to spite me, a spectacular version of the night sky slowly came into view. *'Oh, now you're trying to taunt me with the night sky—prick.'* Internally, I sighed. *'The whole impenetrable darkness thing was much more terrifying. Do you even know how to dark lord properly? Obviously not.'*

A sharp, prickling pain crept through my skull, causing me to nearly black out. Grunting, I mentally berated the fucktard. *'Didn't you learn anything from Batman? You don't start with the head first—plus if I'm blacked out, I can't feel shit, so it's kind of a waste of your time. Fuck, you're terrible at this.'*

That was about the time my spine decided it was time for it to chime in. If I'd been capable of screaming, I would've been doing that. At this point, I couldn't even breathe so yeah, this sucked. Again, I was taken to the very edge of consciousness before my suffering began to subside. Of course, that was when my throat decided it'd pitch in its two coppers and let me know how unhappy it was. This time, I think I actually lost consciousness for a moment, though when my vision returned, most of the pain was gone. I was still paralyzed, but other than some minor discomforts such as several hard sharp things digging into my back, head, and legs, I was fine...well, as fine as I could be, considering my situation.

As I stared up, I found it odd that the devil chose to use the night sky I was familiar with. I mean, it was pretty, which made me wonder where the whole extended day pass to the burning sulfur pits was.

I don't want you to take that the wrong way, I wasn't in a hurry to be tortured, but just lying here looking out into the cosmos wasn't exactly what I was expecting.

Huh, I began to wonder if this was a personnel issue. Hold on, let me explain my thought process. You see, back when the devil rebelled, there were a lot less people...I mean, there are nearly eight billion of us now, and like sixty one million die each year. Now when you take into consideration their vetting process, most people are gonna land in hell, and there are only so many demons to go around.

Then a pungent odor of the dead slammed into my now functioning olfactory passages. Jesus, looks like the devil got something right; it does reek down here.

Anyway, I was starting to think my welcome committee was just tied up with someone ahead of me in the queue. Oh god, did I have to take a number? That would be the worst version of hell I could think of.

Then a random thought crossed my mind. *'Wasn't I supposed to get a handbasket?'*

That'd probably show up with the demon in charge of my prolonged suffering. For now, though, I'd soak up the view and enjoy this for as long as it lasted…as of now, this wasn't so bad.

Thump.

What sounded like a clap of thunder sent tremors throughout the cosmos and shook me to my very core.

7

DID THE DEMONS DOUBLE BOOK

Eventually the vibrations passed, allowing strange sounds to worm their way into my ear canals. It took me several seconds to begin to parse them out. Apparently, hell had crickets. Who knew? Plus, if the devil really wanted to torture people, he would've just used one. A bunch of crickets sound amazing, while a single cricket is the most annoying thing on the planet—wait. I strained to listen a bit more closely and picked up a low-level humming noise. Scratch that, they were the second most annoying things to exist—florescent lights were far worse. Of course, there was one sound that was in a league all its own and couldn't be lumped in with the others... yep, you guessed it, the growling bark of a chihuahua.

An oddly familiar sound pulled me out of my spiraling thoughts. Straining my focus, I tried to make out what I was hearing. It sounded like two people arguing out in the distance. Oh, for fucks sake, did the demons double book? Was that why they were late? Or had I been unfortunate enough to find a demon so bad at their job their supervisor had to tear them a whole new ass before they were allowed to torture me? If it was the latter, I was sure the lower-ranked demon would make me pay for whatever indignity their supervisor was currently heaping on them from a very great height.

Finally, they got close enough I was able to make out what they were saying.

A very hostile sounding male grumped. "Look, lady, I don't know how many times I have to tell you this; it's a local affair and we'll handle it."

The reply came from a female who was clearly fed up with the man's shit and was ready to tear him limb from limb. "Oh, you'll handle it? Really?" She huffed out a breath. "Just how exactly do you plan on doing that? You've got three corpses and one guy in critical condition at the hospital…how in the hell do you plan on handling it?" There was a short pause before her jagged tone cut through the silence. "Do you have any idea who these people are?"

The male demon mumbled something that sounded like a string of curses. "It doesn't matter who they are." There was a quiet thud. "We're capable of handling whatever comes our way." Another set of not quite audible curses were spoken. "Look, I'm curious, just how in the fuck did you get involved in this? If it wasn't for you and your people, this wouldn't be the circus it has become. All this—bullshit is your fault, and I want you out of here."

There was another lull in the conversation, but when the female spoke again, annoyance coated her tone. "Officer Arango, I've been courteous enough to use your name, I'd appreciate it if you reciprocated." There was a long intake of air. "As to us being gone, that's not going to happen."

Hold up just one goddamn minute, was the term officer a rank of some sort or maybe that was what they called their wet work people—those that got their hands dirty. My biggest question was when did Lucifer start naming any of his demons Arango? Hell, I knew a few people named Arango, and they seemed like nice people. I somehow doubted they'd appreciate the devil coopting their name for his minions.

Obviously, Officer Arango heard the implied threat in the woman's voice. "Sorry, Inspector Heredia."

Okay, just back the fuck up, inspector? Was she some sort of quality control person making their rounds to ensure each soul was tortured properly? Or was this something else entirely?

The hard edge in the inspector's voice faded. "That's better." Before he could say anything else to make the situation worse, she continued to speak. "As to how I found out, we at the Policía Federal Ministerial show up where we're needed." There was a long pause before she spoke again. "And it's clear, this is where we need to be, given who's involved."

Wait, the Policía Federal Ministerial had a division in hell? Say what you would about the federal police, they weren't demons, and while dealing with them sometimes felt like hell, I doubted they had a direct connection.

Thump, thump, thump.

What was—was that my heart? Was I alive? Pain crept through me as my muscles seemed to loosen enough to let me turn my head. I was still lying atop the steps of the pyramid. I...huh...I was alive. Glancing down at my blood-covered shirt, I wasn't sure how life was an option. Not that I wasn't grateful, because I was, but that prick practically beheaded me. There's no way I should've been breathing, especially not without choking to death on my own fluids.

Thanks to my confusing thoughts, I missed Arango's words, but I didn't miss the annoyance in his tone.

Inspector Heredia's response to his obvious annoyance was a dismissive chuckle. "We don't swoop in. We assist local law enforcement." Resignation sounded in her tone. "At least that's how it is normally."

Barely controlled anger wrapped itself around the officer's tone. "Let me guess, that isn't how things are playing out today."

She was quiet for a long moment. "No, it's not." There was a low grunt of dissatisfaction before she spoke again. "And as such, this is now under our jurisdiction."

"Damn it." There were a few choice curse words I couldn't hear, but then the man seemed to calm himself. "May I ask why?"

Ice filled her tone. "I don't know. People who shouldn't know I exist phoned me personally to show up here and take control of the situation."

With the sullen tone of a petulant teenager, he growled. "Is that right?"

"It is." Inspector Heredia's tone softened. "Do you really think for one second that I wanted to turn an already long day into a longer one?" She huffed out a breath. "Trust me, I want nothing to do with this. Like I said, people who shouldn't know my name called me... you know how things work, everything moves at a glacier's pace until someone important gets involved."

Sneering, he said, "So, you're telling me someone important is involved."

A bitter laugh escaped her lips. "No, I'm telling you there are at least two dozen people with ranks I've never heard of until today and they're crawling all over this mess." She snorted. "Thus, I've been given an unreasonable amount of authority to make all this go away."

Suddenly worried, he asked, "What are you saying?"

"That's simple. My people are collecting everything you've gathered—reports, evidence, bodies—everything." She was quiet for a half second. "See those people surrounding your cruisers?"

"Hey, what are they doing?"

"They're erasing your GPS data." A nervous laugh escaped her. "There are people erasing the phone logs reporting this incident, and every photo shot by some tourist is being retouched to wipe out any trace of this man or his assailant."

Shock registered in his voice. "You can't do that."

"That's my point. I can't." Weariness coated her tone. "But the people moving can. By the time you get back to the station, there will be absolutely no record of you ever being here." She was quiet for several seconds. "It'd be in your best interest to put this behind you and never think of it again."

Arango blew out a long breath. "Holy mother of god, that's... yeah, okay...I'll get you the files we have."

She cleared her throat. "That won't be necessary...like I said, it's all being handled."

There was a long pause before Arango spoke again. "What is—"

"Don't ask." A tiredness sounded in her voice. "Even if I knew, I couldn't tell you." She was quiet for a long moment. "Please, for both of our sakes, just walk away and forget about all of this."

Arango let out a dissatisfied grunt. "Yes, ma'am."

There was a crunching of gravel then Heredia called out. "I thought you said he was dead."

Annoyance sounded in his tone. "While we may be simple public servants, we're capable enough to know when someone is dead." More crunching of gravel sounded in the quiet. "His head was nearly lopped off by his assailant, so—" There was a long pause. "Damn...medic!"

A woman in her mid to late thirties wearing a dark suit that screamed government official suddenly hurried into view. She had smooth skin, dark brown eyes, and a pleasant face that was marred with worry. "Don't move, Senor Garcia, help is on the way."

Obviously, this was Inspector Heredia.

Closing my eyes, I cleared my throat. Pain radiated through my neck, but I was able to find my voice, though it was raspy and ragged. "Hector?" My hand snaked up my chest to rest on my throat as I coughed. "Eli?"

Heredia shook her head. "I don't know who Hector is, but a man named Eli Aura is currently being transported to the hospital." She took a deep breath. "I'm sorry to say Tiara Curiel is dead...looks like a knife wound to the heart." She glanced back. "Something like you did to the assailant earlier but cleaner."

Goddamn it. Tiare was a wonderful person and highly dedicated to her job, and now she was dead because of me.

"Will Eli be okay?" I choked out.

She rolled her shoulders. "It looks like he'll pull through, but we can't be sure. The blade looks to have nicked an artery, but he's holding on for now."

I laid my head back. "Good."

The inspector gave me a hard once-over and frowned. "Not to be indelicate here, but how are you alive?"

That was a great question I didn't have an answer to.

Before I could think of anything to say, a half dozen paramedics formed up around me. There were far too many to be of use as they got in each other's way. Eventually, they agreed to place me on a stretcher and let one of the teams assess my condition.

The second they were finished, Heredia was on me like a rabid dog looking for a meal. Her tone had turned hostile in the interim. "What were you doing here today, Mr. Garcia?"

I guess now that she knew I wasn't about to die at any second, her true colors came out. "Looking for a friend."

Her fingers danced across the tablet she was holding as she went through multiple forms and finally settled on one. She began checking off boxes at random. "Is that so?"

Given the angle, I was able to read part of the screen. One of the boxes she'd checked off caught my attention. "Hey, I haven't been infected."

Slowly, she lifted her head as she allowed her gaze to track over me. "I think you might be wrong on that front." She gestured at me. "Look at yourself." Folding her arms, she frowned. "Someone slit your throat, and yet here you are healthy as you can be."

I was starting to see why the police, no matter the country, were universally disliked. "I think we both know you're wrong here."

Inspector Heredia gave me a look that said she clearly didn't believe me. "Am I?"

God this was so tiring. "Yes, you are."

Lifting her hand, she rubbed it over her face as if to suppress a string of curses. "Look, I'm sure finding out this way is shocking... and yes, I'll have to take you into custody." Her tone softened. "After a few weeks in observation and testing, they'll know for sure. If I'm wrong, I'll apologize, but right now, I'm just doing my job. Got it?"

A soft voice cut me off. "I don't think that's going to work for us, inspector."

Inspector Heredia whirled around to glare at the much smaller woman who appeared at my side. "Who the hell are you?"

"My name is Gisele Gama." Her expression hardened. "And I think we're done here."

She pointed at her tablet. "The hell we are. I have a mountain of paperwork that needs to be completed."

Gisele's bored tone told the inspector just how little she thought of her. "No, you don't." She strode around to stand between me and the inspector. "In fact, you'll find everything has been taken care of." Pointing at me, she said, "And now, if you'll excuse me, I need to have a talk with Horacio."

The inspector grimaced. "I haven't finished with his witness statement."

The tablet suddenly went dark. "Actually, you have." She gestured out at the scene behind them. Roving teams wearing hazmat suits sprayed some sort of chemical on wide swaths of blood-covered earth, causing white smoke to trail up in the air. Others collected evidence bags, tablets, and anything else pertaining to the earlier incident. "As you can see, my people are tending to any loose ends."

Heredia seemed to swell with rage. "Who do you think you are?"

An envelope suddenly appeared in Gisele's hand. "Here, take this."

She snatched the parcel and pulled out the letter. Her eyes widened as she read over it. "You know I'll have to call to confirm this."

"It's the only reason you've still got your phone." She gestured at the other woman. "Please make your call, we'll wait."

Taking a few steps away, she pulled out her phone and dialed a number. "Hello…" Obviously, whoever was on the other end cut her off. While she listened, she put more distance between herself and us. Eventually, she spoke again. "I see, thank you."

Gisele smiled. "Everything in order?"

"Apparently." She glanced out at the teams rounding her people up like cattle. "So…this never happened."

Gisele strode over and put her hand on the taller woman's shoulder. "I'm glad you understand." Turning, she strode back to me then pulled out a dark cloth to wipe my neck. "Are you alright?"

Was she high? "Someone slit my throat in broad daylight, so that'd be a no."

Dissatisfaction crossed her lips. "Yes, I've been made aware."

Of course she had. "I'm sorry about Tiera."

"Me too." Her words trailed off as she eyed my neck with a frown. "That's...interesting."

How in the hell was she so calm? "What's that?"

She reached out with one of her delicate fingers and touched the base of my neck. "You've got a scar." She used the cloth to wipe away more of the grime. "Damn." Glancing back at the covered corpse, she frowned. "Have you been examined by a doctor?"

What? "No." I pushed myself up into a sitting position. "The only people to examine me so far are the EMTs your people have cornered."

Gisele looked over at the small group of medics. "Alright." She eyed the stationary inspector who was still reading the thick packet in her hands. "And her? Did she get a good look?"

My mind refused to work properly. How was I supposed to know? "I'm not sure, but I don't think so." Annoyed, I said, "But she was all too quick to blame the Gaia Contagion for my survival, even when I told her that wasn't the case."

"Yes, I'm sure she was." Irritation flashed in her eyes. "That's standard practice at the moment."

"What's that?"

She eyed me carefully. "Since the appearance of the Gaia Contagion, the mortals have been filing anything that isn't easily comprehendible under its umbrella." Suddenly looking tired, she sagged against the railing of the stretcher. "I suppose it's easier for them to do that than accept there are other options." She eyed me with curiosity. "Though you are a puzzling case."

"Mortals?" What was she talking about? "And what makes me so puzzling?"

Gisele blinked then stood up straight. "It's not important for now." She took a deep breath and let it out slowly. "I'm glad you're okay, and before you ask, Hector's fine too…he never left home; the text you got was faked, as was the call. We don't know who's behind it, but we'll figure it out."

That was a load off my mind. "Thank god…and Eli, is he going to be okay?"

She gave me a gentle smile. "He'll pull through just fine." Raising her hand, she waved someone over. Jose, Issac, Jamie, Christopher, Luis, and Martin stepped into view. "Jose will be with you from here on out."

I winced. "Sorry to interrupt your vacation."

His assessing gaze passed over me, and he shook his head. "We were just sitting around with our feet up at the office; we can do that at your place…plus, the view is better."

That was probably true. "Thanks for being here."

He gave me a wink. "Any time."

Jose turned to Gisele. "Is he well enough to move?"

"I think so." She eyed me for a long moment. "You are up to moving, right?"

"I sure as hell hope so. I don't want to stay here." Looking over at Inspector Heredia, I paused. "What about the police…and the dead guy?"

Gisele's expression blanked and her voice turned cold at the mention of my attacker. "I'll handle the inspector." The muscles in her jaw rippled as they tightened. "As for the man who assaulted you, that's a matter we're already looking into." She reached out and patted my arm. "For now, go home and rest. Once we have a handle on the situation, Jose will bring you to the office and we'll go over the details."

While her tone was polite, it was anything but a request. I had the distinct impression that it was either go home of my own volition or be forced to do so under less than ideal circumstances. "Ah… okay then."

With a helping hand from Jose, I was on my feet a second later. It wasn't long after that I was in an oversized SUV heading south towards home.

8

BABY METAL

May 3rd

Puebla, Mexico, Earth

Beep, beep, beep.

My mind swam into a semi-wakeful state. "What the—"

Beep, beep, beep.

Aww, fuck it was already time to get up. Another sonic barrage assaulted me. "Christ on a pogo stick, will you shut up already."

Before nearly having my head lopped off, waking up after getting a solid bit of rest was one of the more enjoyable things in life. There was always that moment of bliss between sleep and the conscious world that held a special type of magic. In those few fleeting seconds, anything was possible. It was like being one with the cosmos, and it left me feeling whole.

Now, though, that moment of nirvana was missing. It was almost as if the attempt to unalive me had somehow left me more exhausted than ever before. And no, it wasn't due to some sort of lingering trauma or PTSD or even nightmares. My body just craved sleep. Once I woke up, I was fine, but until that moment, I was a useless sack of shit. Thankfully, a good hot shower had the ability to fix almost any ailment, exhaustion included.

Hey, don't judge—I'd like to see how you felt after someone tried turning you into a bobblehead.

Oh, that isn't where the judgement is coming from. Sorry, my bad. Okay—sure, let me address the elephant in the room. No, I didn't feel a single bit of remorse for the man I'd killed. Simply put, it was self-defense. Not only that, but he'd been the one who'd killed Tiera and wounded Eli, so putting him in the ground was a public service.

Really? You're going to take the moral high ground here? Are you serious? You're telling me if someone killed your friend, wounded another, and tried to kill you, that you'd give the guy another chance?

Wait, that's exactly what you're saying, isn't it? Wow, are you stupid? The guy was obviously very comfortable with killing people, so I'm sure we weren't his first victims. So, yeah, showing the guy mercy in the hopes he can be rehabilitated is just asking for him to try again later.

Now, back to the trauma that was waking up.

Beep. Beep. Beep.

Most people prayed for strength, I, however, was praying for restraint. Rolling over, I slapped at the screen.

BEEP. Beep. Beep.

My fingers danced across the surface trying to find the cursed button I needed to swipe to turn the damn thing off.

BEEP. BEEP. Beep.

Sitting bolt upright, I snatched the phone off the nightstand and flicked the wailing screech into oblivion. I was half tempted to throw my phone across the room, but it'd served me faithfully for five years now, and my inability to wake up wasn't its fault. No, that was entirely on me. Maybe one day, I'd find that bit of magic again, but for now, I kind of hated the world.

Bleary eyed, I tried to make out the details around me through the haze in my mind. Then the room snapped into high definition. Rubbing my face with my hands, I suppressed the urge to scream. "Right." Pivoting, I hung my legs over the side of the bed to rest my feet on the cool tiles. "I need to get going. Today is the big day."

What'd that mean? As it turned out, Gisele had put in some serious overtime digging up facts about the guy who attacked me, and she was ready to share. Which was great, because according to my sources, he didn't exist—no digital records, no physical ID, facial recognition didn't spew anything out of the database, and his DNA wasn't on file.

The last bit wasn't exactly unexpected, since I'd supposedly sent the lab a sample they couldn't use. Seeing how I was a longtime customer of theirs, the official wording of the letter they sent me said the sample must've been contaminated by outside sources. The phone call I got was less kind—something to the tune about them not being amused by what they thought was a practical joke and how I'd wasted their time. To say they didn't appreciate it would've been an understatement.

Enough about them and back to this being a big day.

According to Gisele's email, not only was she going to tell me about the man I'd drawn a blank on but Cain as well…along with the others. I wasn't sure what she meant by the others, but I was far more interested in Cain than the dead guy. Call me crazy but getting to know more about the man felt important. I'd been tempted to reach out a few times, but Gisele always advised against it, citing security concerns. She said when the time was right, we'd approach him together.

At first, I didn't get why she was being so damn cautious, but after seeing what he'd pulled in Romania, I came to terms with the fact she might be right. Then when he went one country over to Moldova and started a small war, I decided we'd need more than the two of us when the time came.

Running my hands over my face, I suppressed a yawn. "Come on man, we got to get moving." Craning my neck to the side, it popped several times. "I can do this." I glanced up at the bathroom door. "It's what…four meters to the shower? That's barely a few dozen steps."

Who was I trying to kid? That was like ten times further than I was currently capable of moving. Sitting there, I closed my eyes and listened. A choir of insects sang their song. Out in the darkness, the chirps of bats could be heard as they hunted their prey. Beyond all that was the babbling river just outside my window.

Sitting here was peaceful—comfortable in a way I'd never been before moving here. Lilith did an amazing job creating this place. No, she didn't create the river, but the island our home sat on was an entirely different story.

Let me explain. Back when we were dating, I borrowed Hector's boat to take Lilith on what I thought would turn out to be an incredibly romantic date. I'm sure you can infer that didn't happen from my previous statement. Yes, I'm a skilled boatsman, so that wasn't the issue, and no, we didn't run out of fuel, because I was smart enough to check first. I really wanted to make a good impression. Anyway, we were cruising the Atoyac River just south of Puebla—right where the island is now—when all hell broke loose.

A police boat glided up beside us telling me to stop the boat, at which point they came aboard and put me in handcuffs before proceeding to search the boat for drugs. About five minutes into the charade, Hector's dumb ass climbed aboard in hysterics. For whatever reason, he thought this was the funniest thing ever.

It wasn't.

I didn't punch him in the face, but it was a close thing.

Thankfully, Lilith found the ordeal amusing, since Hector had orchestrated the whole thing in order to meet her. I'd been cagey about the meeting, since Lilith and I were a new-ish couple. Introducing her to Hector at such an early stage was akin to a single mother introducing a strange man to her children after the first date. It was something you didn't do. Still, though, it worked out in the end.

Needless to say, I didn't borrow the boat again, so imagine my surprise when Lilith did exactly that after our engagement six months later. This time she was the one piloting the boat, but the area didn't look the same in the daylight—plus, there was a new island in the river with a three-story anodized steel house atop it, in the brutalist style. Think old communist Russia with a science fiction flare with a serious side of dystopian warlord thrown in for good measure.

How big was the island? Roughly five hundred meters long and half that wide…so decent size. What about flooding? Well, when your wife is a genius who specializes in every field imaginable, that wasn't a problem. Hey, let me stop you there. I'm a smart guy, but I'm not that smart. The sheer scale of her understanding of the natural world is beyond me. I'm just happy it all works. To hear Hector describe the place, you'd think the island was a miracle of civil engineering made manifest.

And he's right.

Out of nowhere, a heavy guitar riff drowned out the burbling of the river, sent a flock of finches screeching off into the night, and pulled me fully back into the reality we lived in. A split second later, the sound of the wailing guitar dropped into the background as a set of high-pitched female voices began singing in Japanese.

Then everything went quiet, save for a string of curses spewing out of Luis's mouth. There was a long pause before he called out. "Sorry."

I didn't respond.

This wasn't the first time his earbuds died and blasted the entire island with whatever he'd been listening to at the time. After two or three times, you kind of get used to it. The man's obsession with a band called Baby Metal wasn't exactly a secret. At least it wasn't that KPOP song I'd learned to hate. Look, some of it was fine, but the dude played the same twelve songs on repeat, and after three months of being stuck in the house with the man, I'd had enough.

"On that note, I need to get clean."

Getting to my feet, I shuffled into the bath.

Fifteen minutes later, I turned off the water, grabbed my towel, and began the process of drying off. Once my hair was mostly dry, I felt almost human again. Working my way down my chest, I strode over to the mirror.

What the hell was that?

Delicate, glowing, golden lines spread out from the thin U-shaped scar at the nape of my neck. It looked to be a hybrid of native artwork and an incredibly complex circuit that'd look more at home in some quantum computer than inscribed on my flesh. It spread out like some ceremonial necklace that sent chills up my spine. The space between the gilded filigree was a surgical white color that acted as a background for the crimson sigils emblazoned upon its surface.

Then as if it were never there, it winked out of existence.

"Okay—that was freaky." Running my fingers around my scar, I tried to feel if there was anything under the skin, there wasn't. I frowned. "Dude, you're losing it." I closed my eyes and counted to ten then looked at myself once more. Nothing. "Yeah, that's just my subconscious messing with me." Looking back at my bed, I sighed. "Maybe I wasn't as awake as I thought I was…yeah, that's it…that was a dream of some sort."

Hey, I don't recall asking your opinion. Just keep your mouth shut and roll with it, because that's exactly what I'm going to do. I don't care if you saw it too; it's not there now. On top of that, we don't have any photos, and I have no idea how to make it reappear. Now, unless you've got some brilliant idea that'll somehow convince the others it exists, and more importantly, that I'm not a loon, then we're going to drop the subject entirely.

Got it? Good.

Pushing off the counter, I began pulling on my clothes. Most days, my idea of dressing up involved a pair of jeans and a button up shirt—if you were lucky. Today was different in many ways. I was promised answers, important ones, and as such, I would dress for the occasion, up to a point anyway. This meant a dark crimson three-piece suit that looked to be of a classic cut that'd never go out of style with a sleek futuristic flare. It mixed comfort with class in such a way it was an absolute pleasure to wear.

This was one of the pieces Lilith commissioned for me when we were still dating. Even though it was over thirty years old, it looked brand new. The inside of the jacket was lined with white silk that felt cool against my chest. It paired well with the gleaming white button up that made me feel like a million bucks. There was no tie, Lilith didn't approve of the things. She always said that was just a good way to get choked to death...often referring to them as a noose with extra steps.

Seeing how I didn't like ties, I was only too happy to agree. It wasn't just ties she took umbrage with, bolos, bow ties...basically any sort of object that could be used to strangle a person was ruled out.

I was just pulling on the jacket when a knock at the door had me practically jumping out of my skin.

"Hey, you okay in there?" Jose called out.

Setting my jaw, I finished adjusting my jacket. "Yeah, I'm good." I stepped into the bedroom, only to hear the synth pop classic from the eighties echo up from downstairs. "Seriously? Issac's watching another episode?"

As it turned out, Issac seemed to have stolen his entire style, such as it was, from a nineteen eighties television show called Miami Vice. The man was obsessed with the show, watching it at every available opportunity and blasting the music in whatever room he was in.

Jose rolled his eyes. "Yeah, it was the only way he'd make breakfast."

After having to listen to the terrible dialogue and hearing Crocket's theme way too often, I'd asked if he would use headphones going forward. He was fine with that but then he began playing the show on mute on every TV in the house. I didn't even realize it was possible to synchronize individual screens throughout the house in such a fashion. It was then that I asked very politely for him to keep it to one tv, and if he closed the door, he didn't have to use his earbuds.

Then again, the man was making breakfast, so that was a fair trade. "Any idea what he's making?"

Laughing, he shook his head. "Not really, but I'm hoping for omelets."

"Not me." I thumbed back at myself. "I want that puff pastry dish with all the cheese and veggies in it."

His eyes went wide as he pointed at me. "Oh...that does sound good...yeah, I hope he's making that." He rubbed his stomach. "Now that you've said it, I think I might be disappointed with anything else."

I chuckled. "Sorry, man." Patting myself down, I began checking for the important stuff—keys, phone, and wallet. "Okay, I'm good to go."

Stepping back, he waved me through the door. Once I was past him, he quickly followed behind me. Secretly, we were both praying Issac had anticipated our desire for a very specific breakfast.

9

STRANGER THAN YOU REALIZE

I'd half expected Gisele to send the chopper for me this morning, but Jose had nixed that idea, saying flying was far too dangerous. It would seem whatever she uncovered about my assailant gave her pause. Which was why Martin and Jamie had spent the last three hours in scuba gear, going over the boat from top to bottom. They weren't willing to take any chances with my safety, and given how things had gone so far this year, I was grateful.

After we got the all-clear from Jamie, we boarded the boat and began our trek across the Atoyac River. I glanced up at the familiar sky and stared out at the mind-boggling beauty that was the Milky Way. Thanks to the miniscule one hundred kilometers from here to Teotihuacan, the view wasn't noticeably different.

Lilith loved this view as well. She tended to rattle on about things I didn't understand. According to her, there were several factors working in our favor that allowed us to see the universe in all its splendor. It was some sort of weird combo of elevation, the lack of pollution—light and otherwise, and like three dozen other things that paved the way for the galaxy itself to show off.

It really was like she knew everything. Yeah, I know that's impossible, but you don't know the woman. I mean she's special—

no, that's not coming from a love-struck husband who missed his wife, though that may be part of it, but she really was something to behold. I found it uncanny how she seemed to just know stuff as if she possessed vast cosmic knowledge not available to mere mortals, such as myself.

Maybe she was from some far-off future where the things she knew were simplicity itself, like knowing two plus two equaled four. I made a joke about it once—she'd looked fearful for several seconds before giving me a stern look. Then, out of nowhere, grief nearly overtook her before she spoke words that chilled me to my very soul.

"The truth of the matter is stranger than you realize."

It was like she really believed she'd been displaced in time and space by some vengeful god. After that, I was smart enough to never go near that subject again. While anything was supposedly possible, that was stretching it, though there was something there she refused to tell me.

Even as thoughts of Lilith drifted through my mind cool, wet air washed over me as the cabin cruiser ponderously cut through the water. I glanced up at the clear sky above and smiled. It was beautiful. If for no other reason, this made living out in the middle of nowhere worth it.

The two and a half kilometers from home to the docks on the north side of the river passed in the blink of an eye. While Christopher should never be allowed near a kitchen, he was an excellent pilot, be that on the sea, air, or land. Hell, if there were space travel, I was sure he'd be an expert at that, as well. The man seemed to have a knack with machines of all types. As such, he slid into the slip with ease.

Louis and Jamie quickly made their way onto the dock and tied us off. Jose scanned the area before nodding at Issac, who exited next. He jogged up the stairs to the parking lot above, paused for a second then gave a thumbs up.

Jose moved to stand next to me. When he spoke, the jovial tone I'd become accustomed to over the last few months was gone, and in its place was something hard and sharp. "We should go."

Their serious demeanors were starting to put me on edge. Just what the hell had Gisele dug up? "Hey, before we go, is there something I should know?"

Gesturing ahead, he said, "Ms. Gama will go over everything once we get there."

Damn, that wasn't a great sign. "Alright."

With those words, I moved out into the parking lot with Issac taking the lead and heading directly for one of the nearby SUVs. Jose was on my right and Luis was on my left as they purposely put themselves between me and harm's way.

Grunting, Issac said, "I would've preferred the Testarossa, but given the situation, that'd be inadvisable."

Christopher swerved around, headed for the back door and jerked it open. "In."

When we were about three meters from the car, Issac ducked to his left and circled around the front of the vehicle. Luis stepped back, allowing me to climb in through the open door, and Jose slid in right after. The passenger door popped a second later, and Issac hopped in, sandwiching me between the two men. An attractive woman with long black hair and the face of a goddess sat in the driver's seat. The opening of the door opposite her forced me to tear my gaze from the driver.

Jamie got himself situated before quickly buckling up. He glanced back at me, then at the driver, and smiled. "Our driver today is Cassandra Busto. She's the best we have—"

Issac cleared his throat. "Second best."

Snorting a laugh, Cassandra looked into the rearview mirror with her warm, coffee-colored eyes. "Anytime you want to prove that, old man, I'm more than ready to beat your ass."

Smirking, Issac flipped her the bird. "Old? I—"

Jose was quick to cut in. "Children, do I really need to point out this isn't the time?"

Cassandra winced. "Right, sorry boss."

Oh, now this could prove amusing. Leaning to the side, I glanced over at Cassandra. "Are you really that good?"

She gave me a wry smile. "Yes."

Plopping back in my seat, I gave Issac a hard look. "If she wins, you have to make that puff pastry thing I like."

It turned out he'd made omelets earlier, which left both Jose and I very disappointed.

Issac narrowed his eyes. "And if I win, you'll sit down and watch all five seasons of Miami Vice with me without complaint."

Oh, for fucks sake. "Hey, if that's the case, I want all my favorite foods for a month—that's breakfast, lunch, and dinner. I would ask for snacks too, but that'd be a bit much."

"No, that's fine." A confident smile crossed his lips. "I'm not going to lose, so it's all good, my friend."

"Then yeah, you're on."

Cassandra cleared her throat. "And what do I get out of this?"

"The honor of challenging me." Issac snorted.

She whirled around to glare at him. "Oh, hell no." Her tone hardened. "If I win, I want the option to choose my next posting—any vehicle of my choosing."

Issac glanced over at Jose, who simply nodded. "Done."

Jamie tapped his palm against the dashboard. "Focus." He gestured out the window. "We're good to go."

I glanced around. "Where's Christopher, Louis, and Martin?"

Cassandra's gaze passed over each of the mirrors in turn. "Buckle up, we're rolling in ten."

"They're in the lead and rear vehicles respectively." Jamie replied.

Just as he finished speaking, Cassandra adjusted the gearshift.

Then one of the weirdest sensations I'd ever experienced hit me like a freight train and left me feeling disoriented. It was as if the whole world rearranged itself in an instant. like god was playing the cup game but with SUVs. Mind you, no one seemed to be moving, but it sure as hell felt like we were. In the next instant, nine identical SUVs moved in reverse as one. Think synchronized swimming but with cars. While we kept a steady pace, we weaved in and out of the convoy until I couldn't tell which was which. Before I knew it, we hit that long, lonely stretch of highway between my home and the city.

Every so often, I thought I heard a sharp snap like a rock hitting the window, but the glass never cracked. That, in and of itself, was neat. We wound our way through the traffic as if they weren't an actual impediment. Thanks to Cassandra's expertise, the two-hour drive was cut down to an hour and fifteen minutes, and that was without speeding.

I wasn't sure how that was even possible, but somehow, the small convoy of SUVs did it with apparent ease. The building that housed Ōmeyōcān-Mictlān was an eighteen-story affair northwest of the city. Unlike my home, this was a modern whimsical affair that, when viewed from the air, looked like a spiral staircase meant for giants. It was an optical illusion, of course. The white banding, glass, and judicious placement of a strange gray-black metal made it appear like something it wasn't. It sat in the center of a three-by-three kilometer campus with numerous smaller buildings surrounding it. From what I was told, each sector of the company had its own R&D department, labs, and manufacturing plants. How they fit all that into such a small space, I wasn't sure.

The last time I was here, that was like three years ago, they'd had a rather plain-looking chain-link fence surrounding the property. Now, though, they had proper walls made of the same charcoal-colored metal as the main building. It jutted out of the ground some six meters high, maybe half that wide, and came complete with dozens of watchtowers.

I nudged Jose and pointed at the barrier. "When did that happen?"

"A few years back." His expression hardened. "The world at large is rapidly changing for the worse. Due to that, Gisele felt it necessary to reinforce our defenses."

Defenses? Were we preparing for some war I wasn't aware of? Or did this have something to do with Lilith's protective custody situation? "Care to elaborate?"

He shook his head. "Not my place." Gesturing at the massive steel retracting into the earth, he said, "Gisele will handle all that."

Okay, now I was starting to feel some pressure about the upcoming meeting with Gisele, and I didn't like it. There was obviously something they weren't telling me, and I knew once that secret was revealed, everything would change.

"I see."

That was a lie, I didn't, but pressing the issue wouldn't help, plus I was nervous enough as it was.

Cassandra rolled through the checkpoint without so much as slowing and headed directly for the main structure at the center of campus. She weaved through the two-lane highways until she found the underground parking garage. It was weird watching eight other SUVs follow in behind us like little, or in this case very large, ducks in a row.

I glanced over at Jose. "Is all this necessary?"

Jamie didn't bother looking back as he responded. "Yes."

Someone took his serious-O's this morning. "Really? This seems a bit overkill."

This time, he pivoted in his seat to look me in the eyes. "You heard those sharp cracks as we moved through the city, didn't you?"

What was that supposed to mean? "Yeah, and kudos to whoever installed your windows; none of those rocks left a crack in the glass."

His expression hardened. "Those weren't rocks."

Excuse me? "Huh?"

Jamie gave me an assessing look as if he were trying to figure out if I were joking or not. "Those were high-powered rounds slamming into the glass."

No, that couldn't be right. I must've misheard him. "I'm sorry, but I didn't catch that."

"Yes, you did." Issac gave me a reluctant shrug. "And it's true."

"Wait." I blinked. "Someone tried to kill me on the way here?"

Jose gave me a serious nod. "Several people and multiple times."

They had to be messing with me, right? The looks on their faces said otherwise. "We should call someone...the police...we can't leave maniacs with sniper rifles out there to roam the city."

Cassandra pulled up next to an unremarkable door and stopped. "Martin and Louis are handling the cleanup."

I whipped my head around to see there were eight SUVs forming a blockade between our vehicle and the ramp leading up. "Really?" I pointed at the others. "Looks like we're all here."

Jamie chuckled. "Yeah, those two peeled off at the first sign of trouble."

Holy shit, things were quickly getting out of hand. "Oh...but how?"

Jose shook his head. "That's not important right now." He pointed at the door. "Your meeting with Ms. Gama is."

I gritted my teeth. "Fair enough."

Issac popped the door and ducked out. "Follow me."

Scooching over, I ducked my head and hopped out. When I raised my eyes again, I spotted Jose standing in front of the door resting his hand atop the scanner. I glanced back at the SUV then at Jose. "How in the hell did you do that?"

He chuckled. "Relax, everything will be made clear shortly."

How in the hell had he gotten over there? I glanced back...he had been right here and now he was there. I suddenly felt a headache coming on as the things I didn't understand started to pile up around me. "Uh-huh...sure buddy, sure."

A big smile crossed his lips when he saw the look on my face. "Easy there, everything is going to turn out okay."

Easy for him to say. "Lead the way."

Visibly relaxing, he nodded. "Excellent." A click sounded and the door popped open. He motioned me forward. "We'll be taking the scenic route today."

Oh, joy. "Why's that?"

Issac grinned. "Marching you through the lobby would put you at risk, so this may be a bit longer but it's safer."

"Because people are trying to kill me, right?"

Even as I said the words they sounded ridiculous. Who the hell was I? In the grand scheme of things, I was no one important.

Jamie nodded. "Exactly, people *are* trying to kill you. I'm glad to see you're catching on."

The joke was on him; I was confused as hell, but seeing how I didn't know what to do with myself, I played along. "Sure man, sure."

Like I needed more protection. The walls were thick enough to stop an army, and the blast door leading into the underground lot looked like it could take a direct hit from an atomic bomb. Still, though, they seemed a bit freaked out, so I shuffled along. Once inside, the heavy metal door clunked shut with the finality of the grave.

Yeah, I was officially starting to freak the hell out.

Glancing from side to side, I noticed both Issac and Jose were tense. As for Jamie, his normal languid posture was nowhere to be found. Instead, he stood ramrod straight as if he were preparing to step into the biggest battle of his life.

Over the following ten minutes, I followed along as Jose guided us through the maze of hallways and up several flights of stairs. Finally, he stepped forward to pull open a door that spilled out into an expansive mezzanine. If I'd properly kept count, we were on the ninth floor of the building, which just so happened to be the highest one that still included the lobby. Lilith designed the entire structure around the expansive lobby housing a biodome of plants and trees I couldn't identify. I wasn't an expert or anything, but given my job, I was quite familiar with most of what Mother Nature had to offer across the globe.

Even so, the plants, trees, and other flora spread across the massive biome were unfamiliar. I had to admit some seemed to be distant cousins to some of the more exotic plants I'd seen, but they were very far removed from one another. There was a sense of something extraterrestrial about the place, as if it'd been summoned from another world or perhaps plucked out of time to be placed here.

It was awe-inspiring, peaceful, and dangerous all at once. Like, if you weren't careful, one of the vines might sneak out of the foliage and pull you in. I had no reason to feel this way, but it persisted even after all these years.

I had to imagine if some ambitious designer visited this place they would go home and try to replicate it. They'd fail, of course, but they'd try. I mean, who wouldn't? It was gorgeous.

Jose tapped my shoulder. "You good?"

"Yeah." As you might guess, I wasn't. You could probably guess the reasons—Lilith was gone, someone tried to kill me, and well, you get the point. "It's just been a while since I've been back."

His gaze passed over the expansive terrarium and his expression softened. "Of course." He gestured ahead. "Ms. Gama's office is this way."

"I remember."

A sad smile touched his lips as he nodded. "Right, sorry." Pivoting, he strode around the circular landing until he came to a halt. He quickly rapped his knuckles against the door then opened it without waiting for an answer. "Good morning, Ms. Gama."

Gisele stood facing the window looking out at the volcano. "Thank you." Her tone was soft and somber. "Are you sure you're ready for this?"

Even without prompting I knew who the question was directed at. "Hey, you're the one who called this meeting, not me."

Her shoulders twitched up slightly. "True." She kept her eyes glued on the horizon. "Come, it's time we had that conversation I promised you."

Given what'd happened over the course of the morning thus far, I was starting to get a bit spooked. Even so, I screwed up my courage and nodded. "Yeah, okay…let's do this."

Her reflection showed a crooked smile cross her lips. "Good." She glanced over her shoulder. "And as I'm sure you're starting to suspect, this will change your world view on a fundamental level."

That wasn't remotely worrying. "Oh, how wonderful for me." Glancing over at Jose, I asked, "Are you sticking around?"

Rooted to the spot, he gave the question some serious thought before shaking his head. "No—though I won't be far." He thumbed over his shoulder. "I'll be just down the hall, should you need me." Patting me on the back, he said, "Relax, this will answer a lot of the questions you have nagging at the back of your mind. Who knows, once it's over, you might even find yourself in a better place than the one you're leaving behind."

Turning, Gisele gave him a curious look. "You know, you might be right."

Smiling, Jose gave her a curt nod. "I hope so." He glanced over at Issac. "Let's go. They have a lot to discuss."

Issac gave me a look filled with pity. "Go easy on the guy." He eyed Gisele for a long moment. "He's been dancing on the edge of this secret for a while, so it won't take much to tip him over the edge."

Alright, my previous concern jumped to straight up alarm. "Hey, this isn't helping my nerves any."

Placing a hand on my shoulder, Issac said, "It'll be fine." His gaze tracked out the door. "Like Jose said, we'll be just down the hall."

"Uh...dude, this isn't helping." I swallowed the lump in my throat. "I'm starting to panic a little here."

Gisele made a shooing motion. "It's fine, they'll be close at hand if needed, and I'm sure they will be. There's quite a bit to go over, and now that you've had enough time to review the files I sent, you're ready for the next step."

I held out my hands to stop her. "Okay, now this is starting to sound a bit cultish...you're not a cult, are you?"

She burst out laughing. "Oh god no."

Her response seemed genuine enough, so that was good. "Okay, now what?"

She arched an eyebrow at the boys, who turned and left. "Now, we talk." She gestured at one of the wingchairs off to the side. "Please, sit, there's a lot to go over and we should at least be comfortable for what will likely turn out to be a multiday process."

Slowly, I meandered over to the nearest chair and plopped down. It was time to see what she had in store for me.

10

EVIL STEPMOM

Gisele's office was a sprawling room that looked as if Frank Lloyd Wright's edgy cousin designed the place. The midcentury furnishings had a brutalist industrial flare to them with a hint of cyberpunk that pushed the design into some dark dystopian future. It paired well with the overall aesthetic of the building itself and the mountains outside.

A thick, gray-white plume of smoke stood out against the purpling sky as it rose out of Popocatépetl, the most famous volcano in Puebla even if it was technically in Cholula. My gaze tracked up to the church, Iglesia de los Remedios. Somehow, it'd become synonymous with the city and thus adorned the majority of the postcards bought in town. The church had a second claim to fame as it sat atop Tlachihualtépetl, the widest pyramid in the world.

Gisele glanced over her shoulder. "Beautiful, isn't it?"

She was right of course. "It is."

Standing there for a long moment, she seemed to come to a decision. Turning, she offered me a smile as she strode toward me. "There's so much you need to know, and I have no idea where to start." She slipped into the chair across from my own. "Please forgive me, I'm not normally the person in charge of introducing people to our world."

"I'm sorry, our world? Wait a minute." It was then I began to ponder the unthinkable, had I died back in Teotihuacan? I glanced over to see the serious expression on her face. Was she an angel or perhaps a demon? Was she about to tell me I'd died, and this was the afterlife? Waving away the thoughts, I cocked my head to the side. "Hey, I'm sorry but…am I dead or something?"

Her eyes went wide at my words. In that moment, I could practically see the thoughts racing through her mind as she tried to make sense of what I'd said. A moment later she slapped her hand over her face as she let out a groan. "God, I suck at this." A pained moan escaped her lips. "No, you're not dead." She gave me a curious look and sighed. "Is that really what you were thinking?"

"Well—yes." Rolling my shoulders, I began to vent my frustrations. "Since getting my throat slit back in March, my world has taken a very weird turn." The look on her face told me she wasn't convinced. "Okay, think about it from my point of view—I've been sequestered at home with Jose and company. They're all great guys, but they aren't exactly normal." Before I could stop myself, I said, "Did you know Issac is obsessed with a show from the nineteen eighties?" I probably should've stopped long enough for her to answer but I couldn't. "The moment we arrive on the mainland, I'm hit with the weirdest sensation ever. Which, as you might imagine, totally freaks me out. Then when I do get here, the whole place looks like the lair of some evil villain out of an apocalyptic future no one wants to live in." Sucking in a quick breath, I let my words rush out. "Then you sneak me in through the back door like you're trying to hide me from the devil himself." Out of steam now, I warily gestured in her general direction. "Now, here you are talking about how you suck at introducing people to *our world*." Shrinking into my seat, I sighed. "What am I supposed to think?"

Stunned, she sat there, mouth agape as she took in my words. "So, your first thought was, this is the afterlife?"

Grimacing, I held out my hands to stop her. "Hey, look, I've seen my scar—that's a cut I shouldn't have survived, and we both know it."

"Okay, I can see that."

While I was reluctant to do so, I told her about the strange dreamlike state I'd been in after having my throat slit.

Nervously tapping my foot against the floor, I glanced up at her. "That's weird, right?"

Astonished, she nodded. "Very."

Feeling better about my earlier assumption, I puffed up in my seat. "So, yeah, between that, everything that's happened lately, and my arrival here this morning, you can see how I got there, right?"

Bobbing her head from side to side, she frowned. "It's a bit of a stretch, but given your mindset, I can see how you managed it."

Did she just call me stupid? "Hey, you've got to admit it's been a weird year."

She burst out laughing. "Oh, yeah, that it has." With amusement thick in her tone, she shook her head. "Wow, this is the first time anyone's actually going to be disappointed with what I have to say."

"Disappointed?"

Gisele wiped away the wetness in the corner of her eyes. "Yes." She made a valiant attempt to suppress the fit of giggles threatening to escape her lips. "Man...I—"

She burst into another peel of laughter.

Seriously? "It's not that funny."

Biting her lips, she gave me a look that said she thought otherwise. Finally, she calmed down enough to speak again. "Okay, look, I was going to start off with Arturo Nunez." She tossed a folder onto the coffee table between us. "But I feel like I should jump ahead and get some things out into the open first."

"Arturo Nunez?" Eyeing the folder, I asked, "Who's that?"

She waved away my question. "Let's set him aside for a moment. You need to be grounded in reality again before we can go through that."

This was getting a little hurtful. "Hey, come on—"

"I know." She flashed me a genuine smile. "It's been a crazy few years."

Reaching over, she picked up her tablet and multiple images appeared a few feet away. There were the big four—Jade Baker, Gavin Randall, Viktor Warden, and of course Cain. On the far side were photos I'd come to associate with the Twelve—James Matherne along with eleven other names with biblical origins. Next up were the six remaining leaders of the Black Circle—Seth, Osiris, Ashur, Ambrosio, Osha, and Nu Gui. Then there the ones that'd split off to revive the Archive—Deheune and Sargon, along with the followers of a man named Ke'lets that'd died about twenty years ago.

A totally separate group led by a man named Khaos was surrounded by minions—they were a recent addition to the puzzle since they'd garnered power through the Gaia Contagion. From what we could tell, their only goal in life was to spread death and destruction across the globe. But wait, there were more, such as the former leaders of the Gotteskinder, a hate group Gavin Randall worked to dismantle about a year back. Sadly for everyone, there were attempts being made to revive it. There must've been three dozen other factions represented there but my attention was focused on the two men at the center, Edward Munns and Geoffrey Yanos, the co-CEOs of Muzos. Their positioning was new.

Pointing at them, I said, "Why are they there?"

Gisele glared at the photos then turned to me. "We'll get to that." She leaned back into her seat. "Let me make some adjustments." Her fingers danced across the screen and the photos changed ever so slightly. "Now look at them."

Turning, I did a cursory sweep to see it was pretty much the same. They were dressed slightly differently, and the backgrounds were new, but they were the same people. "Okay, that's just a different photo of them, so what?"

She narrowed her eyes. "Look closer."

What the hell was she after? I turned my attention from Cain to Jade and finally Gavin. Their photos hadn't changed. Moving from them, I eyed Viktor. Nothing struck me as odd about his clothes but the rotary phone on his desk was kind of a relic. Huh, wait a second. Leaning forward, I peered at the background. Outside his second story window I could see a parking lot filled with antique cars straight out of the fifties. Weirdly, though, this didn't appear to be a car show but an actual parking lot.

Okay, that was kind of odd, but whatever.

Seth's photo showed him out in the desert near one of the lesser-known pyramids, leaning against an old truck filled with archaeological equipment. He wore a very old timey suit with puffy pants and a cigarette hanging out of his mouth. Leaning against the fender on the other side was Osiris, but he was in traditional middle eastern garb that looked to be off the set of some nineteen forties movie.

Moving around the room, I found the majority of the photos showed most of the subjects being portrayed in period specific clothing as well as other props such as cars and such. The Gotteskinder, James Matherne and several others seemed to be exempt while everyone else in the Twelve seemed to be displaced in time.

Before I could say anything, Gisele tapped the screen again and many of the images transformed into something new. With a few exceptions, the photos were gone, replaced by paintings and or drawings from an even earlier point in time.

Before you ask, Lilith wasn't exempt from this treatment, with her first photo being taken at dinner during our last anniversary together. The one before that was our wedding and now there was a painted portrait of her that looked to be from a forgotten era.

Every time I turned to Gisele, she'd tap the screen again to show new artwork and even a few sculptures of these people. Sitting there, I began to have a sinking feeling that I was in way over my head. She continued to do this until Seth was reduced to a carving on stone surrounded by hieroglyphs.

Many of the names stuck out—Lazarus had a fairly current photo, but his last image was something straight out of biblical times. The weird thing was the image looked to have been lifted from a private museum.

Well, so did the others if I was being honest. The strangest thing about the images was the fact the subjects never seemed to age, no matter the time period they were shown in. I wanted to call bullshit, since art was subjective, but Seth seemed to have the same seeping wound on his chest throughout most of the images.

Sitting there for a long moment, I turned to Gisele and held out my hands to stop her. "Please don't change the pictures again...I don't think I can stand to look at anymore."

She nodded. "That's fair, though you did better than I expected. Most people tap out around twenty, you, however, went through over one hundred images. That's impressive."

"Thanks?" I shook my head. "I don't understand what you're trying to show me here."

Her expression softened. "I know, and I'm getting there." She stood and walked over to the bookshelf to pull down a photo and hand it to me. Pointing, she said, "That's me, Jose, Lilith, Christopher, Jamie, and a few others you can see in the background."

Looking closely, I spotted a half-finished Eiffel Tower. "Where did you find a souvenir shop doing this kind of work back in the day?"

A sad smile crossed her lips as she tapped the glass. "Read the poster."

Peering closely at the image, I spotted a small banner. Futur site de l'exposition universelle. 1889.

Smiling, I chuckled. "Oh, that's a nice touch."

She collapsed into her seat. "What if I told you that picture was taken in August of eighteen eighty-eight?"

Bursting out laughing, I shook my head. "Look, I know you've got some great genetics, but that's asking a bit much." I shook my head. "Plus, what you're hinting at here is straight up impossible."

Leaning her head to the side, she gave me a curious look. "Because it'd make me hundreds of years old?"

"Well, yeah." Why was I having to explain this to her? "The

average lifespan of a human is around eighty, and you want me to swallow the fact that you're several times that?" I gave her a dismissive wave. "Come on."

Her finger touched the screen and hundreds of images swam to the front. Each and every one of them was her throughout the ages. "And what about the images you've seen today? How do you explain that?"

"Photoshop?"

She paused then nodded. "Okay, that's fair, if I were human that is."

The way she said it struck me like I'd been punched. "I'm sorry, what?"

"You're assuming I'm human." She gestured back at the other photos. "The same mistake you're making with them."

Mistake? "Hold on, what?"

Gisele touched the screen again and the letter from the lab I used for genetic testing came into view. "You sent them a sample of Arturo's blood, right?"

I blinked. "Wait, the guy that attacked me was Arturo—Arturo Nunez?"

"That's right." A strand of crystalized DNA unlike anything I'd seen before popped into view. "This is what they found—it took a bit of finesse to crash their system and wipe their databank clean of the results, but we managed it without discovery."

It was absolutely beautiful in its design. "What is that?"

A big smile crossed her lips. "This is the genetic code of a Stone Born, much like myself, and most of the others you've met here."

"So, you're immortal?"

She wobbled her hand back and forth. "More or less, yes, I am."

I turned to Viktor. "And him?"

Arching an eyebrow, she shrugged. "We're not sure what he is, though that doesn't change the power he wields."

Wait, what? "Power? I mean immortality is cool, but what kind of power are you talking here?"

Gisele beamed as she held out her hand to create a purplish-black sphere. "Magic."

My mind felt like it was fracturing. Scrambling back, I shook my head. "Hold on...I can't believe I'm buying into this immortality and magic stuff."

"What about the Gaia Contagion?"

Sitting bolt upright, I gaped at her in horror. "Wait, all of you are infected?" I whipped my head from side to side. "I thought this was a new thing...not something old."

She held out her hands for calm. "No, we're not infected, and yes, the Gaia Contagion is new, but you've seen them use their powers...what makes you think that magic is new? Haven't you ever read the myths of this world?"

This world? "Of course, but—" Then it hit me, what if they weren't myths? What if they were about real people with magic? "Are you trying to tell me those are based in reality?"

Her expression turned disapproving, but she nodded. "Loosely... most of those events were either blown way out of proportion or understated the event to such an extent it's not even funny."

Then it hit me. I turned to Seth's photo and pointed. "Didn't I see some religious iconography there?"

Revulsion swept over her as she eyed the photo. "That's a subject best saved for later."

That was easy for her to say but she clearly wasn't going to indulge me. "Whatever." I pointed at the photos of Edward and Geoffrey. "What about these two? Are they Stone Borns as well?"

She tore her gaze from Seth to look at the two men. "They are." Pointing back at Seth, she said, "The leaders of the Black Circle, however, are not. They're lich lords." Her hand flashed up to stop my question. "They're corrupted abominations brought to life third- or fourth-hand through Dvalinn's power."

Holy shit...there were people out there with enough power to create life itself? "And Dvalinn is?"

Her hands worked furiously across the surface of the tablet then a photo of Stephan Morrigan appeared. "We're not sure what

Dvalinn's true form is, but he's currently in possession of Mr. Morrigan's corporeal body." She gave me a worried look. "I feel we're diving a bit too deep into some of this." Rubbing her hand over her face, she grimaced. "Look, this was meant to show you that the world you know is actually much more complicated than you realize."

Slowly turning my head, I gave her a hard look. "Yeah, I can see that." Hanging my head, I sighed. "And Lilith?"

"Right." Her tone softened. "She is a Stone Born."

Nodding, I lifted my gaze to hers. "Is that why she's so brilliant?"

Gisele shrank into her chair. "Uh...no." Her jaw tensed and relaxed several times before she spoke again. "This isn't the path I'd intended to follow to get to this point, but...we're here, so I might as well address it."

My gut was telling me I didn't like where this was going. "Address what?"

She gave me a cautious look. "To get to the next step, we need to agree that a few things are true first."

"Such as?"

Gisele tapped her screen, then a new image bloomed to life, forcing the others off to the side. It was a multi-columned list marked, 'species.' Below each of the columns was a name, then off to the side were specific traits associated with said species, such as lifespans, known strengths and weaknesses, population densities, along with a host of other technical specs related to said species.

For instance, Stone Borns were functionally immortal, barring any traumatic event bringing about their demise. Their population density was roughly one tenth of a percent due to the difficulty of producing offspring. Their powers were always randomized, and their only known source of weakness was gaining access to their stone, which in and of itself posed significant danger to anyone touching it.

There was a lot more there, but I dropped down to the witches to see they aged slower than humans but faster than weres and their powers were restricted, due to their need for items of power. The list continued to spill onward till I lost count; there must have been a thousand different species listed...not all of them humanoid.

"Such as, magic is real." She gestured at the list. "And there are more than the humans and animals you know inhabiting this planet."

My gaze drifted from the list to Gisele. "How long have people like you been here?"

Running her fingers through her hair, she draped it over her shoulder as she thought about the question. "I don't know—maybe since the beginning." She took a deep breath then let it out. "The fact of the matter is, over time our kind mixed with the indigenous inhabitants of this planet and well, it's hard to say, but this is why some people are stronger than they should be or live longer lives, or—"

"Claim to have magical powers."

She nodded. "Those people were quickly discredited or inducted into the Archive...sometimes they were killed to keep the secret, but now that the Gaia Contagion is here, that's an impossibility."

I held out my hands. "Hold on, what's the Gaia Contagion got to do with anything else?"

"Everything."

Her fingers danced across her screen. Thousands of tiny strands of unique DNA floated out of the list as it faded into the background. A moment later, an almost human double helix popped into view across from those of the list. Slowly, they began to merge to produce something I recognized as human.

I blinked. "Wait." Staring at her in disbelief, I asked, "Are you saying that you guys are the missing link?"

Rolling her eyes, she shrugged. "Maybe...Lilith thinks so, but her theory is a bit more complicated than that, going so far as to say we were responsible for the blueprint this planet used for humanoids."

My brain screeched to a halt. "Wait, why would she say that? Where's she getting the data?"

This time when she looked at me, there was genuine pity and a bit of worry there. "Let's address one topic at a time, shall we?"

I didn't like it, but I nodded. "Sure…tell me what the pandemic has to do with—" Gesturing at the images in front of me, I gritted my teeth. "This."

Her tone turned professorial. "Do you know what the Gaia Contagion does…or why some of those infected develop magical abilities?"

The question caught me so off guard, I didn't know what to say. "Uh…no."

Gesturing up at the strands of DNA, she asked, "Would you care to make some guesses?"

I turned my attention to the image then back to her. "Since the world isn't filled with superheroes, the dormant DNA tends to stay that way." She kept quiet but nodded her assent as I pressed on. "Are you saying the Gaia Contagion somehow activates those recessive genes?"

A big smile crossed her lips. "That's exactly what I'm saying."

"So, when the mutation goes wrong, it kills them?"

The smile turned into an instant frown. "That's the prevailing opinion, yes. Something goes wrong in the activation stage, forcing their body to grow at an accelerated rate. Though we're not sure if this was the intent or not, given those who develop powers need to consume the flesh of those killed by the contagion."

"Since we know the cause, can we cure them?"

Her whole body seemed to relax. "We're assisting Ms. Baker and her associates with such a cure even as we speak."

Relief spread throughout my body. "That's great." Eyeing the holograms, a question formed in my mind unbidden. "How is it this company is so far ahead of the curve in comparison to everyone else?"

Gisele gave me a curious look. "What do you mean?"

I gestured up at the holograms. "Well, this, then there's the Network you've been developing and let's face it, finding a cure for this should take a lot longer to research than what you're implying."

"Oh." Her expression hardened. "That."

I gave her a hard look. "Yes, that."

A dissatisfied expression crossed her face. "You're bound and determined to skip some important steps...jumping to the end in this case isn't a great idea."

"What sort of steps?"

A simple gesture brought Arturo Nunez's image to the forefront. "Don't you want to know about the man who tried to kill you?"

It was his DNA that'd sent me careening onto an entirely new path, so figuring out what he had to do with this was probably prudent. "Can we condense his story and get back to this?"

Frowning, she said, "Fine." She tapped the screen to bring up a form containing his name, address, birthdate, and a short history of his life. "Arturo Nunez, a Columbian native, was born in sixteen ninety-eight to a couple loyal to the Black Circle—specifically Sargon."

Sargon and a woman named Deheune were the two that'd split with the Black Circle to take over the Archive with the Twelve's help. "Okay—"

"Stop." She shook her head. "You wanted the short version, so let me finish." Taking a deep breath, she continued. "Once he came into his powers, he was trained as an assassin and has been deployed around the world to great effect. Roughly a year ago, he was transferred to Puebla and began working for Barry Lawson."

I blinked. "Wait, the same Barry Lawson that's been harassing me?"

"The very same." She leaned back in her seat. "It would seem like he tired of trying to have an in-person meeting and has opted to kill you instead."

My mind seemed to grind to a halt. "Wait...is Barry connected to the Archive?"

"He is." Her tone turned serious. "When he was with the Black Circle, he was next in line to be elevated to the Onyx Mind—that's their elite force that roams the world putting down anyone who opposes their master's desires. From what we can tell, he's completely loyal to Sargon."

"Is that why we couldn't find anything on the man?"

Gisele nodded. "It is. They've been doing this for a long time, and they have the right connections to make his ID as airtight as it was."

This was a lot to take in. "Okay…so I'm being hunted by an organization of immortals or semi-immortals who happen to be fully empowered with magical abilities?"

"That'd be about the gist of it, yes." She frowned. "Now that we've gotten past that little stickler, we can push him aside." With a flick of her finger, Arturo vanished to be replaced with Barry. "There's no reason to think he'll stop trying to kill you now that you've survived the first attempt."

Wasn't that just wonderful. "Great."

Her expression softened and she nodded. "Now that you're aware of your position, let's jump back to how Ōmeyōcān-Mictlān is, as you say, ahead of the curve." The skin under her right eye twitched. "That's because we're working with advanced technology from another timeline."

The room darkened for a second there, and my mind seemed to reboot itself, allowing me to properly focus on the woman in front of me. "I'm sorry, what?" Something cracked in my mind as I tried to wrap my mind around what I'd been told. Stone Borns were immortal, Lilith had been here since the beginning. The room began to lose shape around me. When I spoke, my voice sounded far away. "Just how old is Lilith?"

My mind began to swirl.

Thinking back, I'd seen Lazarus—it'd been that Lazarus. Turned out he wasn't a great guy, but he'd been the one mentioned in the Bible. Then there was Cain and his hatred of vampires. It was only then that the V annotation surrounding those deaths last year made sense. They'd been vampires…that meant the Vampire Courts were run by actual vampires.

The room around me completely vanished as the thoughts consumed me. Cain had a V annotation, as did Eve and Vasile. They were all vampires. Even more interesting, while Adam was Cain and

Abel's father, Lilith was their mother, meaning Eve was the evil stepmom. I...I didn't like where this was going.

Giselle was Cain's daughter, but she'd been a Stone Born, but now she was somehow both? How was that possible...the brief said anyone infected by the parasite that caused vampirism lost their abilities.

My head began to ache, and I felt a bit woozy.

Finally, I parsed out an important statement about Adam—he'd been the one to write the first several chapters of the Bible. If they'd been here since the beginning because they were from another timeline, that'd make sense even if his view was skewed.

A tingling sensation enveloped me, then the world turned dark.

11

THIS ISN'T FAIR

Groaning, I lifted my hand to shield my eyes from the glare of the midafternoon sunlight pouring in through the windows. Sound was a distant memory, and my heart pounded in my chest. Squeezing my eyes closed, I turned away from the harsh light assaulting my senses. My world was crumbling, and there was nothing I could do about it. Massaging my temples, I sat there trying to assert control over my rampaging mental state. Slowly, things like the air being forced out of the HVAC system reached my ears. The trembling in my hands lessened, and my breathing evened out.

Purposely turning my face to the floor, I risked cracking open my eyes. This wasn't my floor. In that moment, the memories came crashing down on me, threatening to drown me once again. Swaying in my chair, it was all I could do to keep from slipping out of it. Even as my vision began to narrow, I fought to stay in the conscious world. I was safe, even if everything I'd once known wasn't quite the way I believed.

Rubbing my hands over my face, I resisted the urge to walk out. This was my reality now...or was it? She'd hit me with a lot... was the point to overwhelm me in such a way I became pliable? No, that didn't make sense. She didn't need me for anything, and it wasn't like she was hurting for money. Plus, if she wanted to plan a coup, it wasn't like the others would remain loyal to me over her.

Yeah, okay, so if she was telling the truth, I needed a bit more detail and hopefully some additional proof.

Finally, I turned my attention to Gisele, who sat there looking like the picture of patience. "Adam—" Before I could say another word, a darkened silhouette of a man's portrait swam to the forefront of the images. "Right…we don't have a picture of him." I gave her a curious look. "Why is that?"

Disgust washed over her face. "Oh, we have a photo, we just keep it darkened." She arched an eyebrow. "Would you like to see what he looks like?"

"Yeah, I would."

With a dismissive wave, the photo revealed itself. Oddly, Adam looked pretty much the way I pictured him—blonde with handsome features that'd make him a movie star here. There was a pettiness in his eyes that said everything I needed to know about the guy. Overall, he was nothing special.

"Huh." It wasn't hard for me to believe everything I'd ever heard about the guy. "He looks like an entitled prick."

Gisele's expression soured. "Yes, he was."

"I take it you knew the man."

She leaned back in her seat then shrugged. "Pre-QDM, yes. Thankfully, I was spared his presence in this world."

I raised my hand to stop her. "I'm going to get back to whatever that means, but I have a few questions first."

Curiosity coated her tone. "Only a few?"

"Okay, several." I glanced up at him and nodded. "Yeah, I can see why you keep it darkened." With those words, Adam returned to shadow. "Thank you." Tapping my chin with my finger, I said, "So, Adam is the same guy from the Bible, right?"

Wobbling her hand from side to side, she said, "If you mean he modeled it after himself and claimed to be a victim while saying he had god's ear, then yes."

Right, the guy supposedly wrote them. "Okay, if that's the case, why isn't Lilith in there as well? Why did he jump to Eve?"

Gisele smiled. "Oh, she was in the earlier versions of the Bible, but she's been edited out. As to Eve, that is his second wife. She's a bit of a psycho stalker who can't get enough of the guy, so they're a match made in hell."

"Speaking of heaven and hell—what's up with that?"

A big smile crossed her lips. "He stole a lot of the ideas from stories or small cults from our previous timeline."

"That's manipulative as hell."

She gestured up at the darkened image. "Please allow me to introduce you to Adam...that was kind of his specialty."

"Point made." Swallowing back the bile threatening to escape my mouth, I stared at Cain. "I'm guessing the story Lilith told me about Cain killing Abel is a bit more complicated?"

Gisele shifted in her seat. "What did she tell you?"

Yeah, I wasn't falling for that one. "I'd rather hear what you think happened."

Her gaze tracked up to Cain then over to the image of a vampiric skull. The latter was something a group called the Sanctified Path worshiped. "Abel wasn't right—his father had him all twisted up inside and the kid worshiped him for it. To hear some people talk, Adam forced him to kill his first victim before he could walk. From there, it spiraled." Even as she spoke, revulsion, hate, and sorrow flitted across her features. "Adam hated Cain, so Abel did too...he used to force them into cage fights in the hopes Cain would slip up and die."

That was some seriously dark shit. No wonder Lilith never wanted to talk about it.

Gisele's gaze hit the floor. "Then after the QDM—Quantum Death of the Multiverse—Abel somehow got worse, murdering his way through the countryside for sport, taking people as slaves and torturing them until they broke. All he ever did was hurt people, animals, and the world itself. If he'd been left to his own devices, you wouldn't have a world to live in." Lifting her head, she eyed me with an intensity that left me feeling vulnerable and exposed. "Cain hunted him for years, then when he finally caught up to the insane little prick, they fought. In the end, Cain killed him, but not before Abel cursed him with an artifact created by the Norns to control Cain."

"What sort of artifact?"

She shrugged. "No one knows for sure; all we know is it allows him to kill his siblings by extracting the parasite that transforms them into the vampires they are. Once that's done, their entire line ceases to exist."

It was then her wording hit me. "Siblings?"

Realization swept over her, and she nodded. "Right, you wouldn't know." She made a small gesture and a number of names popped into view. She pointed at the top line. "We'll start with Namisia. Her particular strain was called Strigoi, and her father as none other than Adam...we're not sure who her mother was." As she flicked her wrist, the list began to scroll by. "Turns out every strain of vampirism known to exist are led by kings or queens who just so happen to be Adam's children. With the exception of Cain, all the others inherited Adam's insanity."

Wow, okay, now it was starting to make sense why Cain was hellbent on putting them down. "So, vampires are bad."

"Most are complete assholes." She shrugged. "Though you get the odd few who are decent folk and break off from their pack."

I chuckled. "I bet that goes over well."

Shaking her head, she said, "Not really. They're either killed by their own, or they find safety with people like Warden Global, the Witan, or vanish into a pocket reality in Paris."

"I see." Okay, it was time to get to the meat of the problem. "Alright, tell me about the Quantum Destruction of the Multiverse. How did we get from there to here?"

Gisele looked thoughtful for a long moment then eyed me with curiosity. "What do you know about the multiverse theory?"

Did she think I was some sort of quantum physicist? "Other than the comic book movies, not a lot." I shrugged. "Which is to say, next to nothing, but I think the gist of it is our universe is one of many where everything exists all at once. Each and every decision made has the potential to spawn entirely new versions of reality."

Her fingers drummed against the arm of her chair. "Okay, so that'd make the Earth the center of all creation, which is great for one's ego but incorrect overall." A second later, her fingers were dancing across the screen of the tablet. "Here, take a look at this."

An incredibly detailed image of the Milky Way appeared before it shrank down as the rest of the universe began to populate. It took several seconds, but eventually, a massive cloud of stars hung in the air in front of us. For whatever reason, I was surprised to see the boundaries of the universe that edged up against the void were misshapen. It looked as if something exploded somewhere deep inside, but the impact zone didn't react evenly, almost as if some of it was more malleable than others. Every so often, I spotted a narrow looking tunnel that jutted off into the darkness as if it were headed somewhere in particular on the other side of the void. Looking at it again, I counted eight of them.

When she lifted her finger and pointed, the outer edge of the map began to glow. "This is the Rim. It sits on the edge of our reality and the void." She made a casual gesture, and the glow faded, but the small tunnels I'd spotted earlier brightened. "These are passages that lead to one of the other connected realms."

My mind wasn't quite able to make sense of her words. "Realms?"

"There are nine known realms, but we suspect there are more." She pointed at the map, which shrank down to settle in the center with eight others branching off in every direction. "Ours has many names, as do the others, but it's home to the human race and all its variants." Another gesture highlighted one of the realms adjacent to our own. "This is a land predominantly inhabited by creatures of the aether—i.e. noncorporal. Then there's the land of the giants, fire, ice—well, there's a lot out there that doesn't neatly fall into a specific category, though for expediency's sake, I'm lumping things together."

Exhaling, I blinked. "Is this important?" I glanced over at the map. "Also, how can you be so sure about—" I pointed. "All that?"

The highly critical look she shot me quickly gave way to realization. "Sorry, I kind of jumped ahead again." She blushed. "This is why I'm not in charge of the introduction process." A nervous laugh escaped her. "Sorry."

A split-second later, hundreds of powerful looking spaceships replaced the image of the nine realms. Before I could ask more about them, they shrank into the background to be replaced with dozens of different types of satellites. Some of them were spheres, others were discs, or spears—there were thousands of designs, so it was difficult to focus on just one.

Then, as if by magic, one of the discs appeared and filled more than half the room. It hovered there as if awaiting instructions. Gisele gestured at the metallic device. "This is a drone from the time before the QDM." She leaned forward and touched her tablet and Earth's solar system appeared. "Just outside of the sun's pull is an Anillo Gate—think of them as warp gates from one of your sci-fi shows here."

Sure enough, right in the middle of an asteroid field was a massive, alien ring constructed of a strange alloy I couldn't identify.

"That's an Anillo Gate?"

Gisele beamed. "It is, and if you know how to activate it, you can traverse from one gate to the other, even if it's on the opposite side of the cosmos."

My gaze tracked over the disc hovering there. "And since you're from some alternate timeline—"

"Dead." She quickly corrected. "Basically, all of reality is killed off, a new one is created, and we start over."

I pointed at her. "But you don't...because you somehow survived the QDM."

Her whole body went rigid. "That's hard to explain—for whatever reason, some of the unseen powers of the universe saw fit to allow certain factions, people, tech, and other things to fall through the cracks of one reality into another." She pointed at herself. "I was stationed on Eden with Lilith as a researcher—" Her words caught in her throat. "A lot of the people you see working here were part of that expedition." Sadness seemed to overwhelm her. Slowly she regained her composure. "Our memories were wiped—though we eventually recovered them thanks to Lilith's help…I'm not sure how she managed to recover hers, but it's my understanding that it was traumatic."

Her grief was so profound it hurt my soul. Clearing my throat, I said, "I'm sorry." My gaze landed on the disc again. "But you know how to activate it and send these drones or satellites through it to map the universe?"

She wiped away the wetness on her cheeks. "Yes." A casual gesture caused the drone to vanish. "So, that's how I know all of this is true."

Curious, I asked, "How did they survive the QDM? I would've thought anything you created before would've been swept clean unless this is one of the exceptions you mentioned."

A small smile found its way onto her lips. "Oh, we didn't build those." She shook her head. "And we don't have a clue who did. The only thing we know for sure is they were far more advanced than we ever were."

"Then how do you know how to use them?"

Gisele's form deflated a little. "Lilith—by some grand design her entire lab along with every data crystal and so much more was sent back with her." She held out her hands to make a large square box. "All contained in a golden cube you can carry in your hand."

That revelation hit me like a brick to the face. "Like what Mab was carrying?"

"Exactly like that." Her voice dropped to a near whisper. "Though you should be aware she is no longer in possession of it." Despair seemed to overtake her again. "Not like it matters, but Cain has it, and it can't be opened again until Janus allows it."

Rage rushed through me as I got to my feet. "Who the hell is that, and why does he get to decide my wife's fate?"

Fear flashed in her eyes, as she glanced around the room as if she expected some dark god to strike me down. "We don't know who he is…but he's the closest thing to a god I've ever met. He's got the kind of power that can wipe a civilization from the map one moment and resurrect something in its place the next." She gestured at the map of the universe. "Kind of like he has trillions of times before."

That stopped me in my tracks. Slowly, I sat back down. "What's that supposed to mean?"

Hanging her head, she let out a groan. "God, I suck at this." She lifted her gaze to mine. "The QDM has happened many times, from what I've been able to pick up, there's some sort of contagion that infected the base code of the universe itself, and he's trying to fix it by rerunning the entire universe over and over again until he gets it right."

I couldn't believe it, she was dead serious. "And what's Lilith got to do with this?"

"Other than she's brilliant?" She shrugged. "I don't know…part of it involves Cain. That's why he's wiping out the vampires, but there's a lot more to it, some of which involves Viktor, but I haven't got a clue how."

"So, I can't do anything about it…I just have to wait for Janus to release Lilith from her captivity?"

Gisele nodded. "Yes…and that usually occurs every four or five centuries."

Slumping back into my seat, I groaned. "Fuck lot of good that does me. I'll be dead by then."

She arched an eyebrow at me. "I'm not so sure about that, but before we go there, I think there's something you need to see first."

"Oh, and what's that?"

Holding up a small crystal, she said, "This is a data crystal, and it has a recording of a conversation she had just before the QDM occurred." She leaned over and placed it in a slot on the table. "Watch."

.   .   .

In a flash, the map that'd been hovering there was replaced with Lilith's face. It was a ghostly image that just hung there unmoving for several seconds.

Her worry and fear were plain to see, then relief spread across her features as if she were seeing something that relieved her anxiety. "Oh, thank the gods. You've survived." She swallowed hard, fighting tears and blotting the corners of her eyes with a tissue. "Hello, Cain, my darling boy. I'm sorry I can't be there with you. As much as this pains me to say, I'm likely dead. Or at the very least, lost." Her voice trembled. "I'm not sure what's going on. None of us are. All I know is that you're the key to saving us from this hell."

Squeezing her eyes closed, light shimmered in the wetness streaming down her cheeks. She used her forearm to wipe them away. "Gods, I wish I could see your face, hug you, and tell you everything will be okay. But I think we both know they won't be."

Hurt sounded in her voice. "From what I understand, you've known that for a long time. I've been told you couldn't tell me because it'd destroy our only chance at peace." Anger flashed in her eyes and her tone hardened. "It was unfair of whoever did this to put such a thing on a child." Her rage burned out. "I love you so much, son. I wish I could do more."

There was a noise behind her.

She jumped as she glanced over her shoulder, then she quickly returned her attention to the screen in front of her. Lowering her voice, she said, "It'll take time for the following files to decrypt to view them. I'm sorry to put this on you, but if Hayden is to be believed, you're the only one who remembers everything that's happened. The rest of us have had our memories either wiped or significantly altered. This is a terrible burden we've placed on you, but you're both the lock and the key to undoing this mess."

Wind whipped in the background, causing the structure to groan, and something slammed hard against the outer wall. "I've got to go. Please know that I love you—"

Reaching out, she tapped the screen in front of her. Resentment flashed across her face. Slowly, she turned. "What happened to the shields?"

Gisele stepped into the frame. "They're failing; no matter how much power we feed them, it's just not enough."

Hanging her head she burst into tears. "He's all alone."

Rushing over, Gisele wrapped her arms around Lilith, hugging her tight. "But the message went through, right?"

Bitterness coated her tone. "Yes, Janus kept his word."

A voice I recognized as Jose's called out. "We've got to go...everything is coming apart."

Lilith gave the screen one last reluctant look before taking his advice and running.

The hologram froze, then faded.

That wasn't Earth...and the tech being used there was far beyond anything I believed existed. Turning to her, I fought back tears as I asked the only question I could. "Why did you show me this?"

She gave me a sad smile. "I wanted you to know what she's sacrificed to get this far. I know this feels personal to you, but there's a much bigger picture here that you need to look at." Shaking her head, she said, "This isn't fair, and I get that, but you're not the only one suffering here. She's waited eons to see her son again, and when she thought she had the chance, she went for it, only to be taken off the board until she's allowed out again."

When she put it like that, I felt like a selfish bastard. "What's the endgame here?"

"We don't know." She shrugged. "It's our hope it all goes to plan, and we're allowed to live our lives as we see fit."

Unable to stop myself, I grumbled. "Yeah, if you're an immortal."

"About that." Her gaze tracked over me and then out at the darkening sky. "I think we need to figure out what you are, because I'm certain you're not human."

I blinked. "Excuse me?"

She touched the nape of her throat. "Like you said, you shouldn't have survived, but you did, and I'd like to know why, wouldn't you?"

After what I'd learned today, I was curious. "Actually, yeah."

She checked her watch. "It's getting late. You should eat then get some rest. We'll start early in the morning."

Suddenly feeling tired, I nodded. "Yeah, that sounds good."

The door opened and Jose stepped into the room. "Done?"

She nodded. "Take him to his apartment."

I turned to look at her. "I have an apartment?"

"Of course." She smiled. "Lilith set it up personally."

Damn, I had to see this. "Thank you."

Gisele gave Jose a hard look. "Don't dally, we're starting early in the morning...bring him up to my lab at three."

What? "Hey, I get up early but that's just stupid early."

Smiling, she shrugged. "Can't be helped. I don't want an audience when I run your genetic code through the system."

Before I could argue, Jose waved me forward. "Just let it go man; you're not going to win."

I guess he'd know. "Alright."

With that, I let him guide me out of the room and into the hall. Turned out, my apartment was actually a penthouse that had a spectacular view of the city. It wasn't quite like home, but there was enough there to make it feel close enough.

12

DEHEUNE IS HUNTING YOU

May 4th

Lying there, I reached over and grabbed my phone: 2:15 a.m. At least I had a reason to drag my ass out of bed this time. After dinner, I barely made it to my bedroom before I passed out. That was around nine last night. Then I proceeded to wake up at 22:15, 23:32, 00:45, and 01:22.

No, it wasn't a bladder issue, thank you very much. Also, who gave you the right to ask about my prostrate health? Last I checked, you weren't my physician.

Speaking of which, I was probably going to need a new primary care physician. Yeah, I was definitely going to need one of those. Fortunately, that was a later problem. Right now, it was time to get moving.

Was I tired? What the hell do you think? I woke up every fucking hour last night and I'm getting up at two fifteen in the morning, so yeah, I'm tired. I know they say there aren't any stupid questions, but I'm pretty sure they're wrong after that one.

Shit, sorry, I might be a bit cranky, I didn't get a lot of sleep, and you have to admit the answer to that question was rather obvious.

Again, though, I was rude, and I shouldn't have been. Sit back down and relax. We good? Excellent.

Part of me wanted to say in bed, but the rational bit of my mind said what was the point, I'd be waking up in about forty minutes anyway, so why not get my ass out of bed now?

Decision made, I pushed myself up into a sitting position then stood and hobbled into the bath. Thankfully, everything from my shampoo of choice to my deodorant, and even my favorite type of razor was on hand just waiting for me to use them. Fifteen minutes later, I was clean and dressed. Seeing how I'd be spending my day getting poked and prodded, I opted for a pair of sweatpants, a t-shirt, and some tennis shoes.

There was a knock on the door as I made my way into the bedroom. "Come in."

The door popped open, and Jose leaned in. "Hey, you're up and about. Good for you." He thumbed over his shoulder. "Issac is in the kitchen making breakfast. He must've felt bad about what you went through yesterday, so he's been up baking for the last two hours."

A big smile crossed my lips as hope kindled in my heart. "Is he making that puff-pastry dish?"

Jose chuckled. "Not the one you're thinking of, but yes."

I furrowed my brow. "Huh?"

"Come on." He chuckled. "This is way better, I promise."

I didn't see how that was possible, but I was willing to take a chance on it just this once. Who knew, I might wind up with a new favorite dish. Turned out, Jose was correct, it was amazing. It was a twist on a French dish called chicken friand with a wild mushroom sauce. According to Issac, the normal version was a lunch or dinner thing, but his version worked just as well for breakfast.

On our way out the door, I grinned. "So, that had to be a lot more trouble than the other puff pastry dish with the cheese, eggs, and vegetables, so why make this?"

Issac gave me a wink. "I try not to make the same thing twice in any sixty-day timeframe." He rolled his shoulders. "This, however, was close enough I thought you'd enjoy it while staying true to myself."

Jose gestured toward the elevator. "Come on, Gisele wasn't kidding about wanting you down there at three."

Reluctantly, I strode over and pushed the button. "Why three?"

"Shift change." Issac quickly interjected.

I guess if she was looking for privacy that would make sense. "Alright." The bell dinged and the door slid open. "Let's get this over with."

We strode into Gisele's lab at five till, though she didn't look happy about it.

Tapping her foot against the ground, she checked her watch. "What did you three do, stop for breakfast?"

A plate appeared in Issac's hand. "Actually, yes." He stepped forward with his hand out. "Want some?"

The plate vanished in an instant. "Of course I do." She narrowed her eyes. "But that doesn't negate your tardiness."

"Hold up, first off you said three and we're early." I gestured at where the plate had been. "Second, how the hell are you guys making things appear and disappear like that, is that some sort of magical ability?"

Everyone turned to look at me like I was stupid. Confused, they looked at each other then back at my dumb ass. Finally, Gisele spoke. "Spatial devices." Tapping her wrist, she said, "Mine's a bracelet." She gestured at Jose then Issac. "He has a ring, and his is… well I don't know."

Issac snorted. "And I'm not telling."

"Spatial device…like a bag of holding from those fantasy novels?"

Slowly nodding her head, she said, "Kind of, but it's far more complex."

Like I gave a shit. "Is there any chance I could get one?"

Bewildered, she glanced between the other two.

Jose reached out with his index finger and lifted my wrist. "You already have one."

"No, I don't." Looking down, I smiled at the black anodized steel box chain bracelet with crimson highlights wrapped around my wrist. "This is just a piece of jewelry Lilith gave me for our last anniversary."

Issac's expression softened. "Do me a favor; close your eyes and think about accessing your inventory."

Were they not listening? "I don't have an inventory."

Jose patted me on the shoulder. "Humor us."

I fought the urge to roll my eyes. "Fine." Closing my eyes, I said, "I'd like to access my inventory."

I'd barely thought the words, let alone got them out of my mouth, before a list of categories popped into view: Housing, Vehicles, Food Stuffs...the list continued on into the thousands. When I accessed the housing there were a number of portable shelters of all sorts, plus a large number of permanent encampments that looked to be designed to create outposts in every conceivable environment. There were a few amorphic clouds that looked to be specialty models that seemed to need to be bound to my person before they could be activated.

If I wasn't careful, I could lose myself in there for years. Pulling myself free, I staggered back and almost fell, but thanks to Issac's steady hand I stayed upright.

He chuckled. "Yeah, it's a bit much." Pointing at the bracelet, he said, "I bet you haven't realized that hasn't come off your wrist since you got it."

I thought about it for a moment then looked at it in surprise. "No, it hasn't." Twisting it around my arm, I didn't see the latch that'd allow me to remove it if I wanted to. "Huh, looks like it's stuck there unless I lose a hand."

Gisele rolled her eyes. "No, you'd still have it." She chuckled. "It's bonded to your flesh, so the only way you're losing it is if you die, and maybe not even then."

"Oh...okay." That was a cheerful thought. "Uh...so, what's the plan here?"

She gestured at a chair on the far side of the room. "If you'll join me over here, we can kick this off by getting a blood sample. Sound good?"

"No." I chuckled. "But I don't think that'll help, so let's do this."

Smiling, she nodded. "Alright, come on."

As tired as I was, the idea of getting stuck, scraped, and inspected over the next several hours didn't exactly sit well with me. "Yeah, yeah, yeah. I'm coming."

The moment my foot left the floor, what amounted to blast shields dropped down over the windows. Judging by the dull, thudding reverberations echoing throughout the building, I didn't think this was an isolated event. A second later, the lights flickered and died, only for the emergency lights to glow to life.

Before any of us could say anything, a general announcement sounded. "Please remain where you are." The announcer's voice was clearly Lilith's. "Do not be alarmed. The facility is currently undergoing multiple upgrades and should be completed within the hour." Her tone softened. "First off, I'm sorry if this catches you at an inopportune time, but due to certain circumstances, I was unable to predict when this moment would actually occur." There was a small pause. "I apologize for my current absence, but I've found a way for me to assist you between now and my imminent return. Thank you for everything you do. I cannot express my gratitude for each and every one of you. It's my hope we'll see each other again soon, and until then, know that you're always on my mind."

Cocking my head to the side, I stared at Gisele. "What the actual fuck?"

Stunned, she only managed to shrug. "I…I don't know."

The console behind her lit up, acting as a beacon in the darkened room. Turning, I watched as a basketball sized orb of golden light poured out of what I'd come to recognize as a holo-projector. A sharp crack sounded as if something broke inside the machine, causing the sphere to stutter before winking out entirely. Now that the light was gone, a pervasive darkness seemed to creep into the room as if it wanted to swallow us whole.

A low bass-like hum began to rise through the building, causing every surface around us to vibrate in an almost imperceptible way. Of course, the tingling sensation inside our bones was a clear give-away something was happening.

I turned to Jose. "Should we be panicking?"

"I—" His gaze tracked around the room. "I don't know."

Issac plopped into a nearby chair. "Nah, man, we're golden." He ran his fingers through his hair. "If Lilith says we'll be fine, we'll be fine."

Gisele gave him an incredulous look then shrugged. "He's right."

"Yeah, alright." Jose's gaze tracked around the room, then he nodded. "This feels a bit off, but if you guys are fine, then sure, I guess we should settle in and wait."

While I appreciated their faith in my wife, this was a lot to ask. "So, we're just going to sit and wait, is that what you're saying?"

Gisele shrugged but gave me a curt nod. "Pretty much." She plopped into a nearby chair and gestured for the rest of us to do the same. "It isn't as if any of us can force our way through Tyridium in a timely manner so, yeah waiting it out is our best course of action."

My subsequent objections were cut short when tiny golden lights began flooding out of the holo-projector nearest Gisele. They began to accumulate in a tall cylindrical shape about the width of a single individual. Over the following seconds, more and more of the gilded sparks continued to spew forth like a fire hydrant that'd been opened on a hot summer day. Then it sputtered to a stop and the floor to ceiling cylinder began to spin. Over the following ten seconds, they condensed into a humanoid shape that glowed bright enough we were forced to shield our eyes to keep from going blind.

Then the room dimmed.

Lowering my hand, I gaped at my wife. "Lilith?"

She didn't respond. Instead, she hovered just above the ground with her hands at her side, eyes closed, and chin tilted forward as if she were in some sort of stasis pod. Her entire form pixelated and warped before settling back into her familiar form. She rolled her head to the side then all the way around before she opened her eyes and looked my way.

"Hello, husband."

This was obviously a recording of some sort. "Ah...hi?"

She chuckled. "Relax, I'm not actually the Lilith you know." Pausing, she considered the situation for a moment. "Think of me as a snapshot of her consciousness that's been turned into a Husvaettir."

I frowned. "Am I supposed to know what that is?"

Gisele cut in. "Think AI, but on a scale you cannot begin to comprehend."

Cutting my gaze at her, I said, "That doesn't help...I mean it kind of does, but it doesn't."

Lilith moved to stand beside Gisele. "It's fine, I'll handle it from here." She turned her attention to me. "I'm a digitized version of Lilith...I have all her memories she had at the time though, she's had additional experiences since then. Meaning she's already diverged from the baseline of who I am. We're already two very different beings but we have a shared origin."

Jose's jaw tensed. "When were you...born?"

A soft laugh escaped her. "About a month before she was exiled." Her gaze landed on me. "She loves you very much...I doubt that's changed...otherwise you wouldn't be here."

What was I supposed to say to that? "Uh...thanks?"

She gave me a wink before turning to Gisele. "I'm sure you're wondering what set of protocols were met to bring me to life years after the fact."

"Actually, yes, I am."

Lilith pointed at me. "You were about to run his DNA through the system, and that's something I cannot allow."

Gisele cocked her head to the side. "And why not?"

Her tone was playful but unyielding at the same time. "Do you really think I'd marry a man I hadn't fully vetted?"

"I..." Gisele gave me a curious look. "No, I guess you wouldn't."

She reached out to pat her friend's shoulder but there didn't seem to be any physical contact. "It's alright." Turning to me, she smiled. "As for you, I've reviewed recent events and I'm sure you've got questions."

This was starting to hurt my head. "Yeah, I've got a few." I held out my hand to stop her. "First things first, would you be opposed to me calling you Lily...thinking of you as Lilith is complicating things for me." She gave me a curious look, so I hurried to explain myself. "You already said you're different...and so is she...so you're not actually her...at least not the one I knew."

She considered the proposal for a long moment before nodding. "That works for me. Thank you for your consideration. It'd be awkward to have to keep explaining to you I'm not her."

Whew, that was a load off my mind. "Okay, so why did you stop Gisele? Do you already know what I am?"

Wonder shone in her eyes, and when she spoke, it was barely above a whisper. "Something entirely new."

Issac leaned forward. "Do you have something more for us?"

Lily gestured at the far wall and dozens of glowing spheres bloomed into view. "Yes, and no." She pointed. "What you're seeing here is living light...it contains the power of creation and oblivion in equal measure, along with so much more. To my knowledge, such an organism shouldn't exist." Turning to me, she smiled. "But you do, and you're amazing."

Eyeing the floating spheres, I couldn't help but compare them to the one I'd seen back in Teotihuacan. "This is me?"

She wobbled her hand back and forth. "Sort of...it's complicated —mainly because I couldn't get your—" Trailing off, she rubbed her chin. "They're not cells but that's what I'm going to call them since I'm fairly certain you don't want me to go into an in-depth explanation that's mostly conjecture, since your essence is based on an entirely unknown, and up until I met you, impossible set of principles that shouldn't be alive at all."

Reaching up, I rubbed my neck. "Then why do I bleed?"

Her expression darkened. "I'm not sure...maybe that's your unconscious mind doing things to help you fit in better." She whirled on Gisele. "Speaking of the attack on my hu—on Horacio, you should be aware Barry Lawson is working on orders from Deheune."

Gisele blinked. "What? I thought he was completely loyal to Sargon."

"Oh, he is." Disgust washed over Lily's features. "Thing is, Sargon seems to have pawned the man off onto her for some reason I'm not aware of currently. Not that it matters, the important part is Deheune wants the company and will do anything to get it. She isn't aware of the safeguards in place, and even if she did, she'd just attack our headquarters outright."

Shock registered on Jose's expression. "Why would she risk that?"

"Deheune is desperate." Lily shrugged. "Ever since her encounter with Gavin last year, things have gone poorly for her."

"Do we know what she's after?" Gisele asked.

Lily shook her head. "No."

Issac got to his feet. "What are we going to do about her interference?"

A nasty gleam flashed in Lily's eyes. "Oh, I've already set things in motion that'll flush her out. It might take some time, but she'll pop out of her hole soon enough."

Gisele gave the image a curious look. "Speaking of setting things in motion." She gestured around the room. "Care to explain what's happening here?"

"Before we get to that, I'd like to ask a favor?"

Shrugging, Gisele said, "What is it?"

Lily beamed. "Not from you." She turned to me. "I need you to promise me something."

I gestured at Gisele. "Same question."

Grinning, Lily said, "Now that you know Deheune is hunting you, I suspect you'll be looking for her as well."

"Well, yeah." I shook my head. "Catching me off guard last time almost got me killed."

She nodded. "That's true." Breathing out slowly, she said, "Don't try to take her yourself. You can't kill her, and it isn't because she's some unkillable machine but there are certain conditions that need to be met to properly put down one of the lich lords. Otherwise, Viktor would've been the one that killed Ke'lets."

Stunned, Gisele nearly fell out of her chair. "He didn't?"

"No, that was Jade." Her expression hardened. "She has an ability that allows her to drain them fully and destroy the corruption that gives them life. Without that power, nothing in this world can permanently put them down. It's also the only reason Deheune is alive. By all accounts, whatever Gavin did to the woman should've killed her outright, but it didn't."

Hearing the news didn't make me happy. "So, while it's within my ability to hunt her down, I'll need Jade to finish the job."

She nodded. "Exactly."

"Fine, I'll do what I can to make sure she's involved." I shook my head. "But I don't think she'll take a call from some random guy."

Gisele held up her hand. "No worries. I can make an introduction."

Lily beamed then turned to take in the room. "As to what I'm doing here, well—" She suddenly looked shy. "I may've been experimenting with samples I acquired from Horacio." Her voice turned quiet. "They just kept reproducing and getting larger so I started to do what any scientist would do and tried to figure out what made them tick." She glanced up quickly. "I failed at that by the way, but I did make some other discoveries."

She launched into an in-depth explanation of what she'd done. The first thing she told us was she had to name my base components something and calling it living light or energy was clunky. Or to have her explain it, it lacked a cool factor, which was why she'd dubbed them Ixlilton. From there, she began playing with the idea of channeling their growth in a specific direction, thus she took two rather large clumps and placed them in a pocket reality located in space on the far side of the moon. All we needed to do was use the locked door in my basement at home to access the pocket dimension.

It took a bit to get the details out of her, but when we did, I was shocked. In her words, she took the design specs for every space-ship, prototype and otherwise, and shoved them into a bunch of data crystals which she then fed to the samples before placing them inside the pocket reality to see what happened. Considering it was a locked environment, there was only so much she could do to monitor the situation, but according to her calculations, they were nearing completion and should finish within the next few months.

As if that weren't crazy enough, she'd used the samples to develop entirely new defenses, power sources, and weaponry. Which was what was happening to the building as we spoke. From what we could gather, the entire structure was undergoing a complete metamorphosis and becoming something new in the process. After seeing what Gisele was doing with the Network, Lilith had been inspired to try something new in that regard and created an entirely new and private form of transferring data throughout the cosmos. Most of the Qucoatl spheres were already distributing themselves throughout the universe under their own power. This was a technology she intended Ōmeyōcān-Mictlān to keep to themselves.

Not meeting my eyes, Lily said, "So, yeah, there are a few other things…but those are the highlights."

Part of me wanted to feel violated by what she'd done, but then again, there was a real possibility I'd be getting a custom spaceship out of the deal. Plus, she'd done this out of her love for me and her wish to keep me protected. I wasn't thrilled, but I couldn't say I was pissed either.

"I'm not sure how I feel about this, but at the moment I'm not livid, so that's a plus."

She beamed. "That's more than I was hoping for." Her gaze hit the floor. "But if you'd been pissed, I would've thrown Lilith under the bus; as I said, we're two different people, you know."

Unable to stop myself, I laughed. "Fair enough."

The lights kicked on and the HVAC system began to blow cool, clean air into the stale room.

Gisele got to her feet. "Well, I guess we should move on with our day." She cut her eyes at Lily. "It appears my plans were a bit redundant."

Jose held up his hand to stop them. "How are we going to explain his existence to the Witan? I know they're under new leadership, but I don't think they'll handle a whole new lifeform well."

Lily smirked. "Oh, Lilith handled that situation years ago." She pointed at me. "According to their records, you're a Stone Born." With exaggerated sadness, she sniffed. "Sadly, all their other files surrounding Horacio here were destroyed. Weirdly though, they didn't seem to notice, thus no one's ever going to come looking."

That was clever. "Thank you."

She winked. "You're very welcome."

With that settled, I wandered back up to my apartment for the day to consider what was next for me.

13

THE NETWORK

January 6ᵗʰ

Puebla, Mexico

Under normal circumstances, eight months didn't sound like a lot of time. In my case, however, the last eight months had been anything but normal. Jose, Issac, and the rest of my security team pushed me through an accelerated bootcamp reserved for their elites. Which meant my days started at two in the morning and ended somewhere around ten thirty at night. The first three months was physical conditioning, weapons training, and martial arts.

Thankfully, I was decent at the latter, given my upbringing. At the top of the fourth month, my physical training was scaled back to three hours in the morning. The rest of the day was divided up into multiple classes to familiarize myself with everything Ōmeyōcān-Mictlān had to offer, and it was a lot.

What was Gisele doing during this time?

Simple, she was busy grinding out the day-to-day operations of the company, making sure it ran properly. Which, given how the world around us had been more or less falling apart, was a hard ask. Thankfully, she'd worked out the kinks for the Network back in November, which was fantastic since the big four—Jade Baker,

Gavin Randall, Viktor Warden, and Cain—put it through its paces a few days back with their simultaneous worldwide announcement from the floor of the United Nations.

What announcement? Have you been living under a goddamn rock? Holy shit, and here I thought I'd had my head in the sand for the last several months. Okay, let me back up a bit and go over some of what I was told. For whatever reason, Jade, Gavin, and Viktor had enough of the status quo. What's that mean? If you'll give me a second, I'll get there. Asking me questions only slows this down.

Anyway, I have no idea what pushed them over the edge, but something did so they banded together and began to lean on the leaders around the globe. One by one, said politicians began capitulating to the big four's desires. Cain was lumped in whether he liked it or not. He'd only gotten onboard since hunting vampires under a one world government seemed more efficient.

Let me guess, you want to know what their ulterior motive was, and I'll tell you it's so much more insidious than you could ever comprehend. Could you hear the sarcasm? No, hardly surprising coming from the putz who asked if I was tired after getting no sleep.

So, what was their dastardly plan? Peace. Crazy, right? I mean that's nuts. Just think about it, people all over the globe would have the same chances as those lucky enough to be born in a rich country. To be clear, the world's population would have access to proper nutrition, clean water, and shelter, all at zero cost to them. But wait, it didn't stop there. Everyone would receive access to proper medical care, free education, and so much more. Then there was the universal income project that'd allow people to buy the things they wanted instead of having to pour hours into companies that wanted to work them to death.

I knew that last bit would make my dad happy. He always thought too much work and not enough living was detrimental to the human condition. Though he wasn't the only one, it was like the people of the world could finally breathe a sigh of relief.

Granted, most of the corporations out there hated this plan, because their business model depended on impoverished employees who, without them, would starve to death. There were rabbler-ousers trying to claim the poor deserved the lives they had because they weren't trying to better themselves. If hard work truly led to being rich, the rich would've monopolized that a long time ago.

The fact they hadn't should tell you all you need to know about the subject.

Of course, the Archive, Muzos, and the like were the loudest and the most violent holdouts. They were pouring cash into terrorist organizations and radicalized individuals they'd been manipulating for years in an attempt to slow the change. They knew they couldn't stop it, but they could disrupt it enough to cause problems.

Even the Black Circle joined in as the new world order threatened to strip away some of their power. Their objections were equally as loud, even if they were subtler in the respect they weaponized their influence over religious leaders. This of course sent ripples throughout the general public, but not as much as they were probably hoping for.

Again, not like it mattered.

Over the last year, Gisele had worked hard to put free devices into the hands of roughly eighty-five percent of the world's population. Thanks to her herculean efforts, it was nearly impossible to stop the flow of uncorrupted information to the average person. She'd made it clear Ōmeyōcān-Mictlān had zero ulterior motives. She stripped away the media's ability to skew the news one way or another, allowing for unbiased facts to permeate the world for the first time in probably forever. Anyway, thanks to all this, the common man was onboard with the whole one world government idea.

These efforts were aided by the housing boom across the globe. Thanks to Cain, Viktor, and Jade, prefab housing of the highest quality was available to everyone. Once-poor villages on the verge of collapse were outfitted with these homes, giving the people access to amenities such as indoor plumbing, clean water, and comfort. The massive food waste in the United States caused by what they called imperfections, such as oddly shaped vegetables, were suddenly in rotation as their resources were beamed across the planet via transporters.

Every independent country that signed on to become a part of a global community saw their fortunes change within hours. Even places such as Canada, the UK, and so many others found their infrastructure revamped in record time. Instant communication proved invaluable when it came to dealing with the malcontents.

It helped to quell riots caused by Muzos' blatant attempts at obfuscating the facts via the internet. While they had access to the Network, they refused to use it since they couldn't lie to the public via its bandwidth. I found it a bit shocking just how many people were torn between what they heard on the internet and what was being broadcast everywhere else on the Network. Thankfully, most of the ruckus being caused was easy enough to clarify, and when force was required, it was done in such a way there weren't any permanent injuries.

One of the biggest surprises to me was seeing the North American countries sign on the dotted line day one. Even more shocking was the fact the majority of Europe and Asia quickly followed their example. There were holdouts, of course. In the United States Alaska, Florida, Texas, and Mississippi were refusing to bend the knee. There were others, of course—Russia, the Vatican, and North Korea were the standouts, but they weren't alone. Sometimes these were cities or states that were controlled by certain religious or political factions that had direct connections to the Archive. This often led to them seceding from their country of origin.

To put it mildly, it was a clusterfuck...but the powers that be were working through the issues in a fairly peaceful manner. Considering what was coming in the next few weeks, I was sure that'd change.

What makes me think that? The Deus Ex Project. And what is that, you ask?

Wow, hmmm that's complicated. It's a lot of things, but we'll start with the first of its many benefits, it'll cure anyone infected with the Gaia Contagion. Impressive, right? I mean, it's a complete and total cure. Yeah, I know what you're thinking, what about those nifty new powers they got? Well, that was tricky. You see, while it removes the contagion in an instant, it also activates any dormant genetic material they might have. So, technically, they'll still have magic abilities, but they probably won't be the same. Though, if you ask me, that'd be a fantastic trade, since the person in question wouldn't have to cannibalize their fellow man.

I mean, that's a pretty big upside, right? On the one hand, you might get a different superpower, but you don't have to eat people anymore. Then again, if they choose to opt out of the program, they'll probably starve to death in about a year when the contagion is wiped out.

Yeah, that doesn't seem like a tough choice if you ask me.

I know what you're thinking, what if someone doesn't have any inactive strands of DNA in their system? Given how prevalent it is, that's unlikely, but on the off chance that's the case, the person in question would be given an increased lifespan before being swept up in a program meant to protect them from harm.

Was this available to everyone? In theory, yes, but in reality, that'd be a hard no. Look, they—the people in charge of this shit-show don't want a bunch of serial killers with superpowers. Which, when you think about it, is a good call. The thing is, who decides who does and does not qualify for the program? I have no idea. I'm not involved with that ethical and moral conundrum in the slightest, nor do I want to be.

Is there anything else that may cause the public some concern over this supposed miracle machine? Welllllllll, now that you've asked, maybe one? What would that be? Are you sitting? Fine, but don't say I didn't warn you. Ever heard of a man named Lucifer? Yeah, that guy. It would seem that his name became synonymous with evil thanks to Seth, Lazarus, and Adam's influence on certain religious texts.

What's he got to do with all this? Well, it turns out he was the driving force behind the Deus Ex machine's design. Him, Jade, and someone named Bae. Hey, don't get snippy with me, I warned you ahead of time.

Anyway, back to the Deus Ex Project itself, it was sending shockwaves through the populace that'd been born with abilities of their own. Okay, maybe that was a bit of an exaggeration. Point was, there were some folks who weren't pleased the playing field between them and mortals were about to be evened out. Given the history of some of them, I could see why.

Rubbing my hands over my face, I let out a long breath and got to my feet. I shuffled over to the fridge in the corner and pulled out a pineapple and coconut smoothie. After taking a long sip, I meandered over to the wingchair and made myself comfortable. Setting my glass to the side, I picked up the latest Exiled Ascendants book. Was it a classic bit of literature? Not even close, but it was a hell of a lot of fun.

After reading for about twenty minutes, I set the book aside and glanced up. "Lily."

Her avatar appeared in front of me. "Yes?"

"Care to give me a rundown on how things are going out there?"

She frowned. "Mostly according to plan." Her tone hardened. "The Archive has deployed forces to hold Russia, North Korea, several of the southern states in the US, and a few other hot spots. Thankfully, the civilians are being allowed, or in some cases forced, to leave."

Damn. "Alright...so, nothing new."

She shook her head. "No, not really."

Figured as much. "What about the refugees? Are we able to lend a hand?"

"What can be done is already being done." She smiled. "Jade has set up a Deus Ex station in each of the camps to help them adapt to the change. Then there's the outreach programs that are transitioning them into new housing and assisting them in either learning a new skill or improving their current ones."

Sipping on my drink, I leaned back in my seat. "And how's that going?"

"Surprisingly well." Her eyes glowed for a moment. "So far, every person fleeing these contested areas has voluntarily gone through the process."

I wasn't sure if that was a positive sign or not. "That's a bit of an unexpected turn of events."

She shrugged. "Not really...they're looking for some sort of control and getting superhuman abilities can give you that."

Rubbing my face, I let out a low groan. "Yeah, sure."

I supposedly had such abilities, but other than not dying when I should've, I didn't know what they were.

Lily gestured at the ceiling. "You've been cooped up in here for days; go up to the roof deck. A little fresh air and sunlight will do you some good."

As much as I hated to admit it, she was probably correct.

Getting to my feet, I motioned for her to follow. "You're right." After polishing off my drink, I set the empty cup on the table. I'd take it to the kitchen later to be washed out. "Let's head up."

Taking the stairs, I headed up to the sprawling roof deck. One of the large, shaded areas on the north side had a particularly comfortable chair. It had the added bonus of having a fridge stocked with fruit slushies of all sorts. Leaning over, I tugged the refrigerator open and pulled out a peach flavored drink.

I set it on the counter and reached for a straw. On the far side of the river, a strange flash caught my attention. In that moment, time seemed to stop. Lily stood there, unmoving. Birds hovered in the air midflight and the river ceased to flow. Even with all that, my only focus was on the flash. My vision seemed to zoom in on the spot. Two men were lying on their stomachs in a thicket of bushes.

The one on the right was looking through a pair of binoculars. Off to the side was a digital readout of the temperature, windspeed, and dozens of other readings I didn't know what to do with. As for the other, a high-powered rifle was pressed against his shoulder. The gun was belching fire and a bullet as thick as my finger hung in the air only a few centimeters from the tip.

Cocking my head to the side, power built up inside me and

forced its way out through my pores. There was a blinding flash, then it was gone. A moment of confusion hit me as I felt different. I glanced down at my hand to see a white gauntlet. My gaze tracked up my arm and down my body…I was covered in futuristic knights templar armor—all white but with red embellishments. The hood of the white cape was pulled up over my helm, while the rest of it fluttered out behind me as if blown by winds that weren't there.

Given the style of the armor, I half expected to find a cross emblazoned on my chest plate, but that wasn't the case. Instead, there was a circular symbol filled with circuitry with a marble-like center that burned with flames.

Glancing up, I eyed the bullet again; it'd moved another centimeter since I'd seen it last.

So, time wasn't stopped, it was just slowed.

Holy shit, I was so fucking tired of people trying to kill me. A cold fury sparked to life in my chest. I wanted to put an end to this shit once and for all. More than that, I was tired of feeling powerless to stop them.

On instinct, I reached out with my hand. The world in front of me twisted and pulled apart. Before I could stop myself, I stepped into the chaotic mess. The next thing I knew, I was standing over the two of them. A net made of white light coalesced around the shooter. Working on instinct, I clenched my fist and pulled it back, causing it to constrict around the man. What happened next nearly made me vomit as he became a pool of viscera and minced meat. A heavy crimson chain wrapped itself around my clenched fist and I brought it down hard. The second man's body exploded like an overfull balloon.

It was only then that the echoing shot that'd raced across the river registered. At that point though, the situation had been handled. There were a few issues, however. First, I was on the wrong side of the river with no way home. Second, there were two very dead people at my feet. And lastly, I was covered in blood.

In a flash, Jamie appeared with fire in one hand and lightning in the other.

Stepping back, I held out my hands. "Hey…wait…it's me."

Both the lightning bolt and the fireball had already left his hands. Time slowed, and I knew for a fact I didn't want to be where I was. Stumbling to the side, I fell into a second chaotic cloud to reappear on the roof of my house. Now that I was safe, the armor surrounding me vanished, dropping blood all over my clean roof.

Jose rushed up with a gun in his hand. "Are you—" His gaze fell on the blood at my feet. "Okay?"

I shrugged. "Yes, and no…the blood isn't mine, but I did kill a couple of people."

Jamie dropped onto the roof a split second later. "Horacio?"

"Yes." I frowned. "Look, I'm just as confused as you." Gesturing across the river, I said, "All I know is, I spotted the shot, time slowed down, and I kind of reacted on instinct—that's a nice way of saying I butchered one guy and crushed another with a chain weapon."

Jose frowned. "Okay, I'm going to need a lot more information to make sense of any of what you're saying."

Lily made a small gesture, and a holographic image appeared. "Have a seat. I caught most of what happened, even if I don't understand it myself."

After a few minutes, she was able to identify the shooters—they were a couple of hitters working for Deheune. Finding her just climbed to the top of my to-do list.

Jose eyed the recording several times. "Before we confront her, we should figure out how to trigger your abilities without putting you in mortal danger."

I winced. "Yeah, that's probably a smart idea."

14

JOIN US

February 1st

Siberia

Hey, I've got a quick question for you, do you think thirteen months is a long time? I mean, there are people out there who plan out weddings years in advance. For them, time seems to fly by, leaving them feeling stressed and totally freaked out. I, however, felt the same way but for a whole different set of reasons.

Like what? Well, over the last year, Jose and company put me through my paces in an attempt to figure out my abilities. You think that sounds like fun? I'd like to see what you thought after getting tossed out of an airplane, and no I wasn't expecting it. We were supposed to be doing some zero-G training, but that wasn't what happened. For the record, I was exceptionally happy I'd already mastered my teleport ability, because I wasn't sure they would've saved me from going splat.

As if the torturous and sometimes dangerous training regime wasn't enough, Lily, Gisele, and many others took it upon themselves to tutor me. In what, you ask? Well, it alternated, one day it'd be the history of the world as they knew it. Seeing history through their eyes put a very different spin on how the mortal population developed. Then there were the politics of the supernatural world, and holy shit, that was a fucking mess.

You're probably thinking I had to be wrong because that sounded awesome, and it does sound pretty neat. But once I realized they were a bunch of petty little shits in a dick-measuring contest where no one got along, I changed my mind. Seriously, it was like a bad telenovela but in real life with terrible acting and shitty plot lines. Ha, you don't believe me? Try this one on for size.

A group called the Gotteskinder was created when a woman named Chandra, a member of the Black Circle, faked a werewolf attack that killed Jacob Grimm's lover. This act inspired him to work with Chandra to form the organization and write the books we know today. Their whole goal was to kill anyone with power while being hyper-focused on the were community. Are you confused yet? Yes, Chandra was a person of power, even if she said she wasn't. Why would she do this? Well, the Black Circle wanted to weaponize the mortals against those with power who didn't toe the line, and for whatever reason, they really hate weres.

So, to sum up, the Gotteskinder, an organization created with the intent to wipe out anyone with magic, was being controlled by a group of magic users. You couldn't write a more obvious plot with so many gaping holes in it if you tried.

See? It was a fucking mess.

Then there was the magical stuff, learning to counter it, recognize inscriptions, and things like that. There were minicourses involving found tech—i.e. the stuff that fell through the void during the QDM. I was also required to memorize a list of spaceships that'd been spotted or presumed intact hidden across the globe. Slow down, it isn't like you can go spelunking and find one for yourself, since the various factions seemed to hide their toys in pocket dimensions only they can access.

You're probably wondering why I'm rambling here, and the answer is, I'm doing everything in my power to distract myself from the fact I was freezing my balls off. Oh, you think that's funny. I'd love to see you out here in this bitter cold and do better.

What was I doing out here? What do you think? I'm hunting Deheune's punk ass.

Seriously, that was the only thing that'd convince me to ever visit the hellscape the Russians called Siberia. Oh, you think you know what cold is? You've been skiing? Do you really think that compares? And you, going to Canada in the winter isn't the smartest thing in the world, but it hardly compares to being out in the frozen tundra with gale force winds, trust me, I've visited as well, and I thought I knew what cold was thanks to that. I was mistaken, and so are you.

Speaking of being mistaken, why in the hell do people live in a place where simply existing is cause for suffering? I mean, it would be one thing if it was just my face hurting, but at this rate, I was worried about my soul becoming a popsicle.

Am I really that cold or am I being dramatic? First off, fuck you very much. Second, it's just that fucking cold. If you haven't been here, you can't really speak on the subject, but trust me, this is so much worse than you can imagine. Which begs the question why did hell have flames when slowly freezing to death is far more painful?

Oh, yeah, they were desert people, so they tended to think burning up was the worst way to go. They, however, were wrong.

Anyway, back to why I was here, Deheune. Two weeks ago, she finally scurried to the surface world in the backwoods of Arkansas and started working her way across North America. None of us were quite sure how, but she jumped the Atlantic Ocean in one go. Her arrival in Portugal didn't go unnoticed, but she avoided most of the traps we'd laid out for her across Europe. Things took a turn for the worse for us when she entered the territory that used to belong to the old USSR. It was there she was able to dramatically pull ahead.

Before you ask, yes, I reached out to Jade—okay, Gisele did. I mean, she knew the woman personally, so it was better she did the talking since I was on the road. Thanks to Jade's involvement, Deheune started making mistakes and lost people along the way.

Still though, we hadn't managed to flush her into the open just yet.

Weirdly, Jade dropped off the radar a day ago. She mentioned she needed to check on something and simply vanished. As of yet, no one had heard from her. Lucifer, though he preferred to be called Luci, said she was still alive and not in any danger as far as he could tell. He did admit his connection to her was sporadic due to some unknown interference.

That was the last thing I wanted to hear when hunting down a very dangerous lich lord who wanted me dead in no uncertain terms.

For fucks sake it was cold.

Being knee deep in snow, hanging off the side of a mountain wasn't helping that situation. Okay, that *was* a little dramatic; we weren't actually hanging off the side...but we were on a steep-ass incline that could prove tricky if one of us slipped.

Glancing around, I found what I was looking for...a big-ass bolder that'd provide cover while I made a slight adjustment to my attire. I felt we were closing in on Deheune's position and being in the best winter gear money could buy wasn't going to stop a bullet. It wasn't keeping me warm either, so at this point, I wasn't sure switching over to my armor would be an actual detriment.

Pressing up against the rockface, I willed my armor in place. I expected the cold to cut through the ceramic-like plate like a knife, but it didn't. Wait...seriously? Stepping to one side then the other, I frowned. What the actual fuck? Oh, you're confused...so am I. For whatever reason, my armor stabilized my body temperature in seconds, and now I was almost comfortable. No, scratch that. I was comfortable. Then the feeling in my toes and feet returned with a vengeance.

"Ouch." I hopped from one foot to the other. "Ouch, ouch, ouch!"

Goddamn it that hurt...but it was nice to be warm again.

Gisele gave me a curious look. "Are you okay?"

"Yeah." I shook my leg. "My feet are warming up...and well, it hurts."

She suppressed a giggle. "Oh, okay."

I narrowed my eyes. "Hey, why aren't you shivering?" That was when I looked at the others. "Hey, none of you seem cold...why is that?"

Issac struck a pose. "Magic."

My jaw dropped, and I stared at them in disbelief. "Are you shitting me?"

Begrudgingly, a tug at the corners of my mouth threatened to pull my lips into a smile. I mean it *was* kind of funny—it was exactly the kind of thing Hector would do to me. So, yeah, they'd had their fun at my expense. There wasn't any permanent harm done, so I'd be laughing about this by nightfall.

Gisele smirked. "We told you before we set out your armor was a better option."

That she had. Unable to stop myself, I burst out laughing. "Yeah, but watching me suffer like that was kind of a dick move."

Issac smirked. "For the record, it's all on video, too...you know, for posterity's sake."

Flipping him the bird, I said, "Like I'm the one who should be embarrassed here." I pointed at him. "Just wait, you still owe me a month of meals and snacks. You better believe I'm going to get everything I can out of that."

He rolled his eyes. "What can I say, she's way better than me and I was wrong for doubting her skills. I mean, I knew she was good, but holy shit that's on a whole new level of amazing."

Cassandra finally got her race...if that was what it could be called because she drove circles around the man.

Gisele cleared her throat. "Do I need to remind you two why we're here?"

Now that I wasn't being threatened with hyperthermia, she kind of did. "Sorry."

Jamie gave us a disapproving glare as he strode over and sighed. "If you two idiots are finished, we've got a couple of shooters on the ridge about a kilometer ahead."

That killed the mood. Striding ahead like he hadn't said

anything, I quickly spotted the would-be assailants. With a thought, the space in front of me twisted into a chaotic, blurry mess. Stepping into it, I appeared behind the shooters. Reaching down, I grabbed the back of their jackets and jerked them up. There was a loud ripping sound that nearly covered up the half dozen dull cracks that followed.

Standing there with long strips of cloth in either hand, I frowned. Both men were lying unnaturally still on the frozen earth. It was then I realized that I'd put a little too much umph into my earlier attempt to surprise them. In my head, I saw this playing out very differently—me yanking them up, maybe slapping them around a little before immobilizing them so they could be questioned properly. Instead, I think I snapped their neck in multiple places along with several other bones for good measure.

Jamie quietly touched down beside me and frowned. "Yeah, you may've gone a bit overboard there, champ."

"Sorry."

Jose jogged up to stand next to me and winced. "Oh—damn... uh...yeah, they're not getting up from that."

I cut my gaze at the man. "We figured that out already, thanks though."

Everyone that followed pretty much had the same reaction. Their gaze would land on the broken bodies, then move over to me as they grimaced and walked away.

You know, being super strong was supposed to be cool, and it was, but seeing how I still wasn't used to my new strength, I tended to break things. The way I went through phones lately, you'd think I hated them.

Hanging my head, I followed the others as they continued up the slope. About five minutes later, I tapped Jose on the shoulder and pointed up with my chin. "What's that?"

He glanced up at the big dark spot on the ridge up ahead. "I'm not sure."

Gisele eyed the spot and smiled. "I think that's our destination." She bumped Jamie with the back of her hand. "Come on, let's get going. I don't want Deheune getting her hands on whatever is here."

We'd walked maybe a hundred meters before Gisele took a knee and wiped away some snow atop a boulder. "Huh."

Confused, Jamie looked at the stone and frowned. "What is it?"

Stepping back, she gestured at the area in front of her. "Can you feel that?"

Closing his eyes he concentrated, then practically jumped out of his skin. "How?""

She shook her head. "I don't know." Glancing back at Jose, she said, "Help us clear this section...I need to see the ground."

Was this the time? "Shouldn't we keep moving?'

Gisele waved off my words. "No, this is important, and if I'm right, it may tell us why Deheune ran to this place specifically. And if it doesn't, it should give us a big hint."

It took a solid five minutes, but between the six people in our group, they were able to melt away the snow and ice. What we found below was a fucking nightmare—scorched earth, mangled bodies, and a corruption seeping into the earth itself.

"What the hell is that?"

Clamping a hand over her chest, Gisele's gaze snapped up to the opening above. "This is where Ke'lets fell."

I blinked. "The lich lord?"

"Yes." She scrambled toward the rockface trying to find a trail leading up. "We need to hurry."

I jogged up behind her. "Slow down. I can get us there." With a flick of my wrist, the chaotic tear in reality formed. "Step through that and we're there."

She did as I asked. The moment we were in front of the dark spot, we could see it was a massive doorway leading deep into the mountain.

"Now can you tell me what's got you so freaked out?"

Jose grimaced. "Deheune is looking for something Ke'lets left behind."

I didn't get it. "Like what?"

"He was a lich lord." Jamie grumbled. "It could be most anything...but you can be sure whatever it is, we don't want her to get her hands on it."

Okay, that I got. "Point made." I gestured into the dark tunnel. "Let's get going and put an end to her machinations."

That made the entire group stop moving and turn to look at me like I was some type of moron.

Shaking his head, Jose sighed. "That." He trailed off. "That...just don't say stupid shit like that...it makes me think you believe yourself to be in one of those awful telenovelas."

Issac snorted. "Like you aren't addicted to those things."

I cut my gaze at the man. "At least he's watching something from this century."

Wincing, Issac mumbled. "That's hurtful."

Gisele sighed. "Gentlemen, as much as this entertains me, maybe focus on the job at hand?"

"Yes, ma'am." They said in unison.

To my surprise, there weren't any guards hiding in the dark, as far as I could see, which was the full length of the two-kilometer-long tunnel. We were about halfway down when I spotted an open doorway. It'd clearly been forced, and the dusty stairs showed multiple footprints leading down.

I gestured at the opening. "If we pick up the pace, we might be able to put an end to this shit sooner than any of us expected."

Gisele nodded. "Let's go. I'll try to reach out to Jade on the way." We hurried down one flight after the other. When we reached the ninth switchback, she growled her displeasure. "It would seem the woman doesn't know how to answer her phone or return one of my many messages."

Weird, but whatever, we needed to get to the bottom of this shaft and figure out what Deheune was looking for. "That can wait, Deheune can't."

"True."

Several minutes later, we exited into a roughhewn hallway that looked like something out of a bad B-movie set with its uneven surfaces. Quietly, we crept through the shadows to what remained of a set of vault doors made of a thick metal I couldn't identify.

Issac knelt and touched it. "Tyridium." He glanced back at Gisele. "What's this doing here?"

She shook her head. "Nothing good."

Slowly, we made our way into a massive chamber. There in the center was an overly large metal protrusion jutting out of the bedrock. Deheune and eleven of her cronies were examining the giant slab of Tyridium looking for something.

Shock sounded in Gisele's voice as she spoke. "A dreadnaught... here? I...I didn't think that was possible."

That must've been spoken aloud instead of over the comms link, because all of them stopped and turned.

Deheune sneered. "Who are you?"

That was my cue. "Until a couple years ago, no one special." I stepped forward. "At that point, I didn't know your name or any of this shit existed, but thanks to you, I've become a giant pain in your ass."

Hate burned across her face as she looked me up and down. "So, you're Horacio." She snorted a laugh. "Somehow, I was expecting something—more." Waving her hand up and down at me, she shook her head. "But this...whatever you are, is pathetic."

Suddenly, multiple golden spikes flew across the room to pin her people to the floor like insects in some museum collection.

Deheune spun around and looked up. "What are you doing here, brat?"

A lithe, darkhaired woman with the face of an angel and four glowing golden wings hovered in the air. Smirking, she flew a little closer as if she were preparing to strike. "I see you're still the same grumpy cunt you've always been."

While I hadn't met the woman in person, I recognized this was Jade Baker without being prompted.

The lich lord surged forward a half meter before she caught

herself. "Watch your tone!" She growled. "Being Seth's pet won't protect you here." She gestured back at the slab of metal. "Do the smart thing...join us."

"And what? Be put on a leash?" She shook her head. "No thank you."

Again, she continued to close the distance between them.

Sneering, Deheune said, "Would you rather die?"

Ignoring the question, Jade gestured at the room. "You've done a good job disabling the glyphs. It would've taken me years to get through all of them." She eyed the woman below. "Thank you for that."

Hate burned in the lich lord's eyes. "I didn't do this for you, girl." She stepped forward. "Decide now: kneel before me or die." Dark flames shone in her eyes. "I hope you choose the latter."

Golden light stretched out across the space as Jade suddenly dropped down to slam her fist against Deheune's chest. CRACK. Deheune's spine bowed as she flew back with such speed, she turned the man behind her into blood mist as she passed through him unimpeded. A second man died when he was crushed between the lich lord and the Tyridium wall. Dozens of cracks sounded as a golden light burned inside the woman. She opened her mouth in a silent scream, and gilded streams of light erupted out of her mouth, eyes, ears, and...other places.

More on instinct, a cloud of inky black shot out at Jade as Deheune fell to her knees. Jade was forced to dodge the attack. Numbly, Deheune pulled something out of her pocket and slammed it against her chest.

Jade rushed over, searching the area, hoping to find the lich lord but failing. "Goddamn it." With a casual flick of her hand Deheune's remaining henchmen died where they stood. A moment later, the golden spikes that'd pinned the others to the ground vanished, dropping their corpses to the floor. "Fuck."

I arched an eyebrow. "What's wrong."

She whirled on me then let out a long breath and pulled out a disc-like device about the size of a frisbee. "This locks down space in a five-hundred-meter area...meaning she couldn't use her ability to teleport out of here." Frowning, she sighed. "Though it looks like Atman Stones have a way of bypassing the barrier."

Gisele's helmet vanished. "Why not just kill her?"

"What the hell do you think I was doing?" Her tone softened. "Look, if taking out a lich lord was as simple as landing a single hit on them, I would've killed them all well before now."

I gestured at the spot where she'd fallen. "She didn't look so hot after you hit her."

"No, she didn't." She beamed. "That's because she's still weak after trying to kill Gavin, and I just made things a lot worse for her."

"Oh." I tapped my foot against the floor. "How long will it take her to recover...and can you track her with whatever you did?"

Jade looked out into the distance as she thumbed a button on the disc. "It'll take her a few months and several hundred followers to heal herself from the wound." Shaking her head, she turned to me. "As for tracking her...it looks like she's ducked into a pocket reality...so, no, she's in the wind until she comes up for air again."

"Damn."

"Yep." She gestured at the slab of metal. "Do you know what this is?"

"Me?" I shook my head. "Not a clue." Pointing at Gisele, I smiled. "But she seems to have one."

Gisele frowned. "It's a dreadnaught vessel." She shivered. "I didn't realize there were any on this planet."

Jade's expression turned serious. "Technically, it's not...it's how they broke the pacts without technically breaking them. All the ships are hidden in pocket dimensions. There's enough hanging out to allow access, but not enough to breach the accords."

Jose frowned. "We can't leave it here."

"No, we can't." Jade looked up at the cavern overhead. "Bea, would you be so kind as to put this in one of our storage facilities?"

A hologram of a beautiful woman with light green skin and

emerald hair appeared. "I'll tend to it promptly." She glanced over at me. "You should probably tell them why we're not destroying it, though."

Jade nodded. "I suppose I should."

Without another word, the strange woman and the ship vanished.

Gisele gave Jade a hard look. "What's going on?"

She hung her head. "It's Muzos...they've stepped up their production of ships. More than that though, they are purposely poisoning the atmosphere with a toxin that targets humanoids."

I blinked. "Why?"

"They're a cult, why do you think?" When she saw the blank look on my face she continued. "They are of the opinion that if they can't have the planet to themselves, no one can. It's why they're building ships...they intend to abandon this world." She was quiet for a moment then sighed. "I suspect we've got about five years left to us here before we're all forced out...maybe less."

That wasn't good. "Why aren't we stopping them?"

She glared at me. "We would if we could find them." Gesturing at the spot where Deheune stood, she growled. "She's been hiding them in one of her pocket dimensions. Until we get her, we can't stop them."

Rubbing my forehead, I grumbled. "Well, fuck."

Gisele patted me on the shoulder. "That about sums it up, yeah." She turned her attention to Jade. "Do the others know?"

Jade suddenly looked tired. "Not yet, but I scheduled a meeting for this afternoon with them. Do you want to attend?"

Gisele thought for a long moment before letting out a breath. "No, I can send a representative if you'd like, but honestly, I need to focus on production and upgrading the tech available to our allies."

Jade considered her words. "Alright, let me know who'll be attending in your place."

"Sure thing...I should have the information to you within the hour."

Smiling, Jade said, "Do you guys want a ride home? Or do you want to take the long way back?"

Gisele thumbed back at me. "We've got a ride, but thanks."

She smirked. "Fair enough."

A cloud of black and gold surrounded her and vanished, taking her with it.

15

I GUESS THIS WAS MY LIFE NOW

May 21st

Northern Ireland - Sperrin Area of Outstanding Natural Beauty

Staring down at the stylized Z emblazoned on the backpack laying on the ground made me think of an old country and western song I'd once heard in a movie. I think it went a little something like: You load sixteen tons, what do you get? Another day older and deeper in debt. St. Peter, don't you call me 'cause I can't go, I owe my soul to the company store.

In this case, the company store belonged to Deheune, as did the dead strewn about the campsite. Gavin happened to be with us when we stumbled upon them, and he went full Grim Reaper mode on them. A dark shadowy cloak surrounded him. Chains that looked to be made of the essence of the dead whipped out to tear the souls of the living out of their bodies, only for them to ignite a second later.

According to Gavin, this was due to the lich lords inscribing the spirits of their followers with sigils designed to keep him from interrogating the dead. Just in case you were wondering, I damn near needed a fresh pair of underwear when it happened, because the guy was absolutely terrifying. Look, I don't care what the image you have of the Grim Reaper in your head is, this guy is way scarier.

Oh, you want to know why he's here. Well, Deheune tried to kill him a little over a year ago and he took that personally. Trust me, that's a bad thing. You really don't want this guy taking up a personal grudge against you.

I shivered as my gaze passed over the mutilated corpses and spectral goo littering the ground around the smoldering fire. The memory of their souls burning in silver flames swam to the forefront of my mind, and I couldn't stop it.

Before all the murder and mayhem, I had to imagine this would've been a beautiful place to visit. Now, though, it left a lot to be desired. Seriously, I was standing in one of the most beautiful places on the planet and it'd been forever marred in my memory by a bunch of fanatics throwing their lives away and for what, to hit a convoy? That didn't make a damn bit of sense.

Turning to Jose, I grumbled. "What the hell is Deheune thinking?"

He shrugged. "I don't know."

Jade strode over shaking her head. "They're after the Deus Ex machines."

"Why?"

She shrugged. "We're not sure...though this is the twelfth shipment they've hit. Thankfully, they didn't get this one, so that's a plus."

Looking thoughtful, Gisele stepped forward. "Is that what's causing the delay in the old Eastern Bloc countries?"

"Them, Texas, and Jerusalem." She replied.

Concern etched itself across Gisele's face. "What's the goal?"

Jade scratched the back of her head. "We don't know...but we'll probably find out soon since they know we're onto them."

That wasn't good, but that wasn't why I was here. "We can speculate about this later." I gestured ahead. "Right now, we need to focus on putting Deheune down."

Reluctantly, Jade nodded her assent. "You're right."

Look, it wasn't like I didn't care about what was happening with the Deus Ex machines but that was more of an Edward and Geoffrey kind of thing. Seeing how we couldn't get them until we got her, I felt like we needed to keep our eyes on the prize. Why couldn't we get our hands on them? Well, they were still hiding in a pocket reality, but once Deheune died they'd be forced out sooner or later.

"Sorry, I know we're all a little on edge here with everything that's going on, but this lady really needs to go."

A bitter laugh escaped Jade. "You're telling me." She pointed. "I'll sweep around to the right and Gavin is headed left...so if you can keep pushing through the middle, I think we can end this today."

I winced. "Oh, now you've done it." Shaking my head, I said, "She is for sure going to slip through our fingers now that you've jinxed us."

She rolled her eyes. "I'm going now."

Gisele waved and we headed off again.

A half a kilometer out and it was all rolling hills with slightly rocky terrain covered in lush greenery. I'd always thought the Emerald Isle was a bit much, but Ireland truly lived up to the hype. It made me feel a bit sad when I thought about what the tourism board came up with for Mexico: Live it to Believe it. What the hell was that supposed to mean? Did they realize just how many ways that could be taken out of context? I'm guessing they didn't think that through properly, but then again, that's hardly the point of today's exercise...kind of like what I accused Jade of doing.

Before I could get my head back in the game, a wave of power swept over me, making me nauseous. Fortunately, or perhaps unfortunately depending on how you wanted to look at it, my abilities gave me a keen sense of my surroundings. What'd that mean? Well, I was one hundred percent certain where the epicenter of whatever vile bit of magic that'd just been cast was located.

Sadly, for the people in that particular village, I was fairly certain that didn't bode well for them. There were about ten kilometers between me and them, so I lifted my hand to create a tear in reality.

The moment I stepped through, I was hit with a sense of dread. Death and sickness hung in the air. Everywhere I looked, darkness seemed to cling to the sides of buildings and houses. But the worst part was the people who'd been outside when whatever happened occurred. They looked like extras off a zombie flick. They shuffled forward, screaming in pain as their flesh melted off their bodies. When they finally collapsed, they simply ceased to move.

Horrified, I mumbled. "What in the name of god is happening here?"

Deheune's sneering voice cut through the unnatural silence. "You can say my name, boy." She casually leaned against a nearby stone building cleaning the gore out from beneath her nails. "I'm the only god here, after all."

The ego of this woman was crazy. "You are so full of shit." Shrugging, I flicked my wrist and called forth crimson chains. "Though I have to admit, putting god-killer on my resume does sound cool." Gripping the links tightly, I chuckled. "Are you ready to die?"

Deheune shot forward. "I could ask you the same."

Her palm slammed against my breastplate. A brilliant flash of white-gold light enveloped the entire village. Though I couldn't see her, I could hear her screams. As the light snapped back into my body, I was knocked off my feet and propelled several meters back at speed. Even crashing through a stone wall did little to slow me down. It did change my trajectory, and I found the sudden stop against a basement wall carved out of the bedrock far more intense than I would've liked. Groaning, I picked myself up and stumbled up the stairs. When I staggered out the door, I spotted Deheune clutching the stump that used to be her hand.

Her gaze fell on me an instant later. Hissing in pain, she got to her feet and rushed into a jagged line of darkness that suddenly appeared in front of her. Goddamn it! I was so sick of this woman running. Closing my eyes, I focused on my surroundings. It was then I picked up a trace of power that belonged to me. Somehow that burst of light had marked her.

Smiling, I turned and looked out at the horizon. "There you are." Tapping my comms badge, I sent a message to the command group. "Zero in on my position, Deheune has been marked and I'm in pursuit."

Sadly, for me and the population of nine other villages, Deheune was fast. I was following as quickly as I could, but it wasn't enough to keep her from sucking the lives out of a few thousand people. Then something happened that'd never occurred before; she vanished. It was only for a minute, but it was all she needed.

Instantly, I jumped to somewhere close to her last-known position and found myself standing above a sheer cliff. Before I had time to figure out what was what, the earth trembled beneath my feet.

"Since when did Ireland have earthquakes?" Back home they were a semi regular occurrence, but I'd never heard of one here. Stumbling back, I landed hard on my ass. "Goddamn it."

Jade suddenly appeared and promptly staggered to the side and fell beside me. The scene repeated itself with Gavin and several others. As one might expect, only the weres remained on their feet, though it was a struggle. Then the earth shattered as a massive Tyridium spire broke through the lush green. A split second later it was gone and all that was left was a monstrous cavern.

Jade pushed herself up to her feet. "Fuck."

Gavin frowned. "She's running." He glanced up. "I'll see what I can do."

Indigo flames wrapped around him, and he vanished.

"Where's he going?"

Jade grimaced. "To chase her down...or at least try." She turned her hard gaze on me. "Can you still track her?"

I thought about it for a moment then nodded. "I can." That was when it hit me, Gavin wasn't the only one with a spaceship. "I think I'll lend Gavin a hand."

A moment later, I was aboard the Roja—the ship Lilith created from my cells—heading for the edge of our solar system in pursuit of Deheune. I was too late; she reached the Anillo Gate and was gone. I wasn't sure if it was her power or the range, but she no longer showed up on my tracking sense.

Lily appeared next to me. "She doesn't appear on our sensors."

Gavin let us know he was headed back to Earth, leaving the tracking to us.

We gave it another hour in the hopes she might show up, but that didn't happen. With no way to track her, we too headed back to Earth.

A moment later, Lily appeared on the bridge. "You need to see this."

The moment she stopped speaking, a press conference that was already underway was being broadcast from Moscow to the Network appeared.

Edward gestured behind him at a large ring that looked suspiciously similar in style to the Deus Ex machines that'd been stolen. "After what happened to one of our investors, Ms. Deheune Byrne, we felt we had to break our silence no matter what it cost us...even if they come after us next."

Was he really pretending to be the victim here? Seriously?

A smarmy looking Geoffery swaggered out onto the stage. "The reason these people are doing their damnedest to hunt us down is because they don't want you to know the truth." He gestured back at the machine as Edward had done. "Part of that truth is we were the ones who developed the technology you call the Deus Ex Project."

Edward swooped forward in what was clearly a well-rehearsed play. "After stealing proprietary technology from us, they have gone out of their way to say WE are the ones destroying the environment." His anger seemed genuine. "But they're the ones flying around in their massive spaceships.

They're the ones destroying this world's uniqueness and forcing you, the people, into a homogenous world faction."

Then right on cue, Geoffery stepped forward. "As anyone will tell you, the lands we've liberated from this supposed world faction have been allowed to keep their national identities." He held up his hands in surrender. "We only want them to be who they are and not become just another cog in the machine."

"We are not the villains here." Edward gestured at his business partner then back at himself. "We are the victims." Sadness coated his tone. "We only wanted to make a better life for the people of Earth, but they've stymied our every attempt. Why? Because they want to play the role of hero where we just wanted to help. They want you to bend the knee and serve them, while we only want you to be free."

Geoffery walked over to pat the giant machine. "To prove our machine is safe, we were the first ones to use it." He puffed out his chest. "We're proud to announce we're both Stone Borns now. We were elevated from mere mortals to the peak of existence."

Well, that was a fucking lie! They hadn't used the machine to become Stone Borns, they'd been born that way. But I had to admit it did play well with the load of shit they were selling.

Sighing, Edward shook his head. "You'll find that isn't the case with the Deus Ex machines. They've manipulated it in such a way that only those loyal to this new world government will reap the benefits."

Hate coated Geoffery's tone. "To be clear, this means only those willing to pledge their undying support to this empire they're trying to build will be allowed such an honor."

Reluctance shone on Edward's expression. "While the percentage is low, there is a chance, with our help, that you too could become one of the elites."

Trembling slightly, Geoffrey held out his hands in caution. "Be careful who you trust. They missed their opportunity to kill Deheune, but I assure you the next time they try for one of us, they'll send Cain." Disgust washed over him. "You've heard of his exploits all your life. This is the same man who brutally murdered his own brother in cold blood out of jealousy. Personally, I think he likes it—the killing, bloodshed, and mayhem."

"The man is perverse, that's for damn sure." Edward seemed to sag on the spot. "Just look at what happened to his poor stepsister, Namisia." A photo of a stunning looking dark-skinned woman appeared on screen. "She was so afraid of this man she went to extremes to protect herself, going so far as to live on a train that was constantly moving in the hopes he wouldn't find her." He let out a dramatic sigh. "But he did...then he hunted down each and every one of her children and murdered them too."

Spittle flew out of Geoffrey's mouth as he practically screamed at the camera. "He's a mass murdering freak that this new world government recognizes as one of its founders." Fury and hate burned in his eyes. "Are you sure you want to follow anyone who counts him as an ally? What happens when he turns his attention on you and yours?"

Huffing out a breath, Edward stomped forward. "It isn't like the others are any better." His index finger flicked up. "Look at Viktor Warden. The press makes him look like some sort of vigilante hero out of the comics and you can't get them to stop talking about his philanthropic endeavors—as if they exist at all." He let out a derisive snort. "If he was so great, why has he amassed such a huge army?" Leaning forward, he lowered his voice slightly. "I'll tell you why...because if you step out of line, his people will be right there to crush you under foot." Shaking his head in disgust, he said, "His own people rebelled against him not more than five years ago." He leaned toward the camera. "Care to guess how he dealt with that? That's right, he murdered their leader Leonard Marcello for daring to defy him." His tone softened slightly as a photo of Kira Warden flashed onto the screen. "He's such an evil man his own daughter ran away, trying to put as much distance between her and him as possible. She even changed her name to Heidr to hide her shame of being related to this—monster."

Geoffrey's face reddened as he clenched his fists over and over again. "Then there's Gavin Randall, their supposed head of law enforcement. He's nothing more than a hitman. Even before getting involved with the magical world, he was murdering his way through most of the Middle East because his lust for bloodletting puts the others to shame. His allies in *the government destroyed most of his files, but there's enough to piece together he murdered thousands of people." He sneered. "Then when he joined the community, he continued the practice, killing anyone who dared stand up to him. His first victims were Walter Percy and his son." His tone hardened. "You might be asking yourself what they said that set him off...well, it was because Walter dared to attend the funeral of his former wife, Martha O'Neil." A picture appeared showing a middle-aged man standing next to an attractive creole woman in a wedding dress. "You heard me right...a man stricken with grief at the loss of his former wife was enough to set the psychopath off because he didn't appreciate his presence."*

Glaring at the camera, Edward snarled. "Then there's the worst of the bunch, Jade Baker. A woman brought into this world by perverse means when Viktor Warden played mad scientist to create the abomination we know today." He harrumphed. "The moment he pointed her at the former head of the Archive, Lazarus—yes, the very same one you've read about. He was a devout man who wanted nothing more than to bring peace to the world, but Jade murdered him in cold blood. As if that weren't insulting enough, she claimed his position and abandoned the Archive and created the Witan. This new organization wasn't content with its own power but sought to gain more." He gestured around the wide-open room. "Which is why there are only a few holdouts...those of us who have stood strong."

Geoffery scoffed. "You left out the most heinous part."

"Right." Edward scowled. "She then freed the devil himself, Lucifer. After binding the demon to herself, she's nigh unstoppable."

Holy shit, talk about manipulating the facts...just, wow.

"Ugh, can we turn this off?"

Frowning, she shook her head. "We should wait." She gave me a hard look. "They haven't gotten to you yet."

I blinked. "Me?"

Gisele pointed off to the side. "Look."

There off to the side sat Barry Lawson. "Shit."

She offered me a sad smile. "Yeah, this isn't going to be pretty."

. . .

Sadness filled Geoffery's eyes. "These people are evil, make no mistake, but understand they are not the masterminds behind the tragedy that brings us here today." He shook his head then waved his hand to show my image. "No, that honor belongs to this man, Horacio Garcia. He's the one behind all your troubles. He's the one killing this planet, providing weapons to the monsters you now call leaders. Horacio Garcia is a madman who wants to dominate every second of your life, and he won't rest until he's crushed us all under his heels."

Edward nodded. "It's true; he's the most dangerous of them all."

Geoffery gave a serious nod as he moved to stand beside Edward. "He is, but that's not the worst of it." Tears ran down his face. "Due to his actions, our world is doomed. We have somewhere between six and twelve months before Earth is uninhabitable."

"The things that man did." Horror filled a grief-stricken Edward. "Well, specifics aren't important, what is, however, is that his actions have left this world on the verge of ecological collapse."

Nodding, Geoffery lay a comforting hand atop his friend's shoulder. "Which is why we are forced to enact the Ark Project." Another wave of his hand caused the hologram of my face to morph into a small fleet of space-ships. "Anyone wanting to free themselves from this insanity...who wants to live as normal of a life as possible should reach out to us at the link in the description. We'll provide transportation to the evacuation points."

Hopelessness filled Edward's eyes. "We're sorry we can't do more." He sighed. "Even as we speak, Deheune is tirelessly searching out suitable planets for us to call home."

Geoffery hung his head. "God has already seen fit to show her the way to one such world, Escarcha. Life there will be hard, but we can start over there before branching out into the stars."

What the actual hell? These two were a real piece of work. "Okay, now I've heard enough."

The hologram winked out as a defeated looking Lily stepped

forward. "They're right, you know?"

"What?"

She shook her head. "Not about you or the others...about the planet." Fear tinged her voice. "The corruption Jade warned us about is spreading rapidly through North Korea, Florida, and all the other Archive-controlled territories, leaving the locals in a weakened state...if their exposure continues to rise at this rate, every humanoid on the planet will die within the year."

"Goddamn it." I gestured at where the hologram had been. "They've done something to accelerate the process."

Lily nodded. "They have...now everyone will be forced off the planet. In time, the truth will come out, but for now...well I'm not sure how you should proceed."

That was just great. "I'll keep a low profile while trying to save as many people as possible." Holding my face in my hands, I suppressed a scream. "Let's return home and see what we can do to help."

"Very well." She eyed the space where the hologram had been. "They've been planning this big reveal for a while now."

Nodding, I leaned back in my seat. "Yeah, I got that."

Gisele grimaced. "I guess we know what they're doing with the machines they stole."

Lily's expression soured. "As much as it pains me to admit, their plan was well thought out."

It was, and sadly, it was going to cause me no end of trouble. I guess this was my life now. Yippee.

16

THIS WAS THE END OF THE WORLD

May 27th

Puebla, Mexico (Earth)

Reaching into the fridge, I pulled out a watermelon and cantaloupe slushie. I grabbed my metal straw and drank deeply. It was sweet, cold, and refreshing. Even as spectacular as it was, it did nothing to relieve the exhaustion threatening to overwhelm me. Part of it was the lack of sleep over the last six days. Most of it though was due to mental fatigue. A lot had happened since Edward and Geoffrey took to the airwaves with their fictional tale of events that never happened.

Moving out to the expansive balcony, I sat down and placed my drink on the table. "Lily."

A somber looking Lily appeared in the chair across from me. "Morning."

At least she had the common sense not to say it was good. "What'd I miss?"

"In the two hours since you collapsed in your bed?" Her tone was more accusatory than expected. "Not much."

I leveled my gaze at her. "Is this the same not much as Iraq, Iran, and Egypt abandoning their agreements with us, to join forces with the Archive?"

Annoyed, she cut her gaze at me. "We both know they weren't really onboard with the whole world government thing in the first place." She wagged her finger in my general direction. "They simply used the broadcast as an excuse to back out."

I could see that. They weren't exactly excited about joining up in the first place. Though Gavin's involvement did complicate things, since there was some truth in the accusations aimed at him. Technically, he did kill a lot of people, though most of them had it coming, from what I could tell. Egypt's problem with him boiled down to the influence of a single man, former general of the Egyptian army named Babu. As it turned out, the incident that soured their relationship revolved around a dirty bomb. The main issue there was who got the disarmed product. By all accounts, Gavin turned it over to his handlers against Babu's wishes.

As for the Iraqis, they were claiming he'd committed some sort of war crime that resulted in the deaths of hundreds of people. Turns out, the real story was very different. After being held and tortured for nearly four months, he escaped, though the aftermath did result in a lot of people dying. Though, that sort of thing should be expected when you build your fortress atop a massive stockpile of explosives. In Iran's case, they didn't have a bone to pick with him so much as they saw a way out and took it.

As for what happened in New Orleans when he first arrived, that was a lot more complicated than what they said. First off, Walter was never married to Martha. However, he was married to a woman who looked almost identical to her named Mary Matherne Percy, but that doesn't actually count. However, Gavin did wind up putting Walter and several others down after they tried to kill him and his uncle. Turned out, necromancers were a bunch of assholes, who knew?

"Yeah, okay." I stifled a yawn. "So…there isn't anything else I need to be made aware of at the moment, right?"

She gave me a flat look. "You could use some more sleep."

Rubbing my face with my hands, I grumbled. "Agreed, but is there anything else?"

"Yes." Her shoulders slumped forward, and her voice was barely above a whisper. "Everyone is scrambling to set up evacuation points around the globe." She shook her head. "Earth will become uninhabitable somewhere around the end of the year, maybe early next if we're lucky." Sniffing, she said, "Don't expect to be here in February."

Well, that sucked. "I can't believe that's still the timeline with all the countermeasures being deployed. I was hoping they would've bought us a few more months."

She sighed. "Me too."

Jade, Lucifer, Warden Global, Ōmeyōcān-Mictlān, and several others had access to advanced tech that in theory could right the world, given enough time. Sadly for all of us, that wouldn't happen anytime in the near future. We would have to leave this world behind us if we wanted to survive.

Feeling helpless sucked. "I see." I took another drink. "What about those leaders that were on the fence concerning the new world government? What's their plan? Will they stay with us or bail like the others?"

Anger flashed in Lily's eyes. "Oh, you can expect them to stay put, at least for the moment. The second they feel safe, either aboard one of our vessels or on some far-off planet that'll change."

That wasn't good. "If that's the case, why not bail now?"

A bitter laugh escaped her. "There was a reason Deheune made a play for the Dreadnaught belonging to Ke'lets."

It took me a second to figure it out, then it hit me. "They're running out of room."

"You got it." She snorted. "The engineers at Muzos don't have access to dimensional technology, meaning their ships can only hold so many."

I huffed out a laugh. "It isn't like Deheune's coming back to pick up stragglers."

Lily shook her head. "No, she's not." She shrugged. "Even so,

Sargon has access to at least two Jotun Class Battleships and Nu Gui has made her move to officially join the Archive."

Like we didn't see that coming. "She realized the others knew she was a mole?"

"Yep."

I leaned my forearms on the table. "Speaking of which, have we figured out who was feeding Deheune information?"

Her expression soured. "We did—it wasn't anyone in our direct employ. They honey-trapped one of our communications people. They spiked his work tablet with a particularly devious bit of malware."

Well shit. "I'm guessing you patched that out."

"Good guess." She leaned back in her seat. "I did a thorough cleaning of our systems and found six other such holes in our defenses."

We both knew she was purposely avoiding those contaminated by the Gaia Contagion. Shortly after the broadcast, a manifesto supposedly written by Jade and me was released onto the internet. It more or less painted the picture we were systematically trying to exterminate the infected and in truth there was no cure. The document was followed up with gruesome photos, several heavily altered videos, and the summary execution of thousands.

Within hours, some of the more extreme groups of the infected began waging war on the public. They were of the opinion that if they were going to die, so would everyone else. This had the added effect of slowing our efforts to try and eradicate the infection. Of course, the Archive welcomed those affected by the corruption with open arms, or so they said. In reality, these people were being taken into custody and put in cells to be experimented on.

Whenever such a laboratory was discovered, Muzos was quick to point the finger at the Witan, me, or one of the others…with the exception of Cain. So far, they'd kept his name out of their mouths.

Lily swallowed hard and cupped her forehead in her hand. "There was another event that occurred about an hour ago." She gestured with her hand and the image of the Muzos headquarters appeared. "And it isn't good."

A haggard, bruised, and beaten Barry Lawson limped into view. Blood ran freely from several cuts across his body, his nose was broken, and one of his eyes was practically swollen shut.

When he breathed, it sounded wet. Coughing out blood, he spat it onto the ground. "Ladies and gentlemen, I've come to you today to show you what its cost us to speak out against tyrants." *Hobbling to the side, he gestured at the corporate offices belonging to Muzos.* "Many of you will recognize this as our corporate headquarters." *He hung his head.* "Now, though, it's a tomb." *He stepped toward the doors then dragged his bad leg behind him.* "What I'm about to show you is beyond shocking." *He stopped suddenly and looked into the camera.* "If there are young children in the room with you, shield their eyes, or better yet, send them out to play, this shouldn't be seen by anyone, but especially not by the innocent."

The doors leading into the lobby had been ripped out of their frames and tossed aside. Chunks of cement were missing from several support beams and the area around him was eerily quiet. A bloody stump of an arm lay in the shattered glass just inside the door.

"What's that?" *A woman said as the camera stopped moving.*

Barry glanced over at the slender appendage and sighed. "An arm." *Leaning over, he pulled a gore covered cloth out of his pocket and wiped away the glass on the pavement before he knelt. With trembling hands, he reached for the severed appendage and picked it up. He eyed the large diamond ring on the woman's delicate finger.* "This is what's left of Rachel."

The camera shook violently as the same woman from earlier shrieked. "The receptionist?"

Tears streaked down Barry's cheeks. Sorrow and grief turned his voice hoarse. "She just got engaged, too, and now she's dead."

Sniffling, the woman behind the camera spoke as her voice cracked. "Who could've done this?"

Looking dead into the camera that was suddenly still, Barry growled.

"Cain." He gently placed the arm down as he stood and stared into the rocksteady camera lens. "Jade and the others finally turned their feral dog on us...this is our punishment for revealing who they really are." Thumbing back at himself, he said, "I barely survived the attack."

"What about Edward and Geoffrey?" The weeping woman cried.

Barry sneered. "They weren't here...he missed them...like everything he does in life, he screwed this up too." He gestured back at the building. "The only thing he's good for is creating havoc and brutally murdering innocents."

What followed was a tour of the twenty-story building as they searched for survivors. Of course, all they found was one bloody room after the other. Whoever went through the place left corpses hanging out of walls, strung up from chandeliers, or beaten into the floor. It was horrific on a scale I couldn't quite wrap my head around.

"What the actual fuck?"

Lily glared at the still image then it was replaced with the faces of the dead. Names suddenly began to appear next to them with a short bio on each. They all shared two things in common. First, they'd been infected by the Gaia Contagion, and second, they'd fled into Archive territory seeking asylum.

I blinked. "They killed them for a publicity stunt?"

"It looks that way." Her tone had a dangerous edge to it. "I've already disseminated the information to every news network, the world government, the internet, and the families of those affected."

My gaze tracked up to the shattered building that'd once been Muzos's home. "And how's that working out?"

She shrugged. "Better than expected, but you know how stupid people are...they want to believe we're the bad guys, and even in the presence of facts that say otherwise, they won't change their opinion."

Yeah, that was a problem. "Keep trying...it's all we can do."

She nodded. "I will." Her gaze landed on the building and fury burned in her eyes. "I want to make them pay."

Lily might be a lifelike AI...she was literally a mental clone of Lilith...but she had a fierce love for her children like any other mother.

I kept quiet as I considered what came next. This was the end of the world as I knew it, and there was nothing that could be done to change it, which sucked.

17

THE RIM

January 9th

1/1/0 AE

Low Orbit, Earth

I found it shocking just how badly the educational system had failed so many. Granted, going forward, the problem should be rectified, but that didn't help in the interim. Still, I had a hard time believing just how many *people* were willfully ignorant about such basic things as the world was round and not a fucking frisbee. Yet, even when they saw it for themselves while in orbit around the planet, they were convinced we were trying to fool them.

According to them, this was a massive hoax being perpetrated against them personally. As if we had nothing better to do with the end of the world at hand. Still, they were certain everything they were seeing was an illusion, or CGI, or some other such thing specifically designed to trick them into believing the big lie we'd constructed.

What did they really think was going on? Oh, you're going to love this. They genuinely believed this was all an elaborate stunt dreamed up so we could take over the surface world while they were banished to the underworld...you know, because the world is flat in their teeny tiny little minds. God, just hearing about it hurt my head. Sadly, there was more to their conspiracy. First off, we were passing them off to our Illuminati overlords who were actually lizard people whose headquarters were underneath the Denver airport. Also, they thought there was maybe five years' worth of air in the underworld, which was why lotteries would be created to see who lived and died...and it only got crazier from there.

So, yeah, their delusions were far stronger than any of us anticipated. If you'd asked me a month ago where I thought any potential uprising would come from, I would've said hidden cultists, Archive agents, or some fringe religious sect. And sure, they were a problem, but a small one. Everything else, though, came from the likes of a small battalion of Karens and straight up tinfoil wearing shits who couldn't be reasoned with. Part of me wanted to drop them back on the planet just to be rid of the idiots, but they were victims of people like Muzos, Seth, and those like them.

My heart ached at the sight of the blue-green marble below.

Lily wore a serious expression as she popped into view. "The last remaining human on the surface has just died."

"Damn it."

It took us a while to figure out exactly what Muzos had done. The self-replicating toxin released in the Archive-controlled territories targeted humanoids, but we hadn't been quite sure how, and now that we did, we knew it'd take centuries to correct. Thankfully, over nighty-eight percent of the Earth's population voluntarily evacuated the planet. Of course, there were a few holdouts, and not all of them were humans. Even though most of the ships were already making their way to the Anillo Gate, I waited. I figured it was the least I could do. The people down there may be stubborn, but most of them deserved one last bit of recognition for who they were, and I was willing to give that to them.

"Anyone else of note?"

Shaking her head, she leaned against the railing. "Anyone with power has left the planet voluntarily or are currently in the final stages of life."

A holographic globe appeared in front of us. There were thousands of small red dots. As I watched, they began to wink out.

"How much longer?"

Her tone hardened. "An hour...probably less."

I nodded. "Then we wait."

"Okay."

She gave me one last worried look before vanishing, leaving the globe where it was.

Turning, I stared down at Earth...it'd been my home, and maybe one day it would be again, but I doubted it.

In the meantime, I had a lot to learn about the new world we were stepping into. For whatever reason, the historians already settled on the verbiage for the new age, AE for After Earth. That wasn't the only thing that'd changed, though. The twenty-four-hour day was gone, replaced by a thirty-hour standard. The seven-day week was reduced to six, every month had thirty days, and the year was now fifteen months long.

They—corporate assholes—decided the change was best now that everyone was superhuman. Though, they didn't get everything they wanted. For instance, the workday was a standard eight hours, the week was now four days long, everyone got three months off a year, and finally, unlimited sick time. The way Jade put it, if someone was so sick a healer couldn't fix them, then they deserved whatever time they needed to recover.

Unfortunately for everyone, money was still a thing. Instead of paper money, it was electronic credits bio-locked to the individual. It was extremely secure with a ton of oversight. Anyone caught skimming money would quickly wish they hadn't. I was fuzzy on the specifics, but telepaths were involved, and certain conditioning was imposed.

It wasn't pretty.

Time passed, and the red dots continued to wink out. Lily had been wrong, it took nearly two hours for the final person, a sorcerer holed up in Turkey, to perish. Now that they were gone, it was time we made our exit.

Lily appeared next to me and eyed the blue marble below us. "Do you need more time?"

I shook my head. "No, I'm good." Clearing my throat, I said, "We should set a course to catch up with the others."

Turning, she gave a curt nod to Cassandra Busto, the navigator. As her fingers danced across the console, Lily gave me a worried look. "Are you alright?"

"No." Closing my eyes, I rubbed my forehead. "That was my home world, and I'm not sure I'll ever be able to return after what they did." I wasn't angry though...I think disappointed and sad covered it. Tearing my gaze away from the planet, I eyed Lily. "You said your home world was destroyed in the war. How did you cope with the loss?"

An old hurt I'd never seen in her settled across her features. When she spoke, her voice had that faraway tone of someone lost in a memory. "Those were the early days...we didn't expect things to turn quite as quickly as they did." She hung her head. "I lost my family—mother, father, siblings—everyone to that attack. Ours was the second of the worlds to fall to the Loki."

The Loki were a hive mind of various creatures that contained the power to challenge the mad god. While I'd been given the basics on both, I had so many questions. This, however, was not the time, so I kept my mouth shut.

In the blink of an eye, Earth was gone.

As we slid through space and time, she quietly watched the chaos pressing against the ship. "I was training at the Asgardian Academy at the heart of the mad god's empire at the time." Sorrow and anguish marred her features. "It took a week for the news to reach us...I wanted to rush out and make them pay for what they'd done, but it was Adam who stopped me." She sniffed. "He told me being a soldier may allow me to fight back, but being a scientist would allow me to change the course of the war."

My jaw dropped, and I couldn't stop the words from falling out of my mouth. "Adam...your ex-husband?" I tried to stop myself, I really did, but I just kept rambling. "From what you've told me about the prick, this bit of advice seems very unlikely."

Regret sounded in her tone. "I don't know what happened to him, but he wasn't always an arrogant, abusive, manipulative prick —" She cut herself off. "Actually, he was all of those things, but they weren't taken to such extremes as they would eventually become." Her tone hardened. "He hid everything but the arrogance well, but when you're a genius weapon-smith, a certain amount of ego is expected."

"You seemed to have missed the whole ego trip."

Her gaze hit the floor. "That's because of Adam as well. He was charming, sweet, amazing really. Then I began to get top marks in my class...I'd taken his words to heart and truly applied myself. My projects were garnering attention, and I was getting noticed. When the higher ups began integrating my innovations to empower the army, things at home began to get rough." She never looked up. "At first, it was bursts of anger, a random insult—at this point we'd been married a decade. The last straw seemed to come when the mad god reached out personally to sponsor a half dozen projects. That was when it turned physical...I fought back...he wound up in the hospital. Everyone knew what happened, which humiliated him even more. That was when he began sleeping with everything in sight."

"Why not leave the man?"

Lily's head snapped up and fury burned in her eyes as she stared me down. "I tried...he refused to leave me alone...he stalked me... when I failed to produce the super soldier the mad god wanted, that was when he banished me into obscurity. Then Prince Munin stepped in with a special assignment...I jumped at the chance to get away from Adam, but he used his connections to follow me to Eden." Shivering, she said, "There are things that happened during that transition that no one should have to endure. The only upside was Cain, he—" Her voice was cut off in a half sob. "He deserved better."

Well, fuck.

She stood there silently, looking out at the convoy of ships carrying mankind into the stars.

I might be a moron at times, but even I knew when a conversation was over, so I stood there beside her with my mouth shut.

After nearly an hour of staring at the ark ship, Skíðblaðnir, she slowly turned to me. "I have an idea, if you're willing to entertain it."

Part of me wanted to just agree with whatever she wanted, but I knew better. "Depends on what it is."

A sly smile crossed her lips. "We need a new homebase." She glanced out the window. "And let's face it, we're not exactly popular with the people from Earth, and believe it or not, we're not alone."

I blinked. "What's that mean?"

"There are other forces in this realm...they're more technologically advanced and not all of them will be thrilled with us encroaching on their territories or even crossing through them."

Shit, I hadn't thought about that. "Okay, I'm guessing you have a solution?"

With a flick of her hand, a map of the universe popped into view. Reaching out, she touched the very edge of the known universe. There, at the boundary between our reality and whatever lay beyond, was a single star...or at least I guessed it was a star as it seemed to fade in and out of existence. Another tap of her finger revealed a single planet with three moons orbiting this luminous oddity.

Lily pointed at the darkness barely three lightyears away from the uncharted solar system. "This is the Rim." Her finger moved to hover over the planet. "And this is Eden."

I blinked. "You mean the desert planet you told me about?"

"The very same." She shrugged. "Though it may look different in this time and timeline."

From what she told me, powerful forces surrounded that world like gnats to a flame. "Is it safe?"

Her eyes glinted in anticipation. "Maybe...but if it isn't, I have faith we can escape without loss of life."

"There's something there you want to get your hands on, isn't there?"

The corners of her lips twitched up into a dangerous smile. "Yes, and if we can solve the mysteries of that place, we may be able to change the course of events."

"And if we fail?"

Her tone came out hard and flat. "Then we're all dead anyway… so it doesn't matter."

I considered her words for a long moment before nodding. "Alright, we'll check the place out, but if it presents more danger than we—I'm comfortable with, we're leaving, deal?"

She practically bounced up and down on the spot. "Deal."

It took two days to settle our affairs with the others, then we broke off from the fleet and headed for the Rim.

18

SO, NEIGHBORS

Nineteenth day of the first month, year zero.

19/1/0 AE

Eden

Up until today, I had always thought brushing up against the edge of reality was something relegated to science fiction or the written word. Thing was, it was a very real possibility—if you were brave or dumb enough to try it. Look, I'm sure someone out there is fuming mad over how unscientific that statement is, and I'm sorry. Unlike my wife, I'm not a scientist. I'm just some guy who is way out of his depth here, so cut me some slack.

Now, you're probably wondering what lays beyond the edge of the Rim. That'd be the void. According to Lily, the void was a pocket of nothingness that didn't play well with physical reality. To be specific, any object from our reality that found its way into the void wouldn't struggle to maintain its integrity for very long. This was why those who lived in the pre-QDM world used the naturally occurring routes between one realm and the next. Some people did try to create vessels meant to traverse the abyss, but those never returned or broke down immediately after launch.

How did everyone survive being pulled through when the multiverse died? That's a damn good question and one no one has a good answer for. Some claim Janus—a god-like being of immense power—had a hand in their survival. Others say it was luck they fell between the cracks from one reality into another—there are hundreds, if not thousands, of other guesses, but that's all they are because no one actually knows how it happened. All anyone knows for sure is, being in close proximity to the void is dangerous.

If that was the case, wouldn't living on Eden propose its own dangers? Yes, yes it would.

Traveling anywhere near the edge of the rim came with the risk of encountering spatial ripples—think air turbulence but with corrosive elements, time dilation, and several other nasty little things that could tear your ship apart in an instant. Then there was the background noise that made navigating by instruments alone impossible. As for long-range communications, that was simply out of the question without setting up satellites specifically meant to combat the problem. All this was to say, being within nine lightyears from the edge of the universe for any reason was a dangerous prospect.

That aside, it was beautiful and more than a little terrifying. Looking at it made me feel like there was a primordial beast scratching at a barrier that was doomed to fail. Every so often, I swore I felt something reach out to brush up against my soul, leaving me feeling sick to my stomach. Lily said I might be experiencing void-sickness, but since the only other people she'd known to experience it were Prince Munin and Cain, she couldn't be sure.

Those weren't the only dangers, either. For whatever reason, there were occasional breaches between our reality and the void. When that happened, a wave of destruction would rush in to wipe out an entire solar system in an instant. The only reason she was willing to risk traveling to Eden was due to its long history of avoiding such catastrophes.

Other than the obvious dangers, there was one other problem I had with Eden, and that was the fact something there was actively preventing us from warping into orbit above the planet. The nearest we could get was a spot about ten days out at cruising speed.

Since I was a fan of the slow but steady approach, it took us seventeen days to get this far. Due to our relaxed pace, we were able to leave a trail of communications satellites in our wake. Two days ago, we were forced into some sort of labyrinth that narrowed our window of approach. The small passage continued to abruptly change directions several times to keep from running into artificially created spatial rifts. Even with all the twists and turns, Cassandra was able to thread the needle and place us in geosynchronous orbit above Eden.

I glanced over at Lily. "Tell me why we're here again?"

She beamed. "Above all else, Eden will keep our people safe."

Her hand flicked out to reveal a holographic map of the space around us. Someone went through a lot of trouble to place layer after layer of protections around the entire solar system. There was a single, narrow path that led us safely through. Had we deviated, we could have been locked inside a pocket reality with time either slowed to a crawl or sped up to the point the ship would've crumbled with decay. And those were the obvious traps; things only became more sinister from there.

Scratching the back of my head, I glanced between the image and Lily. "At a guess, someone doesn't want us here."

She burst out laughing. "You think?" Rubbing her hands together, she let out a maniacal laugh. "Joke's on them, because we made it without incident."

Had she lost her mind? "Yeah, I'm still not sure we should stick around." I gestured at the nearest pocket dimension where gravity fluctuated between lighter than air and the event horizon of a black hole. "What if the people who built this come back?"

"They won't." She said confidently.

Obviously, whatever she wanted on the surface was outweighing her good sense. "How do you know this?"

Lily finally tore her gaze away from the planet. "Because, if they'd ever returned in the other timelines, it wouldn't have become a barren rock." She gestured out the window. "Just look at this place, it's vibrant with life and we'd be foolish to ignore the built-in protections that'll keep our people safe."

Okay, she had a point, especially with the last bit, but I still wasn't convinced. Turning, I eyed the planet for myself.

Eden was easily twice the size of Earth. Even seeing it through the projector, it was clear the people who called this place home had cared for it in a way humans hadn't back on Earth. There was a natural beauty to the place that said it'd somehow been a partner to its previous hosts and not a resource to be plundered. Every now and again, a spot on the map would glow to life to indicate a city. Without the notification, I would've missed it, since the population centers were built in such a way they flowed into the surrounding area without disrupting it.

For me, there were two things that stood out; one was a large onyx platform. Pointing at it, I asked, "What's that?"

Lily glanced over and smiled. "That's the arrival pavilion."

Okay, that made sense. Then I pointed at the one thing that did not, a floating pyramid. "And that?"

Turning, Lily blinked. "What?"

Zooming in, I tapped the pyramid. "This…what's this?"

Concern etched itself across her face. "I—what do you see?"

Wait, had I finally cracked? No, I would've noticed if I'd lost my mind…wouldn't I? Clearing my throat, I zoomed in even more and pointed. "Are you telling me you can't see the pyramid floating near the top of the atmosphere."

Her eyes went wide, then when she spoke, it was in a hurried tone. "Can you describe it?"

Frustrated, I pushed down my irritation since I didn't know if she was messing with me or not. "It's several miles tall and wide…it has four sides…the support beams seem to be made of polished silver Tyridium, and the clear parts seem to be made of the same base material."

Shock registered on her face as she eyed the spot carefully. "I...I can't see it." She turned and waved Jose over. "Can you see anything floating there?"

He eyed the hologram for several seconds before shaking his head. "I'm afraid not."

The way she was acting told me everything I needed to know. "Let me guess, you know what it is, don't you?"

Shifting on the spot, she said, "I can't be sure, but maybe." She lost herself in thought for a long second before nodding. "Since you're the only one that can see it, you need to check it out and relay anything you see."

Really? When I saw the resolve on her face, I sighed. "What am I looking for?"

She shook her head. "No, I don't want to say anything that might taint your perception of what you're seeing."

That was less than helpful. "Alright, give me a moment." Focusing on the structure, I made a gesture to create a chaotic tear in reality. "Here goes nothing."

With those words, I stepped through.

Instantly, I appeared at the base of the pyramid. It was massive on a scale that was hard to explain. Reaching out, I touched the cool, polished metal. Yeah, this had to be Tyridium. A glance through the transparent sheets told me it was more of the same. Peering in, I spotted an otherworldly tree that seemed to stretch out into the cosmos while its roots delved deep into the endless void.

The sight left me completely speechless for several seconds. While I was trying to recover from the sheer beauty of the tree, a lightning flash struck the ground nearby. The brightness blinded me for a split second, but when I recovered, I spotted three women standing where the lightning bolt struck.

The eldest one leaned heavily on a gnarled cane, but her head was on a constant swivel as if she were searching for something. In the middle was a beautiful, darkhaired, middle-aged woman. Her gaze landed on me and did not waver. The nearest was an attractive blonde woman in her twenties who looked lost as to why she was there. Like the eldest, she whipped her head around as if trying to spot something she knew was there but couldn't.

Stepping forward, the middle-aged woman bowed. "Good day to you—uh, forgive me, I do not know how to address you." She gestured at herself. "My name is Verdandi."

The young blonde woman's whole body tensed so hard she vibrated where she stood. Slowly, she turned to look at her companion. When she spoke, her voice trembled slightly as fear and hesitation made itself known. "Who are you addressing?"

As for the eldest of the bunch, she hobbled forward to place her hand on the younger one's shoulder. "Easy, sister." She panned her gaze over the spot where I stood but she didn't seem to register my presence. "I think it's best we allow Verdandi to guide us forward."

"Forward?" The young woman half screamed. "That's my domain." She gestured out in front of her. "Yet all I see is an empty path."

Sisters? Wait a minute, there were three of them—one old, middle-aged, and the last was a youthful woman...were they the Norns? I did my best to recall their names, then it came to me. Urd, Verdandi, and Skuld, the three sisters of fate, or such was the legend.

Verdandi pointedly ignored her sisters. "Is impoliteness commonplace where you come from?"

Impoliteness? Oh, right. "My apologies." I gestured at myself. "My name is Horacio." Leaning to the side to get a better look at the others, I smiled. "Would their names be Urd and Skuld?"

"They would." Clearly unaccustomed to being addressed so casually, she frowned. "Why are you here?" She glanced from side to side before looking down. "Eden?" Her voice was suddenly hoarse. "How?"

At the mention of the planet's name, Urd and Skuld stood unmoving. Worry and fear crossed their expressions, but it was Urd who found her voice first. "Why are we back here?"

Verdandi shook her head. "I don't think we are...not really." She eyed me with suspicion. "Tell me, do the people aboard your ship know we're here?"

I wobbled my hand back and forth. "Not exactly, though I think at least a few have their suspicions after I described this place." Gesturing at the pyramid, I smiled. "Care to tell me what that's about?"

She winced. "What if I said no?"

Something told me they wanted to be left alone. Not only that, they seemed to be lost as to why they were even here. "Then I'd have to figure it out on my own, which means I'd do a lot of poking and prodding."

Verdandi grimaced. "We could stop you."

"Maybe you could." I gestured at the two behind her. "They, however, wouldn't be of much help."

Her tone hardened. "I assure you, I'm more than enough."

My danger sense was usually right on the money with most people and right here, right now, it wasn't even twinging. "Perhaps, but I don't think you want to test that theory."

A smirk crossed her lips. "Oh, and why not?"

My armor slammed into place with enough force the resulting shockwave caused Verdandi to stumble back, and her sisters were knocked to the ground. "Look, I'm not looking for trouble, but if you bring it to my doorstep, I will end you."

Even as her two sisters scrambled to pick themselves up off the ground, shock registered on Verdandi's face. "You're not one of us." She glanced between her sisters and me. "That's why they can't see you...you only exist in the now." Hope sounded in her tone. "You aren't confined by your past or your future, thus they have no sway over you." Reaching out with her hand, she seemed to strain her senses. "And while I can see you with my eyes, I cannot sense you, and my power cannot touch you."

Okay, this was getting weirder than I would've liked. "Uh...good to know? I guess?"

Verdandi snorted a laugh. "I don't know who or what you are, but I welcome the change." She shook her head. "Between the new reaper, Cain, Jade, and now you...there's a real chance the cycle will end." Her gaze tracked over me. "And from our ending, it appears a new beginning may be on the horizon."

I held out my hands to stop her. "That's a whole lot of weight to lump onto a guy in his early fifties...but for now, I'd like to be—well, not friends but at least neighbors."

She narrowed her gaze then glanced down. "You want to settle this world?"

"We do." I gestured up at the ship. "We need a safe place to setup camp, and this seems like as good of a spot as we're bound to find."

"That, and you want to dig out the secrets buried here." Verdandi accused.

Well, I didn't. "Would that be so bad?"

She hung her head. "It isn't like we could stop you."

Shrugging, I stepped toward her with my hand out. "So, how about it? Want to be neighbors?"

"Does that mean you'll leave us be?" She eyed my hand with suspicion. "And by that, I mean allow us to conduct our work in peace."

As I considered her words, I bobbed my head from side to side. "That depends. Will you interfere with my people?"

Her tone hardened. "That sounds accusatory."

Was she really going to play the victim here? "Lady, believe it or not, you and your sisters don't have a stellar reputation when it comes to interacting with others."

A small laugh escaped her. "Perhaps we should define what constitutes your people."

I shook my head. "According to what I'm told, you've set multiple wheels in motion in an attempt to end the loop you're trapped in."

Her shoulders barely twitched. "True."

"Good, we're not gonna play games." I gave her an assessing look. "You can continue your maintenance of the deals you've made but that's it...no new bargains."

Verdandi flinched. "I'm not sure that's a workable solution."

"Really?" My index finger flicked up. "You've trapped Nidhogg, Cain, and god knows how many others in your schemes, and you think you need more?" An unbidden anger welled up inside me as I advanced on her. "Have you ever thought that it's you that's the problem? You and this Janus person? Between the four of you, you've tried to manipulate every possible scenario, and what's that gotten you?"

Stumbling back, she seemed to shrink before me. "We're doing the best we can with what we have."

My tone softened. "Then maybe it's time to try something new."

Her gaze hit the ground. "Maybe you're right." She was quiet for a long moment. "I can agree to leaving you and those you bring to this world alone—unless they're currently in a binding agreement with us."

"Not good enough." I shook my head. "So long as they're here, they're off limits...if you already have an agreement, you can adjust it elsewhere."

She grimaced but nodded. "That's agreeable."

Whew. Relaxing, I offered her my hand again. "So, neighbors?"

Sounding defeated, she nodded. "Neighbors." She frowned at my outstretched hand. "Don't take this the wrong way, but I have a feeling touching you wouldn't work out well for either of us."

That was fair. "Sure, okay." I gestured up at the Roja. "I'll make sure your abode is given plenty of airspace."

Verdandi gave me a curt nod. "Will you be using the planet's true name or the one it was assigned?"

A little insight might be helpful. "Depends, what is it's true name?"

Irritation flickered through her eyes at my lack of knowledge. "Gjöll."

Wincing, I said, "That doesn't quite flow off the tongue, you know." I shrugged. "We'll stick with Eden if it's all the same to you."

Flashing me a contemptuous look, she shook her head and turned to Urd and Skuld. "Come sisters, we should go."

I guess that wasn't what she wanted to hear. Oh well.

Urd gave the other two a worried look but acquiesced to the request. A second later, they were gone. There was no blinding flash of light or slight pop…they were just gone. I gave the tree one last look before returning to the ship. It was time we made ourselves at home.

19

SMARTER THAN THEY APPEARED

Fifteenth day of the Sixth Month, Year Two.

(15/6/2 AE)

Miriam, Oxido

Archive settlements were, as expected, the absolute worst. This was mostly due to their leadership simply not giving a damn about anything that didn't affect them directly. Simply put, the nutters they'd recruited back on Earth had served their purpose and now they were disposable.

What did I mean by that? That's simple, let's take a look at Oxido as a prime example.

Depending on how you looked at it, Oxido was a resource-heavy planet. Specifically, it had a lot of metal ores just waiting to be mined. Seeing how the rest of the cosmos had moved beyond what they considered primitive metals, they weren't interested. To them, Oxido was a semi-barren rock that was more trouble than it was worth. This was a key reason the Solenopsis Empire didn't bother contesting the planet when the Archive settled it.

For whatever reason, the Archive was carving out territory directly adjacent to the insectoid people. Being a hivemind, they didn't like outsiders, so I guessed it was only a matter of time before the Archive pissed them off and sparked a war. Until then, they were the Enclave's problem. Oh, right, the Enclave was made up of everyone from Earth that didn't jump ship immediately to join the Archive.

Anyway, back to Oxido and its many problems. They'd colonized the planet roughly a year and a half ago, and half of the frontier cities had already been abandoned due to supply chain issues. Muzos, being the well-known sacks of shit they were, simply couldn't manage to make timely deliveries. Even when they did, their products were subpar at best.

Don't get it twisted, they looked great, but they didn't last. This was especially true when they weren't constantly being maintained. Then when you added in the harsh desert environment here, the cities that'd been built a year ago were already collapsing in on themselves.

Even with regular upkeep, Miriam, the capitol city, was a total mess. The buildings on the outskirts were closer to the tin shacks you might find back in the poorer countries on Earth. Don't get me started on the sanitation system, because it was practically nonexistent this far out. The people out here were filthy, there was a constant stench of sewage from the open cesspools, and they'd somehow managed to bring flies with them. As weird as it may seem, every planet had its own version of the rat. On this world, that'd be the charku. It was some sort of gray lizard creature that ran around on two legs—which was super creepy.

You're probably wondering how it got this bad so quickly, and the easy answer is the Archive didn't care. More than that, though, they tended to hand over control of planets that didn't mean much to them to the local goons. Here on Oxido, that was the Huffers.

They got their unimaginative name from their drug of choice, an inhaler filled with vespera. It came in almost any form you could think of—injectors, powder, creams, dissolvable tablets...pretty much every conceivable way to get an outside substance into the body was fair game.

Other than a synthetic blood compound, no one was sure what it was or who was making it, but a lot of people were trying to figure it out. As to what it did, was dependent on how you ingested it. For example, if you puffed on the inhalers here on Oxido, it tended to turn the grunts into hyperviolent assholes hellbent on beating someone to death in the most brutal way possible. Of course, it had side effects. It was hard on the teeth, the person's breath tended to smell like ass, and too much caused open wounds to form. There were others, but those were the obvious signs.

A charku ran across my foot, leaving a trail of blackish brown goo I didn't want to think about. Glancing around, I really took in my surroundings. Off to the side in the corner next to an over-flowing dumpster was the third corpse I'd spotted in the last hour. I had to give the Huffers credit, they took their intimidation practices to a whole new level of psycho most didn't bother with, so kudos to them.

Dozens of charkus climbed through the filth looking for—well, I had no idea since they were carrying away random bits of every-thing from cloth or food to literal trash and broken tools. That was weird, and I suddenly had the distinct impression they might be smarter than they appeared.

Waist-high bags of garbage lined either side of the street, and the corners were marked with debris piled twice that. I couldn't fathom how people lived like this. Even though I knew they'd chosen to follow the Archive, I kind of felt sorry for them.

My sympathy quickly evaporated as an old man staggered out of a nearby alley zipping up his pants. Unable to stop myself, my gaze tracked back to the corpse lying spread eagle in the filth. That was just nasty.

Disgust washed over him as he eyed me with suspicion. "I ain't seen you before." I wasn't sure what the accent was, but they were clearly not the upper crust. "Who you?" Before I had a chance to answer, he leaned in and wagged his finger at me and screamed. "Outsider!" Adjusting his crotch one more time, he hobbled forward. "Haven't you people dun a'nuff?"

I glanced over my shoulder then back at him. "You people?"

Sneering, he lurched forward. "Yer one of dem guv-mint folks." Mania tinged his voice. "Ain't you satisfied with the blockade?" Breathing hard, his cheeks burned crimson. "You up there steeling our supplies and now you down here to rub our noses innit."

Did these people actually believe the Enclave was preventing the Archive from sending supplies? "Tha—"

"Shut yer mouth boy, no one wants to hear it." Panting, he continued to rant. "How dare you show yer face down here after you hounded the Archive like you did. Ain't you the least bit ashamed of yerself?" Sadness wrapped itself around his tone. "'Specially since they were kind enough to take us in after what you did." Whipping his gaze up to mine, he snarled. "How can you look at yerself in the mirror after stranding us on this godforsaken planet?" He ripped his shirt open to show his pallid, chicken chest. "If you're gonna kill us, be a man about it and do it where we can see ya."

By this point, several people had stepped out of nearby businesses, alleys, or stopped their skimmers to watch.

I didn't have time for this bullshit. "Contrary to what you believe, I'm a special investigator attached to the Twelve." Raising my voice, I panned my gaze around to the others. "And I'm here looking for one of the Enclave's spies."

Recoiling back as if I'd slapped him, the old man tugged his shirt closed. "Truly?"

"Yes." Lying wasn't great, but it sure as hell beat having to murder a street full of people. With a flick of my hand a hologram of Kira Warden appeared. "Have you seen this woman? She's trying to pass herself off as Heidr to gain access to vital information about the Oxido's defenses to sell you out to the Solenopsis."

His eyes narrowed in suspicion. "How do I know yer not da spy?"

I pulled back the sleeve of my cloak to reveal a very realistic looking twelve-headed dragon. "Because of this."

Dropping to his knees, he bowed his head. "I didn't mean to question yer authority, sire."

One of the women saw his reaction and stepped closer. Upon

spotting the emblem, she too fell to her knees. "She was here three days ago, but she's gone now...one of the local brokers got her a spot on a transport carrier headed for the Andromeda system."

Goddamn it! She'd slipped through my fingers again. "Do you know which one?"

She tapped out something on a screen I couldn't see then sent me the information. "Thank you." I bowed slightly. "The Twelve will hear of your service."

The woman bowed so low her head touched the filthy pavement. "Thank you, my lord."

Turning, I headed back the way I came. The moment I was out of sight, I teleported to the bridge. The moment I saw Cassandra, I flicked her the information. "Prepare to set a course. Copy the information and send it as a priority message to Viktor with my signature."

She nodded. "I'll handle it."

I strode to the door when multiple alarms sounded. Whirling around, I asked, "What's going on?"

Christopher strode over to the communications console and tapped out a series of commands. He listened to something closely before tapping his fingers against the console again. "It's a series of distress calls from Escarcha flooding the Network." His eyes went wide. "They're under attack by unknown hostiles."

Huh, on the one hand it was the Archive, so they kind of deserved to die. On the other, however, it was a rescue mission that'd likely save lives and maybe give us a clue what they were looking for. "Let's hear what they have to say."

A hologram of a man in uniform, marking him as one of the soldiers of the Twelve, huddled beneath a doorway. Thunderous explosions shook the room he was in, showering him in ice, dirt, and debris. There were several cuts on his face, but the bitter cold acted as a bandage, freezing the blood in place. Exhaustion, fear, and resolution wrote itself across his face. This was a man who knew he was about to die.

. . .

"We're under attack—" A burst of static cut the feed and took his words with it. *"Anyone in the vicinity—"* The roar of an explosion drowned out the voice and knocked him onto his side as something heavy fell from the ceiling, severing a leg. Coughing up blood, he wheezed. *"We need to evacuate."* Defeat sounded in his voice. *"Our ships are gone—"*

The following rumble cut the feed entirely. His wasn't the only one, there were hundreds of others, most faring only slightly better than he had, since they were still amongst the living.

A part of me was thrilled to see Edward and Geoffrey's pet project go down in flames, but it was only a small part. A lot of people had been duped by the act, and from what we'd heard, been forced to sign indenture contracts, which was a glorified form of slave labor.

Suddenly, a narrow-beam transmission came through. The image changed to show the space around the planet, and it was surrounded by tens of thousands of eldritch satellites. Even with the more powerful scan performed by the desperate survivors, there was nothing indicating the satellites' origins, specs, or power sources. It was as if they operated somewhere outside of space and time.

One thing was clear though, their weaponry was more powerful than anything I'd ever encountered. They'd wiped out an entire fleet of ships, some of which were Jotun Class Battleships and Dreadnaughts. Perhaps the most terrifying bit of information included was the fact they'd been destroyed so quickly they didn't have time to escape.

To put that in perspective, it takes less than five seconds for most ships to go from having their engines turned off to faster than light speed. Unless you want everyone aboard to die of asphyxiation you kept the power on…which meant they should've been able to press a single button to get clear of this ambush. The fact none of them made it clear concerned me.

Running my hands over my face, I grumbled. "Shit." This was the first time I was sad I wasn't the monster the Archive and Muzos made me out to be. "Sound general quarters, bring up the shields, and set a course." I swallowed hard. "We're going."

Gisele nodded. "Yes, sir."

Her neutral tone left me wondering which side of the fence she was on. She, more than anyone, had been pissed at the Archive's attempt to smear my, and by extension Ōmeyōcān-Mictlān's, reputation. Then again, she wasn't a monster either, so maybe she understood where I was coming from.

Space distorted in front of the ship, then the Roja moved forward. In the next moment, we were surrounded by broken ships being fired upon by strange satellites whose mere existence created a field of existential dread.

Jose's hoarse voice sounded next to me. "What sort of eldritch god dreamt these things into existence?"

"I don't know." I eyed the newly populated map to see the satellites were targeting the settlements now. "We need to hurry or there won't be anyone left to save."

Cassandra's fingers danced across her console as we shot forward, falling into a chaotic orbit above the planet. "Teleports are currently under way."

Nodding, I turned to Gisele. "While they work that out, begin cloning the local datacenters, all handheld devices, basically anything you can hack into."

Even as her fingers began punching out commands, she frowned. "You know we won't be able to get a clean copy of everything."

Lily appeared next to her. "Maybe not everything, but we will get enough." She glanced over at me. "I'll review and clean up all incoming data."

That was one thing off my plate.

Jose gave me a stern look. "Fighters?"

Sighing, I glanced out at the newly created graveyard of ships. "No, tell everyone to stay put."

His tone hardened. "That'll mitigate the number we could save."

"I don't care." For whatever reason, these people chose to be here. I wasn't about to risk my people any more than I already had. "Everyone stays put." I gestured at the floor. "Make sure there are enough people to keep the refugees calm and scan them for anything dangerous."

"And if we find something?"

My tone hardened. "Ask nicely first, and if that doesn't work, then do what's necessary to protect this ship and our people." I balled my hand into a fist. "They're guests, and they will act like it, or they'll find themselves back where we found them."

He nodded. "I'll handle it personally."

Pivoting, he strode off the bridge.

It was weird; I wasn't hearing any reverberations from enemy fire. Scanning the area, I spotted hundreds of ships jumping into the area. The civilian craft were forced out almost as fast as they arrived. Those belonging to Warden Global, the Vigiles, and the Witan itself shrugged off the few attacks thrown their way to make their way to the planet.

Frowning, I turned to Lily. "Have we taken any fire whatsoever from the satellites?"

She blinked. "What—" Her expression faltered then she shook her head. "No, we haven't."

What the hell was up with that? "Okay, focus on what you're doing, I'll see about coordinating with the others."

You might be wondering why such a coordinated effort was so important, well there was the obvious, the planet was under attack, as were most of the rescue vessels. What wasn't well known was Escarcha's size—it was a little over three times larger than the Earth's sun. Depending on your understanding of our home solar system, that may or may not mean much to you, so let me explain. The sun is so large you could fit the entire planet into it, roughly one million three hundred thousand times. Now, take that number and multiply it by three point four, and what do you get? That's right, you could stuff Earth into Escarcha roughly four million four hundred thousand and twenty times.

An hour into the rescue mission, the only ships still in orbit were the newly outfitted cruisers from the Witan and Warden Global. The Vigiles ships probably could've stayed around longer, but given their size, they maxed out their capacity within the first twenty minutes.

"How many more?"

Cassandra eyed her screen and shook her head. "Maybe a few thousand, but we should have them in the next ten minutes."

Thank fuck. "The moment we've collected the last of them, get us out of here."

Without looking back, she gave me a thumbs up.

Gisele stepped away from her console. "We need to talk."

I gestured around the room. "Okay."

Clearly unhappy, her gaze flickered over to the conference room. "Perhaps a little discretion is in order."

Damn it. "Alright." I gestured for her to lead the way. "Let's get this over with."

Once inside the conference room, she gestured for me to take a seat as she brought up an image. "We're not finished sifting through all the data, but there are a few things that stand out."

Leaning forward, I looked at the holographic image of a handsome man in his early thirties with dark brown hair and striking green eyes. He was average height and had the build of a man who visited the gym more often than most, even if he focused on cardio.

"Who is that?"

Her jaw tightened. "His name is James Matherne. He's one of the leaders of the Twelve and sits on the council that answers to Sargon, Nu Gui, and Deheune. According to my sources, he has close personal ties with Deheune, often undertaking tasks for her." She pointed out the window at Escarcha. "Like coming here."

That was weird as hell; from what I was told, they normally only left their sanctuary on matters of the greatest importance. "What the hell would one of the Twelve be doing here?"

"That's what we were wondering. Then we found this." A second image appeared of a large, jagged crystal as big as my thigh. Its surface seemed to be inscribed with some sort of organic circuitry. One end was unnaturally flat and covered in the same indecipherable gold script. "It looks broken."

She nodded. "That's our assessment as well." Her voice trailed off as she read something off the screen on her wrist. "From what we can tell, he brought this artifact with him a week ago when he assumed control of the expedition."

I blinked. "So, they were looking for something."

Gisele's grim expression told me I'd hit the nail on the head. "We're not sure what, but they seem to think this was once a Cintamani settlement."

I held out my hands to stop her. "Slow down, who the hell are they?"

She shook her head. "We're not sure...but if I had to guess, they're somehow related to Janus."

Oh, hell no. "You mean the god-like being who has the power to reset the universe at will?"

"That'd be the one." She reached out and tapped the broken crystal. "They seem to think even in its broken state, this will give them access to the technology left behind."

My gut tied itself into knots. "We need to find James or simply take the item for ourselves. Even if we destroy it, that'd be better than letting Deheune get her hands on tech that advanced."

Her expression fell. "The moment things went wrong, James pulled the crystal and used his Atman Stone...he's gone, as is the artifact."

"Fuck me." I sighed. "Let the others know."

Before either of us could move, Escarcha vanished, only to be replaced by an entirely new set of stars.

"I did tell her to get us out of there fast."

A wry grin crossed her lips. "Yes, you did." She gestured at the images. "What are we going to do?"

I thought about it for a long moment before speaking. "How far away is the nearest Archive settlement?"

She tapped something into an unseen keypad. "Muda is a week away."

Nodding, I frowned. "In the meantime, interview the survivors, clone any devices we haven't and try to dig out as much information as possible concerning their real mission there." I drummed my fingers against the table. "I want to know what they've been doing for the last two years and what happened to cause the attack."

"You think it was some sort of self-defense measure?"

Who could say? "Maybe, but the only way we'll know is if we investigate it."

She rubbed her temples. "You know they're going to stonewall us, right?"

"I do." I gave her my best reassuring smile. "But I have faith in you."

Gisele glared at me. "Thanks for resting this bag of shit at my feet."

Chuckling, I said, "You're welcome."

The following six and a half days were painful for everyone involved. The Archive refugees blamed us for their troubles, saying we somehow planned the ambush that killed eighty percent of their citizens. We had to take on extra passengers when one of the Witan's ships stopped to make emergency repairs. Of course, this caused an uproar because of overcrowding. They couldn't be happy they survived the incident, but instead went out of their way to make everyone as miserable as possible.

Everyone involved was only too happy to be rid of the ingrates. The only positive to come out of the trek was the context provided. Things only started to go wrong once James arrived. The moment he landed, there were power issues, and random accidents cascaded across the surface. There were even a few fires. But everything went to shit the moment he unboxed the crystal near a datacenter they were trying to breach.

The moment the case was opened, reports began flowing in about their fleet being wiped out. Then the satellites began to bombard the surface. It was in this small window James was able to activate his Atman Stone. The teleporters went first, then the entire planet was locked down, preventing anyone else from following James's example. All in all, eight million people died. Out of the two million survivors, there were only a handful of officers amongst them; the rest were indentured servants.

Now that they were all gone, Gisele, Jose, Lily, and several others sat around the conference table. "I don't like the fact James got away with the artifact."

Gisele sat across the table from me. "Neither do I."

Jose shook his head. "They clearly knew about this place before leaving Earth."

"True."

Issac nodded. "Anyone else think it's suspicious Deheune just so happened to have an artifact that set off the defenses?"

I chuckled. "That wasn't her intention." Holding out a hand, I stopped his retort. "She had a device that activated the hub. I think the internal defenses weren't something she accounted for."

He thought about it for a moment before leaning back in his chair. "So, you think she wanted access to the technology but didn't know it'd wipe everyone out in the process."

Smiling, I pointed at the man. "Exactly. There's no way she'd sacrifice what was obviously an ace just to watch everyone die. She's a cruel bitch, but she's also greedy…she wanted something from there, and she didn't get it."

Gisele rested her forearms on the table. "You think she'll try again."

"I do."

"How do we stop her?" Frowning, she gestured at the image of the freaky satellites. "If that sort of power falls into her hands, she'll steamroll the entire realm in a matter of years."

That was a good point. "I don't know." I shook my head. "I say we pass on our suspicions to Jade and the council and let them do their job."

Jose held his hands up as if to say, I want no part of this. "That's good with me."

"Me too." Issac quickly added.

Gisele didn't look happy but nodded. "That's probably for the best."

"Yep." I shrugged. "And while they do their job, we'll keep trying to track her down."

Defeat sounded in her voice. "Do you really think that's possible?"

I chuckled. "Oh, yes." Pointing at the data screen, I grinned. "And we have a place to start...she personally handed over that artifact to James on Apesto. Meaning, we know where she was as of a week ago."

Her eyes went wide. "We should hurry."

I laughed. "We're already on the way." Tapping the star map, I said, "On our way back, I need to stop here."

She narrowed her eyes. "Why?"

"Vetalas."

Jose leaned forward. "You found him?"

"I think so." Cain was looking for the man, and I picked up his trail about a month ago. "With luck, we can check two of our bounties off this month."

Issac beamed. "That'd be nice."

To say things didn't work out as planned was an understatement. Deheune gave me, and by extension Jade, the slip. Cain, however, was far more disappointed than anyone else. Yes, the world I found was filled with Vetalas's children and yes, he had been there, but he'd left well over a year ago. Eventually, though, I knew they'd be found. When that would happen was anyone's guess. Now that we were no longer contained to a single world, they literally had an entire cosmos to hide in.

20

YOU'RE AN IDIOT

2/3/264 AE (Present Day)
  Cosmos Redshift 7

After two hundred and sixty-two years of searching, you'd think I would've had better luck by now, but that wasn't the case. Sure, I'd caught a few small fish along the way, but Deheune was a tricky old bat, and it was a big universe. The fact she could jump from one side to the next, then kick her ship's engines into overdrive to create faster than light speeds, made tracking her down a real problem.

Yeah, I was making excuses for myself, and no matter how valid they were, I didn't exactly feel good about it. My own displeasure about my failings was why I'd risked a jaunt out to the Rim to check the local Anillo Gate. Yes, it was dangerous. Even more so when you realized there'd been a breach that'd wiped the area clean. What little remained felt dead, as if the void had drained the life out of space itself. Thanks to the absence of creation, or perhaps spark of life, there was an unnatural chill that crept through the hull and into my bones.

I would've thought such a wide swath of destruction would've taken out the local gate, but it remained as if the destruction all around it had no bearing on its existence. Thankfully, that meant it was fully functional, which allowed me to pull the logs. It was my hope they'd tell me where Deheune scampered off to.

I'd gotten close a few times in the last decade, but she vanished about five years ago. Since then, no one had heard from the woman. That in and of itself was odd, and her continued absence bothered me on a fundamental level, since the next time she popped up, I was almost certain she'd take another swipe at me.

...Titan Class Container Vessel: Arrival Date 1/15/263 AE: Origin: Mice Galaxies: Departure 1/15/263 Destination: Condor Galaxy.

...Titan Class Container Vessel: Arrival Date 3/14/263 AE: Origin: Condor Galaxy: Departure Date 3/14/263: Destination Mice Galaxies.

...Titan Class Container Vessel: Arrival Date 1/15/262 AE: Origin: Mice Galaxies: Departure 1/15/262 Destination: Condor Galaxy.

...Titan Class Container Vessel: Arrival Date 3/14/262 AE: Origin: Condor Galaxy: Departure Date 3/14/262: Destination Mice Galaxies.

...Titan Class Container Vessel: Arrival Date 1/15/261 AE: Origin: Mice Galaxies: Departure 1/15/261 Destination: Condor Galaxy.

...Titan Class Container Vessel: Arrival 3/14/261 AE: Origin: Condor Galaxy: Departure Date 3/14/261: Destination Mice Galaxies.

Yeah, that wasn't suspicious at all. I mean what container ship captain in his right mind wouldn't take a super dangerous route that just so happened to bypass all those pesky checkpoints? At a guess, everything the mass cargo ship was carrying was completely legal and properly vetted with all the appropriate taxes paid on the goods in question. More importantly, I was sure the added detour that took them weeks out of their way was completely justified by the view.

Still, smugglers weren't my concern. I'd shoot Gavin a message about this after I found what I was looking for. I continued to scroll down and down...and down. Finally, however, I struck gold.

· · ·

...Jotun Class Battleship: Arrival 29/14/258 AE: Origin: GRB 090423: Jump Point Destination: Hamal.

"Ha, ha, ha, gotcha." My excitement quickly waned once I had a moment to think about the destination. When it finally sank in, I slumped in my seat. "Well, shit."

What's the big deal about the Hamal gate? Simple, it's the gate nearest Escarcha. Yep, that was where those strange eldritch satellites wiped out the Archive's fleet in seconds. Sadly, there's a lot more to it. You see, after we vacated the system, it went dormant, so the Archive risked sending a few ships. Their arrival was nothing special, but the moment they pushed beyond the one-thousand-kilometer mark from the gate, they were promptly destroyed. Ships from the Enclave faired somewhat better, only being fired upon once they broke the two-thousand mark. Once everyone realized trying to return to the planet was a suicide mission, people stopped trying.

Okay, the smart ones did. Every so often, the Archive or Muzos would send out a ship, only for it to be turned to scrap the moment it crossed the demarcation line. Though, now that I thought about it, they hadn't tried in the last decade or two, so maybe they were getting the hint.

Now, the question was, had Deheune given it a shot? Was that why she'd gotten so many pricy modifications to her ship over the last century? What sort of modifications? We weren't quite sure. I mean, it wasn't like she could go to a legitimate shipwright for the work, so she sought out the kind of places that catered to smugglers, pirates, and the like. As you might imagine, getting info from people like that would've been tough. But seeing how she didn't leave any eyewitnesses, our info came from fractured data cores salvaged from the smoldering remains of the shipyard. Apparently, she was a firm believer in the best way to keep a secret was if she was the only one who knew about it. That was a roundabout way of saying she killed everyone involved that wasn't part of her crew.

Back in the day, I'd always been told that dead men tell no tales. It was only later I found out that wasn't quite true. Meaning, if people had the right powerset, they could call up the spirits of the fallen and have a quaint little chat. Which was why Deheune made sure that didn't happen. I wasn't sure how she did it, and I didn't want to figure it out; all I knew for sure was it was a nasty bit of business.

Anyway, back to Deheune and her now heavily-modified Jotun Class Battleship. From what little we could piece together, she was focusing on defensive measures, though we had no idea how, but the why was becoming apparent.

Lily suddenly appeared in the chair across from mine. "You found her?"

Gesturing at the symbols hovering in front of me, I shrugged. "Like you don't already know."

She cocked her head to the side and looked at me like I was the stupidest person she'd ever met. "No, I don't."

I thrust both hands out at the text between us. "It's literally right there."

Her eyes narrowed into an accusing glare. "Are you genuinely this dense?"

Glancing between her and the text, I held my hands out in a 'I don't understand what you're talking about' gesture. "What the hell?" I held my hands out like I was a presenter on one of those old game shows. "Are you not seeing the same thing I am? It's literally a log of the comings and goings of all the ships in this area—speaking of which, we should tell Gavin there's a smuggler using this gate to move product from the Mice Galaxy to the Condor Galaxy."

She slapped her hand across her forehead and let out a groan of dissatisfaction. "God, it's a good thing you're handsome, because you aren't the brightest."

My gaze tracked up to the log before moving over to land on her. "Says the woman who is ignoring what's sitting right in front of her."

Her mouth opened then slammed shut then opened again. "I

want you to listen carefully." She threw up her hand in annoyance at the hovering text. "I. Can't. Read. That." A simple gesture created a second hologram showing the exact same text as the one between us. "That's all I see."

I blinked, then slowly moved my head between the two images. "Yeah, it says the exact same thing."

Her expression blanked as she eyed the second image. "Wait, you can read that?"

"You can't?"

With trembling hands, she pointed from one to the other. "You can see text in both images?"

I failed to keep the 'duh' out of my voice. "Yeah."

Lily covered her mouth. "All I see is a static jumble...there's no rhyme or reason to the chaos there."

Was she fucking with me? "You're kidding, right?"

She gave me an odd look. "Haven't you ever wondered why none of us have ever volunteered to help sift through the logs?"

"Uh...no." I shrugged. "I figured you were all too busy with other work to deal with this type of drudgery."

Her fingers rested over her lips as she gave me a long, hard look. "Too busy?"

The way she looked at me made me slightly self-conscious. "Yes?"

Frustration clearly wrote itself across her face. Hanging her head, she rubbed her temples. "I'm a goddamn computer-generated image powered by the most advanced processors ever known to exist." She glared at me. "Do you know what that means?"

This was one of those times in life no matter what I said it'd be a wrong answer. "Uh-no?"

Her long fingers continued to massage her temples as a long breath escaped her lips. "It means I don't have actual nerve endings...I don't even have a real body." She mumbled several words in a language I didn't know, but they sounded very derogatory to my person. "Yet somehow, you have managed to give me a headache." Stamping her foot on the floor, she growled. "How in the hell is that even possible?"

Yeah, I'd missed something very important, and at this point, I wasn't sure asking would be in my favor. That left me with one option, attempting to comfort her. "I don't know, but I'm sorry for causing you pain."

"You don't even know what you've done." Irritation was clearly driving her current state, but she tried to suppress it. Pointing at the text between us, she grumbled. "Okay, so let me be clear, no one..." She cut herself off then pointed at me. "Okay, no one but you, can make heads or tails out of the data streams you're able to tap into." Defeat sounded in her tone. "And you genuinely believed we were just too busy to help when the fact of the matter is we couldn't. But let me address the elephant in the room."

I didn't want to know. "Maybe we shouldn't."

"Oh, we should." She slowly stood then moved over to look down at me. "Not to put too fine of a point on it, you're an idiot. No one here is too busy to help you..." Wagging an accusing finger at me, she continued to lecture. "Since Lilith stepped away, you've carried us forward at every stage. Do you really think we don't see you're the first one in and the last one out in every situation? You bust your ass, and we do what we can to support you...so, no, we're never *too busy* to help you."

Lily was gracious enough to leave the 'you fucking moron' off that sentence, but her tone ensured it wasn't necessary.

Shrinking under her glare, I couldn't help but cringe at my obvious shortcomings. "Ah...okay...thank you...and I'm sorry for what I said."

She shook her head. "It isn't important." Gesturing at the text, she asked, "So where are we headed?"

Wincing, I mumbled. "I kind of don't want to say now."

She pursed her lips. "Don't be a child."

"Fine." I hung my head. "The Hamal Anillo Gate."

The words hit her like a ton of bricks. "Escarcha?"

"That's what it looks like, yes." Nervously, I scratched the back of my head. "Give the ship a onceover; we head out in an hour."

Giving me a curt nod, she stepped back. "I'll get it done."

"Thanks." I glanced over at the mysterious log only I could read. "Maybe I can finally put the woman behind me." Mumbling more to myself than her, I said, "I could use a win."

Arching an eyebrow, she smirked. "What's that supposed to mean?"

"It means, I'm tired of chasing her...I really want to take her off the board so I can focus on the others."

Lily burst out laughing. "God, to be young and stupid again." She shook her head. "The sooner you figure out life is a marathon and not a sprint, the happier you'll be."

Maybe she was right. "I suppose, but right now, this chase feels like a weird obsession that needs to end. I'd like to turn my focus onto some of the others is all."

She nodded. "I can see that." Her tone softened. "You know you've done a lot of good over the years...you've helped a lot of people by taking some of the worst ones off the board."

Reluctantly, I shook my head. "They were small fish, though finding them did feel good."

Lily gave me a sad smile. "I intended to broach this subject at a later date, but since it's come up, we should talk."

Whenever anyone says, 'we should talk', it never ends well.

I gestured for her to continue. "Let's hear it."

She stood there quietly for a long moment before sitting in the chair across from me. "It's about the people you've been hired to find...all of them."

"What about them?"

Smiling, she nodded. "Maybe you should change your tactic going forward."

Where was she going with this? "I'm going to need more than that."

"I'm getting there." Lily waved away my words with her hand. "It's my opinion you should focus on what you're good at...the finding part. Back when you did this sort of thing on Earth, you would locate said item or person…but when it came to apprehending criminals, you turned that sort of thing over to others better suited for it."

That was true. "Okay, but—"

She cut in. "But nothing…you should continue the practice now. Find the person, if you want to be thorough, confirm their location, but let Jade handle the lich lords and let Cain handle the vampires. We both know they have special abilities that'll allow them to actually kill them in a way that sticks."

I'd found that out the hard way with one of the vampire kings—Milos Cicar. He was a nasty piece of work whose origins were shrouded in mystery—from what I heard, he was born after Adam knocked up a Domavoi. Anyway, the point is we fought, I thought I killed him, but he got better and ran away.

My pride wanted to bring them in myself, but having them escape on me sucked. Defeated, I hung my head. "Fine…I can do that."

Smiling, Lily got to her feet. "Thank you." She glanced around the ship. "Give me the full hour, and I'll make sure we're properly outfitted for whatever we find in the Hamal System."

"Alright, I'll meet you on the bridge."

With that, she vanished.

21

ADMINISTRATOR'S REQUEST
GRANTED

Hamal – Anillo Gate

As an FYI, Anillo Gates weren't mandatory for interstellar travel. There were FTL drives which were more or less the standard on even basic models. Then there were the more powerful ships that came with wormhole generators, allowing them to cover vast distances nearly instantaneously. Lastly, there were a few ships, such as Skíðblaðnir, Atet, Valaskjalf, and whatever that monolith of a ship Jade used was called, that worked on an entirely different paradigm. How they worked was complicated, but the fact they could jump across the entire cosmos wasn't.

I purposely left the Roja off the list, due to how few people realized what it could do and its future potential. One of those well-kept secrets was how it traversed the cosmos. While it was capable of FTL speeds, all jumps were made via the ships own version of my power. Meaning it just worked. There was no folding space or wormholes or any other nonsense...we just moved from one location to the other without much of a fuss.

As to why this was important to know, well, that's simple, power requirements to create wormholes were immense, and as such, they could drain the core of power. If they pushed too hard, they'd be left stranded in space somewhere until they could restart the engines. That wasn't something the Roja had to deal with.

What's the point? Well, Jotun class ships had the ability to create their own wormholes, but for whatever reason, Deheune hadn't bothered to use that feature in decades. She'd been using the Anillo Gates almost exclusively for the last fifty years, and I was starting to guess why. All that power was likely being shunted into the shields.

Leaning back in the seat, I closed my eyes, allowing my personal information network, Qucoatl, to connect to the gate. Streams of data began to pour in. It hadn't been used in a few years. The last ship to enter and leave almost immediately was a Vigil ship performing a curtesy check. There were two others before I found what I was looking for.

...Jotun Class Battleship: Arrival 29/14/258 AE: Origin: Cosmos Redshift 7: Jump Point Destination: N/A...

...Please Standby...

Requirements Met—You have been granted Administrative Rights.

Alert: You have searched for the: Jotun Class Battleship—Identification Number: IJN-98X-411-38K-6T1, 1810 times across the Anillo Gate Collective. Due to the special interest shown in this vessel, a log of its final use of the Collective has been made available to you.

Query: Would you like to view the log?

Yes/No

What the hell did it mean by final use? And why was I assigned administrative rights? Shit, that didn't matter right now. I tapped the affirmative and paused the image as I tried to figure out how to convert it into something the others could see.

. . .

...Please Standby...

...Administrator's Request Granted...

I gestured at the viewscreen at the front of the bridge. "Heads up."

Everyone gave me a curious look but turned to the viewscreen without argument.

Gisele sidled up next to me and gave me a hard look. Leaning in, she lowered her voice to a near whisper. "I thought Lily explained this to you." She gestured up at the text in front of me. "We can't see what you see."

"She did." I beamed. "But I think some of that is about to change." Pointing at the screen, I smiled. "Now, pay attention."

Reluctantly, she sighed and turned to look at the viewscreen.

An image of the Anillo Gate flickered into view. Once it stabilized, the center ring began to spin, creating what most referred to as a void ball. No one was sure exactly what it was, but it was so dark it looked like a hole in space, and anything that touched it ceased to exist. After it finished spooling up, a purplish black beam tore a hole in space. Three long seconds passed before the bow of a massive ship pushed its way through. The framework clearly belonged to a Jotun Class Battleship, but this was a very different beast.

Normally, such ships were clean, sleek, killing machines sporting enough armor to shrug off nukes with ease and with enough firepower to lay waste to an entire planet. That wasn't the case here. They'd reinforced the hull, stripped away the weaponry, and covered the ship in what looked to be festering boils filled with a sickly chartreuse, puss-like substance.

It took me a few seconds to place the odd-looking organic additions. While I hadn't encountered the Solenopsis myself, I was semi-familiar with their ships, given their aggressive nature. Leaning in, I confirmed the addition to the hull was an organic exoskeleton made of a chitin favored by the insect species. It was tough, and the puss was actually a fast-acting patch that instantly, or very nearly so, repaired any damage the vessel suffered. As a whole, fighting these guys was not recommended due to the sheer amount of firepower needed to scuttle even the smallest of their vessels.

They were barely through the gate when their shields snapped in place. These weren't your standard fare, being so powerful they caused the ship below to become hazy.

Gisele's hollow voice cut through the quiet. "Are they going to make a run at the planet?"

"No…they wouldn't." Cassandra mumbled. "That'd be suicide."

I kept my mouth shut, but my money was on them trying to punch through the defenses.

Under the fog of the supercharged shields, the ship took on the look of an ancient, dying beast whose hide had been pocked by some sort of wasting disease. The massive vessel seemed to vibrate as additional protections sprang up. Crimson runic script wrote itself across the shielding. Golden sigils glowed across the marred surface, and the pustules began leaking. The sickening yellow-green viscous substance coated the entirety of the ship, illuminating it in the process from the magic just below the surface.

Finally, it ponderously loped forward as if the engines weren't getting enough power. It began to pick up speed, racing toward the point of no return. The moment it passed beyond the unseen boundary, thousands of eldritch satellites phased into existence and began to fire.

The shields surrounding the ship trembled from the numerous impacts. It wasn't as if they could shunt power from one spot to another with the satellites hammering it from every angle. Suddenly, the crimson script glowed brightly then vanished. Less than a second later, the satellites bored a hole through the rear shields as they attempted to damage the engines. Unfortunately, the mundane armor proved its worth. Then green scripts appeared above the ship, returning the shields to full, and the cycle began again. The scene repeated itself, but when the light flared to life this time, one of the thrusters was sputtering as it struggled to maintain power. Once the shielding was in place, the gooey substance pooled above the engine, reinforcing the hull.

By the time the ship crossed the halfway point, there were dozens of plumes of smoke filling the space between the ship and the shields. More and more satellites phased into reality as they continued to tear through the ship's protections. By the time they reached orbit around Escarcha, the shields were no more, and the ship was in tatters. The entire bow of the ship was gone, half the port side, from the bridge back, was missing, and all but the positioning thrusters were dead.

Thousands of heavily modified fighters poured out of the dying beast like an angry swarm of bees. They flew out in every direction, trying to use their pathetic excuse for shields to create a barrier between the ship and the transports fleeing to the surface. The systematic deconstruction of the battleship slowed as the satellites targeted the fighters and transports alike. While the fighters required two or three shots to eliminate, the transports withstood four or more. Thanks to the main ship and the fighters running interference, hundreds of shuttles made it to the surface.

As the last of the shuttles escaped the hanger, the battleship began collapsing in on itself. Explosions sent debris flying out into the vacuum of space as the interior lost structural integrity. In seconds, half of the remaining fighters were destroyed, as was the final shuttle. The satellites continued to fire until the last ship either landed on the planet or was blown out of the sky.

Horror was etched onto everyone's faces as they watched the scene unfold.

A queasy looking Gisele put her hand over her mouth. "Why in the hell would they kill themselves like that?"

A cold fury burned in Jose's eyes. "They're fanatics, what else do you expect?"

She whirled on him then stopped and took a moment to consider what he'd said. "Okay, yeah, that's a good point." Brushing her hair over her shoulder, she lost herself in thought for a second. "Does Deheune really believe that whatever is down there is worth that kind of risk?" Her tone hardened. "What in the hell would drive her to do something so desperate?"

Cassandra gave Gisele a look that said her opinion of the woman had just been lowered. Slowly, she lifted a finger and pointed at me. "Him."

Blinking, Gisele cocked her head to the side. "What?"

"Think about it." Cassandra shook her head in disbelief. "We've hounded the woman for the better part of three hundred years." She shrugged. "And she's been on the run the entire time."

Gisele slowly nodded. "That actually makes sense."

As much as I hated to admit it, her words rang true. I hadn't given Deheune time to put down roots or even breathe for more than six months at a time in all these years. This was an extreme move, but I could see how she got to this point.

"Desperate or not, we can't let her get her hands on whatever is down there." I glanced around at the others. "If she does, she could prove a threat to us all."

Gisele winced. "I know." Her gaze landed on the frozen image of the wreckage. "But I'm not sure what we can do."

I had some thoughts, but they weren't going to like them. "How many do you think survived?"

Issac wobbled his hand. "It's hard to say, but given the size of the ship, it probably carried a full contingent—around two hundred and fifty thousand strong." He scratched his chin as he turned to Christopher. "Thoughts?"

"Probably around eighty thousand." He said flatly.

Those weren't great odds. I looked at Escarcha. "It's been five years. What are the odds they're still alive?"

He wobbled his hand. "Not great…from what we gathered, the surface has its own defenses on top of the bitterly cold weather.

Between those two things, they'd be lucky to have half that make it into the tunnels."

That was still forty thousand potential hostiles. "Since we're too far away to get a proper read on the planet, I have a suggestion." I prepared myself for the obvious objections. "To help mitigate the danger to the crew, I think using the Halcon as a signal booster is our best move. It'd allow me to get close enough so we can scan the surface and let us know what we're walking into."

Lily suddenly appeared next to me. "Absolutely not."

Gisele was shaking her head. "Are you stupid?"

I held out my hands for calm. "Ladies, take a breath and let me explain."

Jose rubbed his forehead. "I'm with them. This is a stupid move."

Taking a deep breath, I began to explain what'd happened the last time we were here. It took a while to convince them, even with Lily's reluctant assistance. Eventually, though, they caved, knowing something had to be done.

Gisele grumbled. "You realize this plan of yours doesn't fill me with confidence."

"Me either." I gestured at the blast door behind me. "Which is why I want to take the Halcon instead of the Roja. If I'm attacked, I can run away faster than you can, and if worse comes to worst, I can jump out of there without endangering the entire crew."

Lily folded her arms. "That's—well, it isn't a great idea, but it isn't the worst, either. The fact you can create your own jump point is a plus, but I'm not sure it's worth the risk."

I gestured at Escarcha. "Letting Deheune get her hands on whatever she's looking for on that frozen rock is a worse idea."

Issac rubbed his hands over his face. "He isn't wrong."

If the looks on Lily and Gisele's faces could kill, Issac would be a dead man.

Gisele glared at him. "Not helping."

"Actually, he is." I blew out a long breath. "Look, I appreciate the whole overprotective thing you two have going on, but sometimes I have to do things that none of you are going to like."

Gisele's glare landed on me. "Fine, do whatever it is you're going to do. It isn't like we can stop you once you get your mind set on something."

Lily's disappointed gaze zeroed in on me. "Yes, at this point, it's best to let you get it out of your system."

Feeling slightly attacked, I thumbed over my shoulder. "You know what? I'm just going to go now."

Both women gave me a dismissive wave, and, on that note, I made a quick exit before they could change their minds.

22

ESCARCHA

Have you ever lost yourself to a thing of beauty? I had. Please pay careful attention to my wording: I said thing, not a person. For some people, it's a sunset or some other natural wonder, and yes, I found those amazing as well, but that wasn't what I was referring to. While Lilith may not have understood how my cells worked, she did have a good eye for how to manipulate their growth. With a whole lot of knowhow, she pushed that knowledge to the limit, creating both the Roja and the Halcon, both of which were works of art in their own right.

At least I saw them that way...for everyone else, it was kind of a mixed bag.

What did that mean? Well, take the Roja for instance, between its black and red color scheme and unusual design, it delicately straddled the line between conjuring up some primordial terror and awe in equal measure. Needless to say, it often left onlookers more unsettled than they'd like. As for the Halcon, it carried over the same color scheme but gave off the sense that it was some ancient bird of prey. Even sitting there on the flight deck, there was a sense it might swoop down and snuff out the life of any who dared think itself superior.

I wasn't sure how much of the final result was due to my wife's tinkering and how much came from the guidelines she'd fed into the template during the incubation period. Though, one of the things directly attributable to her skills was the fact both ships made extensive use of pocket dimensions. This allowed us to make adjustments on the fly, making compartments larger or smaller as necessary.

While I tended to leave the Roja in Gisele and Lily's capable hands, the Halcon was mine. Look, I didn't mind sharing most of my toys, but there was something about the ship that called to me in a way the Roja did not. Even though it had a dozen crew cabins, a large mess, meeting room, and a gargantuan cargo hold, it could be flown by a single pilot. Yep, you guessed it, that'd be me.

Was it selfish? Absolutely. Did I care? Not in the slightest.

Do you really expect me to stand here and tell you I don't love romping around the galaxy in my very own spaceship? Are you mad? Wait, you're serious...what sort of callous prick are you? I mean, it's my very own private spaceship capable of faster than light speeds, it can warp across the entire cosmos in one go, and it has enough firepower to crack a planet in half. If that doesn't excite your inner child, you, my friend, need to seek professional help.

Seriously, call a friend, set up an appointment with a good therapist...hell, do something to fix your broke ass. Remember, working on yourself is a good thing. Somewhere along the line it should turn you into a better person and if you're lucky, rekindle that childlike glee you've clearly lost.

As I approached the Halcon, a ramp lowered to allow me entrance. Striding up, I found myself in a cleanroom. It took less than a microsecond for the scans to allow me entry. Once inside, I could either take the corridor to the oversized cargo space or continue onward into the common room and into the cockpit beyond.

Not wasting any time, I dropped into the captain's chair, strapped myself in, and began the launch sequence. The bay doors slid open, and an excited tingle ran up my spine as I taxied out into the vastness of space. I shifted in my seat, glancing from one side to the next. I didn't know why, but each excursion felt like the first. Barely able to contain myself, I swung wide around the Roja and set a course for Escarcha.

A disgruntled looking Lily appeared on the holo-screen. "Really? You're heading out on your own against unknown odds."

Annoyed, I said, "This is just a scouting mission." I held my hands out for calm. "It isn't as if I plan to land or anything. We just need to know what we're up against." Gesturing back at the ship, I grumbled. "We literally just discussed this."

I swear to god it was as if she didn't pay attention to the script half the time.

She grimaced. "It doesn't mean I have to like it."

"I'll be fine." I gestured out at the planet in the distance. "Let me focus and do my job. You can make me feel guilty another time."

An annoyed acceptance swept over her. "Like that ever works."

Even though she was pretending to be annoyed, I knew she did this just to mess with me. "That should tell you something." Smiling, I winked. "Say what you want, but I'm always good for a laugh." I gestured back at the ship. "Now, if you don't mind, I've got work to do."

Amusement coated her tone as she flipped me the bird. "You can be such an asshole some days."

Laughing, I nodded. "Yep." I pointed at her finger. "You realize only old people still use that, right?"

Rolling her eyes, she ended the transmission.

The moment she vanished, a stray thought sped through my mind. *'This isn't the Roja.'*

Would the satellites know the two ships were cut from the same cloth? Hell, I wasn't even sure they'd avoid firing on the Roja, but I guessed they wouldn't. Now I could only hope the Halcon got the same treatment.

Coming to a full stop, I glanced back at the Roja before turning my attention to Escarcha. My voice trembled slightly. "This is fine." I didn't even sound convincing to myself. "Right?" Nodding, I pressed onward. "What's the worst that could happen? I run? That wouldn't be so bad…I'll be fine."

Was talking to yourself this much healthy? Probably not, but it helped…sort of.

The Halcon crossed over the fifteen-hundred-kilometer mark and I nodded. "Don't ease off…just keep going."

When I crossed the two-thousand-kilometer mark, absolutely nothing happened.

Nervous laughter escaped me. "See…it's fine."

Of course, if I was actually as confident as I pretended to be, there wouldn't be a trickle of sweat running down my back. Things continued to get worse as I pushed passed the ten thousand mark… at that point, I was having to constantly mop my brow to keep from going blind at an inopportune moment. Slowly, though, I began to relax. My white-knuckled grip on the controls eased up. I felt the knot forming between my shoulder blades loosen ever so slightly, and my butt cheeks seemed to unclench. Good thing too, because the big muscle back there was starting to cramp up.

At the one hundred-thousand-kilometer barrier I leaned back into my seat. "Yeah, okay…let's pick up the pace." Opening a channel to the Roja, I said, "How close will I need to get for a proper scan of the surface?"

Cassandra appeared on the holo-screen to my right. "You'll need to settle into orbit to get the kind of information you're looking for."

Oh, was that all? "Uh, okay…I'll be in touch."

Unfortunately, that meant I had a long road ahead of me.

How long? Well, I still had several hundred thousand AU's, Astronomical Units—roughly six quintillion kilometers to go before reaching the planet. That broke down to about a three-hour travel window for me at my current speed.

At the ten-million-kilometer mark, something happened.

A powerful shockwave rolled out from Escarcha's core which rapidly expanded in every direction at once. My whole body instantly tensed. My fingers danced across the console to send more power to the shields while I waited for impact. Weirdly, the wave washed over me like a cool summer breeze. A strangely familiar floral scent I couldn't place hung in the air, even after it was well past me. Eventually, it slowed to a stop about thirty thousand kilometers behind me, blotting out the stars, the Roja, and the Anillo gate.

I winced. "Oh, that's not a good sign."

To say Gisele wouldn't be happy with the situation would be an understatement. Seeing how there wasn't anything I could do about it, I did the only thing I could think of and that was to phone home.

My fingers danced across the console as I tried to open the comms channel but to no avail. That left me one option; with a thought, I used the Qucoatl for its intended use and reached out to Lily. *"Are you guys okay?"*

Lily's face appeared in the holo-screen. "We're fine, but there seems to be some sort of barrier between us."

"Yeah." I glanced up at the solidifying white sphere. "I can see that."

Her arched eyebrow and smug look conveyed the 'I told you so' she thankfully didn't speak aloud. "Perhaps turning around would be for the best."

Reaching out with my hand, I caused the space in front of the Halcon to warp into a chaotic pool. "Maybe, but I still have a way out. I think we should continue with the original plan."

Gisele was quick to join the conversation. "Which is to scan the surface and return, right?"

"That's the idea." I eyed the planet in the distance. "Thing is, it looks like something, or someone, is trying to get my attention, so I might do a little poking around." With a thought, the image of my teleport came into view. "I have options to leave if things get tricky." I held up my hand to cut her off. "If things look sketchy, I'll come right back, but for now, let's just play this by ear."

Her expression said she wasn't thrilled with my assessment of the situation. "I'd like to go on record as being unhappy with said plan."

"Noted."

Ending the call, I focused on what lay ahead.

An hour and a half in, I was perplexed. There weren't any obvious signs of life but there were hundreds of spots scattered across the planet that seemed suspicious—small, shielded sectors that blocked my scans. A lot of these could've been a result of the evacuees failing to shut off the defenses before being beamed to safety during the evacuation efforts. Yeah, most if not all of those would be a waste of time.

Looking at the results again, I focused on the prize, the archaeological site James was so interested in. That was when I spotted what I was looking for, a series of twelve heavily-shielded encampments. The first was a good way from the opening of the cave system, but from there they appeared like a tiny breadcrumb trail that led to his last known location.

Yeah, those had to be new. With that in mind, I had the scans focus their efforts on combing over the area with all they had.

It was my hope it'd give me a clue to Deheune's whereabouts. Barring that though, maybe I could figure out what made this expedition worth the effort. Was there really something down there worth such a sacrifice both in resources and manpower? For the life of me, I couldn't fathom what it could be, but then again, I wasn't an evil prick with a god complex. So, yeah, I doubted I'd ever fully understand her motivation.

Clearing my head of those thoughts, I sat there and really took in the planet. Escarcha was an oddity in every conceivable way. First, it was huge, then there was the fact it didn't orbit any of the local stars. Actually, it didn't move at all, it just sat there, as if it were waiting on something. Then there was the atmosphere, the fact it had one was shocking enough, but all things considered it shouldn't be a thing. According to science, it should be a barren rock, and not whatever this was.

That was when it hit me, was there some sort of intelligent being watching over this place? I thought back to the recording of Deheune's arrival. Even though she'd upgraded her ship, I was almost certain those eldritch satellites could've punched through those without effort, so why didn't they? Were they holding back? And if so, why?

"Holy shit, it let them land." The realization swept over me, leaving me adrift. "Was it luring her in? Shit! Was it doing the same to me?"

Then it occurred to me that I didn't care if it was…I wanted to know what this place was about. Not for any personal gain, but because it was a mystery that needed solving. Speaking of mysteries, there wasn't any debris orbiting the planet.

Where did it go? Did Deheune use it for something, or was this the planet's doing?

These, along with a number of other questions, plagued me till I fell into orbit above the dubious trail of breadcrumbs leading into the depths of the planet. They'd been compelling enough to distract me from the fact I hadn't encountered a single hostile satellite.

Sitting there, I allowed the scans to do their work while I pondered my precarious situation. "A smart man would be suspicious right about now." I shrugged. "Then again so would a dumb one. I mean, it's obvious there's something off about all this."

Pushing that aside, I eyed the readings.

Even being this close to the planet, I wasn't getting a lot of usable information. Though there was enough here to confirm my suspicions that these were new. The quality of the shields and the general design of each of the encampments were enough to point at the fact these were likely pre-QDM models. Seeing how few people had access to that type of tech, it was unlikely they would've splurged for the original residents.

Weirdly, though, I still wasn't registering any life signs. To be clear, that'd be zero, zilch, nada on the living. On the flipside, though, there were a lot of undead. What was a lot? I wasn't sure because I stopped caring once the number surpassed ten thousand.

Of course, they weren't the only things showing up. Nope, there were a metric fuck-ton of droids to go along with them. Then there were the undead constructs, which were such a special type of abomination I couldn't even guess as to what they'd be like. Why? Because each and every one of them were unique, since they were custom built from parts and pieces of the dead. Imagine if Dr. Frankenstein had an unlimited number of bodies to work with, but instead of making something human adjacent, he decided to smash them all together in one big lump.

There was one possible upside to all this though: with zero necromancers around to give the undead orders, they'd likely be directionless. Then again, they normally had that one default setting that made them want to murder anyone that wasn't controlling them, so there was that. As for the droids, I couldn't tell how many of them were of the battle variety and how many of them were workers. Depending on their programming, they might let us pass without incident, or they could swarm us, but that was a later problem. Right now, I was here for recon and that was it.

After another twenty minutes of collecting data, I decided it was time to head back. Lifting my hand, I tried to create a tear in reality, but before it fully formed, it collapsed in on itself and the bubble surrounding the system suddenly contracted, only stopping one hundred kilometers out from my current position.

"Well, shit." Hanging my head, I opened a channel to the Roja. The moment Lily and Gisele appeared, I waved. "Hey there...funny story."

Gisele pulled air in through her teeth. "Does it have anything to do with why that weird barrier just shrank to surround the planet?"

I gave her my best smile. "Maybe?"

She drummed her fingers against the conference table. "Spill."

It took a few minutes for me to transfer over the data and explain my situation. "So, as you can see, I'm kind of stuck."

Lily looked intrigued. "Do you really think there's some sort of intelligence controlling Escarcha?"

"I do."

Gisele frowned. "And you think it wants you down on the surface."

Yeah, she was pissed. "That's my guess."

Reluctantly, she leaned back in her seat. "Let's say you go down there. Do you really think it'll let you leave?"

That was a good question. "It doesn't seem hostile, though I could be wrong." I gestured at the screen. "As you can see, I can't confirm that since everyone down there is either dead or escaped the planet via means as of yet unknown."

Sighing, she nodded. "Alright." She threw her hands up in annoyance. "I don't think you have a choice, at this point, but to make your way down there, but I want you to keep in regular contact with us."

Whew, that went better than expected. "I can do that."

Lily frowned. "Are you sure this is a good idea?"

"Absolutely not." I chuckled. "But like she said, I don't have much of a choice."

Gisele leaned forward. "Don't use my words against me. I'd like to point out I didn't like the plan to begin with, and it's only gotten worse."

I chuckled. "You were right then and now."

She smirked. "As long as you know, that's good enough for now." Waving, she said, "Don't keep us waiting too long before you check in."

"I'll do my best."

The moment the link ended, I began my descent. Hurricane force winds threatened to push me off course, while beachball sized pieces of ice slammed against my shields. Setting down in the open wasn't going to work, so I found a nearby cavern and used it as cover for my landing.

Climbing out of my seat, I allowed my armor to snap into place. Feeling somewhat safe, I strode down the ramp and out into the blistering cold. Thankfully, my gear did a decent job of protecting me from the elements. Sure, there was a chill in the air, but if I kept moving it wouldn't prove fatal.

Reaching out, I touched the landing skid. The Halcon glowed brightly, turning into orbs of light before slamming into my body and vanishing. I didn't want to leave it unattended, and having it with me added extra protections I wouldn't normally have.

Grimacing, I strode out of the cave mouth into a maelstrom of snow, sleet, and hail. If that weren't bad enough, there were hurricane force winds trying to lift me off my feet. Thankfully, one of the protections afforded me by absorbing the Halcon allowed me to stay on my feet. It didn't increase my weight so much as manage certain environmental forces. Then there was the shielding that protected me from being skewered by shards of ice.

Pulling my cape tight, I pressed onward, only to be forced back more than once. After about twenty minutes, I began to learn the rhythm of the dance—four steps forward, two steps back, three steps forward, one back and repeat. Was I being dramatic? Kind of. While I was able to make some progress, the winds, or hail the size of my head, would force me to retreat or jog to the side, and it wasn't nearly as graceful as I was trying to make it sound. Did I look like a very uncoordinated person trying to dance? No, that'd be an insult to uncoordinated people.

Remember when I said it was chilly? Yes? Well, I lied. This wasn't chilly it was fucking miserably cold and beyond anything I'd ever experienced. To make matters worse, it seemed like the heating element in my armor suddenly decided to take the goddamn day off.

23

COME TO JESUS MEETING

Forget what I said about the cold not being lethal, because I was an absolute moron for mentioning it. After spending six hours in subzero temps, pushing through gale force winds, and getting waylaid by chunks of ice bigger than I was tall, I was on the verge of collapse. Why? Because this was fucking brutal, that's why.

Oh, I should've burrowed into the ice to get out of the elements to warm up a little? Look at you, using that brain of yours. Do you think you deserve a gold star for that idea? Do you really think I hadn't done that already? Yes, it helped, but all that did was remind me that being warm and cozy was a good thing before having to go back out and deal with this shit.

Still, it was probably the only reason I made it to the entrance to the cave without freezing to death, but it was a close thing. Shivering, I eyed the dark silhouette that marked the mouth of the cavern network winding its way throughout the planet. So far, my sensors hadn't picked up any of the automated defenses I'd been expecting, so that was a positive. I did have to make my way through a minefield, but that was doable.

Darting out from under cover, I sprinted into the cave's gaping maw. The slanted tunnel was tricky to navigate, especially with the stalactites dropping down from the ceiling forcing me one way and stalagmites forcing me another. This went on for a while, but either by design or luck, it kept the winds at bay, which allowed the temperatures to climb ever so slightly. Somewhere around the two-kilometer mark, I began to warm up. I wouldn't go so far as to say I was comfortable, but freezing to death was no longer on the table.

To be clear, it was still well below zero down here, but my armor was able to compensate without all the additional factors it'd been forced to deal with on the surface.

"This is nice." I flexed my fingers and grunted. "Damn, that hurts." Frowning, I glanced down at my feet and shook my leg. "That's going to take a second to work itself out."

In the end, it took a solid fifteen minutes to feel normal again.

Now that I wasn't absolutely miserable, I checked the map. Ouch, there were about a hundred thirty kilometers left between me and the first encampment. Thank god I had superhuman endurance and speed, because if I didn't, that'd take all day. Even so, that was like a two-hour run...which meant it'd probably take me three. Contrary to how Gisele tended to paint my exploits, I didn't have a death wish. In fact, I loved everything about being alive... mainly because of food. Plus, I wasn't sure the afterlife had bacon. I literally don't know how that could happen, but for whatever reason, it was one of the banned substances in multiple religions.

Oh, yeah, about that, several of the old Earth religions survived the exodus. I'm sure your first thought is why wouldn't they? Well, how do I put this gently? A lot of things came to light during the whole escaping Earth thing. Believe it or not, certain individuals were outed for manipulating mortals through religion for their own gain. This happened throughout the ages, meaning there was more than one person at fault, though one name, Seth's, popped up often.

Anyway, after these revelations were confirmed, chaos ensued, which was quickly followed by the Great Purge. This led religious leaders to prune the proverbial tree. That was a polite way of saying anyone not toeing the party line was expelled from the church or simply killed for the sake of expediency. This had the unintended effect of gutting their influence due to their flagging numbers. Sadly, the ones that remained were the zealous types, and there was always the threat of a holy war looming in the background.

Anyway, this was all an explanation as to why terms like heaven and hell were no longer used, and terms like the afterlife or beyond the veil took their place.

No matter what you called it, I didn't want to be there because of its potential lack of bacon. It was hard enough to come by these days as it was. You have to remember it wasn't like every ark ship made bringing livestock with them a priority. Some did, but most did not thus, there was a lack of bacon, steaks, and even poultry from back home.

So, to put it bluntly, I planned on living forever just so I could enjoy certain foods. Plus, it'd give me an opportunity to spend more time with Lilith, though we needed to have a conversation about keeping secrets. Especially ones that involved her going away for five or six centuries at a time.

Turned out, it took me nearly four hours to find my way to the first encampment, and it was a goddamn mess. The dead were strewn about, and most of the vehicles I could see were trashed. While I'd been right about them being pre-QDM prefab structures, they'd seen better days. Whatever attacked this place obviously didn't give a shit about the Tyridium walls as it'd torn right through them.

It was laid out like any standard research base, a central six story tower with eight domes ringed around it. All in all, this sort of setup could easily house up to sixty thousand people, and double that if they shoehorned them in. Given the fact we assumed around eighty thousand made it to the surface, this should've been sufficient. Now, though, you'd be lucky to find housing for a hundred.

Why? Because this place was wrecked. The top two floors of the tower were just gone. As for the fourth, it was a series of collapsed walls and remnants of the framework that held it together. It wasn't like the other three faired any better, given they weren't in much better shape. All that was before we got to the domed structures on the outer ring. Three of them had been crushed flat. It was like some giant stomped it into the ground. The ones on either side of that fiasco each had one of the outer walls ripped away before someone scooped out the interior. Those that remained were only somewhat intact, though one was clearly in better shape than all the others.

That'd be my last stop...you know what they say, save the best for last. In this case, that was an easy thing to spot.

Turning my attention to the obvious problem, I began to assess the enemy. There were roughly a thousand undead between the temporary base and the cave Deheune used to escape.

Given the scene, I drew a few conclusions, the first of which was this was where the survivors regrouped. I wasn't sure if they'd turned their companions into undead fodder before or after things went wrong, but my guess was before. Think about it, a lot of people probably died making their way down here, so why leave their companions to laze about in death when they could be a good meat shield in case something went wrong?

Obviously, something went very wrong here, and I had to wonder why this group of undead had been left behind. Clearly, they'd been attacked by something incredibly powerful. It had to have been quick too, otherwise, they would've dragged this lot with them. Then again, maybe they were left here on purpose to prevent whatever wrecked this place from following them. Huh, if that was the case, Deheune's goons weren't the only thing I had to watch for.

Here and now, though, the undead were a problem. There was a chance—a very small one—they'd allow me entry without moving a muscle, though I doubted that'd be the case.

Okay, it was time to figure out what I was going to do about this and how to get through them without getting dead, because dead equals no bacon.

Eyeing the scanner, I confirmed once again there weren't any life signs in the vicinity. That was good. Glancing up at the undead, I sighed. What a lot of folks don't know about the undead is they come in a variety of flavors. You've got your basic zombie: the shufflers who can barely move and the only real danger they pose is in numbers or infecting you. Then there's the next step up where they are still dumb as rocks, but they're physically imposing thanks to super strength and that sort of thing. Think barbarians but less articulate. From there, they can scale up in power where they can have magic of their own, communicate, and act like generals on the field, negating the need for a living necromancer. Mind you, the latter is the kind of thing Deheune would make, but depending on the power of the underling summoning the pricks, I could be in real trouble here.

Speaking of which, I needed to think. Hiding behind a rock, I pulled out a cherry flavored slushie and began to work out a plan.

What? The slushie? It helps me think. Yes, I do know it's cold. I don't see how that makes a difference. Oh, you're concerned about the subzero temps and my earlier whining. To answer your question, yes, it's still freezing—it's somewhere around negative two hundred degrees Celsius if you must know. How is the slushie not a solid chunk of ice? Magic—more specifically, each cup has been inscribed with magic to keep it the perfect temperature inside. I could set at the core of the sun, and the drink would still be cold and refreshing, even if I was a charcoal briquette.

Oh, for god's sake, let it go. Yes, it was expensive. Yes, it's a luxury item. Yes, I'm sure there were more productive things that could've been done with the money, materials, and the inscriber's time, but someone chose to do it anyway. If you must know, they were a gift and one I happily accepted. For fucks sake, get your priorities straight. I have a cavern full of annoyingly hard to kill zombies here.

Also, fuck you and your judgmental attitude, this is why no one likes you. You'd like to think it's because you're so smart; it's not. It's because you're a know-it-all prick who wants to make themselves feel important by pointing something out without realizing some of us have thought this through. Now, sit back and let me finish thinking…you know, because some of us do that.

Asshole.

It took me nearly an hour to come up with a plan and a second one to stage the upcoming battlefield.

What? You thought I was going to play fair? Or maybe you thought I was dumb enough to charge into a small horde of undead with just me, myself, and I for support. Come on man, I thought we'd established the fact I was smarter than that.

Well, it was time to implement step one in my underhanded and highly unfair plan that'd hopefully lead to the death of every undead bastard in the camp.

Striding out into the open, I waved. "Hey, how are we doing today?" A big smile crossed my lips as I cupped my hand over my ear. "Glad to hear it, do you have a moment to talk about our lord and savior?" I tossed a concussion grenade up before catching it again. "Because Mr. Explodey Pants loves you."

The words were barely out of my mouth when every zombie turned. As one, they opened their mouths to let out a rage-filled howl. Even as they sprinted towards me, they began to clump together. The moment they got within one hundred meters of me I hurled the grenade at them like it was a baseball. A sickening, shattering crack filled the chamber as it tore through the zombie's chest only to tear through the next one's arm. A split second later, it exploded in the middle of the first group.

Concussion grenades normally weren't lethal, but as you may've guessed, this was anything but normal. Do you remember what I said about the temperature earlier? Yeah, it's stupidly cold. Now, combine that with a bunch of reanimated bodies with zero internal heat sources of their own, little to no armor, and what do you get? That's right, a bunch of meat-sicles. Now, what happens when you set off an explosion in the middle of something like that? Correct, they shatter and take all their shitty friends with them for good measure.

Oh, there's mister smarty-pants trying to show how clever he is by pointing out that if they're frozen then they shouldn't be able to move. And if we were dealing with regular corpses, sure, they wouldn't because they'd be dead. Again, though, we're dealing with necromantic magic that somehow bypasses the natural laws. I would've thought with the fact they were walking about in the first place that'd be evident, but I guess not.

Now, do you have anything else to add or can we get back to wiping out a bunch of undead? You sure? Cool, because having to point this out in the middle of a fight is kind of annoying.

Good lord almighty, some people need to have what they used to call 'a come to Jesus' meeting. That was where they took them out back and beat them within a hair of their lives. Did it work? I wasn't sure, but in this case, I was willing to try it out if they didn't get off my ass.

With the first group down, I dropped back to allow the second to move forward. After two more grenades, they wised up to my tactic and spread out. By this point, I'd fallen back enough to implement step two of said plan. This involved the use of multiple shields, forcing them together or at least slowing their advance. As they were forced into a smaller area, multiple mines exploded, further thinning their numbers.

The problem with mines was the fact they were stupid. Anything landing atop them tended to set them off without taking more of their brethren with them.

Taking a deep breath, I summoned my crimson chains. Sure, I could probably take what was left, but I wanted to test one of my abilities against a large-scale incursion. This didn't exactly fit the bill, but it'd let me know if it was viable for future conflicts.

Lashing out with the long chain, I tore through three of the undead at once. They didn't blast apart in chunks. Instead, their body mass was transformed into crimson spheres. The spheres quickly sought out the nearest shambling corpses they could find before disappearing inside. Then those bodies broke down in a similar fashion as they spread across the cavern seeking out my enemies. It didn't take long before the zombies were gone. In their place, thousands of crimson spheres hovered around the edge of the cavern like watch dogs on high alert.

Okay, that was more effective than I thought.

24

SOMETHING WAS OFF

Thankfully, I had some time before the spheres would dissipate. Though exactly how long they'd stick around was debatable. Why? Well, their power came from the foes they defeated, and since I hadn't fought a horde of shamblers before, I didn't want to hazard a guess. Seriously, they could last a matter of minutes, or perhaps hours; it was impossible to tell.

At this point, I guess I should point out what sort of conditions need to be met to create them in the first place. For starters, I needed to make an attack with the intent to create the spheres. In addition, said attack must be a killing blow caused by my chains, which is why I don't use the other special abilities, such as fire, to enhance the blow. It'd suck for them to die to the fire damage and not the blunt force trauma from the chains.

Anyway, once those conditions have been met, a surge of power flows out of me to the chains and finally into the corpses. There's some sort of exchange where it converts the body mass, residual energy, and if applicable, even a bit of the dead person's soul into a crimson sphere. From there, each of the spheres independently targets a nearby enemy. Yes, this sometimes meant more than one sphere would target the same person or entity. Anyway, once they vanished beneath the flesh of one of my foes, the process began again, thus setting off a chain reaction.

It was some pretty nasty shit, and one ability I'd been hesitant to use often. Now that I was fighting the undead, I had zero compunctions about seeing what it was really capable of doing.

I glanced up at the spheres and smiled. It was my hope they'd last long enough for me to inspect the encampment, because now that the undead were handled, it was time to find some answers. I had no idea what form they'd take, but with a little luck, there'd be something here that'd explain what was going on. Right now, this whole thing felt like Deheune was on a fetch quest. Say what you will about the unstable lich lord—*I certainly had*—she wouldn't put herself through this much shit for a MacGuffin. That was the sort of thing she'd pawn off on a follower.

It was right about then it hit me. I was on my own version of the MacGuffin quest, except she was the prize. I mean she was a rather important part of my life's story, but was she really important in the scheme of things?

Uh...I didn't like where my mind was taking me, and I decided that I'd stick with my actual job title of Finder. I might even lower myself to be called a bounty hunter. Then again, that made it sound like I rounded up petty criminals, which she wasn't. Oh, don't get me wrong, she was petty as hell, but her crimes were kind of a big deal, especially once you looked at all the shit she'd pulled across the centuries.

Yeah, I was going to stick with that and just move on.

It took me five hours to work through the outer ring, which when I thought about it, was incredibly quick. Who or whatever attacked the place played hell with the dimensional pockets inside, either ruining them entirely or leaving one or two rooms intact. Thanks to the rampant destruction caused by such spatial collapse, there wasn't a lot for me to search. Out of the two dozen intact rooms, there was very little in the way of anything I'd call useful, though there were a few things of importance.

One such tidbit turned out to be the name of the site James was so interested in: Dig 49. On top of that, I found a data cache that held copies of the recruitment contracts employing thousands of people from the other lich lords associated with the Archive, even the dead one. To my surprise the terms were generous, so long as the mission was a success. Of course, most of the spoils would be handed over to Sargon, Nui Gui, or Deheune herself, since the individuals involved were little more than vassals of some *greater power.*

While I was somewhat better informed, the goal here hadn't been made any clearer. Granted, there was only so much I could learn from contracts and proposed payouts, but I'd been hoping for more, especially since this had been the most intact of the surviving structures. Glancing out of the hole in the wall, I eyed the tower.

"Goddamn it." Dusting myself off, I stood up and shook my head. "Looks like I need to see what's inside door number nine."

Technically, it was more like one hundred and ninety but that didn't roll off the tongue.

Stepping out into the open, I looked up to the shattered fourth floor. "That's got to be about eighteen meters."

It was doable, but the landing was going to be tricky, given the fucked-upness of the floor I was trying to reach. Thank god for superhuman reflexes, strength, and well, magic. Back in the day, such a jump would've been impossible; now it was just inconvenient.

Seconds later, I was standing atop the mutilated mess that used to be a command center. Glancing around, I frowned. Given the sheer amount of destruction and the speed at which it must have occurred, I found it odd there wasn't any blood—like none. You'd think being caught by surprise would've led to casualties; thus far though, I hadn't seen a single body inside any of the buildings I'd been in. Even the corpses that'd been strewn about earlier seemed bereft of blood, and I had to wonder why.

I'm not wrong here, right? That is odd, isn't it? Well, I think it is.

I didn't know if answers were forthcoming or not, but either way, it was a mystery that'd have to wait. Right now, I had to make my way through this shit show without falling to my death or possibly getting tetanus. Carefully picking my way through the debris, I tried to find the terminal for the floor.

Searching the tower took nearly as long as it'd taken to search all the other structures combined. Finally, though, I found several data crystals, a mostly intact room, and best of all, it looked to have belonged to someone important.

Piling all my loot onto the end table, I dropped into the recliner and activated the holo-screen. "Okay, let's see what we've got."

Not having a better option, I grabbed the first crystal in the carousel and slotted it into the player. There was a long moment before an annoyingly familiar face popped into view, Barry Lawson.

"What's this prick doing here?'

A very disgruntled looking Barry was seated in the same chair I'd chosen. That alone made me want to get up and find somewhere else to sit, but the others were in rough shape, so I stayed put.

Looking slightly constipated, Barry gave the recorder what was commonly known to anyone from Earth, or who'd studied Earth history the nazi salute. "Greetings Lord Sargon, my apologies for not being able to make this report at the time of this recording." Glaring around the pristine version of the wrecked room I was sitting in, he sighed. "But it seems that Lady Deheune either didn't know or purposely mislead us about the conditions here on Escarcha."

Reaching out with a shaky hand, he grabbed a nearby canister and filled the glass in front of him with clear liquid. Then he pulled a heavy-duty vial out of a storage ring and poured its dark red contents into the liquid and swirled it. After stowing the vial, he reverently picked up the glass and sipped. His color seemed to return, and he suddenly looked healthier even if the annoyance was still written across his face.

A long, tired breath escaped him. "It's currently the thirtieth day of the fourteenth month of the two hundred fifty eighth year of your ascension." He took another sip to steady his nerves. "We're thirty hours into our mission, and the losses are far greater than anticipated. Out of the one hundred and fifty thousand intended to reach the surface, only ninety-six made it. But that wasn't the end of our losses; none of us were prepared for the environment—yes, we were expecting subarctic temps, but not the ensuing storms...only eighty thousand of us made it into the caverns."

Suddenly shaking, he got to his feet and began to pace. Retrieving a tablet, he mumbled to himself as he read something on the screen before flicking to another and repeating the actions. Finally, after several minutes, he collapsed into the chair once more.

"My following words aren't meant as heretical, though I'm sure if they are taken out of context they would sound as such." His trembling hand reached for the glass again, this time downing twice that he'd drank previously. "I...I..." He hung his head. "Forgive me lord, but I must admit to having my doubts about Deheune. To me, it appears she lacked the foresight to predict what we'd encounter here, both on our way in and after we landed on the surface." Holding out his hands in a pleading nature, he quickly said, "Please forgive my ignorance, but I have no other way to explain to you or anyone else how she bungled things so badly she lost all six of her personal attendants."

Sweat beaded along his hairline, and he tugged at his collar as if he were burning up. Again, he got to his feet and retrieved his tablet and mumbled to himself.

After a little while, he absently nodded. "And while I'm aware these were mostly new due to the incident in New Orleans involving the heretic, Gavin Randall, their deaths are concerning. If she can't properly guide them through this safely, then I can't see how she'd manage to do better by the rest of us." He shook his head in disbelief. "Sadly, my current problem stems from another issue that's manifested itself over the last few days." His gaze suddenly hit the floor. "I know it's not my place to judge her, but she seems weak. Her control over her own people, not to mention the rest of us, seems to be waning. I can't be sure why...maybe she was wounded...but how can a god—a true god suffer such a wound?"

Leaning over, he all but hyperventilated on the spot. Sweat soaked his shirt and dripped down onto the floor like he was some sort of junky coming off a high, and unable to get their next fix.

He reached for the glass again and took a large drink. "A week ago, I wouldn't have dared voice such concerns, but now...I'm starting to see *things I hadn't before." Pointing at his chest, he sat upright looking completely strung out. "You personally assigned me to her contingent the day we took to the stars, two hundred and fifty-eight years ago...since then, I've served you faithfully...or so I believed." Wiping the droplets out of his eyes, he grimaced. "But I'm starting to think she did something to me...to all of us." His voice cracked. "I think Zmey and the Twelve are in on it... you said as much...warned me not to let my guard down." Tears welled in his eyes. "I hadn't thought I had, but now...now I'm not so sure—"*

There was a panicked knock at the door, and he froze. Swallowing hard, he hurriedly wiped away his tears as he leapt to his feet. Clearly, whoever was out there didn't think he was moving fast enough and pounded again. Stripping off his shirt, he grabbed a towel, then reached over and switched off the recorder.

"Huh, that was odd."

Through a series of *brilliant deductions* worthy of Sherlock Holmes, I was starting to think something was off. Hey, easy there, that was sarcasm, the fact something wasn't right between competing lich lords, Zmey, and the Twelve is blatantly obvious.

It's almost like some of you lack the ability to comprehend a person's tone. Weirdly, up until now, that hadn't been a problem; pretty much everyone I knew was able to recognize my ability to mock not only myself, but others, and situations with ease. You might want to think about what that says about you that you're a bit slow on the uptake.

I glanced down at the carousel, and while I was tempted to go through them all, that wasn't practical. No, the next time I reached out to Lily and the others, I'd transmit them over for them to review. Simply put, this wasn't what I was looking for, at least the part I'd viewed, but it still had a lot of potential value if used correctly.

25

SOLID AND UNMOVING

Two hundred and fifty-two kilometers wasn't exactly a walk in the park to begin with, but when you added in explosive runes, trip-wires, and the like, it got way worse. And before you ask, I only set off like one or two or like nine of them before I finally got the hang of disarming the traps properly. All I can say is, I'm so very grateful my armor was tough as hell. Also, it appears it's fire, impact, and shock resistant, so that's a huge plus.

Quick question: if mistakes were made but no one was there to witness them, were they actually mistakes? The simple answer is, yes, yes they are. What kind of moral code are you operating by? Wow...you're something special. Don't you know that you're supposed to learn from your mistakes and try not to repeat them?

For me, it was that last part that was the toughest bit of advice to follow. Look, I quickly learned rushing through the disarming process was a bad idea, and I shouldn't do it. Which, for the record, I didn't. Sadly, for me, there were a few times I thought I was smarter than I was. Turns out the necromancer in question set up a failsafe or three into some of the sigils, and I didn't realize. As you might imagine, this led to bad things happening, such as me nearly having my head burned off my body. Obviously, I survived, but holy shit was it unpleasant.

I feel like I'm rambling here...maybe the head trauma was getting to me.

Finding a little nook, I propped myself up against the wall and reached out to the others via the Qucoatl. It didn't take long for Gisele, Lily, Issac, Jose, and the others to pop into view. My face-mask slipped away, and I smiled. "Hey there, how are things?"

Lily's eyes narrowed. "What happened to your face?"

Wiping away a few crispy bits of skin, I shrugged. "Would you believe me if I said nothing?"

Gisele grumbled. "No."

Jose snorted a laugh. "Dude, did someone hold a blowtorch to your face?"

"That's not too far off." I chuckled. "I took a fire rune to the face because I missed a few context clues...but I'm fine."

Jamie winced. "That had to suck."

"It wasn't fun." I held my hand out to stop their questions. "Look, I just wanted to check in before I made my way to the second settlement."

"Second?" A very confused Gisele asked.

Rubbing my hand over my face, I wiped away more of the flaky bits. "Yeah, I'm going to beam over a whole bunch of logs from our favorite lawyer turned necromancer, Barry Lawson." I sighed. "I'll tag his last entry...which was the first and last thing I watched...I'm kind of hoping you guys can sift through the rest while I try to track down some more clues."

Gisele didn't look thrilled, but she nodded. "Fine, send them over."

Smiling, I inclined my head. "Thank you."

It took me a couple minutes to transmit the details, but once I was finished, I signed off and focused on the task ahead, the second encampment. Thanks to a handful of drones I deployed earlier, I had a better sense of what I was walking into this time.

A small hologram appeared. The layout was similar to the last, but instead of eight domed structures, there were only six, though these hadn't fared any better than the previous ones. Actually, these were probably worse off, since the tower was only three stories instead of four and only two of the outer buildings seemed to be structurally sound.

It looked as if Deheune tried to learn from her earlier mistakes by deploying multiple automated defensive measures. There were dozens of turrets, a large field of mines...none of which were triggered, along with a small host of battle droids, several constructs, and a host of other nasty bits I didn't want to think about. Yes, there were zombies here, too...probably two or three times what I'd encountered at the previous encampment, so that sucked.

Weirdly though, these had a different look about them—it was almost as if there was a glimmer of intellect in their eyes.

My gut twisted in on itself as I got a bad feeling about this place. "This isn't going to turn out well for me."

Enlarging the image, I eyed the rotten pricks. "Is that fire?" I shook my head. "No, it couldn't be...who would waste fire magic on them?"

That was when I realized the shields surrounding them contained the element of fire within it, but there weren't any flames. What's that got to do with anything? It's a tricky bit of magic that'd require a whole lot of power and even more skill to integrate it the way they had.

A tiny groan escaped my lips.

Yeah, yeah, yeah, you can stop laughing. I know my previous strategy won't work here but thanks for the support.

Gritting my teeth, I eyed the space for a long moment. If I was going to win here, I'd have to get creative. Between them, the traps, droids, constructs, and automated defenses, I was half tempted to just nuke the place before moving on. Sadly, that wouldn't give me anything in the way of actual intel, so, I'd have to fight my way through if I wanted to figure this shit out.

Go me.

Can't you tell how overjoyed I am by the situation?

Do you have any idea what's worse than a bunch of undead? That's right, a bunch of smart undead with access to automated defenses, a small army of combat droids, and a large number of constructs.

Just as a reminder, constructs were pure nightmare fuel created when necromancers weaved in blood, death, and even a little soul magic for good measure. They used their powers to fuse multiple bodies together into a single entity with no apparent rhyme or reason. Occasionally, they came out in a roughly humanoid shape, but most of the time they didn't. I once saw one that rolled across the ground like a weird ball with thousands of whip-like appendages capable of striking most people dead in a single hit. Worse still, they had a nasty habit of absorbing the people they killed into their own body mass to grow stronger.

So, yeah, it's a nasty, ugly, and revolting endeavor that's as much intimidation factor as it is weapon. I mean, who wants to be absorbed into a construct? No one. Especially me. I think we've discussed this before, but I want to live forever. Plus, and I must stress this to no end, I am one thousand percent sure constructs aren't given fruit slushies. So, yeah, that'd be one of the worst ways to go.

So, you can imagine how upset I am that there are about a hundred of those things spread across the compound. Also, whoever made these constructs went the extra mile to graft in makeshift weapons—everything from clubs, to jagged looking swords, to spears, and things I couldn't actually identify.

Yippee.

Thank god Lilith properly stocked my storage bracelet. Thanks to her foresight, I had options; the question was how to exercise them without bringing the cave down on my head or blowing up the encampment.

First things first, I needed to take control of the automated defenses. Thankfully, that was the easy part. Pre-QDM structures were by far the best. They sported Tyridium frames, walls, top-of-the-line automated defenses, and all the creature comforts you could ask for. Plus, they had complex AIs that ran the places with very little to no input from their humanoid guests, meaning you could set it and forget it. Seriously, no matter how you sliced it, they were just cool as hell, though they did have a flaw. Okay, it wasn't so much a flaw as a weakness. What's that, you ask? Well, the entire software package was based on code provided by Lilith.

See, now you're starting to get it, I was going to cheat. By that, I meant I'd be turning those turrets against them the moment I prepped step two of my dastardly plan to take over the world—I mean basecamp. Yeah, not the world; that's a little too ambitious. Plus, this place was cold as hell.

It took me a few minutes to sift through the data to discover one major hiccup in my plan, none of the droids were tied into the central processor. For whatever reason I couldn't fathom, they were working under some sort of independent programming. It also meant I'd have to plan to take them down as well, and that complicated things. It wasn't impossible, but the extra effort here was beginning to bug me.

I guess it was time to see what I was really capable of.

One of the little gifts Lilith provided me was a wearable cloaking device. Yes, it was cool, but it also had multiple limitations; one of which was I had to move slowly. Anything over a casual stroll, and things got iffy—I'd still be mostly hidden but anyone scrutinizing the area would spot me in a second. Then there was the second problem. This involved any sudden movements causing the device to completely fail and revealing me to the world for the sucker I was. There were a few other quirks as well, but those were the ones I was currently worried about.

It took me the better part of five minutes to position myself behind a lone zombie. Inhaling deeply, I steeled my nerves and went for it. In a flash, crimson chains wrapped themselves around my hands. Lashing out, I nearly obliterated the shambling corpse on contact. Thanks to my overzealousness, there was only so much flesh able to be converted into crimson orbs.

Stepping forward, I lashed out a second time, only for my

weapon to be slowed by the shield that suddenly sprang to life. I still managed to kill it in one go, but there'd be no slacking off if I wanted to survive this. The body was quickly converted into crimson spheres which shot out to find suitable victims.

Deciding now was as good of a time as any, I activated the automated defenses which took aim at the backs of nearby droids. My orbs couldn't penetrate the shields, so when they were forced back, they exploded. I wasn't sure what the conversion rate was, but the undead weren't thinning out as fast as I'd like. With a wave of my hand, a large white net stretched out between me and the oncoming horde. At first, their shields pressed against the barrier, only to be quickly whittled away before the bodies behind them were pulped into a fine mist. More and more of the orbs filled the air as they cut through the shields or used the viscera created by the net to increase their number.

The bedrock at my feet shuddered as something loud sounded behind me. Before I had a moment to think, air was forced out of my lungs, and my spine arched backwards. My feet left the ground. The moment I became airborne, pain radiated through my entire form. That was about the time multiple dull cracks sounded throughout my skull, telling me a half dozen of my ribs were broken.

Had I been capable of screaming, I would've, but without the air to do so, that wasn't an option. White light surrounded me, righting my ribs, draining my lungs, and easing the pain. That was right about the time I came to an abrupt and complete halt as I crashed into the ceiling. Woozy from the impact, I realized I was falling, and it was a good three or four hundred meters down. My scrambled brain tried to find a solution, but the pain was far too much. Blood leaked out of my ears, nose, and mouth to slosh down my neck and pool somewhere in my chest plate.

It occurred to me once again, I was falling. Then a wave of nausea was followed by the pain of one of my ribs settling back in place. Barely on the verge of consciousness, I knew I needed to stop myself from hitting the floor. Then my arm snapped, and my spine did its best to twist itself into a C as something knocked me sideways.

A scream was choked off by the blood in my mouth and throat. My arm flopped about in the wind as I slammed into something hard, skipped a couple of times like a rock, then skidded to a halt against something solid and unmoving.

My vision narrowed, and I fought the urge to pass out. If I lost consciousness here, I was dead...even so, my mind refused to obey, and darkness took me.

26

CITIZEN LAWSON—BARRY

While I still wasn't sure how I'd survived, I did, and I didn't really want to question it. Nursing a headache, I hobbled over to the recliner in what I'd come to see as the Barry Suite Special. As for the rest of the camp, there wasn't anything of use, not that I did a great job of checking the place. For the most part, I let the automated system sift through the files for any pertinent data. If it found anything, it'd copy itself onto a data crystal to be relayed to the Roja the next time I reached out.

For now, though, I was hoping the meds would ease my pain. Normally, my healing factor would be enough to put me right within a few minutes, but it'd been over an hour now and I was still feeling it. Apparently, nearly dying to a bunch of constructs wasn't great for one's overall health.

Who knew?

I glanced around the strangely intact room once more before picking up the data crystal I'd found stuffed beneath the mattress. Slipping it into the holo-projector, I waited for it to spin to life.

. . .

Barry still looked rough, but he wasn't sweating, and his trembling was barely noticeable. The thing that caught my attention and held it was the hate burning in his eyes. His fingers angerly drummed against the table, tapping out a tune I didn't recognize. Maybe he was just musically inept, but given the cadence of it, I didn't think so. His features were twisted in quiet rage as he glared at the vial of Sargon's blood in front of him even as he sipped at the crimson drink in his hand.

"My apologies, Lord Sargon, my first briefing on this matter was lost when a small contingent belonging to Ke'lets turned on us." He downed roughly half his drink in one go. "Though, I'm starting to see what set them off." Holding his glass out in front of him, he growled. "But that's only due to the gift you bestowed upon me."

Barry bit off the word gift like he was being force fed cat shit.

Sitting the glass aside, he got to his feet and paced a little as he scrolled through his tablet. Multiple images began to appear on the screen. One was a breakdown of the survivors. By the looks of things, the faction belonging to Ke'lets suffered the most as they'd been assigned to hold the ship together while everyone else escaped. Even so, they still represented the largest faction here by a factor of five. Nu Gui's representatives was the second largest contingent, followed by Deheune's own elite forces.

As a side note, it appeared all but a handful of her people made it to the surface without incident.

Sargon's sole representative in this entire mess was Barry, though there weren't any notes as to why that might be. James Matherne was in a similar situation as he was the only agent the Twelve sent out on the expedition.

"For reasons that are quickly becoming clear to me, I am your only set of eyes and ears on this mission." The last word seemed to leave a bad taste in his mouth. "Technically, the same could be said about James Matherne, but we both know that's not true. Not only does he have his own objectives, but he's benefited from Deheune's protections." Resentment flashed in his eyes. "Something I haven't been afforded."

Another screen popped into view. This one was a detailed list of Deheune's personal attendants. It was a mixture of weak blood witches, powerful telepaths, and one soul engineer. A second screen appeared to show multiple blood witches loyal to Deheune stationed in key positions throughout the battleship, though most of them were assigned to the mess hall. Barry stood there glaring at the text for a long moment before he turned his attention to the recorder.

"Due to luck or design, I had to skip my last two meals aboard the ship to complete the final preparations for Escarcha." Cutting his gaze back to the names, he frowned. "I always thought it was strange James never ate with the rest of us. Now, though, I suspect he knew something the rest of us didn't." He snatched up the vial off the table. "And I'm guessing you had an idea of what might occur once I was aboard."

Rubbing his forehead, he made a dismissive gesture with his free hand and all the data vanished. Stowing the vial in his storage ring, he grabbed his tablet and clicked on it to bring up another screen. This one was a schematic of a device I hadn't seen before. Then he tapped on his screen again to show the battleship in its entirety with literally thousands of these tiny antenna-like things all over the ship.

His voice was barely a whisper as he collapsed into his seat. "I have to assume you know what these are...if not, then let me introduce them to you." He tapped the screen, and the ship vanished to be replaced by the long thin looking device stuck to the bulkhead that led into the engine room. "This is an amplifier." Reaching out with his finger, he flicked it in disgust. "Its sole job is to amplify telepathic commands throughout a predetermined area."

Barry tapped the screen again and he brought up Deheune's personal attendants again.

Karen Highland—S Grade Telepath

Terry Fortnight—S Grade Telepath

Susan Gibbons—S Grade Telepath

"As you can see, Deheune's personal attendants were topnotch mind magicians." His fingers worked the screen again and several pages worth of text appeared. There were occasional diagrams, but most of it focused on an unknown chemical compound. "As you can see here, this is what happens when you combine blood magic with science." Fury twisted his face into something ugly and unrecognizable. "This—" He jabbed at the text. "Is a highly addictive compound that makes you susceptible to *mental magic...something three S Grade telepaths could easily take advantage of."*

A trickle of blood ran freely from one nostril. Irritated, he wiped it away before stalking over to the bath to wash his face.

Once he was sure it'd stopped, he returned his attention to the recorder. "I apologize for the interruption, but the side effects of weaning myself off the compound take a toll on the body." He shivered. "It's like any other drug, I suppose, except this one was designed to dig into my brain, body, and soul like some sort of parasite." Coughing, he wiped some blood off his mouth and frowned. "I think the only thing keeping me upright is your blood. I applaud your foresight, but it would've served me better if I'd had a heads up." Looking more tired than any person had a right to be, he eyed the bath. "Before I say something I shouldn't, I'm going to clean up and get a few hours rest." His gaze tracked to the door. "Deheune has called for a mandatory meeting in a few hours, so I need to have my wits about me for that."

Barry leaned over and turned the recorder off.

Then, as if he'd forgotten something, it clicked back on. The timestamp in the corner showed it was twelve hours later.

A haggard looking Barry slumped in his chair. "I think she suspects something is amiss." He wiped his brow. "I have to tell you, playing the faithful lapdog I've been for the last few hundred years is more difficult now that the compulsions are wearing off." A bitter laugh escaped him. "Though, I have to admit, I'm struggling against them, even as weak as they are." He lifted the vial and shook it gently. His face scrunched up into something curious as he held it close to his ear and listened. "Huh."

Leaning over, he shook it again, but this time there was a gentle clinking against the interior of the container. He brought it close to his face and popped the stopper. His hands shook as he focused on his spatial ring. After several seconds, he retrieved a magnifier, a pair of tweezers, and a needle. Using the point of the needle, he pricked himself then smeared the stopper with his blood. There was a tiny click. Setting the needle aside, he picked up the tweezers and began to carefully retrieve a thin sheet of silica. He inspected it thoroughly, then placed it atop his tablet. A moment later, flowing script hovered before him.

Citizen Lawson—Barry,

I have done you a disservice by not warning you about Deheune's true intentions. Though, if you're reading this letter, you're starting to suspect things aren't quite right with her. It was with a heavy heart that I sent you into the lions' den without making you aware of what you were walking into. Thanks to those damn telepaths she has working for her, saying anything to you would've disqualified you from entry. Thus, I sent you armed with the only tool I knew she couldn't combat, a vial of my undiluted essence.

I know you better than you do, I suspect. When the time calls for it, I know you'll remember this and use it appropriately. Now that you're firmly embedded into her inner circle, please allow me to explain her true intentions and not the rubbish she's been selling the rest of us.

You see, her encounter with Gavin Randall in New Orleans stripped her of her divinity. Now, the only thing that remains is a mere spark of who she once was, and she's desperate to find something to rekindle her waning power.

Yes, I know what she's told the others to gain their support, and it's not true. Escarcha was never a secret lab belonging to Lilith and the Mad God. Not that you should need further confirmation, but I've consulted Heidr who found the proposal laughable. There is no hidden technology that'll give us the edge over the others.

However, there is something else that would, something that both Deheune and Zmey want to keep to themselves and that's Hodr's location. It's their belief there's a map hidden in the data core buried deep in Dig Site 49. I have to admit, after combing through the ancient codices, there's a real chance she is correct. It's for this reason, and this reason alone, that I sent you, my most trusted lieutenant, to oversee the situation.

I know she will test you through the years, but keep the faith, for I am with you always. Know that while she is now one of the false gods, I am not. I will vouchsafe your mind, body, and soul throughout eternity. Even if you fall to her machinations, I will watch over you.

Should you succeed in your mission and bring me Hodr's location, I will bless you even further and lift you into the exalted ranks of the true Onyx Mind. The blood contained within this vile will strengthen your entire being. Once you've completely drained my essence from the vial, you should have the power to seize control of Deheune's operations. Be wary of any of Zmey's representatives, as they have begun using forbidden magic pulled forth from the void by as of yet unknown means.

Lord Sargon.

Barry's mouth hung open as he read and reread the message. Nervously, he retrieved the flimsy bit of silica and placed it back into the stopper. His gaze tracked down to the vial then back at the empty space where the letters hung only moments before.

Suddenly, he took a knee and bowed his head. "I will do as you've commanded, my lord."

Getting to his feet, he strode over to the table and turned off the recorder.

Damn, that was a lot of information all at once, though I was unsure just how much of it I could trust. The one big question I had though, was who the hell was Hodr, and what the hell did he have to do with being able to rekindle someone's divinity—not that I believed she was a god. Even so, she was looking for a powerup and that sounded like a bad idea. Of course, if Sargon was lying and there was a chance for the Archive or anyone else to get their hands on Lilith's unedited inventions and samples of the Mad God's DNA, we were all in trouble. The way I saw it, no matter how this worked out, we were in deep shit if Deheune managed to get her hands on any of those things.

With those thoughts swirling through my mind, I opened a channel through the Qucoatl network and transmitted all the data I had to the Roja. In the same instant, I pinged Lily. Before I could take a breath, a hologram showing the usual suspects sitting around the conference table on the bridge appeared.

Wincing, I raised my hand. "Hey, how goes it?"

Jose frowned. "Are you okay?" He randomly gestured at my image. "You look a little rough."

I retrieved a pineapple and coconut slushie out of my spatial storage and drank deeply. "Trust me, I feel way worse than I look."

Gisele eyed me for a long moment. "Care to tell us what happened?"

"A couple of undead constructs decided to use my unconscious form as a soccer ball." I shrugged and took another drink. "Thankfully, the self-replicating orbs took them out before they killed me."

Lily suddenly popped in to stand behind the empty chair they'd reserved for her. "I'm still reviewing the data you've sent over, but this isn't good."

Unable to stop myself, I laughed. "Yeah, I got that." I shrugged. "On the one hand, they get their hands on some serious tech, access to the Mad God's DNA and go nuts." Leaning back in the chair, I frowned. "On the other, Deheune gets a serious power up and becomes a real problem."

Lily shook her head. "No, you don't understand." She sighed. "Given the seriousness of this matter, I reached out to Mir, Bea, Tomte, and Alfred about what we found here." She shivered. "But it was Alfred who had some answers...and if he's right, this could go seriously sideways."

Issac gave her a curious look. "I'm going to need you to elaborate."

"I second that." I nodded.

Fear flashed in her eyes as she collapsed into her seat. "Hodr is a child of the Allfather from some distant, long-dead timeline. The person we know as the Mad God is merely a splinter of a being so powerful that his existence and subsequent self-imposed punishment are the foundations of creation itself."

What the fuck did that mean? "I'm sorry, but none of that makes even an ounce of sense. Maybe dumb it down for those of us not versed in the entire history of every QDM event known to exist?"

Bobbing her head up and down, she absently wrung her hands together. "Hodr is beyond powerful...he is the source of all the contagion in our reality...not just in this realm, but in all of them. His existence is a threat to us all on a scale I cannot begin to explain and if Deheune can find him and unleash him upon this reality, we will die. To be clear, any hope of fixing this mess will perish if he is allowed to flourish in this reality."

Oh, how wonderful. "So, we better hope she doesn't find him."

I was fortunate looks couldn't kill, given the one she shot me. "Correct."

I finished my drink and pushed myself to my feet. "Alright, I need to find a place to crash, but when I get up, I'll get back at it." Waving, I said, "I'll check in when I'm able. In the meantime, see if there's anything else in there I can use."

She nodded. "I'll handle it."

With that, I ended the call.

27

DEVILS & DEMONS

Gah, I hated everything about this place. Look, maybe you're better than me but being down here was getting on my last nerve. Seriously, everything looked exactly the same. Okay, not exactly, there were slight variations of the color gray from one spot to the next, but that was hardly enough to get excited about.

On my third day down here, everything seemed to blend in such a way I couldn't tell the difference between one alcove and the next. It got so bad at one point I started marking the wall just in case I was locked in some sort of loop. Granted, my map said I was moving forward, and the stops at the encampments were nice, but the rest of this godforsaken hellscape could go fuck itself.

Wait, did I just admit that Barry's home videos were keeping me somewhat sane?

I ran my hand over my face and sighed. "I'm going to need some therapy after this." Was this what it felt like to be a victim of the Stockholm Syndrome?

Even as that horrific little revelation flitted through my mind, I rushed through the halls of the tower, excited to see the latest bit of drama that was Barry Lawson's life. Seriously, I was beginning to see the appeal of the old telenovelas. There was betrayal, unrequited love—between Barry and Sargon, a whole lot of drama, and it was all set to the backdrop of an alien planet. Whether I wanted to admit it aloud or not, the intrigue really was killing me. Would Deheune discover he'd thrown off the mental shackles she'd placed on him centuries ago? Would James betray them all, or would it be Deheune that stabbed them in the back? And could Barry stop them?

See what I mean? It's absolutely thrilling.

Though, each stop meant there was a chance I wouldn't get a resolution to their little performance. At this point though, I was addicted to the tragedy of it all, so I always hoped and prayed I'd get my next fix. As to why it was a tragedy, Barry was dying whether he realized it or not.

How could I tell?

Let's see here, his nose bleeds were getting worse, he'd lost a lot of weight, and his translucent skin was pulled so tight around his body he looked more like the dead than the living. Without seeing the guy and giving him a full once over, it was hard to tell what was causing his rapid descent, though I had my guesses.

My money was on one of, or perhaps a combination of, three factors. My first guess was the vial of Sargon's blood he was clinging to like an out-of-control alcoholic. Think about it, unless you were a vampire, drinking blood wasn't exactly a healthy habit to get into. Then, add in the fact it belonged to a skeezy lich lord, because god only knew what sort of shit was swimming around in there. As to my second guess, I thought it might be due to his exposure to the blood magic that'd been put in his food over the centuries. From what I understood, there was some fairly nasty shit involved in that and going cold turkey could lead to a wasting disease. Then again, maybe it was a latent mental command that was taking its toll on him like some sort of 'if-then' statement in Excel. If the subject breaks free of x command, a subroutine is triggered to kill him.

Lastly, and more likely, it was some sort of weird combo of the above possibilities. In short, there was no way Barry was getting off this planet alive, and for whatever reason, that bothered me. In my own weird way, I was sort of rooting for the guy. Sure, if he stopped James and Deheune from getting what they wanted, that'd make my life easier, but if I was being honest with myself, that wasn't why I wanted him to win.

It disturbed me on a fundamental level that I cared at all, and I didn't like it.

Back to Barry and the last installment of...it was then that I knew it needed a name. Yes, I'm way too invested in this but damn it was just so good. Plus, Barry was really selling it. Don't get me wrong, he was batshit crazy, but he deserved an award for his performance. Oh, I had it: Diablos y Demonios, or Devils & Demons. It isn't like anyone here is the actual good guy, so this kind of fits.

Yeah, it was time to see if the producers were going to give me another episode of Devils & Demons or if they were going to pull a shitty network trick and axe the show on a cliffhanger.

Hey, don't judge me, you spend a week...no, it'd been ten days.

Okay, yeah, I'd like to see how you held up after ten days of being stranded alone on a dead planet while constantly on guard the entire time because of zombies. I bet you'd be looking forward to your next little hit of entertainment too, even if it was the ramblings of an insane person. Plus, you have to admit, Deheune is way worse. As for James Matherne, he seems like an angry, arrogant prick with a god complex. So, yeah, supporting him was out of the question.

Pulling free of my scattered thoughts, I tapped the bracer around my forearm, allowing the sensors to sweep the area. Still nothing. That was kind of shocking, since I couldn't shake the feeling I was being watched. It was a sensation that'd been growing over the last few days, but no matter what I did, I couldn't find the source of my growing paranoia. Maybe watching the noose tighten around Barry was rubbing off.

Then again, maybe it wasn't. It wasn't like I'd uncovered who or what had been attacking the encampments. There'd been that one notation pointing the finger at Ke'lets followers rebelling at the first basecamp but nothing since. Now that I thought about it, it was kind of strange Barry had gone out of his way to avoid talking about it, unless he hadn't.

I'd been working under the assumption the bases were attacked while they were occupied, but what if that wasn't the case? What if they'd been attacked afterward? If I looked at it that way, it explained why I hadn't found any bodies or blood inside. It didn't explain why Deheune chose to leave the undead behind though. Wouldn't she want them around in case something went wrong? The more I thought about it, the less her actions made sense.

I decided I'd leave that part of the investigation to Lily and the others. They had all the files, so if they ran across something I should know, they'd reach out.

Shaking my head, I sighed and settled into Barry's favorite chair. I grabbed the latest and greatest data crystal he'd hidden under the seat cushion. Seemed he liked to vary up his hiding places from one cushion to another. It wasn't exactly safe...I mean think about it, it was like when the kids back in the day used to hide their porn underneath their mattress. If they had a braincell in their head, they'd know that was the first place anyone would look.

Ha, you think I did the same? Joke's on you buddy, I hid my stuff behind the corner of the duct system running to my room. There was no way I was willing to get caught with porn, given how strict my father was.

Anyway, I was curious if Deheune and James had come to blows yet. According to what Barry said last time, they weren't on the best of terms, so maybe I'd get lucky, and they'd kill each other.

Reaching out, I dropped the data crystal into the projector.

Barry was looking thinner than I remembered. Dark blue veins shone through his crepelike flesh that looked as if it'd tear open at the slightest touch. Even though he couldn't see it in a mirror, there were several raw spots that looked to be oozing in the back of his head. One of the absolute joys of being caught in the scope of a holo-recorder was the fact they didn't miss a thing. Dark puffy circles made his eyes appear like they were sunken deep within his skull. Technically, they hadn't moved but they looked as if they'd been pulled back several millimeters.

Just looking at the man gave me the shivers.

His voice was a dry, raspy thing. "I followed James today." He glanced around the room nervously. "I finally figured out what he's doing with the 'volunteers.'" The man actually used air quotes around the last word. "You know I've been curious what he's been up to since he started segregating off certain portions of the faction belonging to Ke'lets." He shivered. "And now I know."

His skeletal fingers danced across the screen and a hologram appeared.

A lithe, well-built man with dark brown hair, brilliant green eyes, and handsome features stood facing a half dozen unconscious bodies. Kneeling, he took what looked to be a thick black coin out of his pocket. Grabbing the nearest one's jaw, he readjusted her position in such a way her face could be seen. She was a pretty, youngish woman with long brown hair, smooth skin, and full of life. The last bit changed the instant the coin touched her forehead. The coin in his hand began violently vibrating as her body shriveled. James grunted as he pressed the coin even harder against her skull. A few seconds later, she crumbled in his hands before turning to dust.

Nodding, he pocketed the coin then pulled out a second, approached the man to his left and repeated the action. Once he was finished, he retrieved the first coin and started over with his next victim. Shortly after James finished with them, the hologram cut off.

"I didn't want to be there when he finished." He shook his head. "For the life of me, I can't figure out why or even how he's overcharging the Atman Stones. Everything I know about the process says adding more than one soul to a coin is dangerous." Shrugging, he sighed. "Anything from having them randomly explode to ripping a hole into the void is possible. That's why no sane person tries it." Disgust sounded in his voice. "Then again, I think we've established James isn't exactly sane, haven't we?"

Reaching up, he dabbed at the oozing wounds on the back of his head. A tear welled up in the corner of his eyes. Sniffing, he brushed it away and looked into the recorder. "I don't know how, but they've poisoned me." He hung his head. "At a guess, it's a thallium base combined with blood magic and multiple other compounds." *He gestured at the little alchemy station* over to the side. "I've been working on a cure, and between my own efforts and your essence, I'm still upright, and that, more than anything, is driving them mad."

His fingers danced across the screen and an audio clip began to play.

"I thought you took care of it!"

Barry hit the pause button. "That's James. The woman in the recording is Deheune."

Deheune growled her response. "I dosed the man myself; there's no way he should still be standing."

Arrogance and scorn flowed out of James's voice in equal measure. "Obviously, you screwed that up, too."

A loud smack of flesh hitting flesh filled the quiet. "Watch your tone, boy. You are not your master...even if you were, I could kill him just as easily as I can you." There was a second muffled smack, and a groan clearly belonging to James sounded. "Remember your place. I won't remind you again."

Coughing and wheezing, James said, "Touched a sore spot, did I?"

There was a long pause. "Boy, don't make me—"

"Make you what?" James hacked out something wet. "You won't kill me...while you might smack me around a little, you won't go too far."

A dangerous edge coated her tone. "Won't I?"

"No, you won't." With a voice full of contempt, he said, "You need me... need what I can do. Without me, you can't escape this place, and you know it."

She was quiet for a long moment. "Keep believing that at your own peril." Her tone softened. "For now, make sure we're ready to go the moment we get our hands on the data core. Understand?"

James snorted his derision. "What about Barry?"

"What about him?" She scoffed. "You've seen the man; he's all but dead already."

A grumble erupted out of James. "I want him all the way there by the time we get to the core."

She harrumphed. "You worry too much."

After a long silence, Barry glared into the recorder. "I'll make it to the core and beyond, just to spite those bastards." He hung his head. "If it's the

last thing I do, I will stop them from getting the information they want."
Looking up, he sighed. "I don't know if I'll have the strength to get it to you,
but denying them is within my power."

Reaching out, he ended the recording.

Well, that was interesting.

And yes, James was just as much of an arrogant prick as I'd believed. I rewound the image to take another look at Barry. I wasn't sure what Deheune had dosed him with, but the results looked nasty.

I jerked back in my seat. "Am I seriously feeling bad for Barry, of all people?" Grumbling to myself, I sighed. "First, I start siding with him against the others, and now I'm starting to feel sorry for the prick. Good lord, I can't wait to get off this rock."

I did my best to shake off my disgust. After failing miserably, I transmitted the data over and opened a channel to the others.

Gisele gave me a curt nod. "Good to see you are well." She glanced up at the timestamp in the corner. "We were becoming concerned." Her pointed look said she clearly didn't approve. "It's been two days since your last contact."

I leaned my head against the seat. "It's been a busy few days." Gesturing out the open wall, I gave her my best smile. "Seems the further in I go, the more heavily they lean on the constructs...and the undead are definitely much smarter now."

Jose frowned. "Seems they've managed to keep the most powerful necromancers alive."

"Looks that way." Eyeing the recording device, I grimaced. "That's not the only thing that's changed." I pointed at the data carousel. "The droids are starting to act funny, and not in a ha-ha way either."

Lily popped into her chair. "What exactly does that mean?"

"They're getting smarter." I shrugged. "Then there's the counter-measures they're deploying...it's almost like they're trying to find a way to neutralize my attacks."

Issac shook his head. "That shouldn't be possible...unless..." He slapped his forehead. "You need to start dropping those jammers at the start of every battle. They've got an open line of communication from one camp to the next; that's the only thing that makes sense."

Lily nodded. "That does fit."

Rubbing my forehead, I grunted. "I really should've thought of that myself."

Gisele huffed out a breath. "Maybe if you had a second set of eyes with you, they may've spotted the problem earlier."

Damn, she was like a dog with a bone. "But I don't." I shot Issac a grateful look and nodded. "Thanks, I'll make sure to deploy the jammers next time."

Lily's face twisted in disgust. "I just finished Barry's last entry." She shook her head. "Unless he's a talented alchemist, I doubt he'll find a cure in time." Her tone hardened. "Though, I'm not sure what'll happen with him in the end."

Cocking my head to the side, I gave her a curious look. "What do you mean?"

An image of Barry's skeletal form suddenly appeared and hovered in the air. "Deheune is correct; whatever she dosed him with should've killed him outright." She flicked her finger, and the vial of Sargon's blood hovered in the air next to Barry. "But it didn't, and I'm guessing that's due to him imbibing Sargon's undiluted essence."

Christopher leaned forward. "Is that important?"

"I think so." Her expression hardened. "It isn't like we know a lot about the Black Circle's blood rituals, but it's speculated the essence is cut with the blood of high-ranking members or that of the dead. This is to prevent people from drinking directly from the tap like Barry is. And seeing how that vial has obviously been converted into a spatial storage, there's no telling how much he's imbibed."

That hadn't been something I'd even thought to consider until now. "Huh...so, we have no idea what's going to happen to him because of that, right?"

She shook her head. "There's absolutely no way to tell."

Gesturing at the still image of Barry, she pushed back into her seat. "To say this is out of the ordinary is an understatement of epic proportions."

Oh, how wonderful. "Alright...anything else we should be aware of?"

"Actually, yes." Her expression hardened as the image of James adding souls to the Atman Stone appeared. "Be aware what he's doing here is extremely dangerous...and without some very specific modifications, it shouldn't even be possible." She gave me a hard look. "If you find one, don't touch it...more importantly, if you see it used, do not attempt to follow. I suspect the forces beyond the boundary will tear you apart."

Did I look that stupid? Hey, don't answer that.

"Yeah, don't worry, I have no intention of getting myself killed." I gestured at myself. "Seriously, that'd leave me on their home turf alone and likely in a very compromised position." Shaking my head, I grinned. "So, no need to worry, I'm actually smarter than that."

Looking way too smug, she eyed me with great interest. "Maybe you are, but have you considered they might try and use it as a weapon?"

That was when it hit me, James or Deheune might want to toss me through to end me quickly. "Actually, that hadn't occurred to me." Nodding thoughtfully, I winced at the thought of being torn apart and never knowing what happened. "Thanks for pointing that out."

"You're very welcome." Glancing over at Gisele, she smiled. "I hope you're starting to see she has a point."

Were they ganging up on me...they were, weren't they? Then again, maybe they had a point. "I'll take that into consideration."

Though, I wasn't sure it'd change my MO.

Lily glanced around at the others. "Anyone else have something to contribute?"

Jamie shook his head. "Not until I review the data. For now, just stay safe and don't die." He pointed at the ceiling. "We don't know what'll happen if you kick the bucket."

I blinked. "What?"

Lily gave me a stern look. "Let me guess, the thought of this vessel dispersing on your death has never occurred to you, has it?"

Pushing myself upright in my seat, I forced calm into my voice. "Why would I?"

Yeah, I failed at keeping the annoyance and panic out of my tone.

Gisele's mouth dropped open, but she remained speechless.

It was Jose who finally stepped in to explain. "Do I need to remind you how these ships were constructed?" He gestured at me. "More specifically, who they're based off of?"

O...oh...ohhhhhh shit.

I held out my hands in the hopes it'd change the outcome of my next question. "Wait, are you saying that if I die, the ship will too?"

Lily grumbled. "It is based off your genetic makeup...it was literally grown from samples of your body and shaped through some rather ingenious engineering on my—Lilith's part. So, maybe? We can't be sure, but none of us want to find out."

Well, shit.

I hung my head. "Yeah, okay." Glancing up at them, I mumbled. "I'll try not to die."

Numbly, I cut the connection.

28

END OF THE LINE

Finally, I'd reached the end of the line—well, more precisely, the end of the encampments. According to the scans I'd done and the maps I'd pilfered while searching the area, there were about sixty kilometers left between me and Dig Site 49. After Sargon's revelation, I wasn't sure what I was going to find at the end of this shit show, but I'd be finding out shortly.

But first, I had one last thing to do. Yep, you guessed it, now that the undead and droids were taken care of, I *needed* my fix. With the way Barry left things, I wasn't sure how all this was going to pan out, and I needed to know.

As I strode through the hall, I pulled out a strawberry slushie and took a long sip. The closer I got to Barry's suite, the more nervous I became. Man, I really needed to get my head checked once this was all over. I wasn't this on edge on my first date or the day I got married, so yeah, I might have my priorities slightly off after being down here so long.

Following the circular passage around to the northern face of the building, I paused in front of the door. It was intact. That was a plus...or at least I hoped it was. I mean it'd been a fifty-fifty shot I'd find something worthwhile inside. Mentally, I started to reach out to the core and open the door, then I stopped myself.

What if he didn't make it? Should I risk finding out or should I just press on? It didn't matter if there was a resolution to this little story I'd been following. Seriously, I needed to focus on the prize, and that was whatever mystery was buried at Dig Site 49, not what lay beyond this stupid door.

Even though I tried to convince myself I should get moving, I couldn't do it. I needed to know one way or another what happened to Barry. I'd come this far, and my answers were just a few meters away, so why was I stalling?

The answer came at the speed of thought. Because, if there wasn't another data crystal in there, I'd never know what happened to Barry, and I wasn't sure I could take that.

Was it rational? Absolutely not. But at this point I was too invested in the man's story not to at least take a look.

Finally, I sent the command to the core and the door slid open. A strange floral scent wafted out of the room, and there was the rustling of something in the far corner.

Before I could wrap my head around what was happening, a raspy voice echoed in out of the dark. "Huh...I hadn't expected company."

My mind ground to a halt, even as chains wrapped themselves around my hands. It was only after I was properly armed that I felt like I recognized the voice. "Barry?"

Confusion sounded in their tone. "Yes?"

No, this couldn't be right. I was frozen to the spot, unable to move. How could it be him? The man was mere millimeters from death in the last projection, and that was years ago. "Barry Lawson?"

It felt like my mind was glitching at the mere thought of it being him. Still though, a part of me was thrilled he might've survived.

A dry wracking cough filled the quiet. "The same." He devolved into another coughing fit, but when it finally settled, he sighed. "Allow me to get the lights." His voice was finally evening out as if it were becoming accustomed to being used again. "As I said, I wasn't expecting company."

Holy shit, it was him, and I was conflicted about him being amongst the living. On the one hand, I'd get my story, but on the other, it was Barry. Just what the hell was wrong with me?

Across the room, roughly about the same spot I imagined the recliner to be, a pair of olive-green orbs glowed to life. Reflexively, I took a step back. "Are you feeling alright?"

A dry laugh escaped him. "That's a funny question coming from the likes of you."

Before I could answer, the room took on a warm glow to show it in much the same way as I'd imagined. The comfy, brown leather recliner sat in the far corner of the room with an end table off to the side. His bed was neatly made and was taut enough you could've bounced a coin off the blanket. To my surprise, the portable alchemy kit wasn't anywhere to be seen, but if he was still kicking, he wouldn't need it...so that kind of made sense.

As for Barry himself, he wore some sort of black ceremonial robe, complete with hood. Somehow, though, he looked even thinner now than he had. You'd think the robe's bulk would've done more to hide it, but it did the opposite by accentuating his narrow frame. There weren't any answers to be found in the darkness of his hood. Between it being pulled so far forward and the way he tilted his head, all I could see were the glowing orbs where his eyes should've been.

I realized I was staring and frowned. "Hey, I know we haven't gotten along over the years, but you did try to kill me."

Snickering, he shrugged his bony shoulders. "After a fashion, I suppose that's true." Slowly, he lifted his gloved hand and gestured at the seat across from the dining room table. "Sit." He shook his head. "I assure you that's all behind us now."

Reluctantly, I stepped across the threshold, allowing the door to close behind me. "What's with the getup? Did I catch you in the middle of something?"

A big belly laugh escaped the man as he shook his head. "No, no you didn't." He pushed himself up to his feet and the robe seemed to hang off him as if it'd been meant for someone several times his size. "I—" Standing there, he cocked his head to the side then chuckled. "A lot has changed since I saw you last."

Unable to stop myself, the thought of his withered form flashed to the forefront of my mind. "I suppose it has." Moving over to the table, I pulled out a chair. "How do I put this?" For whatever reason, I suddenly felt guilty about watching those videos, since it was akin to reading someone's diary. "I've searched all the encampments thus far in an attempt to figure out what's happening down here...and I've been rather thorough about it."

Barry shuffled over to the table and pulled out the opposite chair from my own. He was quiet for several seconds before he nodded. "You've seen the updates I was making for Sargon."

Feeling rather shitty about myself, I plopped into the chair. "Yeah, I have." I gestured at the man. "So, while you look thinner than ever, I've got a good idea about what sort of changes you've gone through."

Cocking his head to the side, he was quiet for an uncomfortably long time. Just as I was about to say more, a dark chuckle escaped him. "Oh, I doubt that very much." He reached into the folds of his robe and pulled it apart to reveal the white and black cow print suit underneath. Then in one motion, he let the hooded cloak fall from his body to reveal a skull with olive-green orbs for eyes and a sharp set of canines. "I've undergone a few extra changes since making those videos."

Shocked by the revelation, I sat there as he tugged off his gloves to reveal his bony fingers. Finally, though, I found my voice. "What the hell, Barry?" Weakly, I gestured up at the man. "Look, I get that you were kind of dying in that last hologram, but once I heard your voice, I kind of expected you to be better, not worse."

A hacking laugh escaped his mouth. "Well, at least I'm not dead, so there's that, right?"

I guess he had a point. "Look, I'm sorry if this is rude, but I'm super curious about how you're able to talk or cough or breathe or anything else if you're a skeleton." Leaning to the side, I eyed the suit carefully. "Unless there's more to you underneath there."

Shaking his head, he made a show of sitting in the chair as if he were some refined noblemen preparing to address a peasant. "I assure you, all that's left of me is bone and—" He pulled back his sleeve to show what looked to be fused stone spanning across his forearm. "Whatever this is." With a bored tone, he continued. "As to how or why I do any of those things, I think it's mostly habit. As for the voice, I'm going to go out on a limb and say it's magic of some sort, because I don't have any other explanation."

That made a weird bit of sense. "Okay, again, I'm not trying to be insulting here, but do you have any idea why you haven't moved beyond the veil? I mean, I think we can both agree, you're super dead."

Barry leaned back in his chair and shrugged. "Not a clue—well, not a good one, anyway." He held up his hand to stop my obvious question. "Before we go any further, do you mind telling me why you're here? To be clear, I'm curious as to why you're on this planet, not in this room."

"It started off with me wanting to track down Deheune." Reluctant as I was to share, I decided to just roll with it. "Now, though, I'm looking for answers." Gesturing at him, I smiled. "Part of that was figuring out what happened to you." Readjusting myself in my seat, I took a long sip of my slushie before inclining it in his direction. "Would you like one?"

A small chuckle escaped him. "I've heard of your fascination with those drinks." He gestured at himself. "But as you can see, I think I'm beyond such things."

I winced. "Yeah, sorry about that."

He shrugged. "It's fine...thanks to my new—condition, I've had a lot of time to think without being influenced by outside forces."

"Care to elaborate?" I glanced around the room. "It doesn't seem like you're in too much of a hurry to return to Sargon's employ."

Flames glowed to life in his eyes at the mention of the name. When he spoke next, there was a cold, unadulterated hate there. "I assure you; those ties have been severed." Tugging his sleeve back in place, he growled. "Even if they hadn't, he wouldn't want me back given what I know."

That was interesting. "And what's that?"

"More than he'd like."

Apparently, he wasn't willing to spill just yet. "Mind if I ask another question?"

Barry's whole form relaxed ever so slightly. "What would you like to know?"

"Why did you try to kill me?"

He chuckled. "I didn't. I hired people for that."

I arched an eyebrow. "Too good to get your hands dirty?"

A long, deep laugh escaped the man. "Please, my hands are plenty dirty. I was killing people before your kind developed the ability to write." He seemed to relax. "No, I didn't want to be the one to kill you because it'd force me to move and rework my identity, again." He shivered. "Seeing how I'd just done that when I left New Orleans, I wasn't in a hurry to do it again." His gaze locked onto mine. "It isn't as if you get to pick your next posting, and there was a real possibility they'd stick me somewhere worse. Do you have any idea how humid it is in the Big Easy? It was awful." Annoyance coated his tone. "Seeing how I liked Puebla, I wasn't in a hurry to leave."

"Why'd you leave New Orleans?"

Leaning his head back, he let out a disgusted noise. "Because of Walter Percy's dumb ass. That moron made a deal to kill off the local vigil and everything went to shit right after...so yeah, that sucked."

I blinked. "Wait, that was less than a year before we met."

"Yes, it was." His tone was entirely too smug for my liking. "Which is why having to pick out a new name only eight months later would've been a pain...plus the weather in Puebla was amazing. I loved it there."

Before I could stop myself, I growled. "So did I, but you kind of fucked that up, didn't you?"

He held out his hands for calm. "Hey, that was all Edward and Geoffrey's deal…and I was assigned to them to keep tabs on Deheune and James Matherne." Hate filled his tone when he said the names. "They were trying to force Jade, Gavin, Viktor, and Cain off-planet." Hanging his head, he groused. "When they realized that wouldn't work, they released that stupid contagion without alerting Sargon—or anyone else for that matter." He wagged his finger at me. "Just so you know, that was some bullshit compound cooked up by Zmey, just in case you're looking for someone to blame."

Wow, the divisions in the Archive were worse than I thought. "Dude, I've got to ask, why stick it out with Deheune and her crazy antics?"

Gesturing around the room, he snorted. "Because I had orders."

"I'm going to need more than that if you want me to understand."

Barry sat there quietly for a long moment before speaking again. "Oof, okay. Let's rewind a bit." He shook his head. "From what I understand, Deheune was part of the squad that eliminated Ra back in the day." Pausing, he glanced over at me. "Are you familiar with the QDM?"

"I am."

Barry absently nodded. "Good, that'll save some time. Anyway, Ra was kind of a big deal with all that because he had a hand in guiding certain individuals through the void to this reality." He bobbed his head from side to side. "It also meant he had access to quite a few artifacts, and Deheune stole one that led her to Escarcha, though the info she had was incomplete."

My gut twisted in knots. "Let me guess, Zmey had the rest?"

"You guessed it."

I sighed. "Speaking of, where are James and Deheune?"

If he'd had lips he would've been grinning. "Oh, they're gone…sadly, they're not dead, but they failed to acquire what they came for."

Oh, thank fuck. "That's good, I guess."

Nodding, he said, "I'd imagine so." His tone softened. "So, you're really not here for the same thing she was?"

I burst out laughing. "No, that isn't anything I'm interested in. Besides, I had no idea what was happening here until you mentioned it in one of your recordings."

Laughter rolled out of him like air. "All this time she was under the assumption you knew about the prize...the grand treasure she wanted for herself." He ran his hand over his bare skull with a loud swishing sound as bone rubbed against bone. "May I ask why you've been so dogged in your pursuit?"

Was he for real? "I thought that'd be obvious."

He shook his head. "No, I have no idea and neither does she."

Pointing at him, I said, "She is the one who ordered you to have me killed."

Barry sat there unmoving for several seconds. "Wait...that's it?" He snorted a laugh. "That's why you've been hounding her every step for almost three hundred years?"

I blinked. "Do I really need a better reason? She wanted me dead, and I didn't want to die." Shrugging, I said, "It occurred to me if I didn't want her to put me down like a dog, I should probably hunt her down and stop that from happening."

Manic laughter escaped him. It took him nearly a minute to regain control of himself, but when he did, amusement was thick in his tone. "Oh, my god. That's...well it's great."

I didn't much like being left in the dark here, so I snapped off a comment I probably shouldn't have. "In your case, isn't your god Sargon?"

His amusement simply ceased. When he spoke, his tone had a dangerous edge to it. "No, it is not." He paused. "Once, I did think of him in such a fashion, but now, I know better."

Yeah, that was a dick move on my part. "You mentioned that earlier...what is it that you know?"

His eyes glowed again. "Far more than I'm allowed to divulge." He settled himself in his chair once more. "But one of the few things I can say is none of the lich lords are gods, no matter what they claim." When he rolled his eyes in their sockets, it left me feeling a little unsettled. "In fact, there are no true living gods left in this world...not in the way we were raised to believe. There are the godlings, but they're infants, and they'll never turn into true divine beings." He paused for a long moment then shrugged. "Once, long ago, in a now dead timeline, one almost existed, but even they were lacking." Spreading his hands in a sorrowful gesture, he grunted. "If they weren't, Hodr wouldn't have been an issue."

That was some pretty heavy knowledge he was dropping on me, and I had to wonder why. "Are you telling me this now as some sort of excuse to try and kill me in a minute? I mean this isn't the sort of thing where knowing the secret is too dangerous to be allowed to get out, right?"

A bitter chuckle erupted out of him, and he shook his head. "No, I'm not going to kill you or even make the attempt." He leaned forward and tapped his fingers against the table. "Though...I would like to make a proposal."

Oh damn, and here it is, the inevitable deal with the devil. "Bargains aren't my thing...that's more Gisele's department and she isn't here."

Barry waved away the words with a dismissive gesture. "No, it's nothing like that...or maybe it is." His tone suddenly turned curious. "Would you be opposed to me coming to work for you?"

What the actual fuck? "Come again?"

"Just hear me out." He tapped his skull with his index finger. "I've got a lot of helpful information stored up here...and not just things about the Black Circle, the Archive, and people like Zmey or the lich lords...though they're not really people so much as monsters in human form."

Well, he went there. "Odd thing to say about your former employers."

"Oh, believe me, they're so much worse than I'm making them out to be."

Pointing at the man, I asked, "And what about you Barry? You said yourself you've killed a lot of people…what makes you any less of a monster?"

Barry gave me a casual shrug of one shoulder. "In a lot of ways, I am…and I look the part…I suspect that's part of my penance for my many sins."

"Penance?"

Surprise sounded in his voice. "Right…that's a conversation best had later."

I shook my head. "Maybe we should have it now."

Barry chuckled. "You won't believe me."

"Dude, I'm sitting in the bowels of a frozen planet talking to a skeleton that used to be a lawyer for one of the worst companies known to exist." I held out my hand to stop his retort. "Not only that, I've spent the last three centuries hunting down a lich lord to keep her from killing me off. So, please tell me, which part of that story sounds believable to you?"

Barry sat there for a long moment before nodding. "I can see your point, though this isn't actually a frozen planet."

"I'm sorry, what?"

Snickering, he said, "This." He gestured around us. "Isn't actually a planet…the grand prize she was looking for wasn't the data core with a map leading to Hodr or Lilith's hidden lab. No, it was a map leading to a being so complex it boggles any attempt to make sense of it."

Either this guy had lost his mind, which given the circumstances seemed likely, or he knew something so profound it was about to change my life. "And you know this how?"

Barry readjusted himself in his chair then steepled his fingers. "You don't believe me?"

"Well." I waved my hand up and down at the man. "You have to look at it from my perspective, you said you've been here for what… three years on your own?"

"Yes."

Giving him a thumbs up, I continued. "Now, you're telling me that this planet, which isn't a planet, is some complex machine the likes that hasn't been seen in our timeline."

Barry tapped his index fingers together. "That's the gist of it, yes."

This guy was way too calm for my liking. "Okay, so if Escarcha is all you claim it is, why aren't you using it to rule the universe?"

His hands froze, then he cocked his head to the side. "Ah, I see your sticking point." Scratching the side of his skull with his finger, he let out a long hmmm. "Okay, before we can address that properly, I need to catch you up on a few things."

"And what might those be?"

Barry huffed out a laugh. "Well, we'll start with what should've been my death, and we'll work our way out from there." He tugged a data crystal out of his jacket pocket and slotted it into the holo-projector. "I'm hesitant to admit it, but by the time we'd made it this far, my paranoia had gotten the better of me."

No shit, he was damn near a jabbering madman in the last recording. "I...uh...yeah, I didn't want to mention that, seeing how sane you're acting now. I thought it might trigger something."

Chuckling, he rolled his shoulders. "Quite right to be cautious, but no worries, I'm much better now that I've seen the way." He pointed at the space between us. "Due to my unfortunate mindset, I began using microdrones at all times to record what I believed to be my final days on this world." He held his hands out in a I don't know gesture. "The way I saw it, either I'd be allowed to leave, or they'd kill me." His olive-green eyes glowed brightly. "Little did I know there was a third option on the table."

Before I could ask anything further, he flicked on the projector.

29

WILL YOU SHUT UP ALREADY

A hologram bloomed to life between us. The drone footage was shot high and to the right, giving me a view of the bland cavern surrounding the man. I kind of hoped he had a good reason he'd chosen this particular angle, because if he thought it was a flattering one, he was sadly mistaken. Between the open wounds oozing goo, the pain etched across his features, and—well, you get the point, he looked like death warmed over. I glanced at the man sitting across from me and noted the skeletal look was a definite improvement.

Barry continued to walk forward, but he seemed to be moving in a wide arc, since the encampment came into view behind him. About a minute later, the cavern leading to Dig Site 49 came into view. All the while, he kept his head on a swivel as he swept the area for trouble. Every twenty seconds or so, he'd slowly turn around as if he were afraid someone would suddenly appear behind him.

A tiny pop sounded to his right. Grimacing, he turned, eyeing the area with suspicion, but there was nothing to be found. His gaze tracked back over to the encampment, where several maintenance droids were working on a heavy-duty ground skimmer.

Nodding, he mumbled to himself. "They'll be moving soon."

The words were barely out of his mouth when a gash in the fabric of reality formed a few meters away. Hanging his head, he blew out a long, wet breath. "Of course it's you." Lifting his hate-filled gaze, he glared at Deheune. "I was wondering when you'd show up."

Revulsion swept over the woman as she brought her hand up to cover her mouth and nose. "God, you reek." She sniffed and wiped her nose. "I think it's time we had a proper conversation."

Swelling to his full height, he squared his shoulders. "Let me guess, you're going to try and kill me, again." A derisive snort escaped him. "Do you really think the others won't notice the attempt this time?" Holding his hands out to either side, he said, "I mean, doing it out in the open like this will tip off the others."

Deheune burst out laughing. "As if I cared what they'd think, though it doesn't matter any longer."

Barry stood his ground. "And why's that?"

She tsked as she stepped toward him. "You're losing your touch, Barry... they're all dead." Her gaze tracked passed him to land on the camp. "Though I guess I can't blame you too much, since you've been so busy trying to find a cure for your condition."

"You mean my poisoning."

Arching an eyebrow, she smirked. "Figured that out, did you?" She gave a non-committal shrug. "Yes, I poisoned you...and I have to admit, your continued survival has puzzled me." Leaning in, she asked, "Would you sate my curiosity and tell me how you've managed it?"

"Why would I do that?" Even though his body twitched this way and that, his voice remained eerily calm. "I may not be strong enough to defeat you, but I can deny you this, and Sargon willing, the core as well."

Hate twisted her face into something ugly. "Sargon!" She spat on the ground. "Do you really think he can save you?" Leaning in close, she growled. "Do you think he, of all people, can stop me? Her hand flashed out so quickly he didn't see it coming and her fingers wrapped around his neck. "Of course you do; you're just as pathetic as he is." Madness filled her eyes as she lifted him off the ground. "This is it for you, Barry, but take solace in the fact Sargon will soon follow you beyond the veil, so you won't be alone for long."

Barry struggled against her grip in a vain attempt to free himself. After a few seconds of watching him struggle, her other hand twitched. A dozen spears of molten stone burst through the ice, piercing his arm, thigh, groin, and multiple spots across his torso. His whole body tensed for a moment before going limp. She let him hang there for nearly a minute before she dismissed the spears. His body hit the ground with a wet thwap. It was clear he was dead, but Deheune didn't seem satisfied. Stepping forward, she brought her boot down atop his head, crushing it flat. Blood and brain tissue splattered against her feet and legs. In a near rage, she continued to stomp and kick until there was little more than paste remaining of what used to be a man.

It was hard to watch, but if Barry could sit there unmoving, I could do the same. I felt like I owed the guy that much.

When she finished, James strolled into view. His judgmental expression said he somehow thought less of her now than he had previously. "Was that necessary?"

Bile dripped off Deheune's words. "Don't question me, fool." Her hand snapped up and she pointed a long, thin finger at him. "I won't warn you again." She seemed to shake off her rage as she eyed the unfazed James. "Are we ready?"

Revulsion filled his expression as he glared at her. "As if I've ever been the failure here."

Power radiated from Deheune as she stalked toward him. "How dare—"

"Will you shut up already." He waved away her anger. "We both know you aren't going to do anything." Thumbing back at himself, he gloated. "Remember, you can't get off this planet without me, so stop with the threats. We both know you're not going to do anything about it." Rolling his eyes, he said, "Do us both a favor and stop wasting time, and let's get on with this."

Trembling with rage, Deheune took another step forward. When she spoke, her voice was barely above a whisper. "Imprisonment here isn't the threat you think it is." Getting up in his face, she growled. "You're young and have yet to realize the passage of time is a small matter to one such as me."

For the first time, James blinked. The look on his face said everything—he believed she'd kill him where he stood. Ducking his head low, he mumbled. "My apologies." He gestured around the cavern. "Being in this place for the last six months must've eroded my manners."

She snorted a laugh. "Wise choice." Huffing out a breath, she grumbled. "But we both know that's not true. You don't respect the old guard, and you believe the lich lords have outlived their usefulness."

His eyes went wide in horror. "I would never say such a thing."

"Of course you would, and you have." She shook her head. "It doesn't matter; we'll finish this joint venture together, but afterward, perhaps we should distance ourselves." Her gaze landed on him like an attack dog. "We both know the goals of the Twelve do not include the lich lords."

The man audibly gulped. "That's a dangerous accusation."

"It is." She gave him a predatory smile. "And one I'll keep to myself, so long as I get what I want. We both know you don't have the power to obtain the items you're searching for on your own...so without me, you will fail." Stepping into his personal space once again, she gave him a knowing look. "Remember how you came to have your position in the first place. If you don't want to be the next head on the chopping block, we'll work together then part ways."

Resentment settled across his face like a mask. "Fine, but I'm not the only one with secrets."

Deheune burst out laughing. "Do you think I care what you tell those groveling peasants? Their lord is dead, and in time, they will become extinct with or without my help."

He paled.

"Oh, you really thought you had me over a barrel, didn't you?" She shook her head sadly. "It isn't as if they don't know my intentions already... this was their last, desperate grasp at power. The moment they realize it's failed, they'll scatter to the winds."

James gave her a look meant to kill, but he nodded. "I'll fetch the skimmer."

A few minutes later, Deheune and James rode off into the distance.

· · ·

Barry leaned over the table and tabbed the fast forward key. "Trust me, you don't want to wait around for this."

The drone hovered in place as the lights cycled in the background. It was going too fast to count, but the timer in the top corner of the video said it'd been about three months. That was when I looked down at the ground and saw his skeleton was reforming. Another month passed when something green flashed inside the reformed chest cavity. It winked out almost as fast as it'd formed, but three or four weeks later, it glowed to life and stayed that way. Slowly but surely, Barry's body finished putting itself back together.

Barry reached out and flipped the switch back to normal speed. Leaning in, he whispered. "This is my favorite part."

His skeletal form lay there for a long moment, then Barry, or at least his skeleton, sat up. Ribbons of green power flowed around his form for several seconds before crashing in all at once. In roughly the same instant, a bolt of pale green lightning fell from the ceiling and struck his skull. The resulting flash hid him from sight for nearly a minute. When it faded away, a very naked skeleton stood there panning his gaze over the now empty cavern.

Without a word, he sped toward the gaping maw that led to Dig Site 49. A small time jump later, and he was standing in front of the data core. Scorch marks marred the walls, while the floor had long, deep grooves dug into it. There were clear indicators there'd been a fight, even if there weren't any clues as to who'd attacked them even though they'd proved victorious. Otherwise, Deheune wouldn't have been so careless as to leave both pieces of the artifact lying on the floor, free for the taking.

Which was exactly what Barry planned to do as he knelt to scoop them up. The moment his hand neared the broken pieces, static filled the screen.

. . .

I glanced over at him. "Do you have them?"

His tone was wistful as he leaned back in his chair. "No, that isn't my path." With a casual gesture, he rewound the image to the point where he'd sat up. Even without flesh to show his expression, it was clear he was filled with a sense of awe and wonder. "As magical as that moment is to see, you can't comprehend how it felt." Tilting his gaze toward the ceiling, he let out a wistful sigh. "In that moment, I glimpsed the secrets of the universe, even if I don't recall them. I felt their power and I knew what needed to be done." Finally, he turned his gaze on me. "What comes next isn't for the likes of me. No, it's meant for people like you. That being said, I must do all I can to ensure the Deheunes of the cosmos aren't the last ones standing." He shook his head. "While you may have trouble believing this, I've seen the error of my ways and wish to make amends. To do that, I must work to serve the greater good."

After watching him basically come back from the dead, I was unsure how to proceed. "And you think that's me?"

"You're a good place to start." He shrugged. "More than most, I know who you are and who you've been. Even before stepping into the world that included magic, you always did your best to help. More than that though, you've gone out of your way to do the right thing instead of the easy one. Believe it or not, that speaks well of you."

"And that's why you want to work for me?"

He seemed to consider the question for a long moment. "It is a large part of it, yes." A bitter laugh escaped him. "Perhaps I just want to be on the right side of history, for once." Shaking his head, he said, "I know it's a hard pill to swallow after all these years, but I assure you, I'm telling the truth."

Man, I really wanted to believe him, but I wasn't sure that'd be a smart choice. "As you say, it's a hard pill to swallow."

"That it is." He leaned back in his chair. "But if you want to make sure my words are true, maybe sit me in front of a telepath. I'm pretty sure you've got a few on the payroll, considering the scope of your operations."

That was a pretty big olive branch to hold out. "Given your condition, are you sure that's an option?"

He shrugged. "Only one way to find out."

Shit, dude was really laying it all out. "Let me think about it." I gestured at the door. "Since you don't have the artifact, we should probably go collect it."

Barry chuckled. "That'd probably be a good idea." Sighing, he said, "Though, that's not a journey I can accompany you on."

I blinked. "And why is that?"

He pulled air in through his teeth. "It's hard to explain, but the simple version is I'm forbidden from returning."

"Forbidden?"

Amusement coated his tone as he gestured at the door. "Trust me, you'll understand once you see it for yourself."

If that wasn't a red flag, I didn't know what was. "Did you rig the place to blow or something?"

Laughing, he shook his head. "Nothing so dramatic." He gestured around the room. "Remember what I said: this planet isn't a planet." Curiosity wrapped itself around his tone. "You must've noticed this place seems to have a mind of its own by now."

I frowned. "I may have a few suspicions, but that's a far cry from saying it's true. Is that what you're implying?"

He spread his hands out in an I don't know gesture. "You'll have to see for yourself."

I didn't like it, but he was right, if I was going to believe something that crazy, I'd have to see it for myself. "You said Deheune and James are gone; do you know how they got out?"

Joy filled his tone. "I have my guesses.... after whatever happened to cause that sort of destruction, I'm betting they jumped into the void in the hopes they'd escape whatever was hunting them."

That wasn't ominous at all. "I guess I'll go see for myself." Eyeing him for a long moment, I asked, "And what will you be doing in the meantime?"

Tapping a skeletal finger against his chin, he waved his hand around the room. "Packing...leaving the intact structures here would be a waste."

Maybe he had a point. "You know if you try anything stupid, I'll kill you for real this time."

"Oh, I'm aware."

I thumbed over my shoulder. "Alright, I guess I'll be going now."

With a dismissive wave, he got to his feet. "Excellent." Mumbling to himself, he eyed the room. "Now, where do I want to start?"

After being not so subtly dismissed, it really was time to go see what this was all about.

30

AS A CONCEPT, YES

Unable to stop it, my mind began to wander. It flashed to a mundane lush green field being warmed under a bright yellow sun that hung in a pale blue sky. Floral scents were carried on spring winds. It was a nice day out, being cool enough to keep you from getting overheated after a long stroll, but warm enough you didn't have to hurry.

Normally, I'd be a bit more on guard, but with James and Deheune absent, the impending doom that'd been threatening to drown me over the last few weeks was gone. Plus, I just needed a fucking break. After being subjected to every shade of gray known to exist, I was close to losing my goddamn mind.

Seriously, I didn't know how much more of this I could endure before something broke beyond repair. That being said, it was probably time to head back to Eden. A bit of fresh air would do me good.

Roughly ten kilometers in, I spotted a large debris pile. The closer I got, the more intriguing it became, since I couldn't quite make out what'd made the mess. Kneeling, I reached out and picked up a piece of jagged metal about the size of my palm. Something about it felt familiar, but I couldn't place it. Moving on to another piece, I began to sift through the wreckage. About a minute in, I found what looked to be a processor. After scanning the code into the database, it popped up as a fragment of the visual cortex belonging to a pre-QDM droid.

"Wow, someone fucked you guys right up."

Now that my curiosity was sated, I could move on in peace. When I happened upon a second, third, and fourth debris field, I barely slowed.

After another thirty kilometers, the passage noticeably began to narrow into a nearly perfect circular tunnel, the wide flat floor underfoot threw that illusion off ever so slightly. It took another two hundred meters for me to realize there was a gentle curve. Stopping, I glanced back only to see the wide cavern I'd been in was nowhere in sight. Cautiously, I pushed onward for another three hundred meters where I finally encountered something new.

Just ten meters away there were a couple of heavy-duty excavators. Their obvious goal was the black hexagons that lined the floor, walls, and ceiling of the tunnel ahead. Judging by the fact none of them seemed to be missing or even scratched, it didn't appear like they'd been successful.

I ran my fingers over the surface. They were smooth, yet I got the sensation they had a woven texture to them, though I had zero idea why. I took out my knife and ran it over the slick surface. It slid across without catching, meaning the weave I imagined to be there was nothing more than wishful thinking on my part. They were super cool, and by the looks of things, incredibly durable. I could see why the previous residents had tried to claim them for their own. Thankfully, that didn't happen. If the Archive could reverse engineer this sort of thing, it could prove problematic in the future.

After taking one last look at the amazing bit of technology, I pressed onward. Eventually, I found a massive vault door with a wheel in the center. Without a moment's hesitation, I strode up to it and pulled. I half expected it to be stuck, but that wasn't the case, as it turned easily.

There was a loud click before it simply swung open. I stepped into the massive room, only to find another door at the opposite end. Easily guessing what needed to happen next, I closed the door behind me and waited. A few seconds later, my ears popped, and the room warmed to about negative one hundred degrees Celsius.

Don't scoff, that's a considerable improvement compared to what I've been dealing with so far.

Once the room reached parity with the atmosphere on the other side, the door unlocked and swung open of its own accord. Steadying my nerves, I stepped through and was instantly irritated, I'd returned to the bland hellscape I had hoped was forever behind me. The only upside was the cavern happened to be smaller, only being twenty meters tall and maybe twice that wide. Seeing how there was only one way forward, I kept right on moving.

Roughly ten minutes later, I was hit with an overwhelming sense of wrongness. Easing around the next corner, I found myself at Dig Site 49. The room looked exactly the same with the deep grooves cut in the floor, a scorch mark here, another there, but that wasn't what'd triggered my oh shit meter.

No, that belonged to the long, jagged, purplish-black crack in reality on the wall just to my right. My instincts told me it led to the void. Barry's little recording didn't do this thing justice because being this close to it left me unnerved and slightly nauseous. I wasn't sure how he'd managed to ignore it long enough to go for the broken artifacts lying on the floor there, but he had.

Kudos to him, because I was transfixed by the damn thing. Eventually, though, I was able to tear my gaze away from it and take in the rest of the room. Seeing nothing of note, I approached the tear in reality and stretched out my hand. Orbs of white light flowed out of me and into the gash. Five seconds in and I felt sweat begin trickling down my back. At ten seconds, I was panting as if I'd run a marathon. Fifteen seconds in and I was on my knees screaming. Finally, the wound in reality closed, and I collapsed into a heap on the floor.

Unable to move, I lay there for a good twenty minutes. Around a half hour later, I scooted over to the wall and propped myself up before grabbing a slushie. The watermelon-cantaloupe mix really hit the spot. Not long after that, I felt like standing up wouldn't kill me, so I did.

Blowing out a long breath, I said, "That's better." I'd love to say I sauntered over and dropped the broken artifact into my storage ring, but that'd be a lie. While I did manage to store it, it took me a minute to hobble the twenty meters required to get them. "Okay, now that you're safely tucked away, I have to wonder what's next."

A distinctly feminine voice sounded behind me. "That's a more interesting question than you realize, Horacio."

My whole body tensed up so quickly my back did the snap, crackle, and pop dance as it suddenly aligned itself.

Spinning around was out of the question, so I slowly pivoted on the spot. When I was fully turned, I was greeted by an amorphic cloud made of silver, blue, and gold lights hovering on the far side of the room nearest what I guessed was the core. "What's that supposed to mean?"

Swirling in a counterclockwise motion, its unspoken intent seemed to bore into my soul. "That all depends on the answer to my next question." The cloud was quiet for a long moment before it decided to speak again. "Aren't you going to try to unlock the secret of this place?"

There was something familiar yet foreign about this entity, and it bugged me that I couldn't put my finger on it. Shaking my head, I held my hands out in a no thank you gesture. "Nah, I'll pass." I gestured over at the core. "I didn't come here for that or your secrets."

The cloud swirled so quickly it made me dizzy before it stopped once again. "If you didn't come here for that, then why did you come?"

I arched an eyebrow. "If you know who I am, I'm pretty sure you already know why I'm here."

Scenes formed within the cloud that made me homesick for a place I couldn't be sure existed. "Oh, but I'd like to hear you say it."

Part of me wanted to freak out, like a really big part of me, but I didn't. First of all, if they wanted me dead, I assure you, I would be. Second, and most importantly, she felt like a long-lost child I never knew I had.

Chuckling, I shook my head. "Technically, I guess the core was what brought me here, but not for the reasons you think."

Her form froze. "Do tell."

A revitalizing sensation swept over me. "Deheune was after whatever is held in that thing, and I have been hunting her for the better part of three centuries." I gestured over at the machine. "That thing there though, means nothing to me."

"Interesting." Their form expanded then contracted. "Would you destroy it if you had the power?"

That was an interesting question. "Would it cause you harm?"

Their response came instantly. "Not in the slightest."

Giving the option some considerable thought, I wobbled my hand back and forth. "I have no urge to destroy it or anything else for that matter, but I don't want the knowledge it contains to fall into the wrong hands, especially anyone aligned with Deheune."

"That's an interesting answer." Her form stilled for a moment before a thin tendril reached out to stroke the spot I'd repaired. "The power you wield interests me."

Nope, I had no interest in becoming someone's lab rat. "While I appreciate your interest, please understand I have duties I need to attend to." I thumbed over my shoulder. "Like getting Barry and myself out of your hair. Turns out the guy is looking for a ride and he's intruded on your hospitality long enough."

Her form stilled. "Ah, yes, the aberration…we should discuss his future as well as your own."

Maybe I hadn't been clear. "Lady, I have no interest in sticking around." I gestured at the empty room. "I missed my chance to grab Deheune here, so I need to get back out there and track her down."

Amusement coated her tone. "Relax, I mean you no harm, nor do

I wish to keep you from your duties, such as they are." She let out a contented hmm. "Though you should understand traveling through the void is a tricky thing and time passes oddly there compared to here. In some places, it moves faster and in others, slower. The route she took, while seeming instantaneous to her will take several more days to complete."

I blinked. "Wait, she's still in the void?"

"She is." Her tone seemed to have a calming effect on me, and I wasn't sure I liked it. "Do you know she's one of the corrupted ones?"

That was a term I'd heard a lot over the years. "I did, yes."

There was a long pause as she seemed to consider my words. "Is that why you pursue her?"

Lying didn't feel like an option. "Partially, though my reasons are a bit more personal. She's tried to have me killed on more than one occasion, and I've taken that a bit personally, so her being one of the tainted is just a bonus." I shrugged. "Though, you should know I've made a career out of hunting these pricks down since they come in all sorts of flavors, including vampires."

Her outer ring swirled one way while her core turned in the opposite direction. "I see." She glowed brightly then returned to normal. "I might have a proposition you may find amenable."

Well, this had the potential to be promising. "Before we get to all that, could you tell me what this place is?" I thumbed over my shoulder. "Barry seems to think this planet that's not a planet is the actual prize...and I'm not sure what to think now."

Her gentle laugh washed over me like a warm summer breeze. "That's a far more complicated question than you know." She spun counterclockwise for several seconds. "It appears the aberration has greater insight than I believed." Her form sparkled then dimmed again. "Are you familiar with the corruption?"

"As a concept, yes." I shrugged. "It's because of it—something stemming from Hodr—that we're stuck in this never-ending loop of creation and oblivion where we try to eliminate the sickness. Once that happens, it's everyone's hope we can move forward to whatever is next."

Her form bounced in the air, and I just knew if she could clap she would. "Very good." She swirled one way then the other before settling. "And it's your job to track these corrupted individuals down and eliminate them, right?"

Wobbling my hand back and forth, I grimaced. "You're half correct." I held up my hand to stop her next question. "I do the finding, people like Cain, Viktor, Gavin, and Jade do the killing. They seem to have a special talent that I lack to put down those filled with this corruption."

Her form spiraled as it began to condense. "Of course, that actually makes a lot of sense." A projection of the known universe appeared between us. Reaching out with a thin tendril, she touched it to zoom in on the Hamal Anillo Gate. "We are here."

She flicked it again and it shrank to show a map similar to the one I'd seen in Gisele's office years ago. The big difference here was it didn't just stop at the nine realms but kept expanding exponentially.

Even as it continued to shrink and expand, she began to speak. "As you can see, there are more than the nine realms you're familiar with."

Stunned, I stood there as I tried to make sense of what I was seeing. "I...I don't understand."

In a flash, the map vanished. "You aren't really meant to; it was a visual aid to explain why the contamination is so dangerous." She paused for a long moment. "The nine realms are the foundation for all the others, and if they become ill and die, that sickness would eventually corrupt the others." Sadness coated her tone as her form dimmed. "This is why I've been assigned to quarantine this sector from the rest. It was only later I realized some of the first ones were attempting to correct the issue, though I am not permitted to aid them."

Cocking my head to the side, I gave her a curious look. "But you want to make a deal with me. Why is that?"

Her form brightened. "Because you are not part of this cycle or any other, though I cannot say what you are or how you fit into the puzzle."

"Can't or won't?"

Every layer of her form swirled in a slightly different direction, making it impossible to look at her without becoming physically ill. She glowed brightly then stopped. "We should move on."

Yeah, that was probably for the best. "By all means."

"Let's address your friend Barry's situation."

I held out my hands to stop her. "Whoa, slow down there, we aren't friends, or at least we weren't. Actually, I don't know what we are right now, maybe uneasy allies."

She chuckled. "Either way, he isn't the same person you knew previously. A number of outside forces happened to come together in such a way it created something entirely new."

That was vague. "Could you be a bit more specific?"

Her form glowed brightly then dimmed again. "Through a series of virtually impossible happenstances, the corruption inside his body was purged through a cleansing process even I can't begin to comprehend. All I know is he is corruption free. More than that though, at the moment of his death and resurrection, his soul was touched by a greater power. Said entity seems to have placed him on a path that'll directly aid you in cleansing the corruption once and for all."

That was a lot to take in. "Uh, okay."

She dimmed ever so slightly. "Though I fear what he has to offer isn't enough, but now that you're in the mix, I'm allowed to directly interact with this reality in a way I otherwise couldn't."

I didn't know what made me special, and she couldn't say, so why not roll with it? "And what does that look like?"

Caution was the name of the game here since I didn't want to get caught up in a Faustian bargain.

Her body dimmed slightly. "I'd like to finish my duties here and rejoin my family." She paused. "To be clear, I want to be free of this place, so, I'd like to assist you in tracking down the corrupted ones."

It was posed as a question, though I didn't think she was asking for permission. "And how would you go about doing that?"

"Give me a moment to slip into something more appropriate, and we can discuss the details." With those words, she vanished.

"Hey, I'm not that kind of boy." I gestured around the room. "You need to wine and dine me first."

There was no response, and now that I thought about it, that was probably for the best.

31

THIS IS GIDGET

One minute turned into ten, which turned into twenty. Yeah, I may've made a mistake there. Just in case you were wondering, it takes one hundred and sixty steps to go from one end of this room to the other, and two hundred to go from side to side. I grabbed a hand towel out of my storage ring and dabbed it against my forehead.

Like you don't sweat when you're nervous.

Stowing it, I glanced around the room and mumbled. "I guess this is what I get for trying to be funny and failing, again."

Another five minutes slid by before I heard something out in the distance.

Click, click. Click, click.

There was an oddly familiar rhythm there with one set of clicks happening in quick succession then the other two a fraction of a second later. It almost sounded like a dog, a small one, making its way across a tiled floor. Of course, that wasn't possible since there wasn't a dog breed alive that could withstand the frigid temperatures on Escarcha.

Click, click. Click, click.

Whatever was headed my way was getting closer.

Stepping back, I grumbled. "I don't like this one bit."

Click, click. Click, click.

Goddamn it, it was really close now. Just what the fuck was this thing? Steeling myself for the worst, I gave myself a once over to make sure my armor was in tip top shape before doing a cursory check of my weapons. The only thing I didn't do was call forth my chains. I know, I probably should, but I didn't want my new friend to think I was overreacting.

Click, click. Click, click.

They were close now. Before my imagination could cook up some terrifying monster, *it* rounded the corner. Recoiling, I pressed my back against the wall. Suddenly, I regretted sealing the passage into the void.

The horrifying creature before me was roughly fifteen centimeters tall with long tufts of patchy black hair across its trembling body. Its bulging, dark, bloodshot eyes didn't seem to fit into their sockets properly. This *thing* had two long canines in the top of its mouth and there were an unusual number of large white teeth between them. Though the way its tongue lolled out of the side, it was missing several teeth meant to hold it in. In short, it was pure nightmare fuel. It was as if someone took a long haired chihuahua and dipped it in radioactive goo. After waiting for it to mutate in the worst possible way, they decided to trot it out to terrify the public.

It stood there looking at me with one of its eyes, the other one seemed to have a mind of its own as it wandered about. Panting, it sucked in its tongue for a split second before letting it roll back out and drooling liberally onto the floor.

Even with a dozen meters between us, I could feel the hate rolling off the vicious little mongrel. It was waiting for its time to strike and tear me limb from limb.

Moving slowly, I edged toward the door in the hopes I could escape with my life.

It cocked its head as if readying itself to strike when it pulled its unnaturally long tongue back inside its head. Then the weirdest thing happened, a familiar, and way too chipper feminine voice sounded. "What do you think?" There was a pause. "Why are you huddled against the wall like that?" She patted forward. "Are you okay?"

None of this made sense and my mind blanked. "Stop."

She did.

Holding out my shaking hands, I let my words rush out of my mouth. "Who are you?"

The little dog sat and eyed me carefully. "My kind don't have names, but that didn't seem to bother you earlier. What changed?"

Wait, was this what she meant when she said she'd slip into something more appropriate? "That was you?"

A gentle laugh escaped her terrifying maw. "Of course." She got to her feet and danced in a little circle. "I thought you'd like this form."

Before I could stop myself, I said, "Well, you were wrong."

Confusion wrote itself across the vicious little shit's face. "I don't understand. I thought your culture liked tiny lap dogs."

"Good ones, yeah." I waved my hand up and down at her. "But not this...you're a fucking chihuahua, for god's sake...that was Earth's most vicious animal."

She narrowed her eyes. "I thought that was the hippo."

"Yeah, it sucked too, but at least it was cute."

Her little tail flicked to the side as she eyed me carefully. "No, I've reviewed the historical records; chihuahuas were loved and adored by everyone—well, maybe not everyone, *you* apparently have a problem with them."

Anger welled up inside me as I took a step toward her. "Of course I do. A pack of them nearly tore me apart when I was a kid. They're little balls of chaos and mayhem, constantly in search of their next victim."

"Don't you think that's a little dramatic?" Her tongue rolled out again as she tried to look cute. "I've decided that it's time you faced your fears, so I'm staying like this."

Raising my voice, I wagged my finger at her. "The fuck you are."

She let out a high-pitched bark, and I flinched back. That got a snicker out of her. "Yes, this will do you some good, and everyone else will love me for the adorable little baby I am."

I folded my arms. "And if I refuse to participate?"

Snark filled her tone. "You'd let Deheune escape because you're afraid of little old me?" She laughed. "I won't even bite you—that much. I mean if you're shitty, I'm going to tear you a whole new ass, but if you're a good boy, I'll sit in your lap and allow you to pet me."

Was she serious? "You'd let the corruption spread just to remain in this form?"

Sitting, she gave me the stink eye or tried to, the one she'd trained on me was a bit lazy and wandered about the room on its own accord. "Do you really want to test my patience?"

Rubbing my hands over my face, I suppressed a scream. "Fine, but you have to tell me why you really picked this form."

"I told you, I wanted to be cute." She jumped to her feet. "Plus, it's symbolic as I'll be the one helping you track down those with corruption."

I groaned. "If you wanted that kind of symbolism, why not go with a bloodhound."

"Because chihuahuas are cuter." She pranced forward. "Not only that, people tend to carry us around."

Stepping back, I held my hands out to either side. "Wait a minute, you don't expect me to carry you around, do you?"

She stopped right in front of me. "Actually, I do. Besides making me more comfortable, it'll help you get over your phobia."

"It's not a phobia." I glared down at the little pup. "I can't help it if chihuahuas are evil little shits."

Stifling a sob, she plopped onto her stomach and covered her face with her paws. "I'm not evil." She sniffled. "Take it back."

Guilt hit me like a freight train. "Oh, for god's sake." Squeezing my eyes closed, I grumbled out a few choice curse words before opening them again. "Fine, you're not evil...as far as I know."

She uncovered one eye and glared at me. "If you're really sorry, you'd pick me up."

That manipulative little shit. "Damn it." Leaning over, I scooped her up in my hand and held her against my chest. "Better?"

Placing a paw on my hand, she pushed her head against my torso. "It's a start."

Reluctantly, I reached out and patted her head. "Okay, the first thing we need to figure out is a name for you."

She whipped her head all the way around like she was the fucking exorcist to look at me. "Is that really important?"

My whole body tensed at the wrongness of the image. "Could you maybe limit your head movement to that of an actual dog...at least for now, because that's freaking me out."

Slowly she turned her head back, before scrambling around to put her front paws on my chest. "Do I really need a name?"

"Yes."

Huffing out a disgruntled breath, she fell back against my chest. "Fine." She lay there for several seconds. "How about Gidget? It means small girl, and since this form is only a small piece of my body, it makes sense."

"Uh...Gidget is fine." Then it hit me what she said. Looking down at her, I asked, "What exactly does that mean?"

A small laugh escaped her trembling form. "You'll see soon enough."

I wasn't sure I liked the sound of that. "How soon?"

She turned around in my hand and pointed with one paw. "After we pick up Barry and return to the ship."

Frowning, I sighed. "Okay, yeah, I could do with a change of scenery."

After returning to the encampment, we found Barry standing there waiting for me, and by extension, Gidget. One moment we were standing in the middle of the cavern, the next, we were in the conference room of the Roja.

Slightly shocked by the sudden change, I glanced around the room and gave an awkward wave. "Oh, hey, I'm back."

Gisele gave the puppy in my hand a curious look. "I can see that."

Then she leaned to the side to look behind me. "Mind introducing us to your new friends?"

Friends? Oh shit, Barry and Gidget. "Right." I lifted my hand. "This is Gidget." Then I thumbed over my shoulder. "And that's Barry." Glancing over at him, I smiled. "You alright back there?"

Panning his gaze around the room, he chuckled. "All things considered, I'm good, thanks."

Issac narrowed his eyes. "Barry...as in the guy who tried to have you killed and by all accounts should be dead right about now?"

Bobbing my head back and forth, I said, "Technically, I think he is dead, though that's a long story in and of itself. Though, if we've got a telepath handy, I'd like them to have a nice long conversation with the man."

Gidget made a whining sound. "I thought we cleared that up."

"With me, yes." I gestured around the room. "But they're going to need a bit more convincing."

She sneezed and a long trail of snot covered my hand. "I suppose that's fair."

I did my best not to show my disgust, but that didn't stop me from recovering my hand towel and cleaning up the mess. "Thank you for your understanding." Turning to Barry, I asked, "You're not going to fight this are you?"

He chuckled. "Of course not."

"Good."

Smiling, Jose eyed Gidget with great interest. "She's sweet. Where did you find her?"

Sweet? She was a freaking hellhound, but I doubted I'd convince them of that fact. "She found me." Thumbing back at Barry, I said, "Let's get him settled first, then we can talk about Gidget here."

Jamie got to his feet. "Brig?"

"No." I grimaced. "Give him his own quarters but place a guard on him till everyone is satisfied with his current disposition."

Gisele grumbled. "Maybe don't tell everyone he's Barry Lawson then."

That was a good point. "Okay, that's probably a smart play,

though I don't want it to be kept a secret forever. For now, though, do what you need to do, without harming him, to confirm he's on team good guy these days."

Barry patted me on the shoulder. "Thanks." He glanced over at the others. "I get why you're leery of me, but I've got nothing to hide."

"Sure, you don't." Christopher said as he got to his feet. "I'll put him in the empty cabin next to mine."

Gisele nodded. "Thank you." She pointed at the puppy. "I want to hear about Gidget here."

Christopher and Luis stepped up on either side of Barry to escort him to his new quarters.

As for Gidget, I wasn't so sure Gisele was going to be happy once she heard who and what Gidget really was.

"Hey." Issac called out as he pointed at the holo-screen at the front of the room. "What's that?"

Hundreds of thousands of thick tendrils of gray mist stretched out from Escarcha in every conceivable direction. Some began to pool into spheres nearly the size of Earth. In the same instant, billions of eldritch satellites winked in and out of existence as they fell in around the Roja.

Arching an eyebrow, I glanced down at Gidget. "Care to explain?"

Several half sneezes escaped her before she finally focused on me, and by extension, the question. "I've reprogrammed the drones to follow the Roja to act as an added layer of protection." She turned to look at the holo-screen. "As for the rest of my body, I'm reworking its configuration into something more manageable. They'll seek out the corrupted throughout the realms and tag them for extermination."

Even as Escarcha broke itself into millions of spheres, Gisele tore her gaze away from the scene. "I'm sorry, did you say that's your body?" Concern swept over her features. "Who or what exactly are you?"

I winced. "That's a very complicated question."

Gidget wagged her tail excitedly. "But one you're welcome to have an answer to, if you're willing to listen."

Nodding, Gisele leaned back in her chair. "I think we can make the time."

Hanging my head, I sighed. "And here I was hoping for a nap in my own bed." I slumped in my seat. "Okay, we're listening."

A very happy Gidget jumped atop the table before launching into lecture mode.

32

TIME FOR A LITTLE VACATION

8/5/264

Tower City, Nocturna

Nocturna was an interesting little planet on the far side of the Needle Galaxy. Due to its positioning behind a much larger planet, it only got a hint of daylight over the course of a week, every eight months. Yeah, so it was dark all the time, day in and day out. Sadly, the same guy who named the planet named the city too. Care to guess what the largest landmark in the city was? That's right, a huge tower sat in the heart of what was now a thriving metropolis, even though the planet was on the far edge of the Collective's territory.

Thanks to its location, it allowed people like me to have a semi-private meeting, which was why I was here. Well, there was that, and Tower City was one of the few places on this side of the cosmos that served a passable steak. It wasn't beef by any stretch of the imagination, but the lizard the locals harvested for food had a similar flavor profile.

Even though the Halcon drew a little attention, it wasn't much. Unlike the big four, I wasn't exactly all that well known, these days. Even so, I took a few minutes to change out of my uniform and into a comfortable black suit.

Exiting the port, I made my way down to an outdoor restaurant I'd visited the last time I was in town. It was a busy place frequented by sailors, businessmen, and criminals alike. They had a strict no questions policy that allowed their clientele a certain amount of anonymity. Between that and the privacy sigils inscribed on every table and all around the pavilion, this was as close as you could get to a one-on-one anywhere in the galaxy.

Fifteen minutes later, Jade strolled up wearing tactical gear that marked her as one of the Collectives commanders. Technically, it was true, but if anyone forced her to reveal herself, they'd be in for a world of hurt.

Her gaze tracked over the tables until she spotted me. Giving me a big smile, she strode over and grabbed the back of the chair across from me. "Mind if I sit?"

Gesturing at the chair, I chuckled. "It'd be a waste of a call if I did."

She gave me a wink before sitting. "Good to see you again."

"And you." I slid a data crystal across the table. She caught it easily. "Everything you need is there."

Jade beamed as she leaned back. "Have you eaten yet?"

"Are you hungry?"

Her tone turned playful. "I could eat."

Chuckling, I gave the waiter a nod and he brought over a menu. "Thank you." He bowed and left without a word. "The steak here isn't bad…then again, that's coming from someone who hasn't had a proper one in a couple of hundred years."

Patting her pocket, she picked up the menu. "Maybe I could convince you to come to Alastor and have the real thing once this is wrapped up."

"That's right, you were smart enough to bring your own cattle when we left Earth." I nodded. "In that case, I'd be thrilled to stop by, steak or not."

She suppressed a smile. "Sounds good." We sat there quietly for a long moment as we considered the menu, and after we ordered, she seemed to relax a little. "What do I need to know?"

"Most of it is on the data crystal." I shrugged. "But she's in the Wolf–Lundmark–Melotte System." She tensed, and I held my hand out for calm. "Easy, the Roja is keeping an eye on things, besides there's little chance of her slipping through our blockade without being noticed."

Jade's expression softened. "Glad to hear it." She gave me a curious look. "What about James?"

I shook my head. "He's still missing...I'm not sure if he's stuck in the void, or if he took a longer route than she did, but the moment he pops his head out, I'll let Gavin know."

She gave me an easy smile. "Good."

Dinner arrived a few minutes later, and we ate our meal in peace. I was fairly sure this would be the last moment of tranquility she'd have until she finished dealing with Deheune.

Once the plates were gone, she got to her feet. "Don't forget, dinner at my place when this is over."

Laughing, I shook my head. "Yeah, I'll be there."

A big smile crossed her lips. "Great, I'll message you when this is over."

"Sounds good."

Turning, Jade walked away, heading for the spaceport. I paid the tab and hurried to follow. It was time for a little vacation before I had to get back to work.

ABOUT THE AUTHOR

Ken Lange is a current resident of the "Big Easy," along with his partner and evil, yet loving, cats. Any delay, typo, or missed edit can and will be blamed on the latter's interference.

He arrived at this career a little later in life, and his work reflects it. Most of his characters won't be in their twenties, and they aren't always warm and fuzzy. He is of the opinion that middle-aged adults are woefully underrepresented in fiction, and has made it his mission to plug that gap.

Translation: he's middle aged and crotchety.

ALSO BY KEN LANGE

Exiled Ascendants

Exiled Ascendants Book 1

Exiled Ascendants Book 2

Exiled Ascendants Book 3

Exiled Ascendants Book 4

Exiled Ascendants Book 5 (Coming Soon)

Hellion Initiative (Novella)

Lord Aegis of the Flame (Novella)

Krampus Day (Short Story)

Nine Realms Saga

Accession of the Stone Born Book 1

The Wanderer Awakens Book 2

Sleipnir's Heart Short Story 2.5

Rise of the Storm Bringer Book 3

Dust Walkers Book 4

Lamia's Curse Short Story 4.5

Shades of Fire & Ash Book 5

Children of the Storm Book 6

Dawning Book 7

Shattered Peace Book 8

Fall of Eleazer Book 9

Storm Fall Book 10

Blighted Book 11

Made in the USA
Columbia, SC
29 October 2024

44942519R00167